Corrupted Pleasure

KINGPINS OF THE SYNDICATE BOOK TWO

EVA WINNERS

Copyright © 2022 by Winners Publishing LLC and Eva Winners

Cover Image Designer: Eve Graphic Design LLC

Model: Darien

Photographer: Wander Aguiar

All rights reserved.

No part of this book may be reproduced in any form or by any electronic or mechanical means, including information storage and retrieval systems, without written permission from the author, except for the use of brief quotations in a book review.

Visit www.evawinners.com and subscribe to my newsletter.

FB group: https://bit.ly/3gHEe0e

FB page: https://bit.ly/30DzP8Q

Insta: http://Instagram.com/evawinners

BookBub: https://www.bookbub.com/authors/eva-winners

Amazon: http://amazon.com/author/evawinners

Goodreads: http://goodreads.com/evawinners

TikTok: https://vm.tiktok.com/ZMeETK7pq/

Kingpins of The Syndicate Collection

Kingpins of The Syndicate Collection

Each book in the Kingpins series can be read as a standalone.

If you'd like a preview to the Villainous Kingpin, make sure to check out the prologue at the end of Corrupted Pleasure.

Enjoy!

Corrupted Pleasure Playlist

https://open.spotify.com/playlist/2ZOW0QyBErPP5ODN7z61Pe?si=vH5dlcV6SSOOm4V2N_2zPQ

Prologue

DAVINA

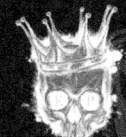

O 8-29-19-98.
My heart pounded with each number of the combination code that I punched in. Blood rushed through my veins and anticipation buzzed in my system. Everything depended on this going right.

With a trembling finger, I entered the last number and a soft click sounded.

My soft gasp broke the silence in the room as I stared, dumbfounded, at the cracked safe door, too afraid to peer inside. What if we robbed the head of the Irish mafia for nothing? It didn't matter that he was Juliette's father... He was a mobster first and foremost.

Swallowing hard, I pulled the door open, and a sharp inhale slipped through my lips. There were stacks and stacks of money. More than I'd seen in my entire life.

Glancing around, I spotted the black backpack that Juliette had said Quinn always left here. I picked it up, unzipped it with shaking hands, and started shoving the money into it. I had no clue how much was in each stack, so I estimated.

Then, as a thought struck me, I paused.

"I should take all of it," I muttered under my breath. "Just in case."

If Wynter's friend didn't come through, I wouldn't put it past Garrett to continue blackmailing us. Again and again.

Determination settled within me. There was no sense in doing it half-assed, so I'd take it all. My hands shook badly. Every so often, I'd miss the bag completely and the wrapped-up stack of bills would end up on the floor.

"Focus, Davina," I scolded myself softly.

Another stack of bills into the bag. Jesus Christ! There was more money in here than most people would see in their entire life.

Once the safe was emptied out, I lowered onto my knees to pick up the ones that didn't make it into the bag. Tugging on the zipper, I attempted to close the bag, but it got jammed.

"Fuck, fuck, fuck," I cursed softly, struggling with the fucking zipper. It finally gave, and I exhaled a breath of relief.

"Filthy words from such a pretty mouth." A deep voice filled the room.

My head shot up, the zipper forgotten, as a little scream shot out of me. Trying to jerk upright, I lost my footing and fell back on my ass, all the while staring into a stormy ocean gaze.

What bad fucking luck to be caught red-handed. This hasn't been my week at all. I could only hope my girlfriends had better luck than I did.

My breathing hitched as I waited for Liam Brennan to call the police. Or kill me. Something. Anything.

Jesus, two crimes in a single week. Could this get any worse? I wondered what the sentence would be for arson and larceny.

Shit!

I couldn't get arrested. I was about to graduate from Yale.

"Let me guess," Mr. Brennan drawled, his tone lazy with the hint of something dangerous and ruthless in it. I imagined the head of the Irish mafia might contemplate tying my feet to a cement block and throwing me into the Hudson River. "The other three were meant to be a distraction while you're in here robbing me," he continued, almost sounding amused.

I looked away, scared he'd see the truth in my eyes. Besides, he was way too nice to look at. Something about him ignited my skin and warmed my insides. He was just as good-looking as I remembered. He was so tall, all muscles and raw strength. God, I bet it would be a treat to explore his body.

Great, now I was turned on *and* scared.

"Fucking wrong," I protested, sounding stronger than I felt.

My eyes glanced at the door he was blocking, wishing he'd move away from it. Maybe I could sprint past him and out of this crazy club.

"Enlighten me then. Why is my safe open, and why are your hands on my money?" he asked.

Wasn't that the question of the century? Of course, telling him the truth was out of the question, so I shrugged nonchalantly, slightly annoyed.

"Safekeeping," I blurted out, because it was the only stupid answer I could come up with.

Hopefully the man wouldn't kill me, his own daughter, his niece, and Ivy.

"I love your sassy mouth." He smirked. "Keep it up and I'm going to find out just how well it works."

I gulped, his words sending heat through my veins. Jesus, why did I find that so hot? Clenching my thighs, I tried to ignore the throbbing in my sweet spot.

Wrong time. Wrong place. Wrong man.

"You're my best friend's father!" I rasped, though I wasn't sure if I was trying to remind myself or convince him that his insinuation was improper.

"What makes you think something so small would keep me away from you?"

I shook my head while a shudder traveled down my spine. I opened my mouth to tell him he was a gross old man, but I was physically unable to utter those words. Because Mr. Liam Brennan was the hottest man I had ever seen. And that shower scene from three months ago had been on repeat in my mind.

"It's time you pay your debt," he said. "The stakes just got higher now that you've stolen from me."

Now he brings up the debt! Three months too late. Unable to think of a single intelligent thing to say, I just stared.

"Stand up," he ordered, and I blinked in confusion. "Now!"

I narrowed my eyes at his rudeness, but I got to my feet, though I ensured I grabbed the backpack and finished zipping it first. I still hoped I'd keep the money. Somehow.

The girls and I needed it to stay out of jail.

"Now what?" I challenged with bravery I didn't feel.

His eyes traveled down my body, and suddenly, it felt like my dress was too revealing. My skin flared from the weight of his stare, leaving a trail of fire in its wake. Then his eyes came back to my face, and something about the way he looked at me stole the breath from my lungs.

The door shut behind him with a soft click and adrenaline rushed through my veins.

This was oh so wrong, but I wanted to see where it went.

He moved toward his desk and casually leaned against it, his eyes locked on me.

The door swung open. "They got away," Quinn told Mr. Brennan. "Wynter took her damn clothes off."

It would seem everything out there was going according to plan. I had to succeed too. For the four of us.

Mr. Brennan's eyes came back to mine, his expression cold.

"Miss Hayes, tell us what it is that you and your friends are up to." This was a man used to getting whatever he wanted.

"No," I snapped.

"Want me to turn in the evidence to the police?" The dreaded question. Why even bother asking it? Nobody sane would say yes.

"Like what? The backpack?" I sneered. I hadn't technically stolen anything yet.

"For starters, yes. That backpack belongs to Quinn, and the money you stashed in it belongs to me."

My eyebrow rose, seemingly unconcerned with his words.

"There are a million backpacks like this, and possession is nine-tenths of the law." I prayed my bluff was right. I was studying business, not fucking law. "So don't touch my stuff." I tilted my chin up, daring him to dispute it.

He pointed to the corner of the room where a camera was. Well, fuck me. Juliette must have forgotten about the security, and I didn't even think to ask. Anyone with that amount of cash would have security cameras.

The. Worst. Criminals.

"See that, sweetheart." His voice was deep and almost seductive. "That's our evidence."

"Shit," I grumbled. "Fucked. Just fucked."

"Pretty much," he agreed.

It was time to run. It was the only thing left to do. Goddamn it. And there were two of them now. I glanced between them, wondering the best way to slip between two men.

"The Italians here?" Mr. Brennan asked.

His man nodded.

"Deal with them and keep them away from here," Mr. Brennan ordered.

Before he left, the man's eyes came back to me.

"I see the girls are following in our footsteps. One hour," he announced, and then left us, shutting the door behind him.

"Let the fucking fun begin," I muttered to myself.

Apprehension twisted in my stomach as I waited for Juliette's father to do something. Anything. A cold shiver erupted at the base of my spine, along with all kinds of scenarios playing through my mind. Our sweat-slicked bodies. His deep voice whispering words in my ear. His strong body pumping into me fast and hard, each thrust breaking me apart.

Keep your head on straight, Davina.

God, I wished he'd make up his mind already. Either kill me or call the police. Or fuck me, so we could end this tension between us.

"What do you want, Mr. Brennan?"

"What do you think?"

It sounded suggestive, making me feel hot and edgy. "Probably your money back," I said dryly, though I wished it was something else. "But it's *our* money."

He released a soft scoff. "You haven't earned it. Yet." So there was a way I could earn it... That was the best news yet tonight. "But we can fix that," he added.

"How?" I asked. The look he gave me seared into my flesh, dark and possessive. "Something freaky probably."

I tried to sound dignified. I really did. But my words came out breathy, something hot burning in the pit of my stomach. Butterflies fluttered through my veins, a heavy anticipation in my every breath.

"Well, I'm not into freaky shit," I breathed, my cheeks burning and my blood sizzling. "Or old men."

Mr. Brennan didn't look old. He was actually the hottest man I had ever seen. Hands fucking down. I couldn't tell him how hot and attractive I found him though. I'd embarrassed myself enough the last time I saw him.

"I'd bet all the money in that bag and in my bank account that you're into freaky shit," he baited me.

I scoffed. I was tempted to bet him, but then I feared his every word was a trap.

"Now what?" I asked instead.

"Are they waiting for you?" My eyes widened slightly. I shook my head, not trusting my voice to betray my lie. He must have read the truth in my eyes though. "Send them a text and tell them to go back to the university without you."

My lungs couldn't get enough oxygen. This man must have been stealing it all. One part of me thought he could also feel this sizzling attraction, and the other part of me thought he wanted to kill me.

"Now," he clipped, and I jumped, rushing to obey his order. There was only so much disobedience I could give to a fucking mobster. "I want to see the message before you send it."

"Control freak," I mumbled, glaring at him. Still, I took a few steps toward him and showed him my phone screen. "Here. Happy?"

He nodded, and I pressed the send button.

Now that I'd taken those few steps closer to him, my heart thundered even harder. The scent of his sandalwood cologne reached me, and I inhaled deeply. It was like extinguishing a fire with gasoline, my body burned for his touch that badly.

"First, you drink my most expensive bottle of cognac," he drawled. I had no idea how he knew that. We just did that yesterday. "Then, you steal from me."

"Sorry." Yeah, sorry would not suffice in this instance.

"Take your panties off," he ordered, and the ache between my thighs throbbed with greed. While my body wanted to obey, my mind warned me against it.

"W-what are you going to do?" I hated that I stuttered. Yes, he was older than me, but I certainly wasn't a blushing virgin.

He let out a breath of amusement. "Take. Your. Panties. Off."

Asshole. "Fine!"

Putting the backpack with cash next to my feet, I reached under my tight mini-dress and slid my panties down my legs.

"Now what?" My cheeks burned, though I suspected it had nothing to do with embarrassment.

He extended his big hand, palm facing up. Did he—

Yes, he did... He was demanding my panties. I threw them in his face, but he caught them.

"Now turn around and bend over my desk."

Holy fucking shit! Would he fuck me now? My body sang *yes, yes, yes*. My mind warned it was a bad idea. I just got out of a relationship that had caused all kinds of problems.

"Are you waiting for written instructions?" he barked.

"Fucking mobster."

I did as he ordered and bent over his desk. He took a step and came up right behind me. His finger traced down my spine, and I had to fight a delightful shiver. He'd barely touched me, yet I felt it unlike anything ever before.

His big hands came down to my thighs and my body reacted, pushing into his touch. God, I was losing my mind. He pushed my dress up, leaving my ass bare for his viewing.

"So beautiful." His voice was like a lover's caress. "I'm going to punish you for stealing from me."

Oh my God. I was so turned on. I wanted to beg him to punish me, fuck me, make me come, but that would be a reward. He must have something else in mind.

"I hope you're not fragile," he said, his voice dark and sinful.

"Bring it on, old man," I breathed.
Did he ever!

Three Months Earlier

CHAPTER 1
Liam

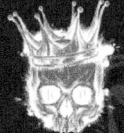

G*unfire.*

I shot out of my seat behind the desk and pulled the .45 from the holster strapped around my chest. The sounds of screams and pounding footsteps traveled from the front of the nightclub.

Fuck, why today? Juliette, my daughter, was visiting me, and I'd asked her to go to the penthouse and wait for me there before we went to grab dinner at our favorite restaurant with Killian, my eldest.

Another shot.

More gunfire and screaming in Russian, Italian, and Gaelic. Obviously the latter were my men, but what the fuck were the Italians and Russians doing here? So far, I'd strictly fought them both separately.

Maybe those two had decided to negotiate and attack together.

I fucking hoped not.

Dread filled me at the memory of my sister in her own pool of blood. The terror I saw in her eyes. It stayed with you forever. Everything I had ever done was to protect my family. I had failed more than one person on that day twenty-one years ago.

It wasn't time for memories. Pushing them all out of my mind, I focused on the situation at hand and rushed down the hallway. My weapon ready, I headed toward the main room, each step bringing me closer to the screams.

The moment I got to the dance area, I saw people run past the corridor and straight out the front doors. It was a damn stampede.

A woman fell down and I wrapped my left hand around her elbow, my gun still in my right, ready to shoot. Yanking her to her feet, I nudged her forward.

I scanned the room. The lounge area was a disaster—tables and chairs were overturned and bodies lying on the floor. Blood pooled around them, turning my white marble floor into a red pond.

I saw three unmoving bodies, lying face down. Judging by the quality of their suits and faint outline of their gun holsters, it had to be the Italians. Idiots never even drew their guns.

"Fuck!" I cursed under my breath. I'd expected an attack to The Eastside Nightclub, but here on the west side of New York, it fucking blindsided me.

This will be a clusterfuck to explain to the police, I thought dryly.

My eyes traveled over the room where I spotted Quinn, my cousin and right-hand man. Our eyes met and he lifted five fingers, indicating how many men were still left. I tilted my head in acknowledgement, keeping a sharp eye. Quinn and I had been doing this for a long time.

I turned and went in the opposite direction. Quinn clearly had a handle on this side, so I headed toward the arched doorway that connected this room to the large dance floor. I kept to the shadows, using the columns to conceal myself. I spotted three of my employees huddled together, hiding at the end of the bar with frightened eyes.

I lifted my finger to my lips, signaling them to stay quiet. All of them stared at me, then one lifted his hand and pointed to the opposite end of the bar. I nodded, letting him know I understood.

Moving to the next column, I kept my steps silent. I thanked God and all the saints that I left the columns as part of the structure when we renovated this place. Otherwise, I'd be left wide open right now.

From my spot, I could see two men in suits crouched down, arguing back and forth in hushed tones. They had to be Italians. It bothered me that I couldn't spot the other three men.

For a moment, I listened to their hissed conversation as they complained about the Russians. Apparently, they'd ditched these Italian men. The question was, why were the Russians working with the Italians at all?

Judging by the idiots here, they were low-ranking men, so I wouldn't find anything out from them.

I whistled, catching their attention. Both whipped around, swinging their guns and pointing them at me.

Before either one of them could do anything, I pulled the trigger, my bullet lodging itself square between the eyes of the first man. Then I pulled the trigger again and hit the other one in the chest.

Rushing to the second one, the faint wail of sirens registered in my brain. We didn't have much time.

I stopped above his body, watching as his eyes bulged out in fear as he gurgled and choked on his own blood.

"What was your mission tonight?" I asked.

He opened his mouth, blood spurting out of it and trickling down his chin. He had only seconds to live.

"Give me the information, or I'll go after your family."

"A warning."

CHAPTER 2
Davina

"**F**our more months."

Our glasses clinked together and our laughter filled the room, mixing with Taylor Swift's album playing in the background and Wynter's humming along to the song.

It was just us, as always. Wynter, Juliette, Ivy, and me. The four of us sat in the luxurious living room of Juliette's father's city home. It was the end of January, and our stress levels had started to escalate with exams. The next several months would be brutal, so the four of us made a last-minute decision to drive almost two hours to New York City and take a long weekend to decompress in the safety of Mr. Brennan's home.

I couldn't help the ball of anxiety in my throat bubbling each time I thought about graduation and what to do afterward. I wanted to be close to my grandfather so I could visit him all the time. He lived in an assisted-living home in Texas since he needed full-time care, but the goal was to move him to wherever I ended up, and the pressure not to fuck it up was immense.

"Another round of shots," Juliette demanded.

Despite acting carefree, I could tell she was tense. I noticed her fidgeting, and she only did that when she was stressed out. I didn't think it had anything to do with our classes, but I couldn't figure out what was causing it. There was something more to it. Something she refused to share with us, which was unusual.

"Maybe you two should take it easy," I recommended, eyeing Juliette worriedly.

Both Juliette and Ivy ignored me and raised their glasses, almost spilling them. Wynter, who wasn't drinking due to her vigorous Olympic training schedule, just shook her head. And me? I'd quit drinking those things three shots ago. Or maybe it was four, I wasn't sure. I just knew I was smart enough to stop before I felt too relaxed or too stupid.

I glanced out the large French windows. The dark skies lurked, and somehow it felt ominous with what was to come. It was stupid, but I couldn't shake the feeling something bad was going to happen. Instead of focusing on the dark skies, I kept my sights on the snow-covered trees and the reflection of the white snow gleaming under the moon.

It wasn't our first time here. Over the course of our nearly four years at Yale, we had frequently come here for weekend getaways. When we had longer holidays, everyone would tag along and come with me to Texas to visit my grandfather. He was the only family I'd ever had, raising me on his own, and the least I could do was ensure I visited him every chance I had.

Unlike me, Juliette, Wynter, and Ivy preferred not to visit their families. More often than not, Wynter was busy with her training. Juliette and Ivy had absolutely no excuses that I knew of. Honestly, they could be brats, but I still loved them. Though, knowing what their families did for a living, I wasn't sure I blamed them for keeping their distance.

The first week at Yale, Juliette and Ivy were more than happy to educate me about their families. Maybe they expected I'd run or refuse to be their friend. I did neither. Instead, I found friends for life. Wynter and Juliette were cousins, and they pretty much grew up together in California under the care of Wynter's mother—Juliette's aunt on her father's side.

Both Ivy and Juliette's fathers ran their respective families in a much larger crime syndicate.

Juliette's father ran the Brennan Irish mafia. According to Juliette, he owned a good part of the westside of New York and the northern part of the East Coast. He also had connections and ran part of the criminal organization in Ireland. I had never met her father, and part of me was kind of glad. I had enough stress in my life.

Ivy's father and brothers ran the Murphy Irish mafia. They mainly stuck to Ireland and European countries. Ivy called them the Irish pricks. And that was the extent of our knowledge—both theirs and mine.

I got the feeling they felt slighted somehow. Neither one of their families included them in any of their business dealings, simply because they were women.

Wynter didn't really care. The only thing that girl loved was figure skating. She won her first gold medal at fourteen at Junior Worlds, Nationals at fifteen and sixteen, and then the Olympics at seventeen. Her mother was her coach, but since she started going to Yale, she'd lost that. In our four years here, we'd visited California twice. Most of the time, the girls preferred to go to Texas with me. My grandfather loved it as much as my friends.

Still, I found it odd that Wynter's mother never visited the East Coast, especially considering she was born here. Juliette mentioned Mrs. Flemming hadn't stepped foot in New York for over twenty years and most likely never would again. There was a story there somewhere, even if none of us knew what it was.

Wynter trained pretty much on her own while at Yale. After winning the Olympic gold medal in singles figure skating, she decided she wanted to compete in pairs skating. Kind of a "been there, done that, on to something else" thing, I guess. The search for her ice skating partner was as stressful to the three of us as it was to her. We'd all traveled to California to support her, but Juliette just about ran off each potential candidate with her questioning.

Have you ever dropped a woman? Ever tried to cop a feel when lifting a partner on ice? Ever groped a woman? Are you a voyeur? Do you take drugs? Any assault charges?

Jesus, I'd never forget that line of questioning. Juliette grilled them and made them feel like they were some kind of sexual predator. I couldn't even imagine how uncomfortable the men were, considering how awkward it'd made me feel just listening.

Wynter had studied their technical and artistic skating on the ice, while Wynter's mother just watched them, muttering something to herself every so often. Ivy and I only stared, our mouths gaped open, feeling way out of our element.

Like Ivy and Juliette, I never knew my mother, but I couldn't imagine she was anything like Wynter's mother. Mrs. Flemming was a peculiar woman, to say the least. She raised both Juliette and Wynter when the two girls weren't with Mr. Brennan, Juliette's dad. Despite that, she somehow always seemed distant. I'd only seen her a handful of times, but that just seemed to be her personality. Maybe it was because not only was she Wynter's mother but her skating coach as well.

Eventually, Wynter picked a partner who lived full-time in California. Right after her last exam, she'd be flying back there to start vigorous training with him for the Regionals, Nationals, and World Figure Skating championships this winter. Juliette was planning to go as well since she pretty much grew up there too.

"I have no idea what the fuck to do after we graduate," Juliette announced, repeating my own worries while wiping her mouth with the back of her hand. We had yet to figure out who could outdrink the other between Juliette and Ivy. Those two were lushes and could drink the boys at Yale under the table. We didn't party as hard as some of the other kids that were graduating with our class though.

"Killian knew what he wanted when he was in diapers," she continued. "And here I am, twenty-one, and have no clue what to do with myself. It's not like I can help Dad like Killian does."

"Maybe ask your dad if you could help out with something at his... ummm, *business*," I suggested.

A shadow crossed her face. "He'll say no," she dismissed me, waving her hand. "He'll say how he wants a safer and better life for me, blah, blah, blah."

"You won't know unless you try," I said, which resulted in an eye roll. "And you can't fault him for wanting a better life for you."

"If I want to do something," Juliette said with a slight bitterness in her voice, "I have to start it on my own. Or with you girls."

I tilted my head pensively. It wasn't a bad idea.

"You could dance?" Ivy suggested, her eyes closed and her head resting against the cushions. All four of us were seated on the floor around the coffee table.

"When you say dance, do you mean as a stripper?" Wynter asked curiously. She had glanced at her watch several times in the past hour, which told me she'd be trying to sneak out later—again.

Ivy, Juliette, and I snickered.

"I didn't mean as a stripper, but now that you mention it... Sure, why not? I watched a show that talked about how women can get good money out of it." Ivy opened her eyes and rolled them, then immediately groaned. "My head hurts," she complained.

"That's not exactly a career," I told Ivy. "And your head will feel better if you drink some water rather than alcohol."

"What show was that?" Juliette asked curiously, as if she was seriously contemplating it. "About strippers or whatever."

"*Heidi Fleiss*. A madame or something," Ivy answered.

I scoffed. "She ran a prostitution ring. Not a strip club."

Ivy just shrugged. "Whatever. She made tons of money."

"Madam Juliette," I played along. "It has a ring to it. And a jail cell. I can already picture you in orange stripes."

"It's all about not getting caught. I'd look awful in orange stripes," Ivy announced like she knew all about it.

Wynter glanced at the clock again. "If you're going to make money illegally, it shouldn't be that way. You'll have to hope every customer can keep their mouths shut or make them sign a nondisclosure agreement, and that seems like so much paperwork. You're better off robbing a store."

The three of us stared at her. Every so often, Wynter would say or do something that would shock us all. Of course, what she said made sense. It just sounded shocking coming from her. If Juliette or Ivy said it, I wouldn't bat an eye. When Wynter uttered it though, the three of us wondered if we knew her at all.

"Just give ballet a serious go," Wynter added, shrugging her shoulders. "That should keep you busy."

Juliette had been taking ballet classes for a while, but she had never performed. She even went so far as to take it as one of her elective classes, just so she didn't have to study another subject.

"I'm not that good at it," Juliette muttered.

"You need to give yourself more credit," Wynter protested.

"Agreed," Ivy and I added in unison.

Juliette didn't look convinced. "No, I'm not good like you, Wynter, and you only take ballet lessons to assist with your choreography." Wynter opened her mouth to protest, but Juliette raised her hand, palm facing her cousin. "Don't."

She tried to look authoritative, but she was leaning so far to the side that I thought she might fall over in a drunken stupor. I was tempted to yell, "Timber!"

Looking between the two, you wouldn't have known they were cousins. They couldn't have been more different in appearance, as well as personality. Wynter, with long golden curls and light green eyes, always stood out. And when she smiled, she captured everyone's attention. But she was also driven and had a strong dose of common sense.

Juliette, on the other hand, had auburn hair that reflected red tones under the light, a dash of freckles over her light ivory skin, and blue eyes that almost looked like a porcelain doll. She was beautiful in her own way. She may have had ambition, but it was usually toward mayhem, and I wasn't sure she could spell common sense, much less that she possessed any.

"I'm not quite sure what to do either," Ivy admitted. "Truthfully, it freaks me out to be a responsible adult." All three of us looked at Ivy. "Yes, Dad has money, but it comes with strings and the expectation to marry someone he approves of. And he doesn't approve of anyone except another Irishman who has connections either to the syndicate or the Irish mafia."

"The syndicate?" I asked, confused.

"Other criminal organizations."

"But why would he make you do that?" I asked.

"To expand their power. Make more money. Form alliances," Ivy explained. "Who in the hell knows? It's ridiculous. First, they keep us in the dark on their business, and then they use us as part of their business transactions."

"Bastards," Juliette spat out, pouring herself yet another drink and then gulping it down.

"Yeah, that's fucked up," I muttered. "Probably why we should ensure we do well on our finals so we can be independent women."

A snort slipped out and my head snapped to Ivy. Her wild red hair came down her shoulders and her cheeks were flushed. "Sorry, you're right. It's a serious matter."

"That's right," Wynter agreed sensibly. "We went to Yale. We can do anything we set our minds to." Wynter took Ivy's hand and gently squeezed. "And if your father or Uncle Liam, or even your sweet grandfather, Davina," she continued, glancing over at me, "try to tell us who to marry, we'll kick their asses and survive without their money. Because we'll have each other."

A round of cheers and agreements followed.

Wynter might have a room full of trophies and gold medals, but there wasn't a more down-to-earth person around. No matter what, she never looked down on anyone. Not a homeless person on the street or annoying rich pricks at our university, even though she didn't take anyone's crap.

"We could open a store together," I recommended. "A figure skating equipment store, since we've all learned so much about it over the last four years. I definitely want to start my own business someday. I just don't know what kind yet."

We all chuckled. It was a running joke how much time we spent in sports equipment stores.

"By now I know the difference between Jackson and Edea ice skates, what polish and E-guards to use, as well as the best blade-sharpening tool," Ivy announced, throwing me a drunken smile. "It's sad really, because the only time I've put skates on, I fell flat on my arse."

"I've been around Wynter for twenty years. I know what blades work best on what ice. Try out-doing that," Juliette teased.

Juliette and Ivy could drink me and most of the male population under the table. It had to be the Irish in them. Not that I ever tried to compete with either one of them. I didn't need a hangover. Not today, not ever. I had a full schedule with my studies and my job at the campus coffee shop.

"Okay, so what do you think about a sugar daddy?" Juliette blurted out of nowhere, shocking the three of us. Wynter, Ivy, and I shared a quick glance before we turned our heads in Juliette's direction. "It could be a way to get some money flowing."

"Sugar daddy?" we asked at once. Juliette's subject changes could give you whiplash.

"Yes. I might want one. Of course, I'll need an interview process." Juliette made it sound like it was perfectly normal to take applications for a sugar daddy. Remembering what she put Wynter's potential ice skating partners through, I couldn't help but feel sorry for any potential sugar daddies.

"Can they handle that? Or even you?" I muttered, thinking I needed a bottle of water to get this haziness out of my brain. Someone had to keep an eye on Ivy and Juliette, because I was certain Wynter would ditch us soon. "You might give them a heart attack."

Wynter shook her head, then stood up. "I don't even know what to say to that, Juliette. If you want a career, I'd rather you consider something else. I'm all for the figure skating equipment store."

"I have to agree. I don't think that's a career choice," Ivy commented, one of her rare sane moments. "However, the older men might know what to do in bed. How to make you scream."

And her sane moment was gone. And so was mine as suddenly I imagined some hot-looking older man bending me over and giving it to me rough. My ex-boyfriend definitely lacked in that department, among other ones.

A giggle escaped through my lips as I pictured that scenario in my mind. And possibly as proof the alcohol lingering in my blood needed more diluting. I took another swig of water.

Juliette laughed. "Let's drink to that!"

"Let's not." I stopped her from pouring another round of drinks. "Let's take it easy. We can just talk and have fun. You don't have to get totally shitfaced."

"Tonight, I need to forget," she answered cryptically. Wynter just stared at her, puzzled.

"Older men can be super hot, you know," Juliette continued, unperturbed by her shocking potential career choice. "They've experimented in their lives and know what works and what doesn't. We could use their experience for our own pleasure. I bet they know how to make you come without having to shove their hand into your pants. With that last guy, I had to show him where my clit was. I mean, what's the point? I might as well do it myself if they don't even know basic anatomy." She rolled her eyes and almost fell over again. Maybe it was time to hide the bottle.

The three of us snickered while Wynter just rolled her eyes right back at her, not dignifying it with an answer.

"I swear, I come harder when I touch myself," Ivy grumbled. "These fucking Yale boys can't find the spot to save their lives."

"Hold on," I grumbled. "Aren't you both still virgins?"

Juliette shrugged. "So? It doesn't mean we've never done anything risqué."

It was my turn to roll my eyes. "I'm surprised you can say that word with so much liquor in your system. You're both hammered."

"Risqué, risqué, risqué." Ivy even went so far as to spell it. "Totally not hammered, as you Americans say it."

"You two are idiots when you're drunk," Wynter muttered, digging through her duffle bag. She pulled out her phone and scrolled through her messages, confirming my earlier suspicion. She'd probably sneak out to go practice her ice skating routine. It was her idea of fun.

"You don't have daddy issues, Juliette, do you?" I questioned before I thought better of it. "I think I might have daddy and mommy issues," I admitted, though for the life of me, I didn't know why. I didn't like to admit to people that not having either parent with me while growing up bothered me.

Juliette paled and a soft gasp escaped her. I couldn't understand what upset her.

"I'm sorry," I apologized quickly, taking her hand. "I didn't mean to upset you."

A shuddering breath escaped her, and for a moment, I thought she'd start crying. In all our four years together, I had yet to see her cry.

"I-I found something," she whispered, her nose turning red from trying to hold back the tears.

Ivy, Wynter, and I shared a glance. "What?" I asked in a quiet voice.

She swallowed hard, then took a deep breath, only to slowly exhale.

"I found two birth certificates," she said softly, her eyes darting to the door as if she wanted to make sure nobody came in. As far as I knew, we were the only ones in the house. "Mine and Killian's. It has our parents listed as Aiden and Ava Cullen."

A round of soft gasps echoed through the room and the silence that followed was deafening.

"Are you sure they aren't your dad's fake documents for you and Killian?" Ivy asked. "You know, in case of emergencies."

Juliette swallowed, and by the look in her eyes, I knew she had given this a lot of thought. She must have been pondering it for a while.

"I thought so at first," she murmured. "But I looked it up, and those people existed. They had children the exact ages as Killian and me. It seems too much of a coincidence."

"Could you ask your dad about it?" I rasped. I didn't know much about my mother, and the identity of my own father was a mystery, so I could relate.

"Uncle Liam would tell you." Wynter seemed visibly upset too. "Tell both of us." When Juliette didn't answer, she whispered, "Wouldn't he?"

"I don't know," Juliette whispered.

"Cullen, Cullen, Cullen," Ivy kept repeating the name. "Shit, my brain doesn't work that great with shots in my bloodstream."

"You think?" I asked her dryly.

She glared at me, though it wasn't quite effective when she was tipsy. Then, as if she remembered something, her eyes popped.

"Cullen was another Irish mafia family," she whispered. "They were wiped out, just like the O'Connors."

"Who wiped them out?" I questioned her, frowning. "And what do you mean by wiped out?"

"An accident," Juliette added. "I read that the whole family died in a fire."

"I think they were murdered actually. Both the Cullens and O'Connors."

Wynter shook her head. "Forget the Cullens and O'Connors. Uncle Liam would have told us. If he wouldn't, then Killian would. The birth certificates have to be fake. They have to be. You know how the Irish are about family. Killian's going to take over the Brennan mafia. If he wasn't family, he probably wouldn't be allowed to."

"Seriously?" I gaped. "That seems kind of unfair."

Ivy shrugged. "Irish are all about family. Fair or not."

"But don't you find it odd we know nothing about my mother?" Juliette questioned.

"And I know nothing about my father," Wynter continued.

"Not that we're competing, but I know nothing about either one of my parents," I added.

"My mom died when I was a kid, but I know way too much about my family," Ivy grumbled. "However, I agree with Wynter."

"Your dad includes Killian in his business, right?" I asked Juliette, squeezing her hand gently in comfort. She nodded her answer. "See, you have nothing to worry about."

"You're probably right," she conceded. "It just freaked me out."

"It'd freak any of us out," Wynter agreed. "But there's nothing to worry about there."

I let Juliette's hand go and took another drink of water while keeping my eye on her. Somehow I had a feeling Juliette would keep searching for her answers. She didn't care for academics too much, but her curiosity would be her downfall.

She never talked about her mother, and Wynter never talked about her father. But I suspected, just as I'd always wondered about my own parents, that they wondered about theirs too.

"Anyhow, back to sugar daddies." Juliette changed the subject abruptly. "I think the interview process should be as rigorous as it was when we were searching for Wynter's skating partner."

Instantly, the rest of us groaned. That was a damn painful process.

"Well, if you want my opinion," Wynter chimed in, hunching down to her knees and putting her phone into her duffle bag. "I don't think you need a sugar daddy. Or more alcohol in your system."

Juliette waved her hand, dismissing Wynter's answer. It was clearly not what she was looking for.

"Just be careful," I told Juliette, hoping I wasn't saying the wrong thing here. "Maybe we should help you with the interview process?" I offered.

"Are you nuts?" Ivy grumbled. "Do you remember what she did to those poor men last time?"

Wynter snickered but didn't comment.

"Well, maybe we can—" Juliette's statement was cut off by the door opening, and all our heads whipped in its direction.

My eyes met the most beautiful blue oceans at the highest pitch note of Taylor Swift's song, "Don't Blame Me." And fuck, if I'd known love would make me crazy, just like the lyrics in Taylor's song, I would have done a few things differently since that day.

The man was gorgeous with a capital G. He had a tall, muscular frame and tan, sun-kissed skin. His dark hair had hints of white at the temples, but nothing about him screamed *old*. His face was strong, a chiseled jawline covered with a short, cropped beard.

God, even in my semi-buzzed state, I could see his clothes were hiding a mouthwatering body, the kind that was created to offer a woman ultimate pleasure. I'd stake my life on it.

His eyes lingered on me for barely a second, yet it seared into me for a lifetime. This man had the distinct aura of danger and dominance, despite his casual attire. Jeans hugged his thighs, and a casual yet clearly expensive button-down shirt offered a glimpse of his tanned chest. My mouth watered as my eyes cascaded from his broad shoulders down his torso to his strong thighs and what lay in between. I had the urge to check if I was drooling.

"Could he be my sugar daddy applicant?" I blurted out, not so subtly. "My panties just melted," I added breathlessly.

Without realizing I had even said the latter words out loud, his eyes flashed back to me and the girls burst out laughing. I felt crimson flood my cheeks as humiliation swallowed me whole. I couldn't believe I had said those words aloud. Of all the times the filter between my brain and mouth had to break... it was now.

And I couldn't even blame it on being drunk. I was buzzed, yes, but not drunk. Any sanity I possessed had obviously been thrown out the window along with my dignity the moment I laid eyes on this man.

I couldn't tear my gaze away from him. A chuckle came from behind me, yet I drowned in his eyes and didn't bother to come up for air. I knew he would bring me pleasure. I just wanted pleasure.

Bend me over, spank me. Anything. Just fuck me. Yep, I was past the point of reasonably tipsy. I'd crossed over into a horny drunk without the use of alcohol.

"Davina, that *is* her daddy." Wynter chuckled, her green eyes shining with amusement.

I think he should be my daddy, I thought to myself. God, I was so hot right now. *Now I kind of want my own sugar daddy. Right the fuck now. Spank my ass. I'll call you daddy and everything.*

I furrowed my eyebrows then placed my cool palm against my cheek. Just one look from this man and I was burning. Maybe Juliette could decide she didn't like this guy.

Judging by the way he was looking at me, I may have said that out loud. Shit!

Ivy's eyes were slightly unfocused as they darted between everyone in the room. "I'm confused. Is this guy a daddy daddy or actual Daddy?"

That question was too confusing, and my brain failed to function properly. Juliette and Wynter burst out laughing, each of them holding their stomachs. Wynter even had tears rolling down her cheeks.

"It's my Uncle Liam," Wynter answered, her voice thick with humor. "Juliette's dad."

Wait. What? *Dad!* Did she just fucking call him Juliette's dad?

My heart sank with those words. I wanted to scream it at the top of my lungs, but I couldn't. Not only was he completely out of my league, but he was Juliette's father, and there were some lines one just couldn't cross.

"Juliette, you didn't tell me you and your friends were coming to stay here this weekend." God, his voice. "I didn't expect to see you so soon after last week's visit."

His voice melted the rest of me, because at this point, my panties were soaked. Holy hotness, I had never seen a man so hot. I wanted to walk over to him, shove him into a corner, and take advantage of him. Or maybe he could take advantage of me.

"You horny graduate," Ivy subtly muttered to me under her breath. Or not. Because apparently everyone heard her. The girls laughed, but Juliette's dad didn't.

"Sorry, Dad. We decided last minute," Juliette said, still laughing. "We needed to decompress."

There wasn't enough alcohol to wipe out this stupid feeling. My eyes slowly turned to Juliette's father, feeling like the biggest idiot on this planet. Horniest idiot, but still a goddamn idiot.

He looked too good to be the rumored criminal. I mean, Irish mobsters weren't supposed to look this good. Right? Whenever Juliette talked about him, I pictured him with a round belly and a whiskey bottle in his hands.

Clearing my throat, I struggled to find my voice. It took me two attempts to finally utter a word.

"Mr. B-Brennan," I choked out, attempting to smile. All the while I stuttered. "S-so nice to m-meet you."

He didn't even acknowledge me. *Ouch*.

"You four stay here," he ordered in a harsh tone, and my heart thundered in an unnatural way when his eyes returned to me. Fuck, it felt like he electrified the entire room. It was as if I had been standing next to a burning fireplace for way too long. "I have a meeting with a visitor downstairs. I don't want to see *any* of you roaming the house."

Why did he look at me when he said any of you? It almost sounded as if he was insinuating I'd search him out and seduce him. Jesus, if he was a stranger, maybe, but he was Juliette's father. Seduction and fucking him was out of the question.

God, my heart drummed against my ribs and adrenaline poured into my bloodstream with images of how good fucking him would feel. I just *knew* it.

The door shut firmly behind him and I let out a breath I didn't realize I was holding. Even if I could find my voice at this moment, I couldn't think of a single thing to say. Except... *I want him.*

The whole idea was ludicrous, yet I couldn't shake the feeling.

"That was priceless," Wynter broke the silence, laughing as she zipped up her duffle bag. "I'm so glad I stayed around long enough to see that."

I glared at her, then stuck my tongue out. "Why didn't you guys warn me?"

Ivy shrugged her shoulders, then took another swig of her drink. "I didn't know."

"I tried to tell you." Wynter smirked. "You wouldn't listen."

Juliette rolled around the floor, still laughing. "The best part was when you said, 'Spank my ass and I'll call you daddy.'" She cackled. "Don't tell me you find him hot?"

"Juliette, your dad *is* hot," I told her. "I have never seen a hotter guy, dad or no dad. Ever!"

Ivy chuckled. "Are you going to ask him for his number?"

"Ha-ha-ha," I retorted dryly. "I'm not asking him for anything. He's Juliette's dad."

Juliette shrugged. "I don't care if you ask him for his number. I'm going to warn you though. He doesn't keep girlfriends around for long. I have yet to meet one."

Maybe he was waiting for me? I thought silently, grateful those words stayed behind my lips.

"Maybe he's been waiting on Davina all this time," Wynter added, as if she read my thoughts.

"Don't be silly." I groaned, embarrassed that it was actually a hopeful thought for me. I still couldn't believe those words that had slipped through my lips, that Mr. Brennan had heard them.

It wasn't every day you see so much hard muscle and a gaze that literally stole the breath from your lungs. I'd never forget those eyes, those lips, that body for as long as I lived. I might even think about this man who was at least twenty years my senior as I pleasured myself tonight. That was a sure way to come undone.

"Well, I've got to go," Wynter announced.

"What?" Ivy and Juliette asked at the same time. I wasn't surprised though because she had been glancing at her watch since we arrived.

"This is a girls' night," Juliette protested. "Stay."

"I know, but I need to take every hour I can to practice," Wynter explained matter-of-factly. I had never met another woman who was that determined. She knew what she wanted, and nobody could deter her from it. Not an intense class load, not Yale faculty, not her cousin, not a friend. Nobody.

"Well, you heard my dad," Juliette replied smugly. "We can't roam the house."

Wynter shrugged her shoulders, pulling on her shoes. She wore black tights with leg warmers over the top and a large white sweater.

"Which is the reason I'll be going over the balcony," she replied calmly. "Someone just throw me my bag over once I make it down."

Ivy blinked, then blinked again. "Is that wise? You could break your legs."

Wynter just waved her hand like she wasn't even worried about it.

Onto the balcony she went, as Juliette poured herself another shot, berating her and assigning her the title of the worst cousin ever. I kept my eyes and ears on the balcony, standing right on the edge so I could jump in and help since I was the only relatively sober one left. Too bad I was scared to death of heights. A lot of good I'd be.

"Throw my bag." Wynter's voice traveled up, and before I could get to her bag, Juliette strode over to it, picked it up, and strutted to the balcony. Barely setting a foot outside, she threw the bag over the railing without even glancing down.

It landed with a loud thud.

"What. The. Fuck?" Was that a man's voice?

I tried to peek over the railing, but I couldn't see anything from my spot. Not even Wynter.

"Damn drunks. Trying to kill us," she spat out.

"Us?" I asked her, confused.

Two heartbeats passed before she answered, "Me and my fabulous self. Us."

I shook my head. Wynter would forever be a mystery to me.

"Are you okay, Wyn?" I choked out, curing my fear of heights. The familiar angst crept up my spine, and I forced myself to take another step, but that was as far as I made it. My palms pressed against the stone wall of the manor as I leaned my forehead against it.

I was such a freak, unable to check on my friend because of this paralyzing fear. I could barely glance toward the marble railing, but it was pointless anyway.

"Yes, I'm fine," she assured me. I heard some shuffling going on down there and I swore I heard a man's grumble, but she said she was by herself. "Let me guess. Juliette's pissed off and threw my precious cargo in hopes it would land on my head."

"Nah," I protested weakly, though I couldn't quite deny it. "Be careful," I told her. "And keep your phone on."

CHAPTER 3
Liam

"What the fuck," I grumbled to myself as I walked down the stairs. The timing of the girls' visit sucked. I didn't want Italians in the same city as them, never mind the same house. "Fuck!"

Juliette was drunk—again. Wynter was stone-cold sober, but I wasn't sure about the other two. At least Davina, that dark-haired beauty, wasn't as far gone as the others, but I doubted she would have said that stuff about me out loud if alcohol hadn't at least loosened her tongue. God, thinking about her tongue and what she could do with it was making me hard.

She was gorgeous. An exotic type of beauty, with long ebony hair that fell down in a silky curtain past her breasts. I knew Juliette and Wynter shared a dorm with her and Ivy. It was my job to keep my family safe, but beyond ensuring she wasn't a threat, I never looked into her further. Now I found myself regretting that.

I had to focus on the threats coming from the Italians and the Russians. A college-aged girl had no business in my life. Besides, the raven-haired beauty was my daughter's friend. I couldn't cross that line.

Shaking my head, I focused on the task at hand—this meeting tonight.

The purpose of the meeting was to come to agreeable terms with the DiLustros about the New York territory. I was tired of fighting everyone for turf. I wanted my family safe, and the warning from the latest attack was clear: the Russians weren't going away.

That meant eliminating war with the Italians was a necessity. It just burned me that I had to deal with these scumbags, the DiLustros, after everything that happened twenty years ago. The world would be a better place without them. At least one of them... Gio DiLustro.

His son, Basilio, had approached me with the idea of a peace offering. The Italians in New York would stick to the east side and the Irish to the west side. No more fighting or crossing sides. There had been too much blood spilled over the last twenty-two years. It had started with my sister and what Gio goddamn DiLustro had done to her.

Nothing would make me happier than to kill that motherfucker and then pin it on the Russians. Kill two birds with one stone.

If I didn't think it would escalate things, I'd take care of it myself, but keeping my family safe was my top priority. If something happened to me, it would leave them all vulnerable, and I couldn't let that happen. I knew Killian would step up, but he had his own ghosts to chase first.

Gio's son and nephews had expanded the syndicate. It now covered Chicago, Philadelphia, Las Vegas, and much to my dismay, a good chunk of New York. Basilio DiLustro ran New York, despite his father still being alive. He had a knack for business and had expanded his wealth significantly.

Basilio's cousin, Dante, Gio's nephew from his brother's side, ran Chicago, while Dante's brother ran Philadelphia. And then there was the kingpin who ran Las Vegas, but I hadn't been able to uncover their identity.

There was also their connection to the Ashford family which had been kept under the radar for the last two decades. Although, that part didn't concern me as much.

Gio DiLustro, on the other hand, did.

Tonight's meeting was just between Basilio DiLustro and me to start ironing out the details. The young man was smart to recognize that working with his father wouldn't accomplish anything. Cruelty in our line of work was necessary from time to time, but Gio relished in it. The fucking monster loved it, enjoyed torture and inflicting pain. It was a well-known fact that he broke his women with a smile on his face.

A muffled laugh filtered through the upper floor just as the music was suddenly turned up a notch.

It's going to be a long night, I thought to myself with a silent groan.

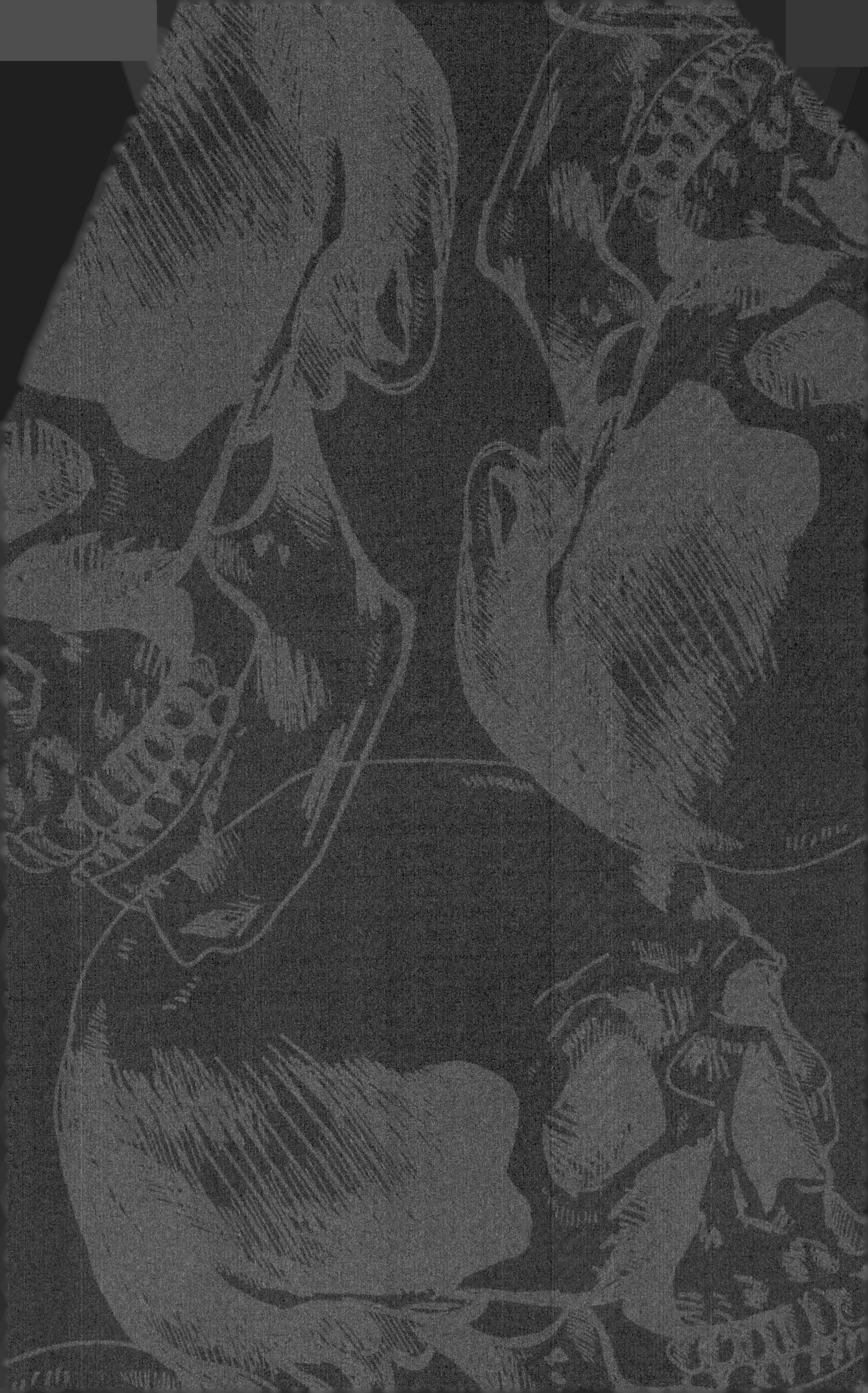

CHAPTER 4
Davina

J uliette and Ivy were sprawled out on the large bed. They snored as loud as drunken sailors, easily able to wake the dead. And also me, apparently.

It was almost midnight, but I couldn't quit tossing and turning. About an hour ago, Wynter snuck back into the house, took a shower, and was now crashed on the lounge sofa. Smart, considering sleeping with the two drunks in the bed was impossible.

"Wynter?" I called out in a whisper. No answer. She was sound asleep. No surprise, since she had been up since before the sunrise.

Turning over, I pulled on the blanket, but the damn thing wouldn't budge. The constant humming of the heating unit should have calmed me, but instead, it made me antsy. My skin felt tight. The room was cool, and you'd think the alcohol would keep me warm, but no such luck. I should have gotten really drunk like Juliette and Ivy. Instead, I was seriously sober now. And fucking cold.

I attempted to pull on the comforter again, but it was like Juliette and Ivy had superglued it to the damn bed.

Sliding off the bed in a huff, I glanced around, wondering if there was an extra blanket around here somewhere. I peeked into the closet closest to the bed but found nothing, and then I checked the other one. Still nothing.

Two closets and no blankets? *I should complain to management about how this place is run,* I thought with a huff. I was getting colder by the minute, so I needed to find a blanket that I didn't have to wrestle monkeys to get.

I padded across the room barefoot, my feet silent against the soft rugs. Cracking the door open, I exited the room and crept down the hallway. The house was so eerily quiet I could hear the wood creak every so often.

"Just looking for blankets," I whispered to myself. The house was covered in darkness, the only light provided by the soft moon. Glancing around the third floor, I listened intently for any sounds. I heard nothing, which had to mean that Juliette's father was gone.

I headed for the door at the end of the hallway, hoping it was another bedroom that would have spare blankets. Placing my hand on the door handle, I pushed on it and the door gently opened. Peeking my head through, I found the room empty and dark.

A thick blanket lay on the large, king-sized bed.

"Perfect," I murmured. It was big enough to keep me warm all night. I tiptoed further into the room, tugging on the comforter just as the sound of the shower registered.

I froze, my head snapping in its direction. The bathroom door was barely cracked open, the sound of water coming from its direction. Somebody was in the shower.

I swallowed hard as my pulse sped up and my breath caught in my throat.

I stood still with my eyes glued to the bathroom door. The smart thing would be to bolt, but no, I stayed, staring in the direction of the bathroom like it was see-through glass.

All I knew was that if I didn't move, I was tempting fate by standing there.

"Fuck." A groan sounded from the bathroom. *Juliette's father.* I was sure that was his voice. An inferno burst through me as I imagined him in the shower. Naked, wet, and big.

My breathing shallowed and my heart thundered against my ribs. I bet that man was magnificent with water cascading down his large body, making his skin slick. Oh, I wanted to see him so badly.

Just a peek, my mind whispered. *Just one peek.*

My insides clenched and fire burned in the pit of my stomach. I just wanted to get a glimpse of the man. Instinctively, I knew nobody would ever compare to him. Those bulky, big muscles. That torso. Fuck, that ass. Everything I saw in those few short minutes, I liked.

With my mind made up, I inched closer and closer to the bathroom door.

Another soft groan.

Another step and my fingers wrapped around the bathroom door handle.

And then a thought struck me. What if—

What if Juliette's father was with another woman? That wasn't something I wanted to see. Unreasonable, poisonous envy slithered through my veins. It made no sense. I'd just met him today, and yet I selfishly wanted him as mine.

The door opened wider. Mr. Brennan came into full view, and my breathing hitched. He looked better than my mind could have conjured. I had never seen something so fucking beautiful. So erotic.

He's jerking off.

My mouth watered. I wished I was the type of woman who could confidently just strip her clothes off and join him in the shower, then get down on my knees and give him the blowjob of his dreams.

Great, I'm delusional too. Still, it didn't prevent me from imagining the wildly hot scenario.

Mr. Brennan was in full view, completely nude. The sculpted muscles of his back and slick, glistening skin were the sexiest things I had ever seen. A single Celtic knot tattoo covered his back, but other than that, he was free of ink.

He was alone. Thank God, because if I saw a woman in there with him, I wasn't sure I'd be able to handle it. His head bowed as he faced the shower wall, and I wished he'd turn slightly so I could see his full front. His dark hair glistened from the water, obstructing my view of his profile.

His bicep flexed with each pump, his movements jerky. Back and forth. My mouth parted, imagining myself on my knees in front of him, his cock in my mouth, taking him in and out. I clenched my thighs, my core throbbing with the need to feel this man inside me.

Braced against the wall, his muscles tensed as he pumped himself faster and harder. The water traced down his beautiful, big body, making my mouth water. I had never felt quite so thirsty in my entire life.

And fuck, his ass.

That was the best-looking ass I had ever seen on a man. Wetness pooled between my thighs and my breathing turned labored. Almost erratic. Greek gods would envy this man of his strong body, lined with muscles. His body flexed with each move as he fisted his cock.

His hips rocked faster, his fist pumped harder. In my mind, I could already picture how good it would feel to have him thrust into me. Mercilessly. Fast. Rough. Rutting me like a beast.

Another soft groan vibrated against the tile. His head tilted back, and I could see his eyes squeezed shut. His moans were raspy and hoarse, seducing me without even trying. My thighs clenched desperately, imagining how he'd feel inside me.

Mesmerized, I couldn't stop watching. I should leave, yet not even the king's horses could've pulled me away. The sight was magnificent.

"Fuck." His biceps flexed as he came with a guttural moan, setting me aflame. All the while, my heart thundered beneath my ribs.

A sound resembling a moaned whimper slipped through my lips, and I instantly realized my mistake. He didn't turn around, but I could have sworn his shoulders tensed slightly.

Slowly and without making a sound, I took a step backward. And another.

When I finally reached the hallway, I turned and bolted. As much as I wanted to see what happened if I stayed, I knew better than to risk it. My body felt as if there were a burning inferno inside me, and I needed *something* to put out these flames.

That man. He was the only one that could extinguish them.

I tiptoed down the hallway, rushing back to my room. The route back to my room definitely seemed longer. My heart thundered so loudly I was sure everyone on this floor could hear it.

Once I made it back to the room, I shut the door softly. Leaning against the closed door, I tried to catch my breath, which was an impossible task as my mind kept replaying what I'd just seen. I couldn't get the vision of him touching himself out of my head. It was so hot, his hand moving up and down.

I wished it was me he was touching. I wished I could run my fingers down that strong body and feel his skin against my fingertips.

My nipples hardened and I swallowed hard as I climbed back into bed, which is when it hit me.

I forgot the blanket.

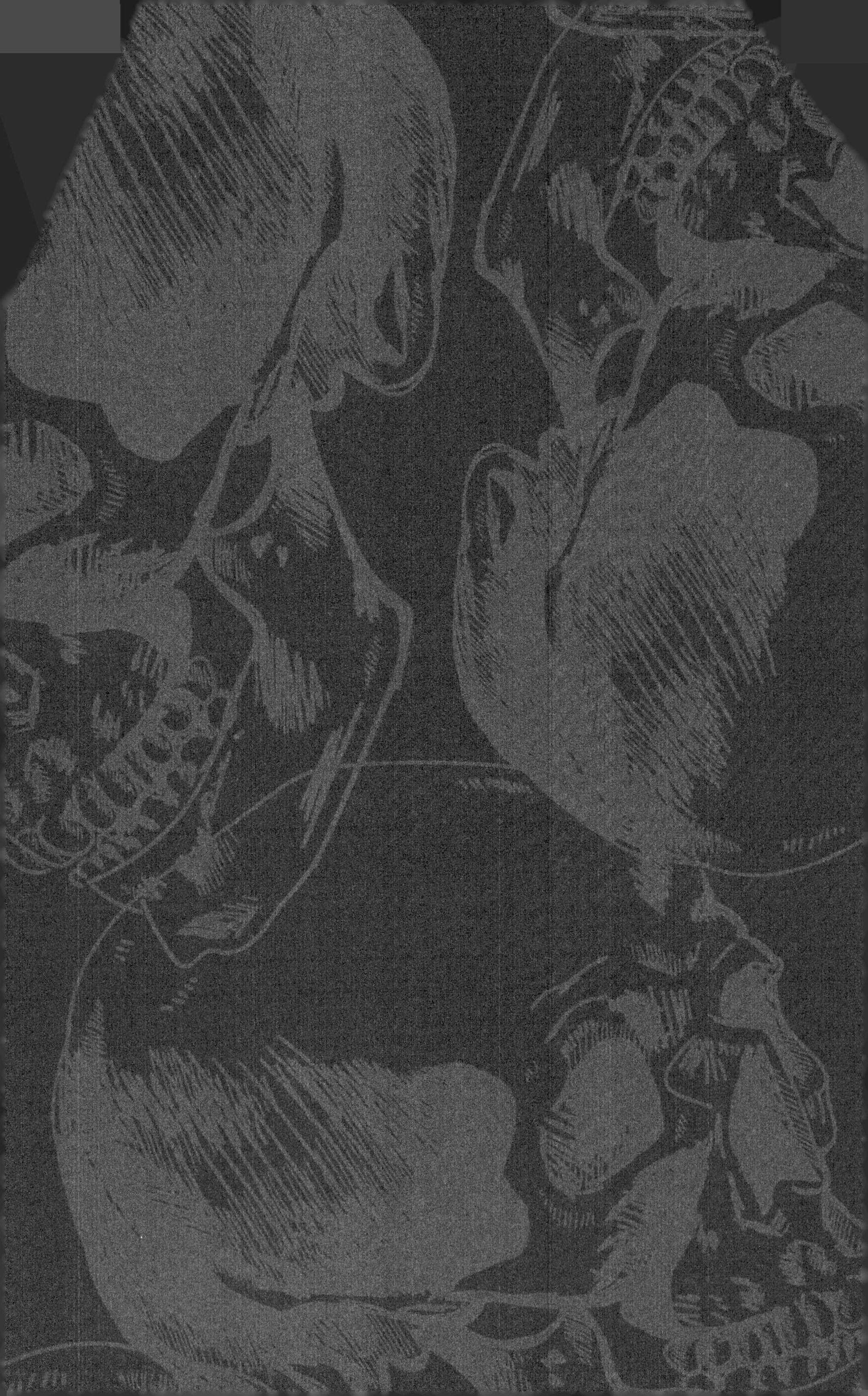

CHAPTER 5
Liam

C*lick.* My head whipped at the soft sound. I stilled, my eyes darting to the gun on the bathroom counter.

I turned off the shower, quickly wrapped my towel around my waist, then grabbed my gun and headed into my bedroom.

More often than not, I stayed at my penthouse. The only reason I was here tonight was for the meeting with Basilio. I didn't like that the girls were here when DiLustro came to visit. I didn't trust any of the members of the DiLustro family.

I couldn't have history repeating itself.

The room was empty and my bedroom door was closed, but I knew I'd heard something.

I pulled on my pajama bottoms and headed straight to the surveillance room. Typing in the code, I unlocked the computer and started to watch the video of the upper floor.

And that was when a shadow creeping around the hallway caught my attention. It was Juliette's friend, Davina. I didn't need to see her face to know it. She had a body unlike any other woman I had ever met. Her hair was like a silky black curtain that made you want to wrap her mane around your hand a few times and hold her close to you.

I watched as Davina walked inside my bedroom, and then I switched to my bedroom camera. It would seem the black-haired beauty was a peeping Tom. And from the looks of it, it seemed she liked what she saw.

Her words earlier this evening had said as much, though I assumed she was hammered, just like Juliette and Ivy. I made it my business to know who Juliette and Wynter hung out with, and I knew Davina Hayes was the most responsible friend. Unlike Ivy Murphy, who could be wild, just like Juliette.

I locked the computer and headed back into my room, hoping to get at least a few hours of sleep.

When I walked out of the room, I ran into Quinn. The alarm must have sounded when I entered the surveillance room, because only the two of us had access to it. When Killian, Juliette, and Wynter were younger, I had a man staffing it at all times. Not that the latter two spent much time at all in New York. But since they'd started college, it was rare for anyone to stay here, so only Quinn and I had used it.

"All good?" Quinn's brows were knitted with worry.

"Yes. I had to check the cameras of the upstairs hallways."

"Huh?"

"I thought I heard something. It was just a midnight mouse creeping through the house."

This time, his eyebrows shot up. "Mouse, huh?" I nodded. "You need to get some sleep, Liam."

I chuckled, unperturbed, and headed up the stairs back to my bedroom. As I passed the bedroom where the girls were sleeping, I couldn't help but feel satisfaction that little Miss Hayes enjoyed the show in the shower. I'd send any other woman packing, but something about that one tugged at me.

The next morning, I was drinking my coffee in my office with the door wide open when Wynter passed by. It was barely six a.m.

"You're not going for a run at the crack of dawn, are you?" I called out to her. "Alone?"

She took a step back, her eyes met mine, and a wide smile spread over her face. God, she looked so much like both her mother and the grandmother she was named after. Some days it was like seeing a ghost.

"Morning, Uncle," she greeted me with that smile that could brighten a whole room. "I am, in fact, running alone. Unless you want to join me?"

"Wouldn't you rather join me?" I asked her. I'd already spent an hour in the gym and was enjoying my coffee before jumping in the shower, but letting Wynter run alone wasn't an option. "We could have a cup of coffee and you can tell me what trouble you girls have been up to."

Wynter walked into my office and sat on the desk. "And then you'll go for a jog with me?"

"I might."

"Then this should be quick," she started, a little mischievous smile on her lips. "We've just been studying. We haven't been attending many parties lately. Yesterday, we just wanted to relax for a bit, which is why the drinks were flowing, but today we'll be back to hitting the books. That pretty much sums up our life. We are boring as fuck." She stood up, straightening her legs. "Now, let's go and burn those miles," she announced.

"Trickster." I was certain she hadn't told me even half of it. "And I'd bet my life your lives are anything but boring."

She shrugged. "You're assuming we're doing stuff," she objected. "We aren't."

"What was the whole thing about a sugar daddy yesterday?" I asked her curiously.

My niece threw her head back, her curls bouncing wildly as she laughed. Her musical laugh rang through the first floor, and I hoped it'd wake up the rest of the girls. It'd give me time to catch up with Juliette, and there was a part of me that was hoping to see Davina again.

The sadistic part of me wanted to call her out on what she witnessed last night and watch her face turn crimson. Of course, not in front of the other ladies. That'd be just for her ears.

"That was just a joke that you showed up at the right time for,"

Wynter explained, chuckling. "Or the wrong time, depending how you look at it."

I shook my head. "I better not find out any of you are doing anything with men—sugar daddies or otherwise." Except for Davina. If she wanted a sugar daddy, I'd sign up.

Wynter just rolled her eyes. "Okay then," she mumbled. "We'll be nuns." For a few seconds, I noted the turmoil reflected behind those big, light green eyes.

"Say what's on your mind, Wynter."

She chewed on her lower lip. "I know you have secrets related to your business." I cocked my eyebrow at her unexpected statement. "But you'd tell us personal family stuff, right?"

I held her gaze. "Like what?"

She shrugged. "Like stuff about my father. Or stuff about Juliette's mother. You and Mom both never talk about it."

"They're hard memories to talk about."

I knew curiosity would kick in. I expected it years ago, when she was a kid. Certainly not now.

"It's just weird, you know," she continued. "I see this name on my birth certificate and know absolutely nothing about that person." I kept my face stoic. "Same with Juliette."

"It's only natural," I tried to put her worries to rest, "when each of you never knew one of your parents."

For a few moments, she watched me pensively, then stood up. "Are you ready now? Or are you worried you can't keep up?"

The abrupt change of subject didn't escape me, but I went along with it. The alternative wasn't an option. Not yet.

"Oh, now you've done it," I teased her. "I'm going to beat you to Central Park and back."

"You're on." She grinned. "Hundred bucks?"

The girl could go through money, but at least I knew it all went to her ice skating equipment.

"How about five hundred bucks?" I challenged.

We shook on it, and out the door we went.

CHAPTER 6
Davina

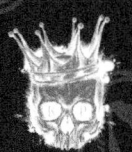

I woke up the next morning, and the first memory that hit me was of last night's image of Mr. Brennan taking care of himself in the shower.

Oh my God! That was a sight to behold.

On one hand, I was mortified that I stood there and watched him like some creepy stalker. And on the other hand, I wished I'd seen more. I couldn't shake off the desire that was burning in the pit of my stomach.

My phone started to ring, and I groaned when I saw it was my ex-boyfriend. I chose not to answer and sent him to voicemail.

"Man, who's calling you so early?" Juliette groaned, burying her face into the pillow.

"Nobody." Glancing at the clock on the side table, I continued, "It's almost ten, definitely not early. Let's get up, eat, and get going. I have an afternoon shift at the coffee shop."

Besides, I couldn't risk running into Mr. Brennan. I'd had my share of embarrassment to last me the entire year, and this year had barely gotten started.

"You should have taken Sunday off," Ivy mumbled.

I glanced at the spot where Wynter slept last night and found her seated, her face in her book. She probably already did a ten-mile run, ate breakfast, and came back to study.

"Morning, sleeping beauties," Wynter drawled. "I thought you three would sleep the day away."

"You should have woken us up," I told her.

"I was about to," she admitted, smiling. "I waited for the three of you so we could eat together. So hurry up, I'm starving."

Ten minutes later, we all made it down to the kitchen for brunch. Juliette and Ivy looked pretty rough. I probably did too, but more from lack of sleep than the alcohol I'd had the night before.

That image of Mr. Brennan in the shower played on repeat in my mind, over and over again. All night long. What I'd seen—and not seen. I'd been up half the night fantasizing about what his cock must look like and what he could do with it.

All the right things, my mind whispered. I was going to hell. There was no doubt about it.

When we entered the kitchen, the smell of food instantly filled my lungs and my stomach growled.

Thank God Juliette's dad had a chef or we'd be out of luck this morning. Ivy and Juliette skipped the fresh fruit and lunged for the crispy bacon and grease-filled sausages, learning a long time ago that fat was the best cure for a hangover.

Wynter, on the other hand, was loading up on carbs so that she had something to burn while she practiced later today. I grabbed a banana and a bagel with some cream cheese. I wasn't exactly hungover, but I didn't want to risk the wrath of the gods by putting something in my nervous stomach that might not want to stay there.

I was pretty sure that Mr. Brennan had left the house. I wasn't sure I could face him after what I'd witnessed.

We sat down around the large dining room table and dug into our food. I'd barely gotten the first bite down when I felt a presence behind me.

"Morning, ladies," a decidedly masculine and very familiar voice called from the entrance to the dining room, and I instantly stiffened. *Fuck my life.*

It was bad enough that my big mouth had made a total fool of myself last night. Couldn't I get a break today? At least he didn't see me. There was comfort in that. I'd never tell a soul about it.

"Morning," Juliette, Ivy, and I mumbled, avoiding looking his way. Probably for all different reasons.

"Morning again, Uncle Liam," Wynter said, grabbing another banana.

"Morning, Davina." Mr. Brennan's voice was relaxed, and I was painfully aware of him in the room.

I glanced his way but kept my eyes to the left of him. I couldn't meet his gaze.

"Morning." I barely got the word out, my throat suddenly dry.

My heart hammered against my ribs and heat colored my cheeks, remembering the glistening of his skin under the shower droplets, the grunting noises he made as his fisted hand slid up and down his cock. A cock that, unfortunately, I didn't see.

A throbbing ache pulsed between my thighs, and I squeezed my legs together, needing to kill this sensation before it became too uncomfortable.

He didn't see you, Davina, I comforted myself as I focused on avoiding looking in Mr. Brennan's direction.

He sat down next to me on my right, and I silently groaned. So much for getting out of here before I ran into him again.

"How did everyone sleep?" he asked, and attention shot up my spine. My paranoia was taking full effect.

He didn't see me. He didn't see me. The chanting in my brain did nothing to make me feel better. My eyes were on the food, but my entire body was hyper-aware of him next to me. I swore his eyes were burning a hole into my right cheek.

I hoped someone would answer the question and save me any conversation opportunities with him.

"Fine," Juliette grumbled, rolling her eyes. "Would be even better if Davina's phone didn't wake us up."

A heartbeat of silence. "And how did *you* sleep, Davina?"

Oh my God, someone kill me now! My body was set aflame. Desire burned so strong it made my hand shake as I reached for my orange juice.

I didn't dare to look at him, yet every fiber of my being was on alert, aware of him. From the corner of my eye, I could see him watching me.

"Good, thanks," I murmured, still refusing to look his way. I took a sip of my orange juice and then set the glass back on the table, landing it a bit harder than I intended.

Juliette's and Ivy's eyes came to me for a moment, but then went right back to staring at their phones. Even Wynter's eyes flicked my way before returning to her book.

"That's good," Mr. Brennan continued, his deep voice sending shivers down my spine. "We want you to feel comfortable here. In *any* room."

I swallowed hard and my eyes widened. Did he—?

No, no, no. Don't panic.

I snuck out of his room and went straight back to my room. He didn't see me peeping on him. *Right?*

"Thanks," I croaked, hoping my smile didn't look like a painful grimace. I still refused to lock eyes with him. I feared it would send me spiraling into a deep abyss and I'd never come back up for air.

"You're studying business, right?"

I wished he'd just ignore me, but he kept talking, acknowledging my presence. It was better last night when he didn't even bother looking my way.

"Davina is the best in her class," Juliette chimed in, elaborating on my behalf. "She's really good, and one day, she wants to start her own business."

I silently groaned, wishing the focus would shift to someone else.

"What kind of business?" Mr. Brennan inquired, curiosity in his deep voice.

"It definitely won't be along the lines of your business." Ivy snickered, and then as if she realized she'd said it out loud, she slammed her hand against her mouth. "Umm, I didn't mean that. It came out of nowhere. The alcohol must still be in my veins. I need to detox."

"You do that, Ivy," Mr. Brennan scolded her. "And go easy on the alcohol next time. All of you."

Ivy's cheeks turned so red they matched her hair color. I had to be a horrible person, because I was glad Mr. Brennan's attention was on her and not me.

Though, it was short-lived.

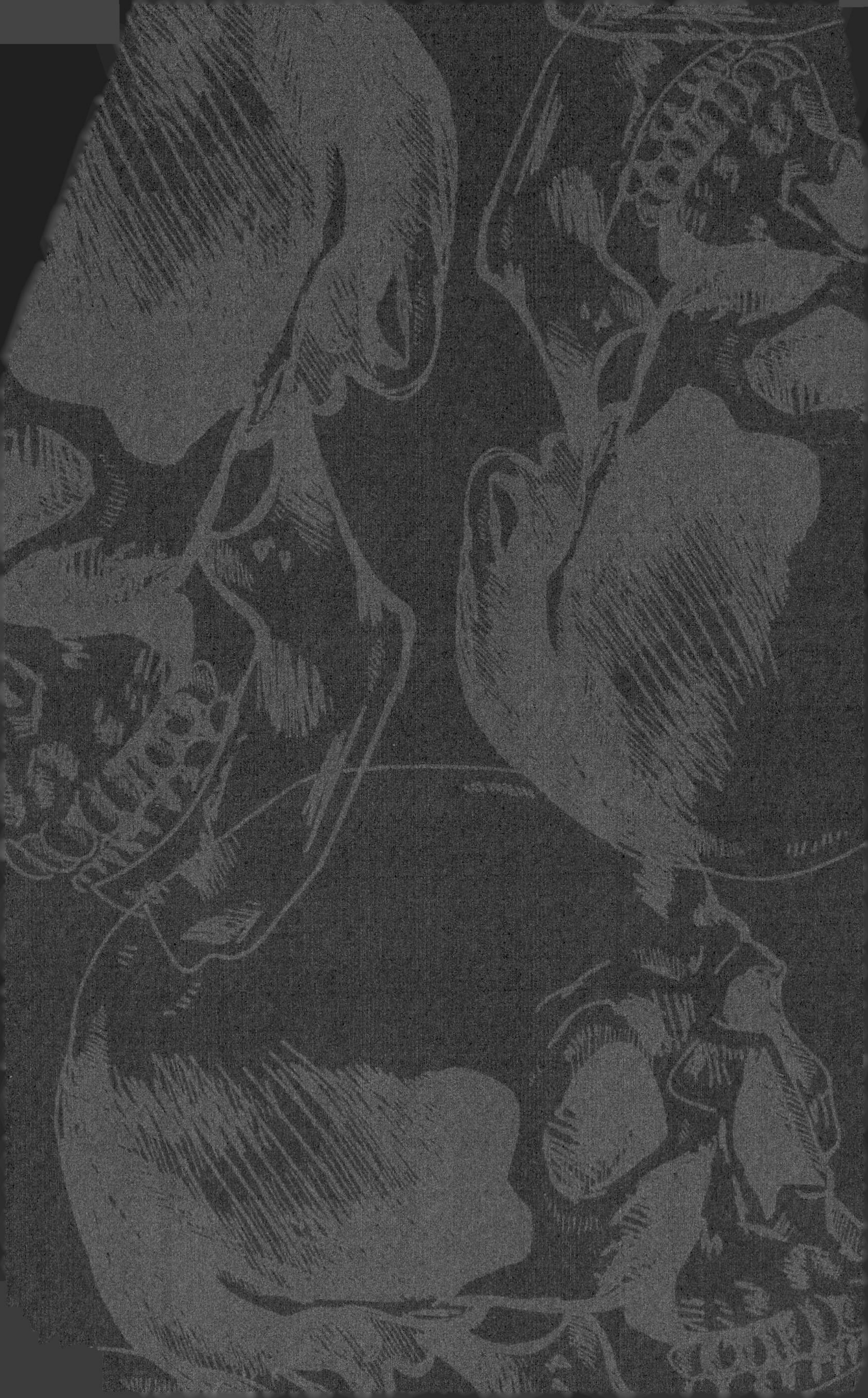

CHAPTER 7
Liam

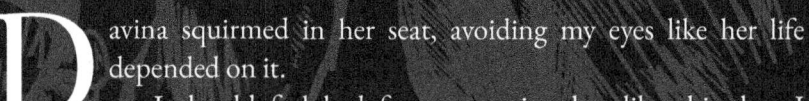

Davina squirmed in her seat, avoiding my eyes like her life depended on it.

I should feel bad for tormenting her like this, but I didn't. I quite enjoyed seeing emotions flash across her expressive face. She may be doing her damndest to not look in my direction, but I knew she was aware of my every move. Each time I moved, I swore she shifted too. Like there was a magnetic field between us.

For all my years on this earth, I had never experienced it. I'd seen it, yes. With my own father and the woman he'd started a war for. It was ironic, really, because at this very moment, I could understand it. I would have done anything to protect my family—Juliette and Killian.

Never a woman. Until today. Because I knew I would for Davina. It was right here and now that I decided she'd be mine.

I watched the beauty with raven hair reach for her glass, her fingers trembling slightly. Did Ivy's comment scare her?

Not everyone could stomach this kind of life. It was the reason I'd sheltered Juliette and Wynter at all costs. Even when Juliette had asked questions over the years, I kept her out of it. I promised Aiden I'd keep her safe, as the same promise I'd offered to my sister.

The same way I'd protect Davina. The resolve had already formed in my mind.

For a fraction of a second, Davina's eyes flicked to me, and I saw a hint of desire lurking in them. Something in my chest rattled with satisfaction. Her pink tongue swept across her bottom lip, and I had to ignore the heat running to my groin. The gesture was innocent, yet hot as fuck.

Wonderful. I'd better get a grip. Otherwise, I'd find myself wrapped around her finger.

"Do you have plans after you graduate, Davina?" I turned my attention back to the woman that fascinated me.

"The only one that has plans is Wynter," Juliette chimed in, her voice tense. "You won't let me help you with your business, and Ivy's family won't let her help with their business. Davina is trying to figure out how to take care of her grandfather and be a responsible adult."

Juliette had been behaving strangely lately. Initially, I'd chalked it up to the changes that she knew were coming once she graduated, but I was starting to think it was more than that. It was true that Juliette had offered to help with the business, but the risks associated with it outweighed the benefits, so it was a firm no.

"I'm so glad you were able to answer for Davina," I told my daughter dryly.

"You all just wait and see," Ivy added. "We'll beat all of you... you..." She tried to come up with a creative name but apparently failed, because she blew a piece of her red hair out of her face with frustration and continued with a "You criminals. And we'll have an even better gig going."

"Yeah, with the figure skating equipment store," Davina mused, her eyes meeting mine. "We'll rule the world with that one. Or maybe just the United States."

And then, as if she realized she'd inadvertently inserted herself into our conversation, she blushed and diverted her attention.

Amusement filled me. I really liked the girl. Sensible with a hint of fire to her.

"Well, we could be a world-renowned figure skating equipment store," Wynter chimed in helpfully.

"It's possible," Davina answered. "Especially with a double Olympic gold medalist as part of it."

"I hope," Wynter added. "Don't jinx me. I still have a ways to go."

"You'll get there," I assured my niece. She was determined when she wanted something. So was Juliette, except that the latter liked to rebel when she hit a bump in the road. And when she was stressed, she tended to shut down.

When Juliette was younger, Killian and Wynter were always the only ones that could get through to her during those episodes.

"And so will you, Juliette," I told my adoptive daughter. Juliette had a golden heart but a temper that was fit for a redhead. It was the Irish in her. "I promise you. I'll help you achieve your dreams, but it has to be something safe."

Juliette had dark hair and blue eyes, so it was easy to sell to the world that she was my biological daughter. I hid both her and Killian from the underworld to keep them safe. I wouldn't let it all be thrown to the wind. Unlike their parents, Killian and Juliette would live into old age and see their children grow up. And, God willing, their grandchildren.

It was my promise to Aiden, my best friend.

I locked gazes with Juliette, and to my shock, there were unshed tears glistening in her eyes and an alarm immediately shot through me.

"Juliette, what's the matter?" I demanded. The silence and tension around the room was palpable, but all my focus was on my daughter.

I waited for an answer, but then her lips curved into a mischievous smile.

"Got you," she drawled, and for a moment, all I could do was stare. The expression she gave me reminded me so much of my late best friend. He'd play pranks on me all the time. His wife was the serious one in their marriage. Killian might look like his father, but he had the temperament of his mother.

Twenty-one years had gone by. All those years, and their lives still hadn't been avenged. Killian and I were working on it, but it wasn't moving fast enough. For either one of us.

Truthfully, I wished Killian didn't remember that day so I could have spared him the knowledge and pain. I'd rather hunt for the guilty ones on my own so he'd stay safe. But Killian remembered too well, and over the years, he had been nurturing his thirst for revenge.

Much to my regret.

Even after all these years, the anger at my best friend's death clawed through me, right alongside guilt. I should have never pulled Aiden into the shit with the Russians. He was the only one I trusted, and it cost him everything, including his own life. And it was all my fault.

Juliette and Ivy stood up and the sound of the chairs against the floor pulled me back from my thoughts.

"I'm going to take a quick shower," Juliette announced, then rolled her eyes at Davina. "It seems my friend took the Sunday afternoon shift at the coffee shop."

Davina shrugged. "You'll live. Make it quick."

"I'll go pack up our stuff," Ivy added. "I know what a dick Mr. Foger can be if you're late. I lasted a week with him. How you've survived four years, I have no fucking clue."

"He's all bark and no bite." Davina stood up as if she was going to leave too, but her breakfast was still unfinished.

"Finish your breakfast, Davina," I encouraged her. She had amazing curves, and selfishly, I wanted her to keep them. Was I getting ahead of myself? Yes, probably. But hey, life was short, and we had to have something to look forward to.

"Yes, stay and finish," Juliette encouraged her friend. "Wynter isn't finished either."

Juliette lacked observation skills, because my niece had been done for the past five minutes.

"Just finish your breakfast," Wynter told her, never lifting her gaze. "My coach always says breakfast is the most important meal of the day." Then she snorted and continued, "Though, to this day, I'm not certain if that was the coach speaking or my mother."

"Both," I told her.

Davina reluctantly sat down. It took another minute before Wynter stood up and left too.

We were finally alone.

Davina took another bite. I watched her with interest, even though she was doing her best to look anywhere but my way.

I leaned back in my chair and focused on her. She picked up a butter knife and readied to spread cream cheese on her bagel, though her movement almost seemed exasperated. She wanted to be anywhere but here.

"How did you like last night?" I asked her, and she dropped her knife with a loud clunk. Her dark gray eyes flashed to mine, her mouth slightly parted. I could see the blotchy blush on her chest that her tank top did nothing to hide.

"Did you enjoy the show?" This time, a sardonic kind of amusement filled me, and I was probably a bastard for not letting it go.

She took a deep breath, then exhaled.

"Y-yes," she stammered, and then quickly added, "I mean, no." She swallowed hard. "It was an accident."

I raised my eyebrows. "It was an accident that you found yourself in my room." She nodded so vigorously I worried she'd give herself whiplash. "And it was an accident that you peeked through the bathroom door." She nodded again and her eyes hazed with lust. *Good!* "And I'm sure it was an accident that you stood there and watched me jack off."

A soft gasp filled the room and her gray eyes turned a shade darker. She really had the most amazingly colored eyes. They were the color of clouds right before a thunderstorm. Something about them cooled the heat burning inside me.

Suddenly, she stood up, slamming the chair behind her with a loud thud.

"I have to go," she breathed, her cheeks flushed.

She readied to bolt, but I grabbed her right wrist. Her eyes snapped to where my big hand wrapped around her small wrist, and a visible shudder rolled down her body. And when her eyes came back to mine, they were molten silver and full of desire.

Davina reminded me of an enchantress sent to seduce a mere mortal, one of the stories my short-lived stepmother used to tell me. One night, and I was under her influence. What the fuck would happen if I was around her for months?

"First, we settle this," I told her, my thumbpad brushing her soft skin. Another shudder and her breathing turned shallow. "After watching me last night, did you touch yourself?"

She licked her lips, then shook her head. "The girls were in the room," she breathed the explanation, and then she looked mortified that she let those words slip between her lips. "I-I mean... of course not."

Too late, I thought smugly. God, she really was gorgeous.

She gently tugged on her wrist, but I refused to let go.

"Someone might come in and see," she whispered, her eyes darting around. I didn't give a shit who saw me holding her hand. "I don't want someone to get the wrong impression."

"It's my house," I told her, a hint of possessiveness edged in my voice. "And I don't give a shit about anyone else's opinion."

"I have to go," she feebly attempted again.

"First, we'll come to an agreement," I drawled. "You owe me a favor for the free show last night."

Her eyes widened and she shook her head like a deer caught in headlights.

"Fuck no. I told you it was an accident." I'd give it to her, she was brave.

I tsked her. "Maybe it was an accident that you walked into my room, but it wasn't an accident that you stayed and watched."

She closed her eyes for a moment and then opened them. She looked calmer now, stronger, with resolution simmering beneath her expression.

"What do you want then?" she asked.

Did she really have to ask?

"You."

CHAPTER 8
Davina

Three Months Later

After that night three months ago, I was on pins and needles for weeks, waiting for Liam Brennan to cash in on the debt I owed him. But then a few weeks by, and then a month, and then another, and nothing. I finally decided he must have just wanted to teach me a lesson and had never meant to follow through. Much to my disappointment.

So, I decided to continue my life, trying my best to forget the Irish mobster. I had gotten back together with Garrett, my on-again, off-again boyfriend. He had been actively pursuing me at least. Unlike a certain Irish mobster who probably forgot I existed the moment I walked out of that kitchen.

It was almost midnight on Sunday night when I pulled into the driveway of Garrett's home. I guess it'd officially be my home too. Soon. Most of my stuff was moved to his place two weeks ago.

After taking a break, we'd decided to give our relationship another go about six weeks ago. With graduation coming up, he wanted me to move in with him, but even though I had taken my stuff over, I still stayed at the dorm most nights. It was more convenient, and the girls were way more fun than sitting at Garrett's place.

After all, scheming about world domination was more important than a boyfriend. Right? And we studied too, so I had a perfect excuse. If I was smart, I'd have stayed back at the dorm tonight and been sound asleep by now.

But I knew avoiding Garrett wasn't actually a good start to our cohabitating, and I haven't had sex in weeks. Six weeks, to be exact. After we first got back together, life kept getting in the way. And so did the fantasies about Mr. Brennan. The way he pumped himself in the shower.

Now that we'd decided to get serious about our relationship, Mr. Brennan would forever remain a fantasy. Cheating was a hard no for me.

But tonight was the night I was going to break my six-week sex drought, and Garrett better deliver. No more fantasizing about Juliette's father.

I turned the key in the ignition, the motor of my little Honda Civic going quiet.

Rubbing my burning eyes from hours of studying, I opened the door to my car and stepped out into the cool night air. I still had a few days until the last of my finals were complete.

And then this will be home, I thought silently.

I still struggled with that idea. Wynter would go back to California; Juliette would follow. Ivy was trying to decide what she'd do. She didn't want to go back to Ireland and be married off. The girls tried to convince me to move to California, but housing there was ridiculously expensive.

We even contemplated sharing an apartment, but I didn't have enough to cover my share of the first few months of rent, and I wouldn't until I found a job there. I didn't want to be so broke that I'd go a long time without seeing my grandpa. The girls insisted they'd cover me, but it made me feel inadequate.

So here I was. Nothing like committing yourself to someone in exchange for housing. I liked Garrett, I just didn't know if I loved him.

I stretched my arms and legs after being cooped up in the Honda. Glancing around, I noticed Garrett's car was missing, but that wasn't strange given his work hours. Though, he'd said he was getting off work earlier than normal today.

My eyes locked on the sleek, red Tesla parked at the curb in front of the house. It had me raising a brow in question. Maybe it belonged to one of our neighbors. It certainly didn't belong in Garrett's driveway. Shrugging it off, I made my way to the front door, pushing my key into the lock and turning it.

Garrett said since I had the key to his home, it was my home now too. To be honest, I struggled with that concept. My grandfather's place was my true home, and my dorm felt more like home than Garrett's house. I suspected it had something to do with my relationship with the people I shared the space with, but I kept ignoring the niggling thoughts in the back of my head.

I always overthought things way too much. Life wasn't a fairy tale. If it were, my parents would have planned for me and been overjoyed to have me. Instead, they got rid of the responsibility. Thankfully, I had my grandfather who took care of me and was the most loving parent.

I walked through the door. All the lights on the first floor were off, the moon shining through the wall of large windows outlining my path. It struck me as odd that Garrett turned off all the lights because he regularly left at least one light on.

I walked through the foyer, then up the stairs, and with each step I took, the dread in the pit of my stomach grew.

Something is off.

Every single fiber of my being screamed the warning. My brain had alarms going off, red flags and sirens blaring. *Turn around. Turn around.*

Yet, I continued. Each step closer to our bedroom, the faint voice grew clearer.

"Fuck yeah." The sound was muffled.

I pushed the handle of Garrett's bedroom door open, and my eyes locked on the empty bed. The room was dark, the only light coming through the slightly cracked door of the bathroom. The sound of the shower finally registered.

Maybe Garrett is jerking off, I thought to myself, amused. In retrospect, I wasn't sure whether it was my faith in him that made me so stupid or hope that I'd picked a better man than my mother, who had gotten pregnant by a married man.

I heard a soft moan and my heart gave a painful thud. That moan hadn't come from Garrett. That was a feminine moan by someone who really liked what was happening to her.

Don't go in there, my mind whispered. I ignored it. I'd never been one to choose ignorance over truth.

One step. Another step. The door was ajar, and I gently pushed it open further, then stepped into the large, marble-tiled bathroom.

Betrayal twisted my heart as I stood frozen, staring at the scene in front of me. Garrett was indeed in the shower, but not alone. A woman's head bobbed up and down as he grunted and moaned through it.

Rage shot through my veins, draining every other emotion out of me. I stumbled backward from the bathroom. My eyes caught on the crystal vase full of flowers he'd bought for me.

Blooming flowers for our love, he'd said. My fucking ass.

In one swift move, I lifted the vase and threw it across the room, watching it fly through the air and crash through the large French window. The loud buzz in my ears dulled the noise of the shattering glass. Things blurred together, yet I couldn't stop myself from continuing. A painting followed. Another vase. A little side table that I'd brought in from my dorm room. It was the only piece of furniture that Garrett would allow me to bring in, and even then, he insisted I hide it in the corner of the room so nobody could see it. What a self-absorbed prick!

I lifted it up, the cheap table barely weighing a few pounds, and threw it through the window, following all the other items.

"Here, let the fucking neighbors see the cheap table," I hissed.

Behind me, I could hear Garrett and the woman scrambling, but I didn't care. I didn't wait. I couldn't stay in this place for another goddamn minute, or I'd lose my shit and set this place on fire.

Sometimes, it was the irony of the universe that caught up with us.

"That piece of shit," Juliette hissed, still pissed about what that son of a bitch did. I barely got through my exam without bawling my eyes out. Juliette, Wynter, and Ivy finished ahead of me and waited, then we headed back to our dorm.

Now we were seated on the floor of the half packed up dorm room, boxes surrounding us. It was Friday, and we'd just finished a full week of exams. Some seniors had already emptied their rooms and were about to begin their lives. Mine had already started to fall apart before it even really began.

Way to start off all wrong.

"I want to go murder him," Juliette added in a decidedly scary voice. "Like take a gun and shoot him."

It had to be her Irish mafia upbringing talking. I had to talk her out of breaking out the whiskey. I didn't need to get drunk with exams this week, though I was sorely tempted. I also didn't need to try to deal with a drunk Juliette on top of everything else. Juliette always kept multiple bottles of whiskey for emergencies, and this was a goddamn emergency according to her.

I needed to get my stuff from Garrett's. I'd already moved most of my clothes and other possessions to his place, and I needed them back. The only things I still had in my dorm were books, little knickknacks, and a change of clothes.

The icing on last night's shit cake was my fucking car. It died halfway between Garrett's place and Yale. In the middle of the goddamn night. Thankfully, Wynter was a light sleeper and answered her phone. The girls came and got me, and now I was back at square one. And on top of everything, I was careless too.

At least it felt like it.

I glanced around the room that had been our home for the past four years. Since we were always together, the four of us had turned two small dorm rooms into one larger one our first year of college. This place felt like home because of the friendship we shared.

"I'm not much for violence," Wynter muttered, "but I have to agree on this one. I think that piece of shit deserves to be tortured and then killed."

"We hadn't even officially moved in together and he already cheated," I muttered. I was so humiliated.

My phone dinged and I winced. I didn't have to look to know who it was. Garrett had been blowing up my phone since I left his house last night. *His* house. It was never mine. It was never ours.

"We have to go get your things," Ivy reasoned. "At least your legal documents and stuff."

She was right. Of course she was, but I was worried about going there. The anger that simmered in my veins was unlike any other I had ever experienced. It had my ears buzzing, my temper flaring. Apparently I destroyed ten thousand dollars' worth of property on my way out, if Garrett's texts were to be trusted. Must have been a Ming vase that I threw out of that window. I'd laugh if I wasn't about to cry again.

"Stupid," I mumbled. "I'm so stupid."

I shouldn't have lost my temper so badly. I always kept a tight rein on it. Maybe it was a combination of being sexually frustrated, betrayed, and furious.

"No, you're not stupid." Wynter took my hand and shook it gently. "Don't you even say it. He's a cheating, dirty bastard. He's the stupid one."

Tears pooled in my eyes and threatened to start rolling all over again. "I was swayed by living in a nice house, by the chance to have my paycheck go toward Grandpa's retirement home costs for a place here in New York instead of Texas. When I found a corporate job here, I'd planned on bringing him. And now..."

The worst part was that I wasn't even in love with Garrett. We'd dated on and off for over a year, and with college nearing its end, it made sense to talk about the next steps. Going back to Texas was an option, but I'd have to take a job at a diner or a bar as a waitress. In Port Aransas, options were limited. The little fisherman's dream town on the Gulf Coast was a haven for anglers and beachgoers, as well as retirees. It was a great place to grow up, but when it came to applying my Yale degree, not so much.

But with a job in New York, on the other hand, I'd be able to afford to bring Grandpa here and take care of him. Just him and me, just like the old days. I'd miss the girls though. He would too. He'd started to care for them almost as much as I did.

"So fucking stupid." I pressed my fingers to my temples. I should have listened to my gut that warned me moving in with Garrett was wrong. I evaluated it like a business transaction, remembering that I studied business because sometimes it was the only thing that made sense.

An idea shot through my brain. "What time is it?"

Three sets of eyes blinked in confusion at such an abrupt change of topic.

Wynter answered while Juliette and Ivy just stared, confused, muttering under their breaths, "Is that a trick question?"

"It's three o'clock," Wynter answered, eyeing me curiously. "Why?"

"Garrett doesn't get home until after six," I rushed. "If we go now, we could get there, get my stuff, and be gone before he gets home."

We shot to our feet, Juliette and Ivy grumbling we should wait for the cheating bastard to get home and then kill him.

Wynter and I just rolled our eyes and pushed them toward the door, hoping we'd be able to keep them under control long enough to get my stuff and get the hell out of there before Garrett got home. I never wanted to see that bastard again for as long as I lived.

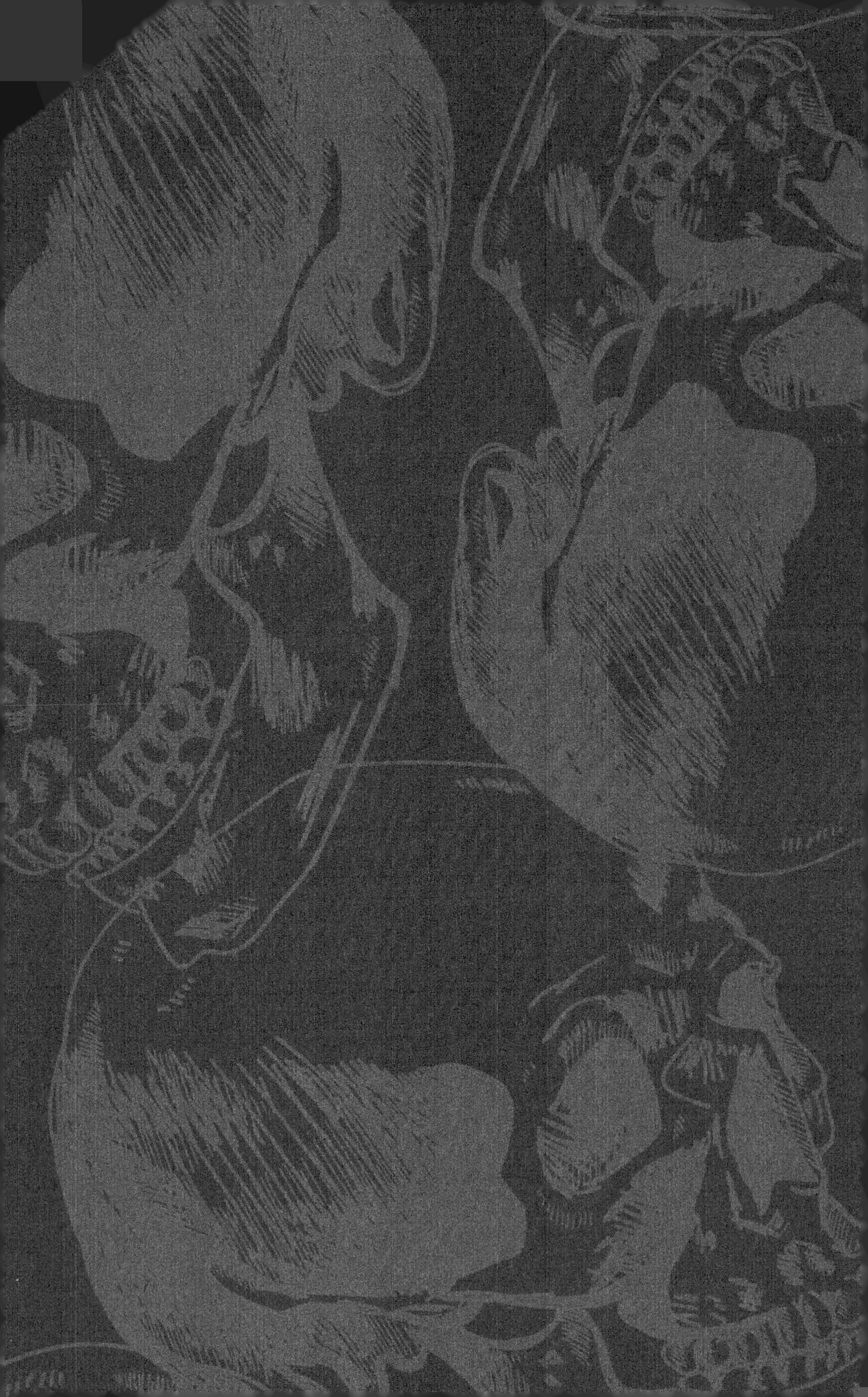

CHAPTER 9
Davina

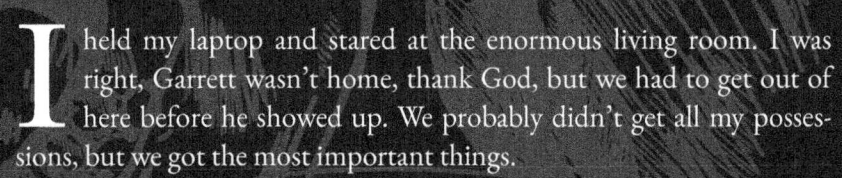

I held my laptop and stared at the enormous living room. I was right, Garrett wasn't home, thank God, but we had to get out of here before he showed up. We probably didn't get all my possessions, but we got the most important things.

The picture of my grandpa. My legal documents. My laptop. Most of my clothes.

"Don't be sad, D," Juliette murmured sympathetically, wrapping her arms around me.

She knocked me off balance and I wasn't strong enough to support both of us, so we fell backward, the couch catching us.

"I'm not sad, Juliette," I told her quietly. "I'm mad. So fucking mad that I want to burn this fucking house down. So fucking mad that I want to cut his dick off. So fucking mad that I could scream until my throat turns raw."

Three heartbeats passed, the silence stretching with my admission. It was lunacy. It wasn't me. Yet, something about this whole situation was rubbing me the wrong way.

He'd sent me over fifty text messages since I caught him last night, begging me to forgive him and give him another chance, saying it was a mistake and he'd never do it again. Except, I was a firm believer that once you were a cheater, you'd always be a cheater. And as the hours went on and I refused to respond to him, his messages turned nasty, blaming me and calling me a cold bitch.

His last message to me was

> Your parents didn't want you. Nobody else will either.

If there was an ounce of a possibility that I'd forgive him—and there wasn't—I certainly wouldn't go back to him after that hit my phone. That statement hurt, and he knew exactly how personally I'd take it. My parents were my sore subject.

"Then let's burn the place down," Juliette concluded.

I blinked my eyes. Once. Twice. Three times. "What?"

She stood up and walked over to the little mini bar. She knew where everything was in this house. She and the girls had helped me bring my stuff over and unload it.

Searching through the mini bar, she dug out three bottles of vodka.

I sighed. "This is no time for a drink, Juliette. We need to get out of here."

Juliette shook her head. "This isn't to drink."

I was too tired for all this. Going on two hours of shitty sleep after all this shit, I just couldn't keep up.

"Then what?" I asked, though I didn't really care.

"To burn down the house," she explained, like she was announcing it was about to rain. Then she glanced at the label. "Look at that. It's actually flammable. Everclear Grain Alcohol. It even sounds cheap, just like Garrett."

"What?" Ivy asked casually, and my head whipped behind me. I didn't hear her enter the living room. "We're burning down the house?"

"Yes," Juliette said.

"No," I shouted at the same time.

"Come on, D," Juliette shot. "The prick deserves it. You know he does." I shook my head. Garrett deserved it, but we didn't. We'd get in trouble for destruction of property or arson. "It's either this, or we cut off his dick."

"Well, fuck," Ivy chirped. "I have a sensitive stomach. So if we're taking votes, I vote we burn down this house."

"Me too," Juliette exclaimed, happy to have someone on board. "Cutting off a dick would make me puke."

Then she gagged, making me believe she'd throw up if we continued this conversation. Definitely not murderer material.

"Let's burn down his house," Juliette insisted. "We can't let men treat us like dirt."

I couldn't believe she was seriously considering doing this. Even Juliette wasn't that insane, was she?

"What's going on?" Wynter's voice sounded alarmed.

"We're burning down the house," Juliette replied without missing a beat as she tried to give me one of the bottles of vodka. I backed away from her with my hands up. No way was I taking that.

"Are you fucking nuts?" Wynter hissed, her blonde curls bouncing wildly as her eyes darted between the three of us. "We'll get caught. Not to mention it's illegal to burn someone's house down."

Thank God for Wynter, the voice of reason.

"We won't get caught," Juliette told her confidently as she handed Ivy a bottle, rag, and a box of matches. Where in the fuck she found rags and matches, I had no idea.

"Don't leave bodily fluids behind," Ivy muttered. "They'll trace that shit back to us."

While Juliette and I stared at Ivy for even knowing something like that, Wynter groaned out loud, probably ready to murder us all.

"Juliette, don't be stupid," Wynter reprimanded her. Though only by a few months, she was the youngest one out of the four of us, but she acted the most mature. "The neighbors saw us. The police will know it was us. He has security cameras outside."

Ivy was no longer paying attention to anything but the bottle of vodka she'd opened and placed on the coffee table, waiting to find out when she could start to wreak havoc. She kept playing with the matches, an almost bored expression on her face.

Swipe, light, blow out. Swipe, light, blow out. It was like watching a kid play with a brand new toy. And each time she lit the match, the embers of it reminded me of her hair.

"Wynter's right," I urged. "Let's just go before we get into trouble and end up behind bars."

Ivy hissed and all our heads turned to look at her. Fire from her match had burned her finger, making her jump and bump into the coffee table. I stood up, and in the next heartbeat, all hell broke loose. The bottle of vodka on the table dropped to the ground, crashing against the hardwood, vodka spilling across the decorative rug. The scent of the alcohol in the air was instant. The four of us watched in horror as the lit match flew out of Ivy's fingers and dropped into the middle of that growing puddle.

It was like watching in slow-motion as her burning match fluttered through the air, falling lower and lower until it hit the rug. A sharp inhale and then swish... the flames spread and screams started. One second it was a flicker, the next it was an inferno.

Ivy tripped over her own two feet and Juliette caught her before she could faceplant on the floor. I grabbed a throw blanket and started fanning the flames, but it only made it worse.

While the three of us screamed, Wynter kept her head.

"Are there fire extinguishers here?" she yelled, trying to be heard over Juliette's and Ivy's high-pitched screams.

"I don't know."

My eyes widened, watching Juliette pour her bottle of cheap alcohol directly on the flames like she was emptying a water bottle. I'd hoped her attempt was to extinguish it, but that was a dumb move.

"Juliette," Wynter scolded her, screaming. "What the fuck! Stop pouring alcohol on the fire!"

Her cousin didn't move. Ivy screamed, shaking her hand while Juliette just stared at the flames like some kind of possessed voodoo doll. Grabbing her other hand, I yanked her away from it.

Ivy yanked the blanket of my grip and threw it over the fire, but the flames still got bigger.

"Shit, that didn't work," Ivy screamed.

"Extinguisher?" Wynter shouted.

"Try the kitchen," I told her, pulling Juliette further out of the fire's reach.

Wynter ran into the hallway and in the direction of the kitchen. Juliette's gaze came to mine, and there was something unsettling about the look in her eyes.

"Where's the other bottle?" she demanded, suddenly strangely calm.

I blinked. "Why?"

"Because I'm going to burn this motherfucking place down," she said, eerily calm. "And then, I'm going to find the people that killed my parents."

Shock had me forgetting about the raging inferno that was sure to kill us if we got too close.

"Killed them? But your dad—"

Before I could finish the statement, Juliette found the cheap alcohol bottle and threw it against the heart of the flames.

Boom.

I jerked back, pulling Juliette and Ivy along. Ivy's screams pierced my ears. Juliette's reason finally caught up and her screams joined Ivy's, though there was a certain edge of anguish and anger lacing her screams.

We had all lost our goddamn minds. And the fire extinguisher came too late.

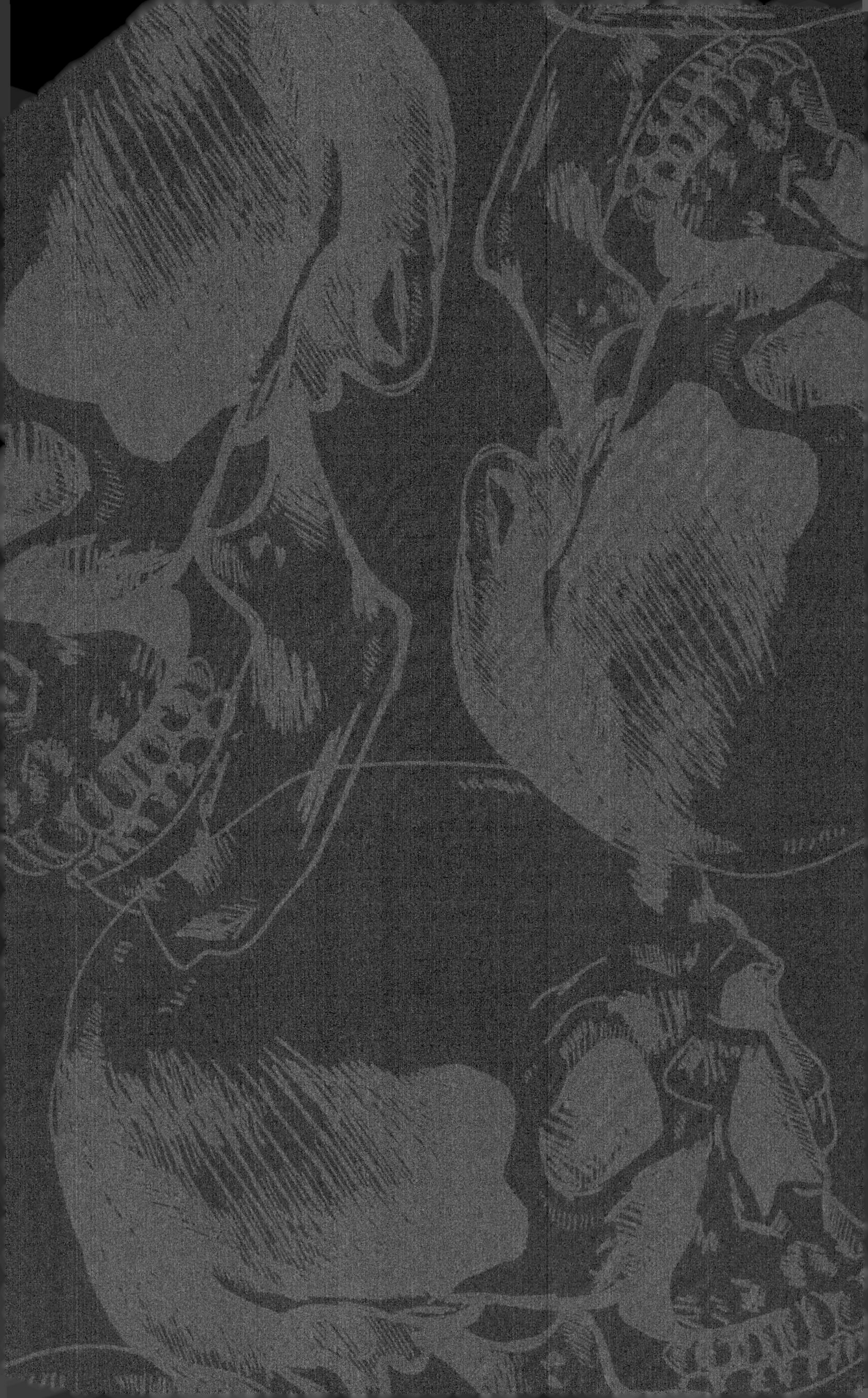

CHAPTER 10
Liam

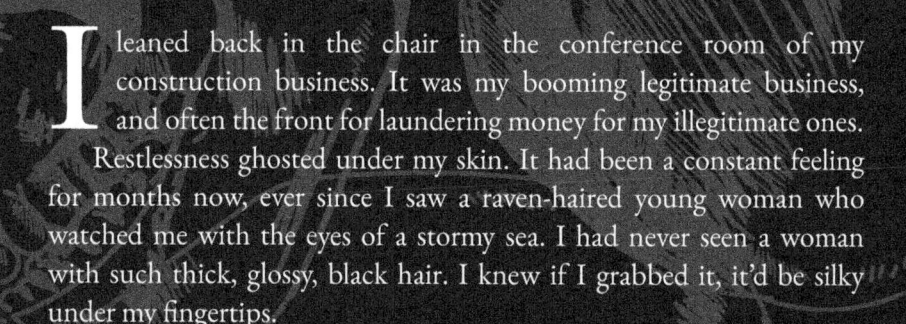

I leaned back in the chair in the conference room of my construction business. It was my booming legitimate business, and often the front for laundering money for my illegitimate ones.

Restlessness ghosted under my skin. It had been a constant feeling for months now, ever since I saw a raven-haired young woman who watched me with the eyes of a stormy sea. I had never seen a woman with such thick, glossy, black hair. I knew if I grabbed it, it'd be silky under my fingertips.

Then why aren't you going after her? I kept asking myself.

Maybe there was a sliver of decency in me that recognized I should keep my distance. Especially since I knew a war with the Russians was brewing. It was inevitable. Or maybe instinctively, I knew that if I took her, there'd be no going back. I'd want her forever.

And it was hard to squash decades of worrying that another person would end up hurt because of this war I was fighting, courtesy of my old man.

Each time I thought about her, the hollow space in my chest filled and my heart beat wildly. She was stunning. I wanted her. To fuck her senseless. To hear her moans as I thrust into her tight pussy. Hard and fast.

Could he be my sugar daddy applicant? Davina's soft voice had a permanent spot in my brain.

I wasn't fucking old enough to be anyone's sugar daddy. Fuck, would she call me daddy as I fucked her? I hoped not. I wasn't *that* much older than her.

Okay, okay.

Maybe compared to her age, I could be classified as a sugar daddy. Though it made me feel too goddamn old, so I fucking objected to the label. The business of melting her panties was an entirely different topic. Yeah, I was totally up for that one.

At a minimum, I needed to let her graduate. Then if I still couldn't get the woman out of my mind, I'd figure out how to cash in the favor she owed me.

Of course, after that day three months ago, I took it upon myself to look into Davina in more detail.

Boyfriend. A grandfather back in Texas who raised her. Surprising connection to the Ashford family. Parents not in the picture. Majoring in business.

I glanced at my phone. Still no response from Juliette. I sent her three messages today, and still nothing. She wasn't usually the type to ignore my messages, regardless of what was going on. I tried Wynter too and got the same result. Though, the latter one tended to forget to reply. Between her training and studies, she often ignored her phone altogether.

I needed to talk to both of them. They frequently went to the Eastside, and with what I was about to do, I didn't want them anywhere near that place going forward.

Killian, my eldest, strode into the conference room.

"They're here," he announced.

I nodded, glancing behind the large glass walls. Our security patted down Gio DiLustro first. His son Basilio was next. Then his nephew, Dante DiLustro, who was part of the Chicago Outfit.

Three months ago, right after the attack on my club by the Italians and the Russians, Basilio approached me with a peace offering. The Italians in New York would stick to the east side and my organization to the west. No more fighting and crossing sides. There had been too much blood spilled over the years. It started with my father and Winter Volkov, then escalated with my sister and Gio goddamn DiLustro.

"Have you heard from your sister or Wynter?" I asked him, keeping my eyes on the rival Italian family.

"Just one message." Killian kept his gaze on the Italians too. "An emoji of a middle finger."

At least he got that much.

"Juliette and Wynter are up to something," I muttered under my breath.

"When aren't they?" he said begrudgingly. "After this meeting, I'm catching a flight overseas."

I turned my head to meet his eyes. I understood why he needed to do it, and I wholeheartedly supported him. I just wished he'd let me help.

Killian was ready to take back what was his and avenge his parents. He remembered them. Juliette didn't. She was an infant when their parents were murdered. Sometimes I wished Killian was too. No child should see what he'd seen.

It was the reason why I sheltered Wynter and Juliette at all costs. I had Nico Morrelli hide both their footprints on the web and make them untraceable. It was harder with Wynter due to her achievements and popularity in figure skating, hence the reason for hiring Nico.

"I'm worried, son." We might not be biologically related, but I thought of him as mine. Both Killian and Juliette. I promised my best friend before he took his last breath that I'd take care of them as if they were my own.

And I did.

There used to be four families that ran the Irish mafia in Ireland: Brennans, Murphys, O'Connors, and Cullens. The O'Connors had been wiped out. The world thought the Cullens had been wiped out too, but the truth was that I had adopted two of them and kept them under my protection.

Killian had a genius IQ. He also saw how brutal life in the mafia was at an early age, and that altered him forever.

The two of us made a pact when I found him and his sister hiding in the secret passageway of their home in Ireland that we'd keep it all hidden from his little sister. For their protection, I was their father. Juliette was raised with Wynter, hidden from the mafia. Killian was raised under me, learning and growing stronger each year.

"I should go with you," I added. "If you wait a bit longer, I can eliminate the threat here, and then we can go together."

"I'll be careful," he promised. "Besides, we can't both be gone. Who'll protect the family?"

Our conversation came to a stop as the three Italians strode toward the conference room, all three wearing black, top-notch, three-piece suits. I bet those suits were made in Italy too. Italians were all about dressing up. I liked to wear a suit, but every goddamn day was a bit too much. Even for a mobster. It was easier to fight and kill wearing jeans. But what the fuck ever.

The door opened and Quinn strode in. "They're clean."

I nodded. "Gentlemen, sit down."

The three pulled out their chairs, and I watched as they all unbuttoned their suit jackets and sat themselves down. Jesus, did they go to school and rehearse that? Gio sat in the middle, his son to his right and his nephew to his left.

My own son and cousin sat to my left and right, respectively.

Tension crept through the room, though it didn't bother me one bit. There were over twenty-two years of animosity between the Irish and Italians. Specifically, the DiLustros and Brennans. Gio had fucked up when he touched my sister, and it was something I'd never forgive.

Gio and I held gazes. DiLustro looked the same as he did twenty-two years ago—arrogant, cruel, and ruthless. The man had no humanity left. I wasn't certain if he ever had any to begin with.

"Liam, let's get this over with," Gio spat out. "I don't have a whole fucking day for this truce."

My lips curved into a cruel smile. "And here I thought you'd cherish it, considering it was you that started this clusterfuck between our families."

The surprise that flashed in his son's and nephew's eyes didn't escape me, though it was barely a flicker, and both schooled their features immediately. It wasn't surprising that Gio would keep the details of how this war between the Brennans and DiLustros started to himself.

He panted after my sister like a dog in heat. Everywhere she went, Gio would find himself there. When my sister rejected the man's advances, the fucker couldn't take it. So, he shot her in the knee and killed her partner. The two had been rising stars on the ice. He destroyed all my sister's dreams and robbed my niece of a father.

"You brought the documents?" I asked him. I didn't want to see his ugly face for longer than I had to anyhow.

A folder sat in front of me and we exchanged the documents. As he inspected my titles of transfer for the east side sections I owned, I examined the titles to the west side. I was tired of this constant war, and Wynter and Juliette were about to finish Yale. This was for my family. I didn't want to worry about their safety twenty-four seven.

After what happened, I had Nico Morrelli set up Aisling and her daughter with a new identity. I trusted the man, and he had incredible resources.

To everyone else, Aisling Brennan died, and Aisling Flemming was born. To the world, my niece was Star Flemming, an Olympic figure skater. To me, she was Wynter, a girl I'd protect at all costs. And God, she was the mirror image of her grandmother. My sister looked like her mother. But Wynter... She had her grandmother's laugh, her voice, her kindness. Even her mannerisms. My father came alive around her, even after decades of mourning.

Little Wynter pulled him out of it.

My sister raised Wynter in California, away from all this bullshit, and I could see that both of them were better off because of it. More often than not, Juliette ran to them, eager for normalcy in her life.

"Tomorrow night, you'll pass the Eastside Club to us," Gio gloated, convinced he'd won this fight.

Far from it. I was securing the long-term safety of my family. Juliette's and Wynter's future. We couldn't fight the Italians and Russians. The attack three months ago highlighted that any kind of alliance between the Russians and the Italians had to be squashed. Basilio swore that it wasn't the DiLustros who attacked the club, but they wanted to focus on the Russians too.

It would seem Gio kept many secrets, even from his own son. Otherwise, Basilio would know that the Russian Pakhan was looking for clues to his daughter's descendants. If I knew the Pakhan's ways, he hoped to find a man that he could torture any information out of on his daughter, granddaughter, and great-granddaughter.

"Basilio will be there tomorrow to take over," Gio drawled, unaware of my ulterior motive to make peace with the Italians so I could focus my energy against the Pakhan. "He has a way to turn anything into gold. A businessman and a ladies' man. Just like his Papà."

I didn't comment. I didn't trust myself not to reach across the table and wring Gio's neck. There would be nothing more I'd take pleasure in than seeing the light extinguished from his eyes.

Twenty minutes later, the Italians were gone.

And there was still no message from my daughter or niece.

CHAPTER 11
Davina

T he four of us stared at the text message.

> Stupid bitches. I know it was the four of you. The cameras were on. Five hundred thousand dollars. Twenty-four hours. Bring me the money by 10 p.m. tomorrow, or I'm going to the police.

We sat in the Whole Foods parking lot on the Upper West Side in New York. Wynter's bright red Jeep top was down, the four of us a mess after the fire we started in Garrett's home mere hours ago.

Wynter had tried to extinguish it with the mini fire extinguisher Garrett had under the kitchen sink, but it didn't help. The fire was already too big, consuming and spreading. It was safe to say that the alcohol poured into it certainly didn't help.

On the other hand, Juliette had definitely gone rogue. Whether we meant to do it or not, we were still responsible. Well, Juliette and Ivy were responsible. Wynter and I were just along for the ride, so to speak.

Wynter held her head between her hands with her forehead on the wheel, and I was wondering how my life had gotten so fucked up when I hadn't done anything but trust a guy I shouldn't have.

"I'm sorry," Ivy cried. Her light freckles could barely be seen from the dirt on her face. "It was an accident. Maybe we can explain."

"Explain what?" Juliette muttered, her eyes wide with shock. I guess her temporary insanity and whatever the fuck that statement meant about her parents had worn off. We'd have to talk about that later. Not now. "We had matches and alcohol. We had intent."

"*You* had intent," I spat. "I just wanted to get my stuff and then get the hell out of there!"

"Davina's right," Juliette muttered, looking slightly defeated.

"I shouldn't have let y'all go." A string of curses left Wynter's lips. "I shouldn't have driven you. I should have made us all stay back at the dorms. We should have called Uncle Liam and asked him to send someone there."

The mention of her uncle shot adrenaline through my veins. *Bad timing*, I warned my body.

Wynter's blonde curls framed her face. She straightened up, soot smeared on her cheek and her pupils dilated from adrenaline that still pumped through her veins.

"Maybe we ask Uncle to help us now," Wynter suggested, pushing trembling hands through her blonde curls. Not that my hands were steady. "We're out of our element here."

"No!" Juliette screeched, her eyes bulging out of their sockets.

"No," I agreed. We couldn't involve Wynter's hot, mafia uncle. Especially considering what happened the last time I saw him. "You have all done enough. I should go to the police and just tell them I did it, tell them I was mad and lost my temper."

Three sets of eyes turned to me. "Fuck no," all of them exclaimed at the same time.

"Besides, that fucker said he has all four of us on tape," Wynter reasoned. "No sense in admitting anything with such evidence."

"That weaselly little fucker," Juliette snapped. "We should just kill him."

"Yeah, let's add murder to the destruction of property and arson charges," Wynter added dryly.

"But the tape will show that it happened by accident," Ivy tried to reason.

I swallowed. I didn't think it would show it was an accident. The events leading up to it showed Juliette preparing to torch the fucking place and us seemingly along for the ride.

"Juliette, we should get out of town," Wynter finally announced, determination on her face. "Let's go to Uncle's beach house in the Hamptons."

"You want to go on vacation *now*?" Ivy questioned, disbelief in her hazel eyes. I didn't blame her. I didn't think it was the right time to go to the beach either.

"You might be onto something," Juliette agreed with her cousin. They shared a nod, and then Juliette explained, "We might be able to find something of value and pay this prick off. Or at a minimum, lie low until we figure out how to get out of this mess."

I took a deep breath. That was all well and good, but somehow, I didn't think it would be the end. Garrett would hold it over our heads forever. And besides, was stealing from the head of the Irish mafia any smarter? He'd kill us. Well, definitely me. Ivy, Wynter, and Juliette were somewhat immune.

"And what about when he doesn't stop at just five hundred thousand?" I questioned. "At this point, I wouldn't be surprised if he blackmails us for the rest of our lives."

"Then we kill him," Juliette, ever the mobster's daughter, concluded.

"Let's not become killers quite yet," Wynter reasoned, rolling her eyes. She started her Jeep and pulled out of the parking lot.

"God, I need a drink," Juliette muttered from the back seat.

"Me too," Ivy agreed.

The two started discussing the need for alcohol to forget what had happened today, while Wynter and I sat in the front in silence as she drove. Guilt ate at me. Wynter was right, we shouldn't have gone to Garrett's house in the first place. I shouldn't have voiced my anger. There were so many fucking things I shouldn't have done, starting with giving Garrett another chance.

Speeding down the streets of New York, Wynter kept her lips

pressed tightly together. It was her telltale sign that she was thinking through things. I knew she had the most to lose if this got out, like making it to the Winter Olympics.

We came to a red light at a four-way crosswalk, and I laid my hand over her white knuckles that were gripping the steering wheel.

"I'm sorry, Wyn," I murmured.

Her big eyes turned my way, the wild curls bouncing around her face, and she shook her head, resigned and tired. Unlike the rest of us, she got up at four in the morning to start her day.

"It's as much my fault as it is yours." She offered a feeble smile, our gazes locked. "Everything happened so fast."

A car behind us sat on the horn and the four of us jumped in our seats. Like true New Yorkers, Juliette and Ivy turned around to glare at the car behind us and yell curses at them. Wynter drifted through the crossroad, and I noticed her eyes widened at the car passing us, going the opposite direction.

The driver of the sleek black sports car stared at Wynter, and I couldn't distinguish if it was because she had soot on her cheek or if he was admiring her beauty. With the doors taken off the Jeep, he probably had a good view of her long legs wearing white snug shorts and a pink off-the-shoulder blouse, both now slightly soot-stained thanks to her insane cousin. Or maybe he knew her.

"What is it, Wynter?" I asked her. I glanced over my shoulder and noted the driver looking back our way as he drove off, his eyes still on Wynter.

Maybe he recognized her as one of the top athletes in the country, possibly the world.

"I-I have an idea," she muttered, as if she was talking to herself.

"What?" the three of us asked her.

Our answer was the screeching tires as she made a sharp U-turn in the middle of the city, violating multiple traffic laws. Speeding up, she passed two cars before we found ourselves behind the black sports car.

McLaren.

That car would pay for Garrett's blackmail. Maybe we could hijack the car? With the driver still behind the wheel, it was a questionable plan. Four against one odds were pretty good though. We might be able to beat him.

Jesus, has it come to that? I wondered silently.

Wynter pushed on the horn. "What are you doing?" I asked her, glancing around. The last thing we needed was to bring attention to ourselves. All four of us were a mess. She ignored me and pushed on the horn again.

Honk. Honk. Honk.

The car in front of us came to a stop and Wynter slammed the brakes.

"What are you doing?" Juliette inquired.

"I have an idea," Wynter told us all. "There might be a way to delete the surveillance."

"How?"

She jumped out of the Jeep. Even with dirt on her cheek, her wild curls cascading down her back, and ash stains on her clothes, she still shone.

Her eyes traveled over the three of us. "Just trust me."

We gaped as we watched her stride away from us and toward the sports car.

The three of us watched her, holding our breaths. With a trembling hand, she tucked her hair behind the ear. Her lips moved as she stared at the driver, and I cursed that we couldn't hear what she was saying. There were a few back and forths, and then the next second, the McLaren car door opened and a man stepped out.

A gasp sounded from the back seat, but I couldn't tear my eyes from the guy that towered over Wynter.

Holy mother of God and all the saints above.

Tousled, coal-black hair. Strong jaw. Gorgeous face. Beautiful mouth. High-cut cheekbones throwing shade over a fierce expression. He cocked a brow as if surprised by what he'd just learned. Dark eyes traveled over to us, and suddenly it struck me that this man could be charming and ruthless at the same time. His whole persona screamed power, and his sex appeal oozed all around him. I could practically taste it from here.

My eyes roamed over his black, three-piece suit, which made him look like an Italian devil who would tempt you and destroy you with his devastatingly handsome looks. This guy was dangerous, deadly, and he knew it. Something akin to amusement crossed his expression as his eyes flicked back to us.

The next second, all emotion disappeared from his face and shifted to an unreadable mask that was focused on its prey. *Wynter.*

He wanted her.

There was no doubt about it, but I didn't think he was the right man for her. Wynter was too soft and warm underneath her ice-princess persona. Things wouldn't bode well for her, because this man had ruthless written all over him.

He tucked his hands into his pockets as his eyes zeroed in on the golden-haired woman with soft curls that matched her personality. There was something dark and possessive in his gaze as he watched her, and I got the distinct feeling it was too late for Wynter.

Because this man had already made up his mind when it came to her. Though the question remained, what had he decided?

"Jesus fucking Christ," Juliette and Ivy muttered at the same time.

My eyes darted to them. "What?" I asked, wondering what got them upset.

"Wyn, get away from him," Juliette hissed even though Wynter couldn't hear her. "He looks like a damn Italian."

The three of us watched in fascination as the guy took her right forearm and ran a thumb over her burnt skin, then pulled out a handkerchief and wrapped it around her forearm.

"Who carries handkerchiefs anymore?" I whispered.

"Fucking Italians, that's who." Juliette made it sound like being Italian was bad. I knew the Irish and Italian mafias didn't get along, but I didn't realize her hate extended beyond that. Unless…

"Is that guy in the Italian mafia?" I asked her.

Juliette shrugged. "He looks like it, but I'm not sure who he is. I spent more time with Wynter in California than I do here in New York. All Italians are scumbags though."

It seemed a bit excessive for Juliette to apply her dislike of the Italian mafia to all Italians. Especially one as good looking as the guy in front of us.

He offered Wynter a pen and she took his hand, turned it over, and wrote something on his palm. Once she was done, she held it for a moment and lifted her head. The two locked eyes, and the intensity of his stare was so strong it pulsed in the early May air. Somehow time seemed to slow and sharp breaths inhaled as we all watched the exchange. A pink flush rose on Wynter's cheeks and she glanced down to where his thumb brushed over her skin.

A smile and a tilt of her head, and then she rushed back to us. His eyes followed her all the way, and only when she got into the Jeep did he get into his own car.

Something told me that the handsome Italian stranger had fallen under the spell of Wynter Star.

And he would never let her go.

"Try this code." Juliette offered another combination as she took a swig of her drink. Ivy and Juliette had gotten into the liquor cabinet, like we weren't in enough shit as it was.

I punched in the numbers. *Beep.*

"Nope." The four of us had been at it for hours. Short of taking everything out of Juliette's dad's house, there was no way to pay off Garrett.

"Do we need the money now if Wynter's guy will take care of the surveillance footage?" Ivy asked, twisting her hands nervously. She worried if this got out, her family would make her go back to Ireland and marry some Irish scumbag. Her words, not mine.

"Bas couldn't promise to get it done within a day," Wynter commented. "We'll need to shut Garrett up until we know all the surveillance has been wiped."

"Bas?" The three of us cocked our eyebrows. "You're already on a nickname basis with him?"

She rolled her eyes. "Stop it, you three."

"Stop what?" Juliette challenged, her lips curved into a smile.

"Stop assuming," she said coolly. She sat on the couch, her feet tucked under her while she was studying. How in the world she could study with all the commotion, I had no idea.

"How do you know him?" Ivy asked. "He looks Italian. Is he Italian?"

Wynter shrugged. "I didn't ask him for his heritage."

"You two stop discriminating," I ordered Juliette and Ivy. "We need to be grateful he's helping us."

"The question is, what is Wynter doing for this favor?" Juliette smirked before mimicking a blowjob with her hands, suggesting Wynter's repayment for the favor.

"I volunteer as tribute," Ivy screamed out of nowhere, making us all screech and scaring the living crap out of us. "Italian or not."

"You are all talk and no action." Juliette snickered.

Ivy didn't miss a beat. "Oh, and you're all action, right?"

"Quit it, you two," I snapped. "Both of you are all talk and no action. Stop obsessing over men while we have a bigger problem at hand."

"Well, that man is fine, and you know it," Ivy grumbled, rolling her eyes like a little brat that lost her favorite piece of candy.

Juliette shrugged her shoulders. "I'd rather find an old man to fuck. Italians are not my thing."

"Oh, we're back to sugar daddies?" Ivy snickered. "I thought you changed your mind when you saw the picture of the first sugar daddy. His skin was extra wrinkly." Juliette rolled her eyes. We all heard her screech when she went through candidates. None of them were as hot as her dad. Ugh, I still got hot thinking about him. "And I bet you that fine piece of Italian ass has more stamina," Ivy added smugly. "So, yeah, I'd pay that man any fucking way he asked me to if it menat he'd wipe out that surveillance. Fuck my ass, my pussy, my mouth. Whatever the fuck he wanted."

"Stop," I chided them, shaking my head, though I couldn't resist smiling. Then worry shot through my mind and I glanced at Wynter, frowning. "Y-you're not..." I trailed off hesitantly. I didn't want her to sell herself to save us. Wynter shut her book with a thud and glared at all of us.

"No, he's not making me pay him in the form of a blowjob," she snapped, annoyed. "Or any form of sex. You freaks."

Juliette and Ivy shared a glance, a heartbeat passed, and then they burst into laughter. They laughed so wildly, they giggled like two girls discussing the first cute boy they'd ever seen.

"Then what?" Juliette asked, offering Wynter her bottle of whiskey.

"None of your business," she answered, glaring at her cousin. "Now, let's focus on the real problem. We fucking suck at this breaking-into-safes business."

Juliette exhaled, exasperated, then took another swig of her drink. "I know," she agreed, which had us all snapping our heads her way. It was unlike Juliette to admit defeat. "I'd hoped Dad..." she trailed off, her eyebrows furrowing. Again, her behavior struck me as odd. "I'd hoped the combination would be the same here as in the club."

I frowned, wondering what she meant, but before I could open my mouth, Wynter beat me to it.

"The Eastside Club?" she questioned Juliette, and the latter nodded. "You're sure you know that combo?"

"Yes, I know it by heart. Though it's not helping us here," she retorted dryly.

Wynter glanced out the window, a pensive look in her eyes. The night was dark, but occasionally, you'd catch a glimpse of shimmering white foam from the waves when the moon glow hit it just right. Juliette's dad had to be loaded, because this house was even nicer than the one he had in the city.

Wynter placed her book down on the couch and stood up, then strode to the liquor cabinet. She skimmed the assortment until she found what she wanted. Grabbing a bottle of wine, she opened the drawer and pulled out a corkscrew.

"What?" Ivy asked, fidgeting. "Your silent thinking is freaking me out."

"You have an idea," I mumbled. "A good one."

After four years together, I knew Wynter well. All four of us knew each other very well. We were so in tune even our professors and peers often thought the four of us had grown up together. And while our personalities were different, they also complemented each other. And we always had each other's back. Always.

The sound of the cork popping broke the silence, and the three of us flinched at the sudden sound despite watching Wynter open it.

"It's simple," she started, locking her incredibly big, beautiful eyes on us. "We go to the Eastside Club and distract Uncle in the bar area while one of us goes into his back office and opens the safe. Take the money, and then we're clear."

Bum-bum. Bum-bum. Bum-bum.

I choked out a laugh. She had to be joking. "Nobody keeps five hundred grand in cash on hand. Even in a safe," I reasoned.

"Uncle does," Wynter assured me, though it didn't feel comforting.

"He really does," Juliette grumbled. "There are always large amounts of cash around. I guess for emergencies or something."

"We'll have to do it tomorrow," Wynter added. "I have practice in the morning, but then we can get dressed up and go to the Eastside and rob him. It would probably be better if we do it early in the evening."

I had to be hallucinating. There was no other explanation for this. Wynter would never suggest a robbery. She was the golden child among us.

"We'll rob him while he's there?" Juliette asked hesitantly.

Wynter shrugged. "We'll have to do it whether he's there or not. We're running out of time."

How could she be so damn calm?

Stealing from an Irish mobster while he was nowhere to be found was one thing, but stealing from him while he was in the building was something entirely different. This should have been my first clue that I had lost my mind, because I should have been objecting to stealing from him at all.

"I swear, I feel like I'm living in the *Good Girls* show right now," I muttered under my breath, shoving both my hands through my hair. I gripped the strands and tugged on them, the pain reminding me this was real.

"Is it a fun show?" It was Wynter who asked the question, curiosity in her eyes.

"That's not the point, woman," I snapped, probably portraying the panic I felt. "Stealing from a mobster while he's not around is one thing, but while he's in the building?" I voiced my concern.

I felt like I should put ten question marks after that to emphasize my point.

Besides, if I saw the Irishman, I might just combust. I'd seen the man jack off. Even after all these months, my panties still melted when I thought about it. *Fuck!*

"Dad won't do anything to us," Juliette protested.

"He won't do anything to *you*," I objected, though my insides were hot and bothered. "You are his family. Ivy is another mobster's daughter. But I—"

Oh my God! The four of us were idiots. Probably the worst criminals to walk this earth. Maybe if I got out of this alive, I could start a school for up-and-coming criminals and teach kids what not to do. *It actually isn't a bad idea*, I congratulated myself.

"Maybe we should just ask him if we can borrow it?" I suggested, hopeful.

"And what? Tell him we burned down a man's house and now he's blackmailing us?" Ivy rolled her eyes. "He'd torture us. And Garrett." Ivy's brothers were enforcers for her family's mafia in Ireland and she picked up a thing or two.

How in the fucking hell did I end up surrounded by mobsters and their relatives?

"He would kill Garrett. Literally," Juliette muttered. "Then he'd kill us, figuratively speaking. Maybe literally."

Oh my gosh. This was bad. Suddenly, my mouth was too dry, and I was parched. I rushed to the liquor cabinet, in desperate need of a drink. Wynter offered me her glass of wine, but I needed something stronger. My eyes roamed over the selections, and then I saw it.

Croizet Cognac Cuvée Léonie, a one hundred and sixty thousand dollar bottle of cognac, give or take a few thousand.

My grandfather had a small liquor store when I was a kid. I knew brands of alcohol, and I recognized expensive bottles. I climbed up on the little bar counter and reached to the top shelf where the cognac bottle sat all on its own. If he had two more of those, we could take them and sell them without going to the club and stealing cash out of the mobster's safe while he roamed the building.

Jumping off the counter, landing with both my feet firmly on the ground and a cognac bottle in my hand, a loud cheer broke out behind me.

"You go, Davina." Juliette giggled. "Go for the best."

Unscrewing the bottle, I took a swig directly out of it. The alcohol burned down my throat and straight to my stomach. Wiping my mouth with the back of my trembling hand, I offered it to Wynter, who shook her head.

"I'll take it," Juliette reached out. She drank out of the bottle then passed it to Ivy, who then offered it back to me. "Wow, no wonder dear old dad was keeping this one for himself."

"It probably has something to do with its price tag?" Wynter said, teasing her cousin. "Back to the topic at hand. We need to pick one of us to get into the safe and you, Juliette—"

"I'll do it," I cut her off. Three sets of eyes locked on me. "This all started because of me. I'll break into the safe, and you three distract the Irish mobster."

Because I needed to avoid that man.

"But—" Juliette tried to protest, and I stopped her by raising my hand.

"No buts," I cut her off. "I'll do it. You just keep your father distracted."

"Someone's got the hots for older men," Ivy teased. "I'll remember to keep you away from my father."

I scoffed. One hot criminal was quite enough for me. Not that Juliette's father was mine, but I'd be lying if I said he wasn't on my mind. All. The. Fucking. Time. When I needed release. Or in my dreams.

Fuck! It'd be best if I never saw him again.

"So this is how we do this," I started. "The three of you make a commotion in the bar area. I don't know, get on top of the bar and shake your ass or something. The crowd will get wild and excited. In the meantime, I'll sneak into the room with the safe." It sounded like a reasonable plan. "Where is the safe?" I asked Juliette.

"It's in Uncle's office," Wynter answered in her cousin's stead, since

Juliette was too busy taking another gulp of her alcohol. "Behind a painting. His office is the last door down the hallway. You can't miss it. Double door, dark mahogany wood."

I took a deep breath and slowly exhaled. "Okay, then I take the money while you guys distract him by making the crowd wild. I'll need fifteen minutes. We'll meet back in the parking lot by Wynter's Jeep."

"When you leave his office, take the back door," Juliette chimed in. "That way you're out of the building and less likely to get caught."

Shared glances. Silent prayers. Although I wasn't certain God would listen to a bunch of drunk girls.

"Undercover job number one: diversion," exclaimed Juliette. "Shake our asses. No problem."

With a chuckle, that was set.

Tomorrow, we'd steal money from the safe of the head of the Brennan Irish mafia.

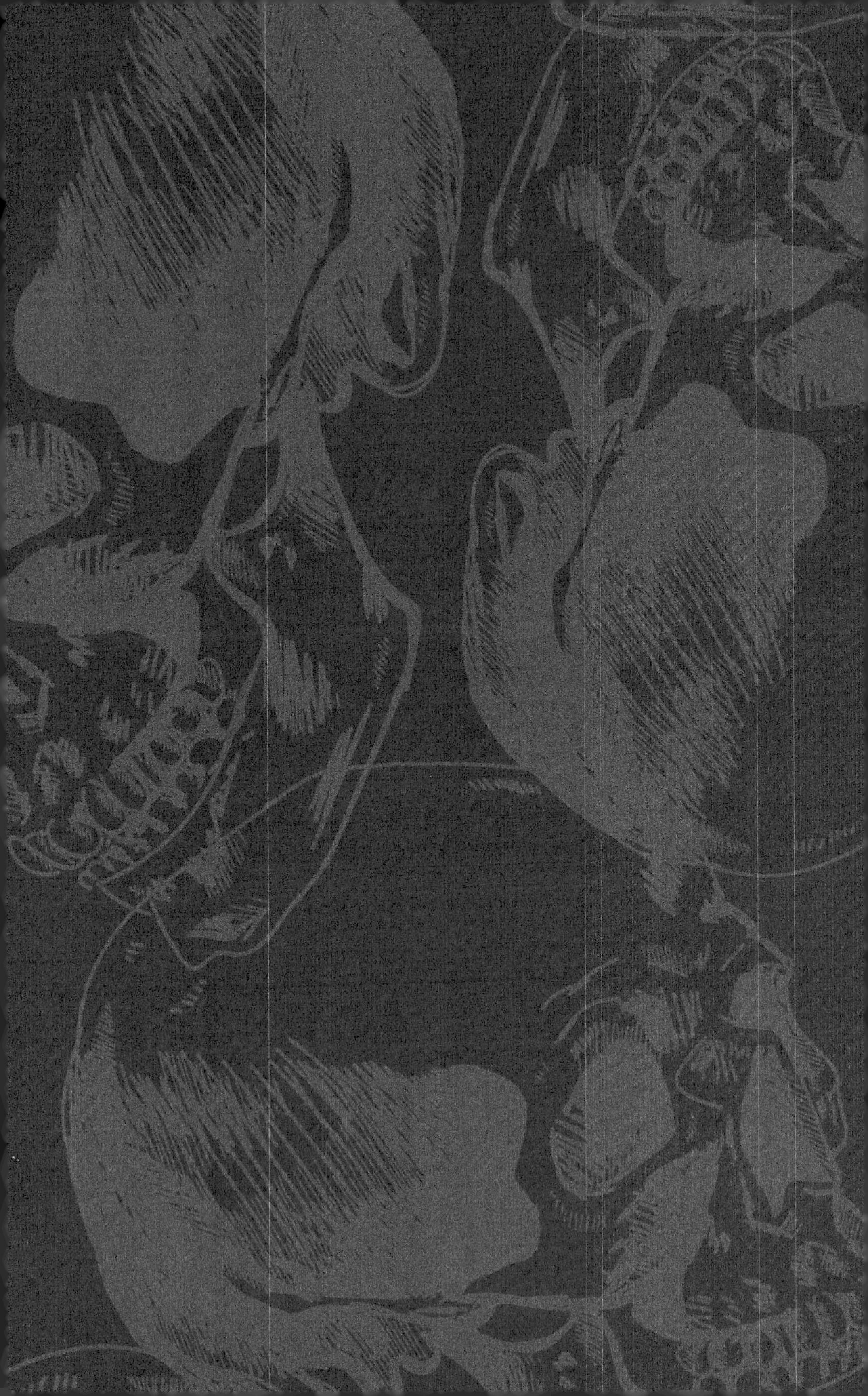

CHAPTER 12
Liam

Riiiing. Riiiing.

There was nothing I wanted to do more than throw my goddamn phone into the wall. It had been a never-ending cycle of calls and shitstorms of one wrong thing after another all damn day.

A seized shipment of my guns. An attack on my dock warehouse—the legal one of all fucking things.

It didn't take much brain power to figure out it was either the DiLustros or the Russians. It was always the DiLustros or the Russians.

Though, this time, I didn't think it was the DiLustros. Not if they were smart. They wouldn't jeopardize our deal before it was final, and that wasn't happening until tomorrow night.

Which left me with the only other logical conclusion. It was the Russians. God, I didn't feel like dealing with the Bratva. Why in the fuck did my father get into bed with one of them and then leave me to clean up the goddamn mess?

I glanced at the caller ID to see an Ireland area code.

Fucking lovely! Just what I needed today.

"Hello, Athair."

"Liam, I hear you're working up an agreement with the Italians?" my father greeted me. Yep, right into attack mode.

How in the fuck my father even heard about this shit from across the ocean, I had no fucking clue, but he always heard everything. I was going to eventually update him. *Eventually!* Probably when the deal was sealed and behind me to ensure he didn't do something crazy.

And my father was famous for his batshit crazy moves.

After all, he thought himself invincible and went after the Pakhan himself by taking his precious daughter. Yes, he fell in love with her, but that wasn't part of his plan. He almost got us, and everyone connected to us, killed. A normal person would have known how far was too far. Any fucker would know that going after someone's child or wife was too far. The trouble was that my father wasn't like any other fucker. And neither was Gio DiLustro. My father took from the Pakhan. Gio took from my father.

Ironic how the wheel goes round and round.

My father made so many wrongs against the powerful Pakhan, we had to take shelter back in Ireland. I was Killian's age when shit went down. It was the reason I could relate to the boy.

And when I got strong enough, I came back to reclaim what was ours.

"Nice to talk to you too, Athair," I retorted dryly. I wouldn't comment on my dealings. I ran the business here. I was the head here. He liked to act like he was, but he hadn't been part of this business in a long time, thanks to chasing his cock. He maintained control in Ireland, but here in the States, he'd made too many fuckups, and I was the one to earn it all back.

"Why didn't you consult me?" he asked, his voice shaking with anger.

"Because this territory is mine," I told him calmly.

"I obtained that territory first, boy." And here we went. "You'd do well to remember that."

"And you lost it too," I reminded him. "I'm doing what's best for my family."

Fuck, wrong choice of words. Even before I heard his next words, I knew I'd fucked up.

"What family?" he barked out. "You have no wife. No children."

"I have two children and a niece," I reminded him.

"You have a niece." I could hear his scowl even over the phone line. A damn ocean between us wasn't enough. "Those children are not yours."

My father only understood blood. If you weren't blood, you were nothing. Regardless of who you were and what you had done for him.

"Liam, unless you marry," he grumbled, "you can't retain control of the Irish in New York and here in Ireland." I kept my mouth shut. Arguing with my father was like going to war. I was too tired for that shit today. "The Irish here are very traditional. They'll see you as a futureless leader." He had a point there, though I didn't voice my agreement. "Wynter has been kept sheltered. Aisling wanted to give her a different life."

It was my turn to scoff. Now he cared about Aisling and what she wanted. He was two decades too late. Though I agreed with him on Wynter. She wasn't built for the criminal underworld. Just like her mother wasn't. Aisling lived it and paid a high price for it.

"Killian can lead when I'm gone." I was wasting my breath, because I knew he wouldn't acknowledge him.

"Those two are not your biological children, Liam. Be reasonable. Find a wife, get her pregnant, and then do whatever you want. It will keep your sister and niece protected."

Just like my father did whatever he wanted once he got his son. After all, it was how Aisling came to be.

"Go to sleep, Athair. It's late there," I answered instead. "I'll talk to you tomorrow."

Or maybe I could get a week's reprieve before I talked to him again.

I ended the call and leaned back in my chair. I was still in my downtown office, my shell for the legal business. I swung around in my chair, my eyes locking on the wall of windows overlooking the city that never slept.

Manhattan, New York City.

This had been my playground for as long as I could remember, but I understood my father's point. Unfortunately.

You fought power with power. By becoming more powerful. My

best friend and his wife could attest to it. They paid for it with their lives. The memory of that day from twenty years ago kicked in and I swore I could feel the heat of those flames on my skin to this day.

The flames burned, the heat of them licking my skin.

Dread filled my chest.

Nobody could survive this. The smell of gasoline lingered in the air and mixed with the rage I felt burning in my veins.

They killed my best friend and his wife. My godson. Their newborn daughter. All dead.

I failed them. I should have gotten here sooner.

The ashen taste of smoke lingered on my tongue as my heart squeezed tightly in my chest. The last year had been hard.

First my sister, and now this!

"Why didn't you run, Aiden?" I whispered quietly, my voice carrying in the hot breeze. March in Ireland was cold, but the rage burning inside me and the inferno in front of me felt like I stood among the fires of hell. Except this was the ninth circle of Hell caused by treachery. And fuck, my chest felt frozen.

My fists balled by my sides as I rushed forward. I had to get in, see if I could retrieve their bodies. They deserved to be buried properly. Not like this. I owed them that much since it was my family who had started this war with the Russians.

I rushed to the rain catcher barrel that Aiden's wife insisted on. Even in this remote, hideaway cabin, she'd insisted on environmentally friendly methods. Taking my shirt off, I dipped it into the water, then pulled it back on and charged forward.

Despite the heat surrounding me, the metal of the handgun that was tucked in the back of my pants was cool against my skin. Grounding me. Pushing me forward.

The fire spread too quickly as I sought out the bodies of my best friend and his family.

Flames devoured the wooden staircase leading to the second floor. It was the only way up, so I searched through the living room. Nothing. Then I rushed into the kitchen and that was where I saw Aiden and Ava. Both laid in a pool of their own blood, their hands reaching out to each other.

Lowering onto my knees, I searched for a pulse. First, I pressed my fingers against Ava's bruised and bloodied neck. Nothing. I shifted to Aiden, whose face was almost unrecognizable. My blood boiled and my heartbeat pounded in my ears.

I'd find every single one of those motherfuckers and I'd make them pay, I vowed.

"Liam." *My name was barely a whisper and my eyes snapped to my best friend.* "Get the kids. Keep them safe."

My eyes roamed the room. Where were the kids? Did they take them?

My ears rang, the buzzing sound almost deafening me. I gasped for breath, keeping the lid on my rage. There'd be time to fume later. Now it was time to save my best friend.

"Your arse better not die on me," *I warned him. Smoke burned my fucking lungs. Fear fisted my throat, making breathing almost impossible. Though the guilt was even worse.*

Meeting my friend's eyes, the terror I saw on his face gutted me. "I'll get you out," *I vowed, lifting him up.* "I'm so fucking sorry."

It was all my fucking fault. I didn't play my cards right.

"Too late," *he said. He kept glancing over my shoulder, and I followed his gaze. Why was he staring at the blank wall?*

"Too late for me. Get my kids," *he begged, his breathing erratic, blood running down his face.* "In the wall."

My pulse thundered and I forced my heartbeat to ease so I could focus. That was when I heard it.

Muffled cries filled the air, mixing with the pop and crackle of the raging fire.

I saved Juliette and Killian, but I couldn't save my friends.

If we grew weak, Aisling and Wynter could end up paying for it. My sister had already paid the price, and it was all for the debts of our father's sins.

Gio learned who Aisling's grandparents were on her mother's side. And just as my father aimed to use the Pakhan's daughter, Gio had the same exact plan. He wanted to get closer to the Pakhan. It sickened me to work with the DiLustros, but I had to pick the lesser of two evils.

It was always the weak that paid the price. Aisling's mother. My sister. My niece would be next, unless I kept her protected.

If I did it for anyone, I'd get married to protect them, as well as Juliette and Killian. My father might not consider them family, but I fucking did, and they'd forever be my kids.

My phone rang again. Unknown number. Fucking hell, I just couldn't get a goddamn break today. My phone was like fucking Grand Central Station.

"Hello?" I barked into my phone, agitated as fuck.

By now, I was convinced both Wynter and Juliette were ignoring my calls. And those of my sister, because I had Aisling call them too. At least I had a few moments to catch up with her. I didn't go out to see her much, and she hadn't set foot in New York in over twenty years.

I had a feeling that no matter how safe I made it, she'd never be back.

"Mr. Brennan." This better not be a fucking sales call, or heads would roll. Everyone in our family had burner phones for a reason—being untraceable and the perk of not having sales calls.

"This is Sergeant Matthews from the Hamptons police, calling about your house."

"What about it?"

"The alarm was set off and the alarm company alerted us. It seems the alarm stopped, but they lost connection. They believe there's a chance that someone cut the connection. Would you like for us to go check it out?"

I frowned. Nobody would dare break into my beach home. It was well known that it was ours.

Unless... Unless my rebellious daughter and niece decided to.

"Thank you for letting me know," I told him. "No cause for alarm."

If it was an actual burglar, I'd deal with him my way. If Juliette and Wynter went to the beach house, I'd deal with them too. I didn't want them in trouble with the police.

"Very well, sir. Thank you."

I glanced at the clock. It was almost nine at night. If I got in the car, I could be there by ten.

There were eight bedrooms in my Hamptons beach home, yet I walked in to find four young women sprawled all over my living room floor. It looked like either a fucking hurricane swept through or there was a wild ass party that I just missed.

Bottles of whiskey, wine, and beer laid all around the floor along with pizza boxes and Starburst candy wrappers. Juliette wore a fucking bathrobe with goddamn candy stuck to her hair. Wynter wore pajama shorts and a matching tank top with slices of pepperoni stuck to her clothes. Ivy had her face planted on top of the pizza.

What in the actual fuck was wrong with this generation?

They trashed my beach home. A slice of pizza was stuck to my goddamn ceiling and a whipped cream trail smeared my French windows overlooking a million-dollar ocean view.

My eyes shifted to the fourth young woman. Davina.

She was hammered. No food smashed on her face or clothes, but her shirt was backward, and she had odd socks on. The large writing on her shirt said FUCK ME, and then a finger pointing south. I imagined if she wore it right, it'd point to her ass.

My dick instantly hardened at the image of her bent over and me taking her ass. *Hmmmm.* There'd be no objections here.

Even trashed, the woman was exquisite.

Her silky, ebony hair covered a part of her perfectly symmetrical face with a smattering of freckles across her nose. The thick, long black lashes threw a shadow over her cheeks. Her lush, pouty mouth was parted, and her breaths fanned the strands off her face with each exhale. I stared at her for a moment, fascinated with the peaceful, relaxed expression on her face.

Her back rested against the living room wall, her legs stretched out in front of her with her hands in her lap, holding a bottle. It took me a second to realize it was my most expensive bottle of cognac.

I lowered to a kneeling position, and right at that moment, her eyelids fluttered open. Her gaze collided with mine. Gray with flecks of gold and brown. Last time I saw her, she was too far from me to notice them, but I could see them now. Along with her faint scent under all that alcohol.

Pineapples. She smelled like the sweetest pineapple.

"Heeeey," she drawled, her eyes unfocused and her smile lazy. "Melting panties."

I shook my head. Juliette and her friends drank way too goddamn much, even by Irish standards. And my friends and I could drink. Though, I was starting to suspect we might not be able to compete with these four. At least not anymore.

"That's my most expensive bottle," I told her, tilting my chin toward it.

She lowered her eyes to the bottle in her hand and grinned drunkenly.

"Good taste," she commended.

"I know." Her eyes lingered on my mouth, then trailed down my body. The girl was hammered. Instantly, my groin objected to calling her a girl. She was a woman. A young woman, but still a woman, and the most beautiful one at that.

"I'll totally volunteer as tribute with you," she slurred, her eyes locked on my groin area, and my cock responded right away. I was a forty-seven-year-old man, and the last thing I needed was temptation in the form of a barely twenty-one-year-old woman who was friends with my daughter.

Yet, I wanted her. Since I'd laid eyes on her, I had been fighting the temptation in the form of raven-black hair and storm-gray eyes.

"Tribute?" I asked her, not understanding the reference.

"Yeah." Obviously she wouldn't elaborate. Her eyes closed for two heartbeats, then opened again.

"What happened here?" I questioned her.

"A paaarty," she drawled, smiling stupidly. And still, she looked beautiful. "A recovery. I dunno."

"How big of a party?" This place looked like a whole goddamn college attended.

"Four." It couldn't be. She had to be lying. Four women couldn't do so much damage and drink so much alcohol.

Could they?

"That cognac cost over a hundred grand," I reprimanded her.

"I-I'll pay you back," she muttered, shifting to lay down onto her side. "Tomorrow."

And she was out like a light, hugging my special edition cognac.

Taking the bottle out of her hands, I put it on the floor and lifted her up into my arms, then headed for the bedroom. She felt small in my arms. Fragile even. Her body leaned into mine, as if she sought out comfort or heat even in her slumbering state.

"You're dangerous for my self-control," I murmured against her hair, laying her down onto the big bed of the master bedroom.

A soft sigh slipped through her lips.

"Same," she murmured, rolling over and taking my arm with her, as if it was her own cuddle toy. "Lie with me. You never collected the debt."

Has she been waiting for me all this time to come and collect?

Fuck, I wanted to. But not like this. She'd have to be sober before I slid into bed with her, and definitely when I fucked her. I knew once I had her pressed against me, there'd be no stopping until I was buried deep inside her.

So, I tucked her into the comforter and left for my penthouse. There was no sense in waking them all up to reprimand them right now.

They were too drunk, and I had a plan to put in motion for Davina Hayes.

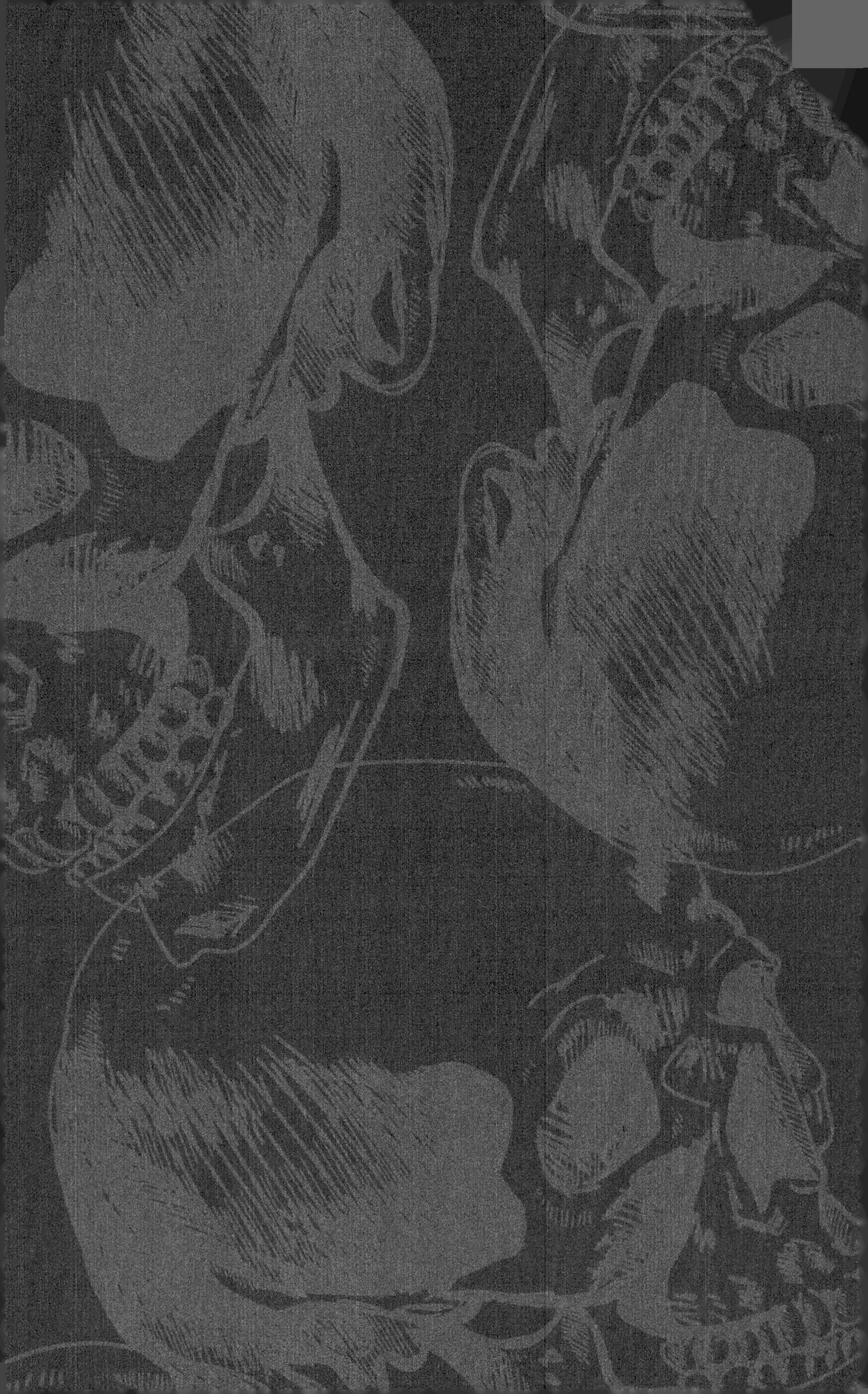

CHAPTER 13
Davina

The trip to the beach house was fruitless, though we came up with a plan. Whether it was good or not remained to be seen. We cleaned up the living room this morning. Lots of bottles of alcohol would do that to you. I thought I fell asleep on the floor of the living room, but this morning I woke up in a warm and comfortable bed. My friends weren't so fortunate.

I must have been drunker than I thought to make it into the bedroom without remembering it. Though I remembered plenty of my dreams from last night—Mr. Brennan carrying me into the bedroom, sliding under the covers with me, his big hands roaming my body. I knew, *just knew*, he'd be an amazing lover.

Unfortunately, it was just a dream. I woke up soaking wet, unsated, and hungover. Horrible combination.

"Okay, we stick to the plan," Wynter muttered under her breath, striding confidently like she owned this city. "Draw all the eyes away from Davina so she can rob Uncle while we shake our booties."

"Sounds like a solid plan," Juliette voiced. "I wish my head didn't hurt so fucking bad."

"Your head?" Ivy whined. "Everything hurts. My neck, my head, my stomach." She had spent her morning throwing her guts up. "I can taste the puke. Do I smell like puke?" she asked, throwing us a side glance.

I shook my head. My stomach didn't feel so great either, but it was more the nerves for what I was about to do. Stealing from a fucking hot mobster was a stupid idea, but I didn't have a better one.

"Stop complaining," Wynter hissed. "We'll be in and out. Let's just get this done and we'll be on our way. And no more drinking."

"At least for a month or two," Juliette agreed, but then thought better of it. "Actually, we need to order at least one round of drinks here. Otherwise, it'll be suspicious."

Wynter and I gave her an exasperated look. "That reason makes no goddamn sense," I mumbled.

"We drink every time we come," Ivy grumbled, looking slightly greenish at the thought of drinking alcohol. "If we change our behavior, it'll be obvious."

"We're going to be dancing on the bar," Wynter choked out. "That's changed behavior."

"Whatever," Juliette grumbled. "Just stick to the plan. We order drinks and toast. Davina disappears, and Wynter climbs on the bar as Ivy's bluetooth connects her iPhone music to the stereo. Then, Ivy and I follow."

Wynter sighed heavily. "Fine. Whatever."

The four of us entered The Eastside Club without any hiccups, even though Wynter wasn't officially twenty-one for another few weeks.

Juliette wore an orange sparkly mini-dress, Ivy wore an identical green mini-dress, and Wynter wore a white one. They looked like a walking Irish flag together. I wore a black mini-dress that hugged my curves. The four of us decided it was best if I wore black so I could blend in with the shadows while I sneak into the back office.

Did it make sense? Fuck if I knew. None of us knew, but in every movie we'd watched with thieves, they wore black leggings and shirts. I mean, we watched *Entrapment* with Sean Connery and Catherine Zeta-Jones this morning. It only confirmed the need to wear black. Except, this club wouldn't allow me to enter in a bodysuit like Catherine Zeta-Jones wore.

We strode to the bar like we belonged here.

CORRUPTED PLEASURE

"A round of fireballs for us," Juliette ordered. The bartender glanced at us all one by one and ended up on Wynter.

"That one is not twenty-one," he said, his eyes on Wynter. Of course the guy would know. Her uncle owned the club.

Wynter pushed her curls out of her face and smiled. "That's okay. I can just get a glass of water."

Ivy looked a tad bit too green. "Actually, can I get ginger ale?"

"Me too." I jumped at the opportunity. My stomach couldn't handle any more alcohol.

"Make it another," Juliette chimed in. This must attest to how bad she felt too.

Three glasses of ginger ale and one tall glass of water, the four of us grabbed our glasses and clanked them, then drank them down.

Ivy whistled the mockingjay song and my head snapped to her. Ever since the first tribute comment, *The Hunger Games* had become the theme of our stupid discussions.

"Why are you whistling?" I asked her.

"It'll be our signal," Juliette answered, then giggled.

She followed up with another mockingjay whistle. Wynter frowned, and the two of us shared a glance, then she shrugged one shoulder. At least I wasn't the only one confused. Either that, or Ivy and Juliette had gone off the deep end and become *Hunger Games* fanatics. Or maybe they were still drunk from yesterday.

"Okay, Wynter," Juliette murmured, suddenly serious. "Time for you to get on top of the bar."

"Climbing up will be a bitch with this short dress," she whispered under her breath, downing the rest of her water then slamming it down onto the bar. It was all for the show. Only the four of us and the bartender would know she was drinking water, not something stronger.

"A fucking Olympic medal winner and you're complaining about climbing a bar stool." Juliette scoffed, rolling her eyes. "Get your ass up there."

I noticed Wynter's guy lingered at the door, talking to another man who had his back to us. I turned to alert Wynter, but it was too late.

She was already climbing onto the bar, giving us all a glimpse of her perfect Olympic ass. Juliette snapped her fingers, and Selena Gomez's song "Hands to Myself" came on at full volume.

Juliette's loud three-toned whistle pierced the air and grabbed everyone's attention instantly. Men whipped their heads around, and it took no time at all for all the attention to be on Wynter dancing on top of the bar. The three of us watched as men leered at her moving sensually on top of the bar to the song, her golden curls catching the light with each move.

"Quinn is on the move," Juliette murmured under her breath, never glancing my way.

That was my cue. Juliette and Ivy climbed onto the bar next, one on each side of Wynter. Now they truly looked like an Irish flag up there. I slipped through the crowd as the cheering became louder and louder. Right as I exited, I glanced over my shoulder and caught my best friends' eyes on me. They pressed three middle fingers of their left hand to their lips and then held them out to me.

We were taking *Hunger Games* to a whole new level with this shit. It was undoubtedly overboard.

Fuck it.

I returned the greeting. Might as well go down in flames, just like Katniss. From the corner of my eye, I caught the face of a man in jeans and an impeccable button-down shirt at the farthest end of the room. He looked furious and was still panty-meltingly hot. His presence alone commanded the place, and for a fraction of a second, I lingered there and stared, admiring the view.

The song switched to "Legends Are Made" by Sam Tinnesz, and I knew all hell would break loose any minute. If anyone could rile up the crowd, it was Wynter. And Juliette's performance wouldn't be far behind.

With an exhale, I moved through the hallway and toward the office where Juliette said the safe would be. Ignoring everyone I passed, I kept my head low and ensured I didn't make eye contact with anyone.

Finally at my destination, I pressed the handle of the office door, and to my surprise, it opened. Glancing over my shoulder, I confirmed nobody was looking my way and I slipped into the office with a soft click behind me.

Without any delay, I rushed to the painting Juliette described. Authentic Picasso. Jesus, we should just steal the painting and we'd get the money we needed for my ex. I never thought having an ex would be so goddamn expensive.

Removing the painting off the wall, my hands trembled nervously as I raised them.

08-29-19-98.

I should have known things weren't going to go the way we planned.

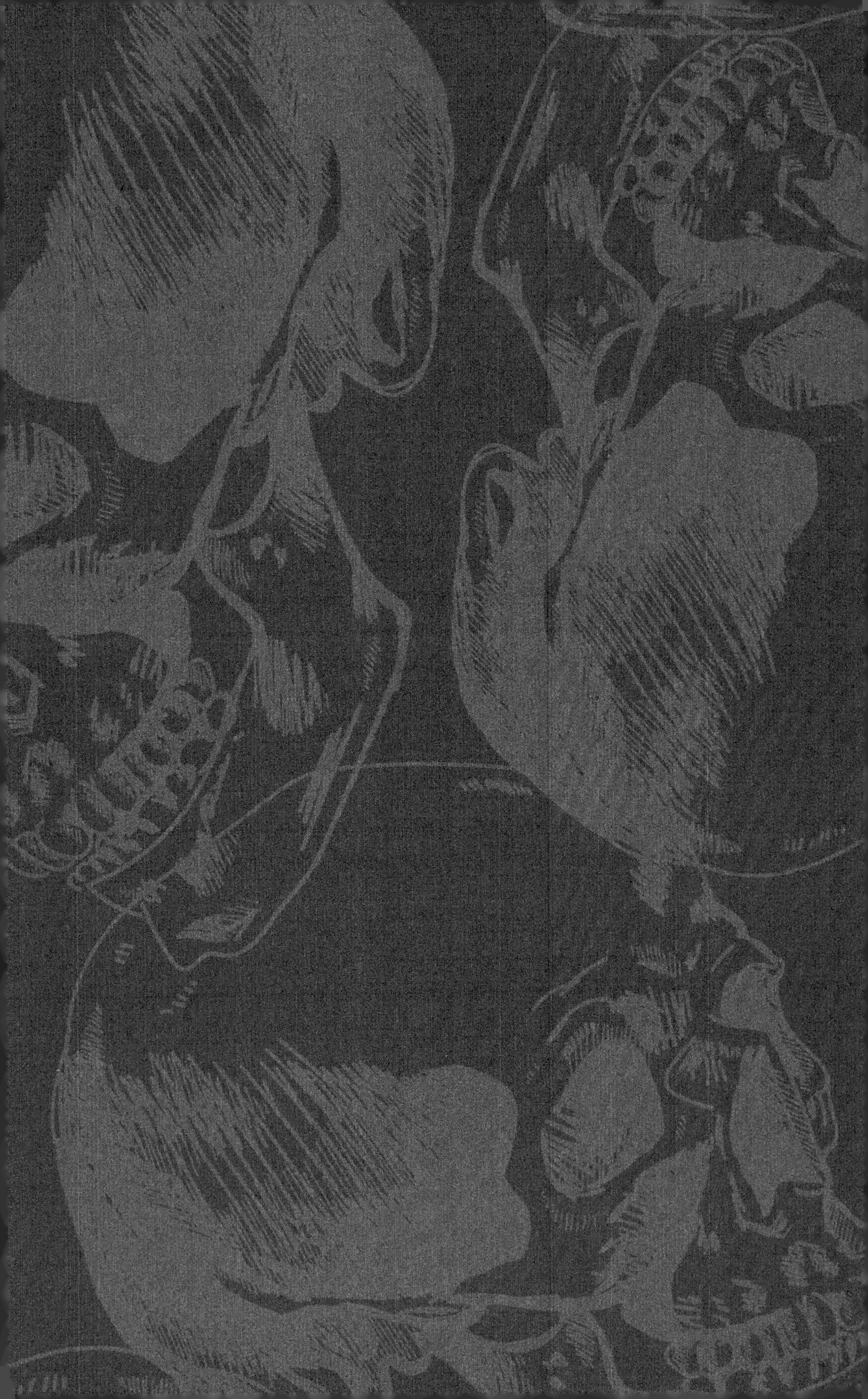

CHAPTER 14
Liam

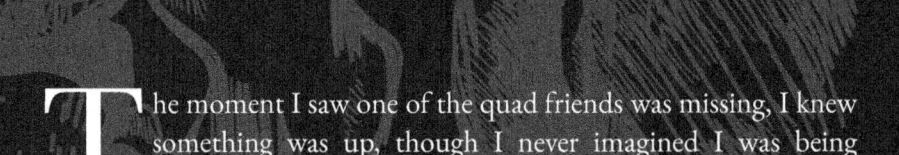

The moment I saw one of the quad friends was missing, I knew something was up, though I never imagined I was being robbed.

By a raven-haired beauty that thought I'd be a good sugar daddy.

"Fuck, fuck, fuck." Davina's soft curses filled my office as she dropped a stack of money.

My resolve to move forward with the plan firmed up. I knew exactly how she'd settle her debt.

"Filthy words from such a pretty mouth," I drawled.

I strode to Davina who was still ass-down on the floor, her little panties on display and her eyes full of terror. She blushed crimson, and the only sound filling the room was her heavy breathing. The loud music of the club was drowned out by the soundproof walls I had installed in this office.

"Let me guess," I started. "The other three were meant to be a distraction while you're in here robbing me."

Her shoulders slumped and her gaze darted away from me. I could practically see her thinking as her eyes roamed the room. She contemplated her scenarios on how to get out of this situation. There were none. Her only way out was blocked by my frame.

Then her lips thinned, and her eyes flashed in defiance.

"Fucking wrong," she said in a sultry tone.

Sassy little thing.

"Enlighten me then. Why is my safe open, and why are your hands on my money?"

She shrugged, her eyes narrowing on me in displeasure. I guess her comment about me being panty-meltingly hot only stood to reason when the girl was drunk.

"Safekeeping."

I honestly had to bite the inside of my cheek not to laugh. She and her friends, including my own daughter and niece, were robbing me, and she called it safekeeping.

"I love your sassy mouth," I drawled. "Keep it up, and I'm going to find out just how well it works."

It was time for this woman to repay the debt she owed. *Debts* now.

She gasped, her eyes widening. "You're my best friend's father!"

I drawled. "What makes you think something so small would keep me away from you?"

She shook her head, though I wasn't sure whether it was at me or herself.

"It's time you pay your debt," I said. "The stakes just got higher now that you've stolen from me."

I watched her luscious mouth open then close. I was almost disappointed there wasn't another sassy remark.

"Stand up," I ordered her. When she didn't move, I barked, "Now!"

I wasn't accustomed to not being obeyed. Except for Juliette and Wynter, of course. Hence why they spent more time in California than here.

Davina watched me warily as she got to her feet, grabbing the backpack where she stacked the cash and zipped it up.

God forbid my own cash fell out of the bag. Though, I might just let her earn it.

Straightening up, she tilted her chin defiantly and shot me a glare. "Now what?"

The corner of my lips tugged up. The woman had courage, that was for sure. My eyes roamed down her body, taking in the black mini-dress that covered barely anything but still left plenty to the imagination.

I shut the door behind me. It was better we didn't have witnesses for what'd follow for the young black-haired beauty.

Pushing both my hands into my jean pockets, I strode over to the desk and leaned back against it. She watched my every move, waiting. She pursed her lips as if she was annoyed that I interrupted her.

The door to my office swung open and Quinn entered.

"They got away," he snapped. "Wynter took her damn clothes off."

What the fuck was going on with these girls? Robbery? Didn't I give them enough damn money? Maybe Juliette wanted a new car. After all, she had been a little brat after she totaled her last one and I refused to buy her another until she underwent driving classes all over again. For fuck's sake, it was her tenth totaled car in the span of twenty-four months.

"Miss Hayes, tell us what it is that you and your friends are up to," I told her coldly.

"No," she spat back, lightning flashing in her eyes, and fuck if it didn't appease me. She was like a goddess of lightning, ready to fight me. It got my cock hard for sure.

"Want me to turn in the evidence to the police?" I asked, watching her for any telltale signs.

She shrugged. "Like what? The backpack?" That sassy mouth of hers made me want to put a belt to her ass.

"For starters, yes," I told her, keeping my face unmoved. "That backpack belongs to Quinn, and the money you stashed in it belongs to me."

She cocked an eyebrow. "There are a million backpacks like this, and possession is nine-tenths of the law." Jesus, how many times had this girl been arrested to know all that? Or maybe she watched too many movies. "So don't touch my stuff."

She pushed her shoulders back, raising her chin in defiance. I almost regretted shattering her defenses.

I pointed to the corner of the room where the camera was. She didn't need to know that it had been disconnected since we were turning this club over to the Italians tonight.

"See that, sweetheart," I purred. "That's our evidence."

"Shit," she spat out, her shoulders slumped slightly. "Fucked. Just fucked."

"Pretty much," I agreed. She shifted from one foot to the other, her eyes darting between Quinn and me expectedly. And it was then that I made my decision. I turned my eyes to Quinn. "The Italians here?"

He nodded. It meant I had an hour to teach this brat of a woman a lesson. A gorgeous brat.

"Deal with them and keep them away from here," I ordered him.

Quinn's eyes traveled over the office, the open safe, and the black backpack, drawing his own conclusions. He'd been around long enough to witness Wynter and Juliette's grand schemes, though this one topped them all.

"I see the girls are following in our footsteps," he muttered, amusement crossing his expression. In his almost fifty years, he had seen and experienced everything. There wasn't much that surprised him anymore.

Davina's shoulders tensed and she muttered something unintelligible under her breath. She kept inching away with each shift of her feet, her eyes ping-ponging between me and Quinn. The smart girl was probably evaluating who was a bigger threat.

Keep your eyes on me, sweetheart, I mused silently.

"One hour," Quinn grumbled and left the room, shutting the door behind him.

Her face fell, probably having contemplated bolting through that door and trying to escape.

Silence stretched, though it didn't bother me in the slightest. I quite enjoyed it, watching her squirm, though she tried her hardest to hide it.

"What do you want, Mr. Brennan?" she finally broke the silence.

"What do you think?"

Her eyes narrowed suspiciously on me. "Probably your money back," she responded wryly. "But it's our money."

I scoffed at that. These Gen-Z girls were out of their mind. "You haven't earned it," I deadpanned. "Yet. But we can fix that."

"How?" Her voice lowered by a few notches, and her neck bobbed as she swallowed bravely. "Something freaky probably."

Damn if she wasn't right. I wanted to bend her over this desk and spank her ass, then fuck her senseless for being so goddamn reckless. I'd been fighting the urge to stake a claim since the night I first laid eyes on her. She was the same age as Juliette, for fuck's sake, yet I couldn't get Davina goddamn Hayes out of my mind.

"Well, I'm not into freaky shit," she added, her cheeks turning an even darker shade of red, which told me she'd thought about it before. "Or old men."

This woman would be the death of me. Not because of her beauty. Not because all the blood that shot straight to my dick and had it straining against my jeans. It was her sassy mouth and her courage to talk back to me that captured me more than anything else.

There hadn't been a single woman in all my life that dared to speak to me this way. Never mind being disrespectful.

"I'd bet all the money in that bag and in my bank account that you're into freaky shit," I challenged, baiting her.

This time, she scoffed but didn't respond. *Smart girl.* I'd enjoy teaching her freaky shit and seeing her face as she enjoyed it. Suddenly, I wanted to see what my touch did to her. I wanted to feel her shiver. Take it all from her.

"Now what?" she bit out.

"Are they waiting for you?" I asked instead of answering her question. She swallowed hard and shook her head. *Little liar.* "Send them a text and tell them to go back to the university without you."

Her gaze burned through me, her breathing hitched.

"Now," I clipped when she didn't move.

She jumped and dug into the backpack. I watched her pull out her phone and her graceful fingers move over the keyboard.

"I want to see the message before you send it."

She narrowed her eyes on me. "Control freak," she muttered.

She had no fucking idea. She took two steps toward me and pushed the screen into my face.

"Here." I read the message.

> All good. Go without me. I'll meet you back at the dorms.

"Happy?"

I nodded my approval, and she pushed the send button, then shoved her phone back into the backpack.

Her gaze flared my way and she waited. She was so close I could smell her. Intoxicating.

Oh yes, this spitfire was a freak. She just didn't know it yet.

"First, you drink my most expensive bottle of cognac," I deadpanned, and surprise flashed in her eyes. It appeared she was too drunk last night to realize she'd seen me. "Then, you steal from me." She bit her bottom lip, and I had to fight the urge to take her mouth.

"Sorry," she muttered, like that would make it all better.

"Take your panties off," I demanded, deciding how I'd punish the little thief. I wanted to spank her ass red, and the moment she opened that safe and stole from me, she granted me permission. Whether she knew it or not.

"W-what are you going to do?" she stammered, trying hard to hide the anxiety in her voice. It was as if she couldn't decide whether she was scared or aroused.

"Take. Your. Panties. Off."

Anger flashed in her eyes again. "Fine!"

Ouch.

This was certainly a downgrade, and not the good kind. Though, she obeyed. She lowered the backpack next to her feet, then she reached under her dress and, careful not to reveal her pussy to me, slid her panties down her gorgeous legs.

My cock throbbed, eager to get out and bury itself in her warm pussy. But I ignored it, intent on delivering my punishment.

"Now what?" she spat out, eyeing me like I was scum, her cheeks crimson.

I extended my hand in silent demand, and she threw her panties at my face. God, I loved her fucking fire. I caught them before they hit my face and stuffed them into my pocket.

"Now turn around and bend over my desk."

Her eyes widened and her throat bobbed. I wanted to fuck that mouth. From the moment she uttered those first words three months ago, I wanted to fuck that pretty mouth of hers until she couldn't remember a time before me.

"Are you waiting for written instructions?"

"Fucking mobster," she muttered as she twirled around and bent over my desk. If she had watched me for a fraction of a second longer, she would have caught me smiling. I loved her fire and her backbone. Unlike other women, she was hot when she pouted.

Her back arched and her ass jutted out toward me, leaving her perfect ass open for my taking, but the flimsy material of her dress still hindered her from my view. I took one step and was directly behind her. I skated my finger along her spine, tracing a line from her shoulders to her hips, then all the way down her thighs.

My nostrils flared as her scent hit me. *Arousal.* My little thief was aroused, and she'd already lost her bet.

Trailing my hands up her soft, naked skin, I slowly pushed her dress up, leaving her bare ass completely exposed to me.

"So beautiful," I purred, my palm rubbing the cheeks of her ass, and I swore I felt her muscles relax a notch.

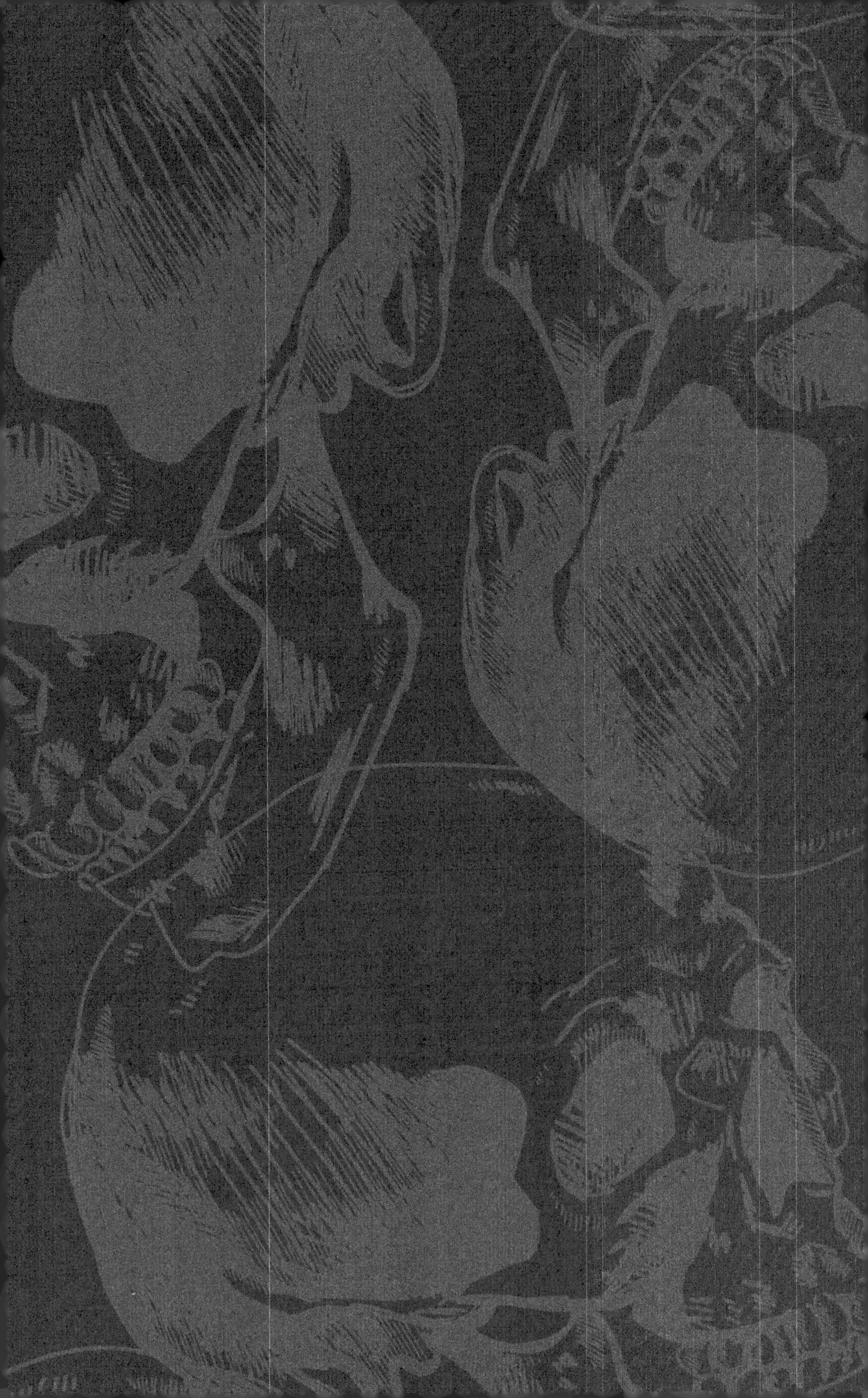

CHAPTER 15
Davina

My fingers gripped the edge of the desk and my insides quivered in anticipation. I had officially lost my mind, or the cognac from last night was still swimming through my bloodstream.

It was the only logical explanation for this.

"I'm going to punish you for stealing from me," Mr. Brennan drawled in his sexy voice.

God, I was so wet. And I *ached*. That delightful throbbing between my thighs intensified with each heartbeat. His rough palms on my thighs felt so goddamn good on my soft skin, and I felt a trickle of arousal on my inner thigh.

So damn embarrassing.

I prayed he wouldn't notice it.

His palms rubbed my ass and I bit my lip to ensure a moan wouldn't escape me. Though I realized too late that my ass pushed into his touch.

"I hope you're not fragile," he added, his voice a notch darker than his earlier statement.

"Bring it on, old man," I breathed. The attempt to sound defiant failed miserably, my level of turned on evident even to my own ears.

His hand came down quickly and the smack of his palm against my ass echoed through the empty room.

Slap!

A light fire spread across my butt cheek and my forehead leaned against the cool surface of the mahogany desk. To my horror, a moan slipped through my lips and my insides clenched in anticipation.

In my whole life, I had never been hit. Not a spank, not a slap. Nothing.

Until now, and I was aroused unlike ever before.

My brain screamed I should fight, I should feel ashamed, but my body refused. I fucking liked this.

Slap!

Another spank to my ass, and this one had more of a kick to it. My body jolted and my breathing came and went in quick bursts. His palm rubbed the sting, and I pushed my hips into him.

"I'm thinking this is more punishment for me than you," he grumbled. Warmth bloomed in the pit of my stomach, and I felt his one hand spread my thighs. He inhaled deeply, his finger traced my entrance, and a loud moan vibrated through the room. "Well, fuck me," he muttered.

Oh my God, I wanted to fuck him. Needed him to fuck me. I felt his fingers catch the slickness of my arousal between my thighs, then come back to my entrance and push the tip of his finger into my pussy.

"Ah... Ah... God," I moaned, my pussy clenching greedily around his finger.

I didn't know if I should die of embarrassment or beg him not to stop, though I couldn't muster the energy for either.

I glanced over my shoulders and caught him adjusting his stance. The look on his face told me he wouldn't stop, and I didn't want him to. The awed and hungry look in his eyes almost had me begging him for more.

Our eyes met, and whatever he saw in my gaze had him land another smack on my ass. Then another. My whole body shifted forward and I pressed my cheek against the cool wooden desk as I stared at the Picasso painting.

I couldn't understand why I was enjoying this. I had never been so aroused. This was degrading.

Wasn't it? Then why did it feel so damn good?

"Want me to stop?" His voice was guttural, and his breathing had turned ragged, as if he was struggling to hold himself back.

"Give me your all, Mr. Brennan." I gasped as my heartbeat drummed in my ears.

He growled, actually growled, as he lowered and bit my right ass cheek.

"Filthy girl." This was so damn hot.

Smack. Another slap followed. The tempo varied and each smack alternated sides, and then he'd rub the burning skin as a muscle deep in my belly clenched in pleasure. This had to be what I sensed the first time I saw him.

Some kind of sexual kink that matched my own.

A deep moan slipped from my lips, and I looked over my shoulder to watch him as he punished me for stealing from him. Yet, it didn't feel like a punishment at all. My hair was a mess, cascading over my face, but it didn't hide the desire clouding my eyes. I had never seen anything so fucking erotic and sexy.

This powerful man was hungry for me.

Blood rushed in my ears, my entire being focused on the gorgeous man behind me. In the blink of an eye, I felt the heat of his body warm on my back as he leaned over, bringing his mouth right beside the shell of my ear.

"Have you done this before?" His voice was raspy and so goddamn sexy. I shook my head and my long hair shimmered, dragging across the desk. "When was the last time you had sex?"

I blinked my eyes. It was hard to think with the heat of his chest against me, his hot breath in my ear. I wiggled my hips and my ass brushed against something big and hard. A gasp escaped me and heat flared in the pit of my belly.

Oh my God! I knew he was big from when I saw him jacking off in the shower, but if the impressive bulge against the zipper of his jeans was anything to go by, he was fucking huge.

My pussy throbbed with the need to feel him inside me.

"Answer me," he demanded, biting my earlobe.

A whimper left my mouth, and through the haze of desire, a shred of reason pushed through. This man wanted me. I could use it to negotiate with him.

"If I tell you," I breathed, my voice sounding strange to my own ears, "and let you do whatever you want to me, will you let me keep the money? And the favor from peeping on you in the shower is settled too."

There. I said it. Okay, the choice of words was stupid, but I couldn't retract them now. If there was something I didn't like, I'd just tell him. And if he pushed, I'd kick him in the balls.

Good plan, I gave myself a pep talk.

His fingers lazily roamed my inner thigh, smearing the evidence of my desire over my skin, and a shiver ran down my spine. I had never been so turned on in my life. Hot and bothered took on a whole new meaning around this man.

"Maybe," he answered, bringing his finger to my lips. They parted instinctively, and he pushed his fingers through. I sucked them clean with a moan.

It felt dirty. It felt forbidden. And so goddamn good that I thought I'd combust into flames right here and now.

He hummed his approval as my mouth worked his fingers, mimicking sucking like I had my lips wrapped around his cock. God, the need to taste him was gnawing at me. Overwhelming me.

"I'm very demanding," he added. "You'll submit to everything and anything. Only with me."

Say no, my mind screamed. *Don't be an idiot!*

"P-please, yes," I begged, though I wasn't sure whether it was for him to fuck me, demand my submission, or let me keep the money so my friends and I could shut Garrett up.

"Answer my first question," he ordered.

I struggled to remember what he asked. My mind was in chaos. "W-what question?" I breathed.

"Have you done this before?"

"No, I haven't," I breathed out. "I haven't had sex in over six weeks."

Fuck, I moved in with Garrett and sex instantly stopped. No wonder I was horny, acting like a damn bitch in heat for Liam.

Liar. I had been attracted to him from the moment I first saw him.

CHAPTER 16
Liam

*S*ix weeks.

She hadn't had sex in six weeks.

"Don't you have a boyfriend?" I demanded. That was what her report showed. She grumbled. "What was that?" I asked.

"We broke up."

"Good." One less thing to worry about.

And the fact she hadn't done something like this before made me want to growl with satisfaction. The possessive streak I hadn't felt before made me want to claim all her firsts. The thought was ludicrous. I was in my forties; demanding any firsts was out of the question.

In one quick motion, I spun her around to face me and searched her expression. Her flushed cheeks matched the red skin on her ass. Her hazed eyes reminded me of the dark clouds of Ireland, right before the spring rain.

Fuck, she was sexy as fuck. Too young.

The bastard in me didn't fucking care. I struggled to rein in my control, to drag air into my lungs. I was ready to pin her down and thrust ruthlessly into her. Fuck her until she forgot everyone's name, including her own.

I strode to the couch and sat down.

"Come here."

She hesitated for a heartbeat and then obeyed. Her hips swayed as she drew closer. Her dress was still bunched around her waist, her breathing heavy, and I watched in fascination as her generous breasts rose up and down with each inhale and exhale.

The dim lights of my office reflected against her glossy dark strands. God, that hair. It was my weakness. Long enough so I could wrap it around my fist twice and hold her firm as I fucked her mouth. *Jesus Christ!*

She stood in front of me, her pussy in full view. Her inner thighs slick from her arousal. I could lose my goddamn mind around this woman and not mind one bit.

Too late, I mused. I must have already lost my mind, because I didn't forgive people who crossed me, yet I couldn't bear to see any harm come to this woman. In the past four years, I'd heard so much about Juliette's "ride or die" friends. Until today, I didn't really believe her until the four of them attempted to rob me.

Now I was inclined to think there was merit to Juliette's statement. Because the performance the three women pulled in the bar as a distraction, wearing the colors of the Irish flag at that, was a sure sign the four women worked well together. The question was why rob me? What did they need money for?

Davina stood still, waiting for the next instruction, and it pleased me she didn't try to take the reins. I preferred to take charge in the bedroom.

I stretched out on the couch, my eyes never leaving her. "Sit on my face."

Davina gasped in shock, and I pulled her closer, then slapped her ass. "Now. I want your pussy on my mouth."

She scrambled onto the sofa, straddling me, and scooted farther up my body. My fingers gripped her thighs, pulling her closer, but she hovered over my face.

"I said sit on my face. Otherwise, I'm going to have to spank that sweet arse of yours."

I tilted my head upward and inhaled deeply, then licked a slow path over her entrance.

"Oh my God," she whimpered, her thighs quivering.

Fuck! She was dripping wet. Her arousal perfumed the air, and it was the best kind of scent. I scraped the scruff of my beard against the delicate skin of her inner thighs.

I grabbed her hips and jerked her down until her pussy sat on my face.

"Fuck," she breathed, and finally sat all the way down. Her eyes locked on me as my mouth sucked on her pussy. Call me perverted, but I liked that she didn't look away. She stared at where my mouth and her pussy connected, her lust-filled eyes shining like diamonds.

I ate her like she was the last meal I'd ever get. Like the world would burn down at any moment and we both needed this last bit of pleasure to get to heaven. I sucked and licked, her hips rocking against my tongue.

Her moans were the sweetest fucking symphony. There was nothing fake about her reaction, her hips rolling with each lick I gave her pussy. I nipped her clit and a loud whimper vibrated through the air.

"Oh my God," she groaned, the desperation in her voice spurring me on.

She was wet and slippery, the flesh of her pussy swollen. The little thief was needy and greedy. I lapped at her, drinking my fill, and shoved two fingers inside her.

"Mr. Brennan," she exclaimed on a moan, rocking back and forth, fucking herself on my hand. I couldn't help but chuckle against her pussy at her calling me Mr. Brennan.

Her movement stilled and she attempted to shift away from me. The fingers from my left hand dug into her hip.

"Where do you think you're going?" I growled. "We're not done."

She blinked, a storm brewing in her eyes.

"Y-you laughed," she accused, her tone slightly breathless.

She thought I was laughing at her? Didn't she know how fucking beautiful she was when she owned her pleasure? It was the best high, the best adrenaline. In all my forty-seven years, I hadn't experienced anything better than this very moment.

"You calling me Mr. Brennan made me chuckle," I told her softly.

"Oh."

"Liam," I told her. "Call me Liam when I'm eating your pussy."

Her mouth parted in shock, but I knew she liked my dirty words. The color that spread over her chest and her cheeks was my confirmation. She watched me as if debating whether I was possibly laughing at her. "You are fucking beautiful when you're aroused," I purred.

She licked her bottom lip, then whispered, "Liam."

Her voice was soft, tentative, as if she was trying it out.

I nodded my agreement. "That's right, baby. Now, give me back that pussy so I can finish what I started."

Fuck, if she flushed so attractively every time I said something dirty, we'd be having a lot of fun together. I slammed her pussy back down onto my face and drew her clit between my lips. She moaned, rocking back and forth. Relentless and eager to see her come, I pushed my tongue inside her entrance and her thighs tensed around my head.

I hummed my approval as her hips rocked hard against my face. I sucked relentlessly, like my life depended on this. Her fingers threaded through my hair. Her eyelids fluttered shut, the most magnificent blissful expression on her face, and I knew I was hooked for life. She pulled on my hair, her body jerking and trembling as she came on my face. Her thighs had my head in a chokehold, but I didn't care. If there was a way to go, this would by far be my favorite one.

Davina Hayes's climax was the most gorgeous sight I had ever seen. She owned it, she felt it, and she definitely enjoyed it. She slumped over and shifted down my body.

"Holy shit," she murmured breathlessly, her face buried in the crook of my neck.

My cock was painfully rock-hard in my pants. It throbbed to be inside her. But fucking her here felt wrong. I just ate her out with the door unlocked. Anyone could have walked in on us. It was unacceptable to lose my head like this at my age.

I ran my hands down her back, her breathing slowing down. This girl was so small and soft. Too vulnerable and breakable. If the Italians would have caught her stealing out of the safe, they would have snuffed the life right out of her. The thought made something tighten in my chest.

Now that I had a taste of her, I was certain I wouldn't let her go.

CHAPTER 17
Davina

My muscles quivered like jelly.

This had been the most intense orgasm of my life. Given to me by Liam Brennan, my best friend's dad. Her *dad*. My reason sunk in, and panic rose.

What the fuck have I done?

I scrambled, pushing off of him. I got to my feet and pulled my dress down, reality finally setting in. I had the most intense orgasm with Juliette's dad.

Holy mother of God!

My eyes searched the floor for my panties, and then I remembered he tucked them into his pocket.

"Ummm, I'm going to need my panties," I murmured, looking anywhere but at him.

Juliette's dad. Of all the people in the world, why him? Though I loved every second of it.

"No."

My eyes flickered to his gaze, and I glared at him, annoyed. He shifted on the couch, adjusting himself, and I couldn't help but notice the impressive bulge still pressing against the fly of his jeans. He was hard, yet he didn't try to fuck me. Was all this meant to punish me?

It wasn't much of a punishment.

"I don't want to sit in an Uber for two hours without panties," I snapped. "Give them back."

"You're right," he retorted, and I sighed. At least he had some sense. "You'll be sitting in my car for two hours without panties."

Wait. What?

He stood up and his hand came to my lower back, nudging me forward.

"Mr. Brennan, you—"

He cut me off. "Liam."

"W-what?"

"Davina, I just ate your pussy like my life depended on it," he drawled while his words lit a match throughout my body. "You'll call me Liam."

I opened my mouth, then closed it and opened it again, but no words came out.

"That's settled." A small smile tugged at his lips and my heart fluttered. It fucking fluttered. A little orgasm and oral sex, and I was a simp for this man. What was wrong with me? I was a strong, independent woman.

"Grab the backpack with my stolen money," he urged me, and I blinked my eyes. I almost forgot about the damn money. It was the whole reason I was in this situation. God, the girls and I really were the worst damn criminals to walk this earth.

I took two steps and picked up the backpack, then let him lead me out of the office and down the hallway. Halfway through, we ran into two men—Quinn and another that I didn't recognize.

I avoided looking at Quinn, worried he'd read on my face what his boss and I did back in that office after he left. My eyes shifted to the man next to him.

"Holy smokes," I muttered under my breath.

This guy was fucking hotness on two legs. Tall, about six foot three. Dark hair and even darker eyes.

"Don't get any ideas, a mhuirnín," Liam whispered into my ear, his tall frame pulling me into him.

I turned my head to watch Liam's profile. Whatever he said, it was hot as fuck to hear him say it. I wanted to hear him say it again, but this was hardly the place for it.

"Where's Basilio?" Liam asked, his voice cold, I was sure I misheard him. Just a minute ago, he was growling and chuckling, and now he looked downright threatening. But at least it wasn't toward me. "Dante, I asked a question," Liam snapped.

I blinked, my eyes darting between the three men. I had no fucking idea who Basilio was, but it was apparently who Liam wanted, and I had a feeling whatever Liam wanted, he got.

"He had some business to attend to," the dark-haired man replied calmly. He looked Italian. "I'll get him the papers, don't worry. His papà will get a confirmation tonight."

If his tanned skin tone and dark eyes weren't enough proof of his Italian heritage, the way he said papà certainly was.

"Don't fuck with me, Dante," Liam told him coolly. "The deal was Basilio gets the deed. I won't have any of you DiLustros fucking it up."

Dante DiLustro.

Hmmm, the name sounded vaguely familiar, though I couldn't quite place it. But I knew one thing for sure from Juliette: her family hated the Italians. She called their mafia ruthless, evil, and cruel, but she never expanded on it, and somehow that made me nervous as hell.

"He was here initially, but then he left," Quinn added. "He was in a rush. So I assumed his cousin was left to pick up the paperwork for him."

"He left alone?" Liam questioned and I thought it odd. Obviously the man left alone if his cousin was still here.

"As far as I could tell," Quinn grumbled. "The bar area was riled up. It was hard to see."

Quinn shot me a glare, clearly blaming me right along with my friends.

"I assure you, Liam. You have nothing to fear," Dante drawled, though everything about him screamed a sophisticated, raw danger. "The deal is sealed the moment you hand over the deed."

I held my breath as my eyes darted back and forth between the two men. The silence stretched and with each second that ticked by, I felt panic rise inside me. I shifted, but Liam's hand tightened around my waist as if warning me to stay close.

Quinn was the one that finally broke the silence.

"Where did Basilio go anyhow?"

"None of your business." Dante didn't even glance his way, his voice cold.

My heart thundered under my rib cage and my mouth went dry. All the movies I've seen about the mafia indicated that killings and conflicts happened all the time. Danger always lurked.

"I-I have to go back to school," I stammered, and it wasn't until the words left my lips that I realized how stupid it sounded. It made me sound like a high schooler.

Dante's eyes flicked my way, and I offered a feeble smile. This was so fucked up.

"Umm, not high school," I added, sounding even dumber. "College. I have finals tomorrow."

Ugh! Stop talking, Davina, I scolded myself.

Dante's mouth twitched. "I'm sure you'll do great," Dante answered, though I couldn't quite figure out if he was being sarcastic or a smartass.

"Thanks," I murmured, glancing at Liam and instantly stiffening.

The look he was giving Dante was murderous, and I wondered what I missed.

CHAPTER 18
Liam

Damn Italians!

They never kept to the plan. Basilio DiLustro was supposed to pick up the last deed, and the fucker wasn't here. I had a suspicion the little bastard was chasing his dick.

"Are we having a meeting without DiLustro's head of the famiglia?" The voice of Gio DiLustro came behind Dante. The latter didn't move, but an expression flickered in his eyes that told me he hated the old man.

Well, get in fucking line. I hated him more. Gio DiLustro belonged six feet underground. I owed it to my sister, and it fucking burned me that I couldn't deliver that justice for her without causing a war. Fuck, if I could get a guarantee that it wouldn't mean Aisling's or Wynter's deaths, I'd do it.

"I decided to witness the passing of the Eastside Club to the syndicate," Gio gloated. "Another Brennan down. After all, it's a cause for celebration for DiLustros. A victory."

I growled, ready to snap Gio's neck. The nerve of that fucking moron.

"You Brennans thought yourselves too good to connect to DiLustros." Gio's voice was bitter. Even after all this goddamn time, he held a grudge.

The itch to wreak violence and shoot him right now flooded me. Like a rush of water after the dam had broken. Davina must have sensed it, because her hand wrapped around my forearm, her grip tight.

A simple touch by her and calm washed over me. Her touch grounded me unlike anything else I had ever felt before. I took a deep breath, reining in my anger threatening to spiral out of control.

"We're passing each other on Brennan's way out," Dante said.

My right hand snaked to the back of my pants where I had my handgun tucked in. Hell would freeze over before I trusted any DiLustro.

"Basilio has the deed?" Gio questioned, his eyes on Davina, which I hated. Her little body stiffened next to me, and the regret washed over me. If I hadn't kept her in the club, Gio wouldn't have laid eyes on her. She wouldn't have been exposed to the DiLustro family, the syndicate, or any Kingpin.

Goddamn it! I should have taken the money she attempted to steal and sent her on her way.

"Well, does he have the deed or not?" Gio barked, and Davina startled, almost jumping in her spot. Her hands were trembling, and she quickly pushed them behind her. She had good instincts. You never show a DiLustro your fear, because they always exploit that shit.

Dante's dark eyes, so much like the rest of the DiLustros, glanced my way before he answered, "Yes."

If Gio wasn't eyeing Davina, he would have noticed his nephew was lying. And because it was that fucking guy that ruined my sister's life, I had no intention of ratting Dante out. Maybe the next generation of the DiLustro family would be better than the last one.

"And you're one of the staff?" Gio asked Davina, taking a step closer to her. "Fucking the boss, I see." Davina's eyes flared with anger, but at least she didn't snap at him. Gio thrived on challenges and breaking women. I pulled her closer to me. "She'll remain," he added, confident to get his way.

"She's not staff," I told him coolly. "And she's none of your concern, so keep away from her."

I ensured there were no women on my staff before I went ahead with the deal. I'd never put any woman within arm's reach of that sick bastard. In fact, I hated that Gio DiLustro had ever laid eyes on Davina, that I was to blame for it. And to think Wynter and Juliette were here a mere hour ago.

"The Italians out of Hell's Kitchen?" I changed the subject. Starting tomorrow, the territory would be divided into east and west. No more turf wars.

His dark eyes flashed angrily. I forced his hand by buying out all the land and buildings around him until all he had was just a worthless building remaining. He ran my sister out of the city, and it took me over twenty years to finally contain the damn Italians to their side.

"Yes," Dante answered for his uncle.

I nodded. "In that case, enjoy the club and the east side. Your son is now the proud owner of the best club in New York. The richest Kingpin, huh? Or so I hear."

My last jab at the old son of a bitch.

Holding Davina close to me, we passed them with Quinn at our back and left the club without a backward glance. It was good while it lasted, but I wouldn't miss it. My only regret was that Gio continued to live and walk this earth. He was scum of the scum. I bet it burned him to know his son now owned more property in New York than his father ever had, the man who started the syndicate. The first Kingpin.

Davina shuddered, and I noted goose bumps dancing across her skin. I rushed her toward my black Mercedes Benz G-class, opened the door, and she slid into the passenger seat. Then I handed her the car keys.

"Start the car and warm up," I told her quietly. "Something happens, you get in the driver's seat and drive."

She nodded without question before taking the keys, her eyes darting next to me. I didn't have to turn around to know it was Dante. I'd expected him to come after me.

I shut the door and turned around. Quinn had my back, but it was never smart to leave yourself blind to the enemy. Especially a DiLustro.

Wearing his three-piece-suit, Dante looked very much like his cousin and his uncle. I had yet to see any DiLustro man out of a suit. They probably fucked their women in suits too.

I watched him cross the street, and in five strides, reach us.

"Thank you," he grumbled. I knew from the intel that Basilio and Dante were close, like brothers. This proved they had each other's backs. With one running the Chicago syndicate and one in New York, they would be a force to be reckoned with one day. Probably too soon for my own liking. That would make it hard for the Russians, the Irish, or anyone else to go against them successfully, unless forces were joined.

Except, the Russians would never be an option due to our history. When my father kidnapped Winter Volkov, Aisling's mother, he had burned that bridge. Fuck, he blew up all bridges to anyone in Russia.

Though that would have to be a matter of concern for another day.

I pulled the deed out of my back pocket and handed it to Dante.

"Basilio's name is on there already," I said. "See that he gets it, and tell him not to fuck it up."

He put it inside his jacket with a nod, and just like that, the deal was done.

CHAPTER 19
Davina

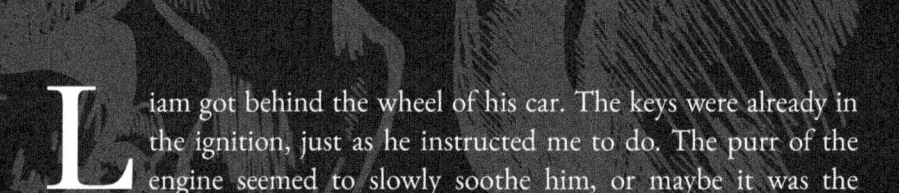

Liam got behind the wheel of his car. The keys were already in the ignition, just as he instructed me to do. The purr of the engine seemed to slowly soothe him, or maybe it was the distance between the club and us.

For a while, I just watched his big frame. His sculpted muscles packed every inch of his powerful figure. I felt it as I rode his face. God, he'd felt good. And for someone so large, he moved gracefully. Lethally.

The car smelled like him, clean with a mixture of citrus and cedar, and I found that I loved the scent.

Sitting so close to me, I kept resisting the urge to tilt sideways to be closer to him. Like a gravitational pull.

"You good?" His deep, gravelly voice after what we shared rolled down my spine like a soft caress. He sounded concerned, and something about the fact that he would care had a swarm of butterflies fluttering in my stomach.

"Yes." Strangely, I felt safe around him. Maybe it was some crazy side-effect after the week we've had, or maybe it was my instincts. *More likely the orgasm he gave me*, I mocked myself wryly.

"Are *you* okay?" I asked him tentatively, unsure whether I should venture into a territory where I cared whether Juliette's father was okay or not. "I would ask if those were friends of yours, but if that's how you treat your friends, I'd hate to see how you treat your enemies."

"Definitely not friends, and today hasn't been the best day," he drawled. I winced, remembering what we did. "I just transferred the club to the Italians." I cocked my eyebrow, surprised he told me. "That last hour with you was the best way to part with the club. It made the memories of it that much sweeter."

I felt the flush burn my cheeks, and suddenly, the car was too small. Too hot.

"But it is important that you and the girls don't go back to the Eastside Club," he continued. I gave him a questioning look. "The club belongs to the Italians now. You girls can no longer venture there. It's too dangerous. Understand?" I nodded.

His hand reached for me, skimming along my thigh before taking my hand into his. And I melted. I fucking melted. No man had ever held my hand or interlocked our fingers as he drove.

"He saw me," I murmured.

"I promise you, Davina. I'll always protect you, just as I do Wynter and Juliette."

His promise sent warmth spreading through my chest. I knew if he vowed protection, he'd follow through. Liam Brennan was a man of his word. Juliette and Wynter always said that if he made a promise, he kept it.

"Umm, I don't..." I cleared my throat, my mouth suddenly dry and thick with emotions. "You can drop me off at the bus station, and I'll take a bus to Yale."

"I don't think so," he mused, as if entertained.

"You can't drive me all the way there and then back," I protested weakly. I actually wanted to spend more time with him. "It's late."

He scoffed. "It's a little after eight o'clock. I know you and the girls can party half the night."

I winced. "Ugh, about that—"

"You have good taste, I'll give you that," he replied, unconcerned that I opened a one-hundred-thousand-dollar cognac bottle.

My eyes traveled over him, and my thighs clenched.

"I know," I rasped. The words left me before I realized how they sounded. I tugged at the hem of my dress, shifting uncomfortably. Around him, arousal seemed to be a permanent side effect. Almost as if I had been deprived until the moment we crossed paths, and now, I was infected by his filth. Even worse, I freaking loved it.

I quickly continued talking to ensure I didn't do something stupid. I wouldn't be able to resist him for the entire drive back to Yale. I'd end up begging him to pull over and make me his.

"It's a long ride. I'll be fine," I spoke fast, my words sounding breathless. "And I have plenty of money." Okay, maybe I was really stupid to remind him I had stolen from him today. "I can text you to let you know I got there okay."

He chuckled softly, but there was a dark edge to it. "Firstly, I am taking you to Yale. Nobody else. My boat will be ready by the time we get to the docks. Secondly, your body will be mine whenever I say. This is one of those times. I will fuck you senseless until we dock in New Haven." Oh my gosh, I was totally on board for that. Jesus, this tribute was totally worth it. I felt like I was getting rewarded, not punished. "And thirdly, if you and the girls are going to steal from me, I'll ensure my money doesn't end up in the wrong hands."

Okay, as far as reasoning goes, this was a good one. Pleasure and security. What more could a girl wish for?

Except...

Unwilling thoughts crossed my mind. "You're going to throw me overboard, aren't you?" I whispered, my hand still in his. "I'm going to go swimming with the fishes." It happened in *The Godfather*.

His booming laugh filled the small space. His body actually shook from it, and inadvertently, my hand shook too.

"Davina, throwing you overboard would be a waste," he rumbled, and my sharp sigh vibrated through the air. "I plan on getting my money's worth. I will fuck you so hard you'll never want another man. You're mine now."

Holy fuck, I loved the possessiveness etched in his voice. He was equal parts dominant and possessive.

"If you're going swimming with the fishes," he concluded, "so am I. The fish can watch as I thrust into your tight little cunt and fill you with my seed."

Wetness pooled between my thighs and I shifted uncomfortably, an ache pulsing with the need to have him deliver on those words.

"Are you always so controlling?" I asked him curiously.

"I've never been that great at sharing," he admitted without any hint of guilt. Not that he should feel any. "Does it bother you?"

I tilted my head. "No, not in this matter."

"When does control bother you?" He seemed genuinely interested.

"Hmm." I thought for a moment. "Well, my grandfather always says that when I set my mind on a goal, no amount of wild horses can hold me back. So, I guess you better not try to control me then."

His deep chuckle filled the space between us.

"It means you're determined," he said, glancing over at me. "It's a good quality to have."

"Thanks. It drove my grandfather crazy at times." To this day, I still remembered when I decided it was time I knew who my parents were. I nagged and researched until he finally had to sit me down and tell me that my parents didn't want children. He refused to reveal much else, but he did it gently, and assured me I was his greatest treasure.

"So, just to be clear," I added. "I give you what you want, and you let me keep the money. No chance of taking it back. Correct?"

"Correct."

I had to admit it didn't feel like a hardship really. I'd been fantasizing about him for the past three months, waiting for him to come and collect his debt, but he never did.

Until now.

Yet, it felt like I was getting the better deal again.

"You're very close to your grandfather," Liam said.

"I am. He was my mom, dad, and everything in between," I admitted softly.

"What are your plans after graduation?" he asked casually.

A tiniest flicker passed Liam's expression, but I couldn't hone in on it.

"I'm going to get a job, preferably using my degree, and then I'd like to move my grandfather to wherever I am."

"Hmmm."

"Did you go to college or did you..." My words faltered. I didn't want to sound rude.

"I went to Princeton," he answered. "So did my father."

"Oh, I thought your father lived in Ireland." I was fairly certain that was what Juliette told me.

"You're right, he does now. But back then, he only visited Ireland and spent most of his time here in the States."

"Does he visit?"

His jaw ticked, and his fingers gripped the steering wheel before he loosened them.

"No, he doesn't," he answered, his voice hardened. "He hasn't in a very long time."

I sensed a story there, and it didn't sound like it was a good one.

"I'm sorry," I murmured. "That must be hard. Is that why Juliette spent most of her time in California with Wynter?"

He chuckled. "You girls really keep no secrets between each other, huh?"

I grinned. "Actually, we do," I said. "But I promise whatever they tell me, I'll never repeat to anyone else. And..." I paused for a moment before I continued. "And I'll never repeat whatever you tell me either," I promised softly. "To anyone."

We came to a stop and his hand took mine. Raising our interlocked fingers, he brushed his mouth against my knuckles and a shudder ghosted down my spine.

"Thank you, Davina." A fragile trust started to build. "You're mine now. Every single inch of you, inside and out."

I gasped, my fingers tightening around his. "Don't you think I'm too curvy?"

"Davina Hayes, you're perfect," he said. "Every single inch of you is gorgeous. Your plump arse, your pussy. Every single fucking inch of you is perfect."

I had lost my words. My thoughts. My mind.

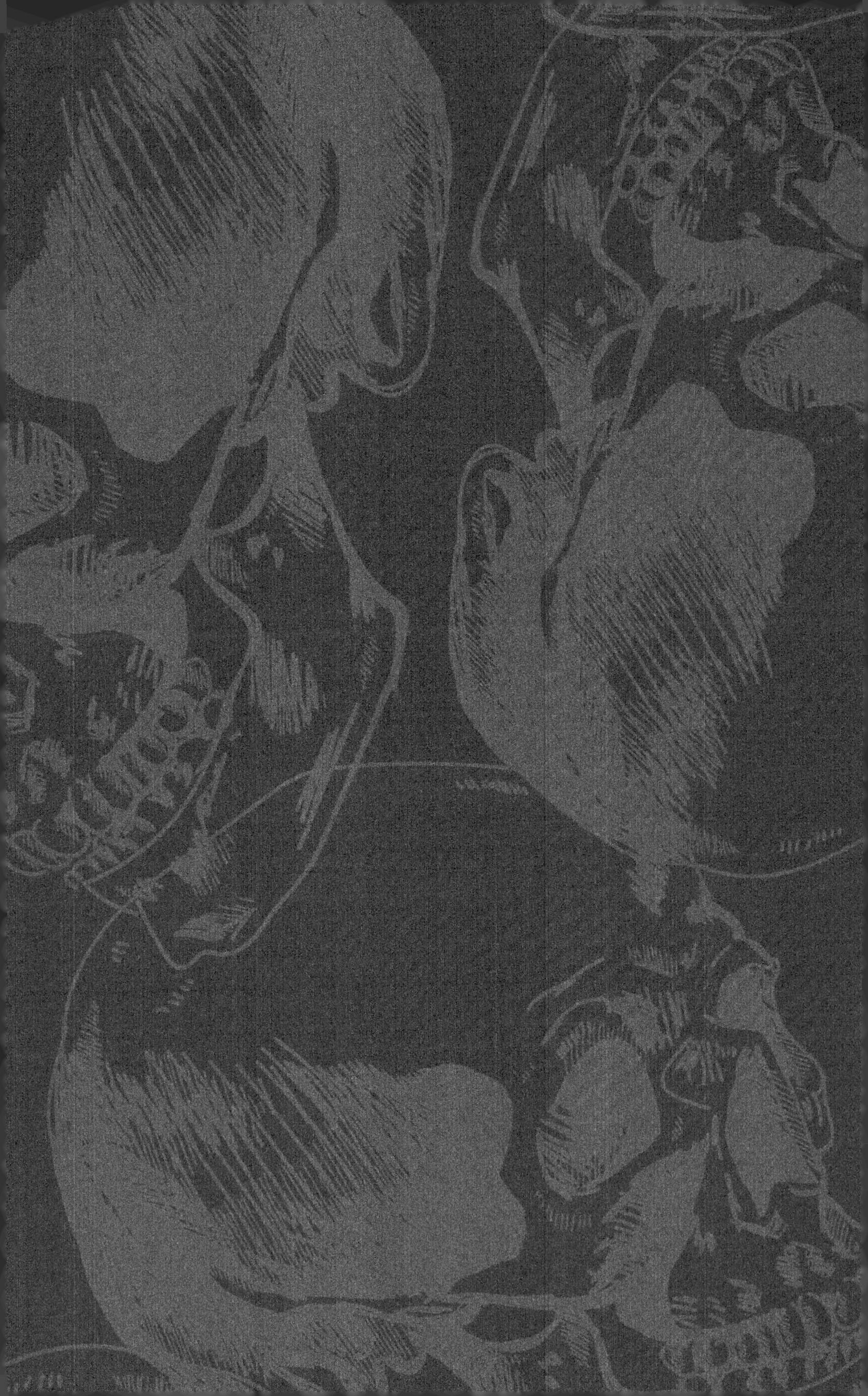

CHAPTER 20
Liam

I could smell her arousal.

She fought it tooth and nail, but Davina was turned on by my filthy words. Maybe I had found my match in her.

"Show me your pussy," I said, my eyes on the car in front of us. "But just to me," I growled. "Like I said, I'm not exactly the sharing type."

"I'm starting to see," she murmured, her eyes darkening. "You still have my panties."

I watched her from my peripheral. She was flushed, her chest rising and falling. God, she was fucking gorgeous. I saw the indecision cross her face. "Make sure I'm the only one with the view."

She sighed in resignation. She struggled with admitting to herself that she loved this.

She lifted her dress up her toned thighs but kept her legs together.

"I can smell your arousal." I glanced over at her. "No sense in hiding it."

"Oh my God," she huffed.

"No, God is not making you soaking wet," I drawled. "I am. Now give me your foot."

"Why?" she asked suspiciously.

"I want to ensure I'm the only one with a clear view of your pussy," I murmured. "Now obey me."

She kicked off her shoes and stretched her leg across the console of my car. I caressed her soft foot and ankle, skimming my fingers up her leg.

"You're so hot. I want to pull over and fuck you." My fingers reached between her thighs and I brushed them over her slick core. "So fucking wet."

Her choked laugh was my answer.

"I've never done anything like this before," she squeaked out.

"No? Tell me you don't like this," I demanded, circling around her clit but never touching it. She writhed, trying to get me to touch her there. "I want to give you everything."

She trembled at my words. "I want to give you everything too," she murmured, watching me through her lust-filled eyelids.

And fuck, her words pleased me. A lot.

As a reward, I brushed my fingers over her clit, then brushed it again before I started slowly rubbing it. The scent of her arousal filled my car, and fuck, I wanted to taste her again.

I stopped and her complaint came in the form of a whimper. "Liam," she protested. "Y-you can't tease me like that."

Her hand came around my wrist, and she started grinding against my hand. "Stop torturing me."

I smacked her cunt hard enough to make her cry out.

"What the fuck?" she whimpered, but she didn't remove my hand from her pussy. "You can't do *that*."

"Whatever I want," I reminded her, smiling darkly. "And you like it."

"No, I don't," she protested.

"Then why are your thighs clenched around my hand, and why are you dripping wet?"

Her breath hitched and her eyes flared as if she hadn't realized until now that maybe she liked having her pussy slapped.

I pushed my finger into her. Her insides clenched around it, and she squirmed as she fucked it. I pumped into her once, twice, then I pulled my fingers out.

"Let go of my wrist, Davina." She instantly obeyed, and I brought my finger to my lips.

"Mmmm," I praised. "I can't wait to have you ride my face again. I want to bury myself so deep in your pussy that you'll feel me for days after. Ride you so hard that no other cock will ever do it for you. Mine will be the only one to ever bring you pleasure."

A whimper full of desire escaped her. "You can't say stuff like that, Mr. Brennan."

I let out a dark chuckle. "We're back to Mr. Brennan, huh?" I brushed my fingers along her naked pussy, making her shudder. "Do you know how many times I've thought about you since that night?"

She watched me through heavy-lidded, lust-filled eyes. "I-I thought about you too," she confessed as her cheeks tinged pink.

"I've thought about you every goddamn night," I admitted, brushing my finger against her soaked core. I was rock-hard, and doing this was a torture to my dick. But fuck if I cared. I wanted to touch her, inhale her scent deep into my lungs. "I imagined how you looked when you watched me in the shower. You are even more beautiful in reality. The way your lips parted as you watched me eat your pussy was magnificent. And your panting noises... Fuck, it's enough to make me spill right now."

I decided right then and there, Davina Hayes would be my wife.

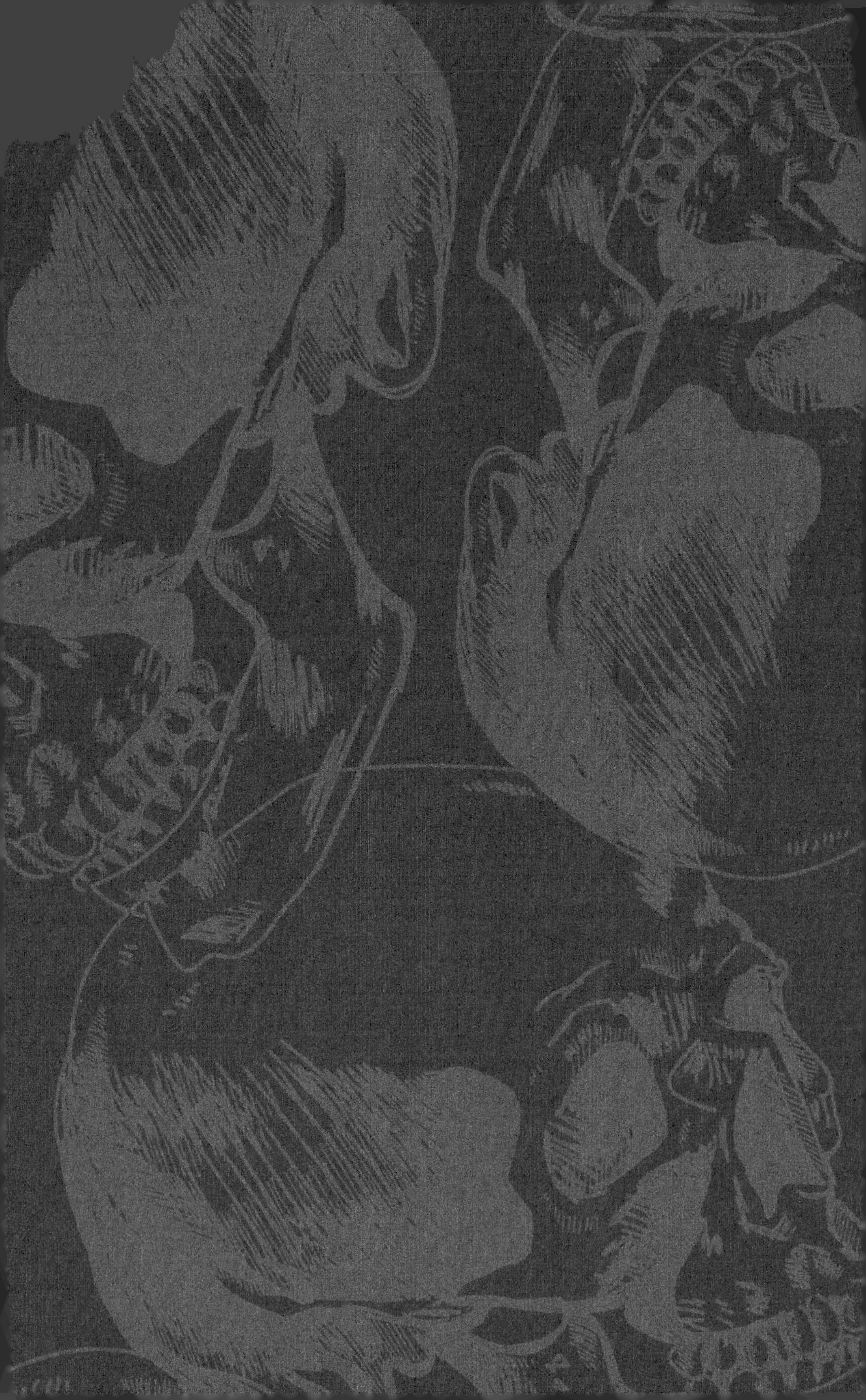

CHAPTER 21
Davina

We pulled up to the docks, and even from here I could see the row of huge, luxurious yachts. Not that I expected a small, dingy boat, but I certainly didn't think we'd take an enormous yacht that looked so pristine and spotless even under the starry night skies.

When we parked, Liam came around and opened my door before I had a chance to slip on my shoes. Tugging on my dress, I ensured nobody would get a glimpse of the fact that I wasn't wearing panties.

We made our way to the docks, and within minutes, we climbed up the ramp to board. Another five minutes and the yacht jolted as it started to move.

Liam placed his hand on the small of my back as we made our way around the deck, like I was his and he'd never let me go. The part that bothered me was that I liked it. Somewhere deep down, I felt he wouldn't just turn me over to the police. Not after promising to protect me.

"What would you like to drink?" he asked, the deep timbre of his voice making my insides grow warm.

"Water," I responded.

He chuckled. "How about a glass of champagne?"

"No, I'd rather stick to water." He turned to a man at the bar on the deck. A freaking bar. He gave him a nod and then returned his attention to me.

"Are we celebrating something?" I asked curiously.

He gave me a big smile, and something about it made me feel like I had fallen into a trap. One full of pleasure and sinful, filthy deeds.

Juliette and Ivy would never let me live this down if they found out. Assuming Juliette could get past the fact I was attracted to her father. I found him incredibly good-looking, and somehow I knew this thing between us was a unique attraction.

"We're celebrating you and me, Davina." He grinned.

One of his crew members showed up, and Liam was quick to hand me my water, dismissing him. I took a long sip, hoping it'd calm my nerves. It had been a strange evening, but I felt like I was floating.

Liam brought his own drink to his mouth and took a sip. His blue eyes trailed over me, and a light shudder ghosted down my spine. I loved the way he looked at me. It made my stomach flutter. Liam Brennan was devastatingly attractive, but it was more than that.

"Would you like a tour?" he offered. "I want you to feel comfortable on this boat."

"I'm fine with boats," I told him. "I spent a good amount of my childhood days on my grandfather's."

He took my hand in his, linking our fingers together as we headed deeper down the deck. The butterflies swarmed in my stomach. In the past few hours, he'd held my hand twice, and I loved it. It kind of sounded pathetic, like a little girl starved for attention.

It wasn't though. It was the effortless way he was intimate with me.

It was impossible to fall for someone so quickly, right? It must be all the alcohol the girls and I consumed this week still impacting my judgment.

As we walked through his massive yacht, he pointed out the kitchen, the bar, the bedrooms, the living room. You could live on this boat and have everything. Then I followed him up the stairs to the upper deck. There was another parlor up there, but a more intimate one. And without any crew hanging about.

The room was surrounded by glass on three sides, and currently, the windows were open. The light breeze swept through the room, followed by the sounds of waves breaking against the massive yacht.

Then the hum of the engine roared, signaling that the boat had throttled to full speed.

I felt his eyes on me the entire time, and something about the way he watched me made my heart squeeze until it felt like it might explode. Maybe it was the result of the out-of-this-world orgasm I'd experienced earlier. Or maybe this man simply had the most peculiar impact on me.

Liam stalked toward me, and something about the way he watched me had my heart beating fast and hard.

I stood still, unwilling to move. Truthfully, maybe I wanted to experience more of whatever pleasure he had to offer. So, call me greedy, but it'd been a hard week. It was a good stress reliever.

I think.

Liam's large hand cupped the nape of my neck, possessive and firm, and lowered his mouth to mine. Our first kiss was explosive. Life-altering. He swallowed my next breath in his mouth as he pushed his tongue into mine, and my blood sizzled.

I couldn't breathe. The hard press of his lips against mine stole all my thoughts. His muscled body had me losing all my senses. I wanted more of him.

He nipped at my bottom lip and then licked it, soothing the sting with his warm tongue, and raw need shot through my veins. He slid his tongue deeper inside my mouth, like he wanted to consume me.

And God help me, I wanted to be consumed by him as much as I wanted to consume him in return. Shivers ghosted down my body at the feel of his large palms roaming my body. He slid one hand down over my hip to the curve of my ass and gripped it firmly, all the while his other hand remained on my throat.

Firm. Unyielding. Possessive.

As if he was my magnet, my opposite pole, my body leaned into him. The magnetic pull between us was impossible to resist. A stronger woman wouldn't yield to it, but I was far from strong.

He grabbed a fistful of my hair and tilted my head so he could kiss me deeper. Harder. Sucking on my tongue like his life depended on it. It certainly felt like mine did.

Everything about this man stole my breath, my thoughts, and my reason.

His mouth trailed down my neck, nipping and licking as if he wanted to mark me for the entire world to see. Drawing my dress upward until my whole lower body was on full display, he broke the kiss so his eyes could soak in my bare thighs.

"You're perfect," he purred.

My heart skipped a beat at his praise.

"My thighs are too thick," I breathed. Garrett always slipped in remarks about my thick thighs.

"They're perfect," he repeated. "When you straddled my face, your thighs offered heaven."

The heat of his gaze seared through my skin. He hadn't touched my core, but with his words and heated gaze, it was as if he had. Heat tugged in my lower stomach, and suddenly, I needed to close the small distance between us.

He was the only one that could ease this ache inside me.

I rolled my hips, closing the space. A rumble sounded in his chest, as if he appreciated my body flush against his. His palms roamed every curve on my body, first my ass, back to my hips, and then right back at my ass.

"And your fucking arse," he rasped, his Irish accent suddenly coming to the surface. "Fucking perfect so I can hold you when I fuck you deep and hard."

A moan slipped through my lips at that image. I wanted him to do it. His palm slid lower down my ass, and then he slapped my ass cheek. Next, he caressed the sting with his big, rough palms. He rubbed my ass, up and down.

My entire body was on fire. You'd think after the orgasm he'd delivered earlier, I wouldn't have the energy for this. Fuck that! I had all the energy in the world. If the apocalypse or death came knocking at the door, I'd ignore them just to finish what we'd started.

This man was making me hotter than I'd ever been. Desperation and desire were eating away at me, clawing at my insides and demanding this pleasure.

"Please..." I breathed. I wanted him so badly, I trembled. "Liam, please."

My hand slid down his body and cupped his erection. Jesus, he was big. Huge, if the heavy length under my fingers was any indication.

He drew in a rough breath, a rumble resounded in his chest, a growl on his lips, and his eyes blazed with fire as he stared down at me.

"I want it," I begged. A hazy wave of lust swam in my veins and there was no stopping it.

He pulled my hand to one side and pressed his face into my neck, right below my ear.

"No going back once I have you," he warned on a groan. His mouth traced the edge of my ear with his tongue and a shudder erupted beneath my skin. I was hot and cold, the combination making me delusional.

"Okay." One word. Acceptance.

I should have known at that moment I'd never be able to go back to before. There was no before or after Liam Brennan.

Only him.

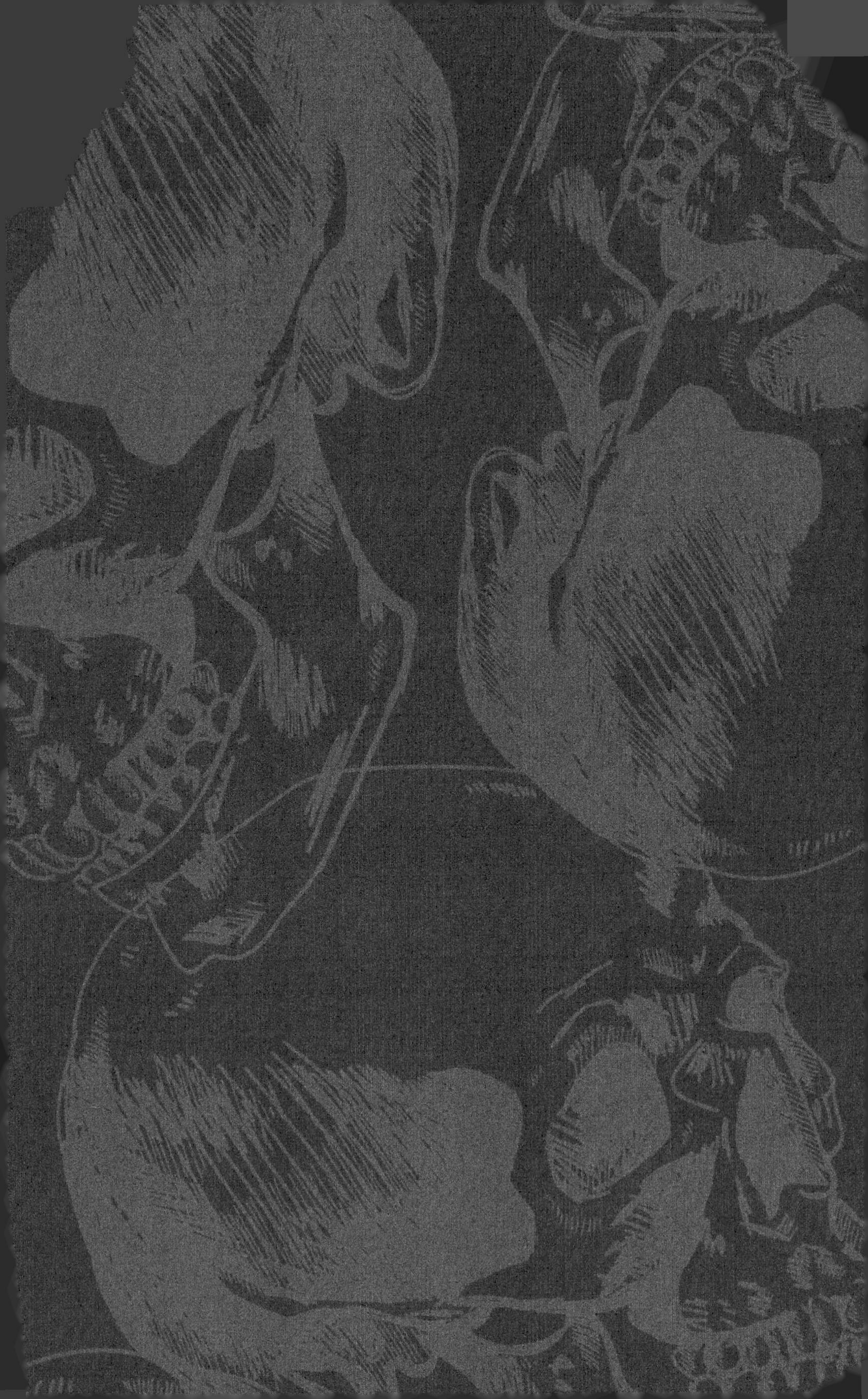

CHAPTER 22
Davina

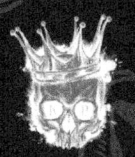

A growl of satisfaction vibrated from his large body and straight to my core.

"Wrap your legs around me."

I listened to his command, eager and hungry for this sensation. Heat bloomed inside me and goose bumps ran down my arms.

His hands held me up as he walked us over to the couch. The breeze coming off the sea cooled my skin, but it did nothing to extinguish this fire burning in the pit of my stomach.

He sat down on the couch, and I straddled his hips. He watched me through heavy eyelids as I ran my hands up his chest, then up his neck and into his thick dark hair. The moment my eyes landed on him three months ago, I became infatuated with him. Then the scene in the shower forever ingrained itself into my mind like a tattoo on my skin.

I undid the buttons on his shirt, my fingers shaking with urgency. I couldn't wait to feel his skin. He pulled his shirt from his pants, eagerly assisting me. My hands traveled over his hot skin and the ache between my thighs increased with each second that passed.

I leaned in and pressed my lips to his skin where his neck and shoulder met. It was my turn to mark him. I nipped, sucked, and licked, hoping I'd leave a mark on him as he had on me.

I ground on his erection, rocking my hips back and forth. He gripped the nape of my neck and yanked my head back. His deep blue eyes locked with mine as I continued riding his erection. Jesus, he wasn't even inside of me and I felt my release building brighter and hotter.

I gasped, a needy whimper slipping through my lips. My breathing was harsh, each exhale higher in pitch.

"Stop," he growled. "This time, I'll be inside of you when you come."

A shudder rolled through me and lust licked my skin. "P-please," I whispered, desperation lacing my voice. I didn't recognize this woman that desperately needed him. Not just physically, and that admission scared me to death.

He pushed the sleeves of my dress off my shoulders and pulled down the cups of my bra to bare my breasts. I watched him through a half-lidded heavy gaze as he admired them.

"Perfect," he praised. "Your tits are just as perfect as your thighs."

He captured a nipple in his mouth and our loud moans traveled over the warm spring breeze. His other hand reached for my other breast and squeezed while he continued with his nipping, licking, and marking.

I couldn't handle this sweet torture anymore. I needed to feel him inside me. I reached for his belt buckle, my hips rolling against him, causing friction.

"Are you greedy for my cock?" he groaned.

"Yes." No sense in pretending. I pulled him out and wrapped my fingers around him. He was rock-hard, hot and heavy. And so big.

In one swift move, he gripped my hips and pushed me down onto his length.

"Fuck," he gritted. "So fucking tight."

I gasped. I felt so full, my thighs quivering.

"I can feel your greedy cunt clenching around my cock," he groaned. "You'll take all of me. Won't you?"

"Yes," I whimpered, sliding down and letting him fill me to the hilt.

His eyes burned, looking down between our bodies where we were connected.

"Grind that sweet little pussy on my cock," he commanded, and my body trembled with the promise of pleasure.

I pressed my face into his neck and rocked my hips, rolling them in a circular motion. My clit ground against his pelvis, sending shudders down my back. His hands were all over me, and each time I ground against him, a moan slipped through my lips.

He felt so good inside me. So addictive. So right.

His hands locked on my hips, gripping them, and he started to grind me harder and faster against him. His mouth sucked on my throat, his teeth nipped my neck, his palm slapped my ass. I was reaching for brand new heights.

"I want to hear your screams." His voice was hoarse, like he was on the brink of losing control. For me.

"Fuck, so good," I panted. "God, please. Don't stop."

I kept grinding against him. Hard and fast. Deep then shallow. And then his hips thrust up, hard and deep inside me in one forceful move. I rode him harder, his eyes trailing over me. My neck. My full, bouncing breasts. And ending at where our bodies were connected. My arousal dripped down my thighs. The sounds of flesh smacking against flesh and my whimpering moans filled the air.

My hand reached for my clit, but he smacked it away. Instead, Liam's hands gripped my hips and bounced me on his erection like his life depended on it. Up and down. Hard and deep, his pelvis grinding against my clit. His length hit the spot deep inside me just right.

He was consuming me. Filling me.

"Fuck. Fuck. Oh my God."

I came so hard that spots danced behind my eyelids. He finished right behind me with a last thrust while my pussy clenched around him. Milking him.

Languid heat spread through me, my breathing erratic. I felt like I had died and gone to heaven. I rested my forehead against his shoulder as the world came back into focus.

Our heavy breaths filled the silence. I rested my face in the crook of his neck, full of contentment and bliss as my fingers curled in his hair.

He nipped my neck. "You're a filthy girl, Davina."

I scoffed, too high on post-orgasmic bliss to act insulted. "Says the man who can't seem to keep his hands off me."

A deep rumble shook his chest, and I couldn't help but smile. "You're right, wise arse. I love your arse." Then as if to emphasize his words, he squeezed my ass. "Which is the reason you'll be available to me whenever and wherever I wish."

The hum of the yacht engine came back into focus and reality slowly settled. I stole from this man. Yes, he brought on amazing orgasms, but it didn't diminish how dangerous he was.

As my reason came back, so did my doubts. Why did he want me? I was certain with his looks, obvious stamina, and knowledge of how to give incredible pleasure to a woman—and let's not forget his wealth—he had no shortage of partners.

"Why do you all need the money?" he asked, and my spine stiffened.

I couldn't answer that one truthfully. Not without giving him more ammunition against me. I was solely responsible for getting us into this situation. If I hadn't uttered those stupid words to Juliette, she would have never even thought to burn down the house.

His palm roamed my back, and I found my tension at his question was slowly draining away. This man had dangerous control over my body. Even worse was that I didn't exactly mind it. I still couldn't share this secret with him though.

I pressed my lips together, all the while my muscles relaxed under his palm that rubbed my back. Up and down. Left and right.

"Is it about Juliette's car?" he asked softly, but I wasn't fooled. He was fishing for information, hoping that under the bliss of his touch, I'd tell him everything.

"Yeah," I murmured, my lips brushing against the skin on his neck. It was better to lie to him without looking into his eyes. "A car for all four of us," I added, lying shamelessly. "Juliette agreed to take lessons."

"Juliette is a horrible driver," he commented. "She cannot drive until she passes driving school."

He was right about that. Juliette was the worst driver I had ever seen or ridden with. Nobody dared to sit in the car with her after experiencing her driving and be lucky enough to escape unscathed.

"I should take that money so that doesn't happen."

Fuck! And this was the reason I didn't lie.

"You can't take it back," I protested weakly. "Otherwise, I won't be available to you whenever you want."

He chuckled. "You're brave."

More like stupid.

But I had a lot more to lose if Garrett didn't get his money. All four of us did. We'd end up behind bars.

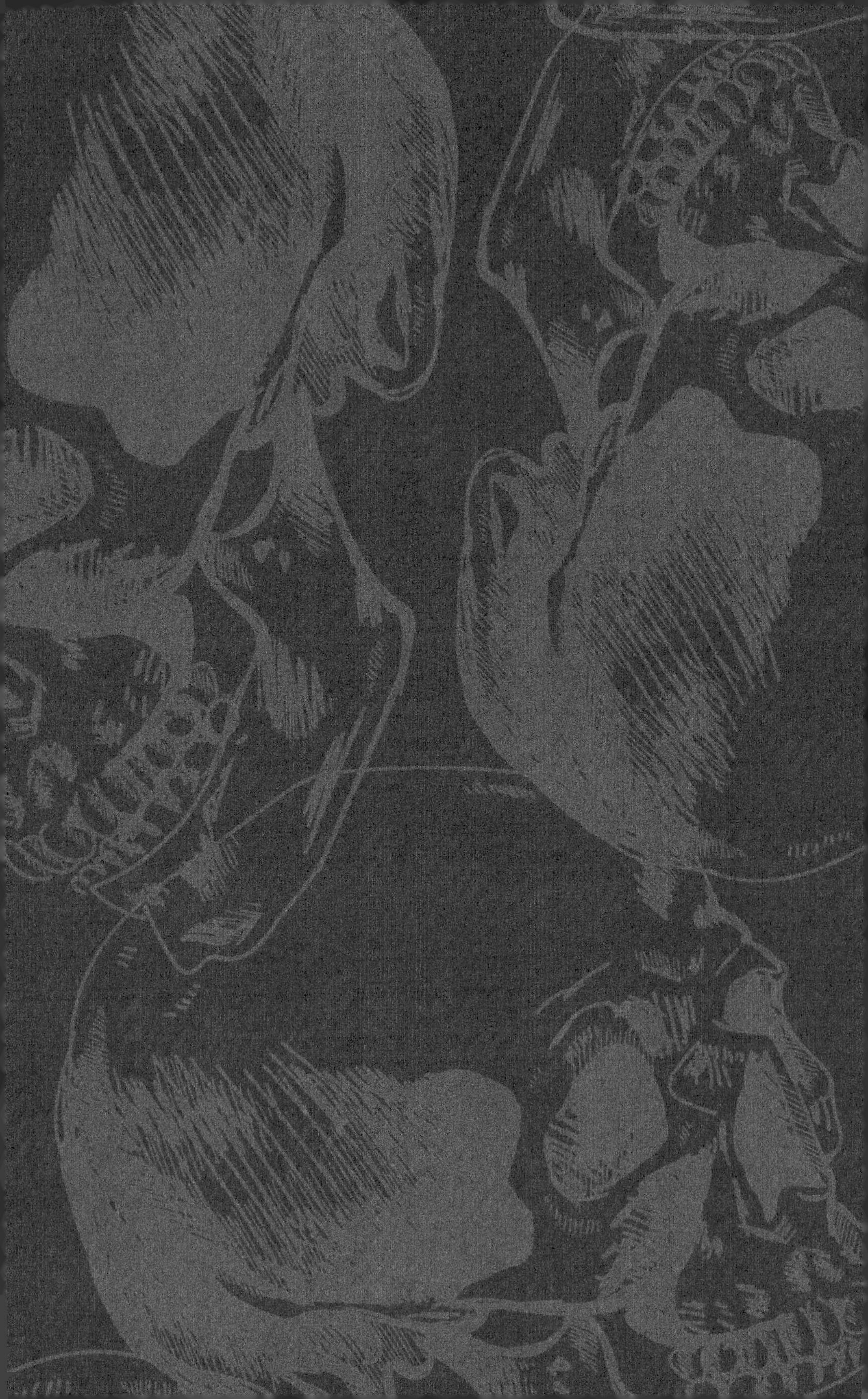

CHAPTER 23
Liam

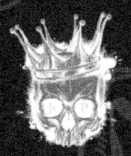

The moment she disappeared from my view into her dorm, I dialed Quinn.

"Boss," he answered. It never mattered what time of day or night it was, he always answered. It was the reason he had been my right-hand man for decades.

"I need you to send me candidates best suited for tailing," I ordered.

"Who are we following?"

"Davina and the girls."

A chuckle filled the line. "Those girls are trouble, I tell you. All four of them."

"I'm aware," I responded dryly. Though Davina was a whole different kind of trouble—the kind that might be dangerous for my heart. "For now, I just want candidates. How are your hacking skills these days, Quinn?"

"Aye, not that great," he muttered. "I'm getting too old to keep up with technology."

"Old arse," I joked.

"Your arse is not far behind me, Boss," he pointed out. Unfortunately, he was right.

"We'll have to find someone we can trust," I said. "Killian will be out of pocket for a bit, and there are certain things he can't do for me."

"I'm guessing you'll want to track the girls and Killian would be against it."

"Or he'll give a heads up to Wynter and Juliette," I added. Killian was close to them and always felt extremely protective of them.

"I'll start looking for candidates we can trust," Quinn announced.

"Thank you."

I ended the call just as I pulled back into the marina where my boat waited. I'd had this arrangement going with the marina for as long as Wynter and Juliette had been going to Yale. And tonight, it had proved very beneficial.

Just as I stepped on the deck, my phone vibrated.

> Cassio King: Where the fuck are you?

> Me: New Haven. Miss me?

> Cassio King: Terribly. So get your ass over here.

> Me: Where is here?

> Cassio King: My compound. It's our game night.

> Me: Busy.

> Nico Morrelli: The fucker forgot. Old age, I assume.

> Me: You're right behind me. Fucker!

It dawned on me that I had been so wrapped up with the DiLustro issues and the threat from the Pakhan, I hadn't been to the game in months. Cassio had his own gang, but occasionally I joined them. Alliances were important in my line of business, and Nico Morrelli had come through for me more than once.

Then it hit me. It was actually perfect timing. Nico might have some hacker recommendations, and Cassio might have some guys I could use to tail the women.

> Me: I'll be there.

It didn't escape me how Davina stiffened when I asked her why they needed the money. She'd lied about the reason, and I'd find out why.

One hour later, after a boat and helicopter ride, I was in Cassio's private compound. As soon as I exited the cabin of my helicopter, I headed straight to the security guard, who recognized me and opened the gate.

Since he'd had children, Cassio kept his game nights in a separate house that wasn't connected to his mansion. He took the security of his family seriously, not that I blamed him for it.

When I stepped inside, a loud roar filled the room.

"We had a bet going that you wouldn't show," Nico announced as I took the last spot around the table. They were already deep into the poker game.

"I said I'd be here."

"I didn't doubt you," Cassio said. "And thanks to my faith, I got myself a pretty penny tonight."

Luca, his brother, snickered. "Like you need it."

"Right on time to lose it to Liam." Nico laughed. "It has to be something in the Irish waters that feeds his poker skills."

"More like your poker skills are lame." Luciano, also known as the Ruthless King among Cassio's gang, scoffed.

My eyes roamed the room. You never knew who you'd find at Cassio's table. Sometimes it was the Russian guys that ran Louisiana. Sometimes it was the Canadians. Other times, the Colombians.

We played a round, and I won. I had a lifetime of practice with my father. Wynter was good at the game too. Excellent, in fact.

"How is the family?" Nico asked. He was the only one at the table who knew of Aisling and Wynter's true identities. His company had a daily schedule for removal of any digital footprint on anything related to my family.

"Good," I answered tightly. "I hear you're expanding your family."

"Fucking again," Luca muttered. "At this rate, the Morrelli family will run the world."

Cassio chuckled. "The Kings won't be far behind."

"Having another bambino, huh?" I asked.

Cassio nodded. Everyone knew his wife and children were his weakness. He didn't give a fuck. He just armed himself with extra guns. Truthfully, family was a weakness for all of us. We'd do anything to protect them.

"I need a hacker I can trust," I told Nico, then turned to Cassio. "And a man who can tail four women without being seen."

Both their eyebrows shot up.

"Killian is good at hacking, last I checked," Nico commented.

"He is," I confirmed, lying down a royal flush. "But this one he can't do. He's too close to the women."

"Ah." He took a moment to think. "I have one person in mind, but let me get back to you on that."

"Alexei Nikolaev is one of the best men to stick to shadows," Cassio chimed in. "He's expensive though."

I shook my head. "Money is no object, but it can't be any member of the Nikolaev family."

Surprise crossed Cassio's expression, but I wouldn't risk Davina crossing paths with them and her half-sister until she had a choice.

"Okay, let me think about it," Cassio said as the cards got shuffled again.

"It has to be someone trustworthy," I told him. "Whoever you recommend, I'll run another check on my own. I can't risk it with this one."

A nod, and that was that.

CHAPTER 24
Davina

"He said he deleted all the surveillance?" Juliette asked Wynter again.

The four of us were packing boxes of stuff we wouldn't need for the next few weeks, like kitchen supplies, since none of us seemed to ever find our way into the little kitchenette. We'd trek across the campus or even to the nearby town, but not into our own kitchen.

"Yes, Juliette," Wynter answered in an exasperated tone, packing up the cabinet with glasses. An open book sat next to her on the counter and her eyes skimmed the pages as she stuffed newspaper into each glass, then wrapped it in bubble wrap.

"Then why are we giving Garrett the money?" Juliette questioned, and all four of us stopped what we were doing to look at her.

"What do you mean?" I asked her, furrowing my brows.

"Why are we giving Garrett the money?" she repeated. "Wynter's boyfriend—"

"For the hundredth time, he's not my boyfriend," Wynter cut her off.

Juliette didn't even miss a beat, while Ivy and I snickered. We all knew that this guy was forevermore Wynter's boyfriend in Juliette's mind.

"Whatever," Juliette retorted. "As I was saying... Wynter's non-boyfriend"—the three of us rolled our eyes because it was so typical for Juliette to find a way to egg her on—"erased all the evidence of us being involved with that fire. So what are we paying Garrett for?"

I blinked. Juliette could be slightly entitled, and her moral compass was slightly skewed, but she couldn't mean that. Could she?

"Because we burned down his house," I said slowly, ensuring she understood the words.

Juliette shrugged. "Well, he shouldn't have been dicking around and sticking his cock where it doesn't belong."

"Mmmhmmm," Ivy hummed her agreement.

My eyes snapped to Wynter, who was always the calmest and the most reasonable of the four of us, and I found her with a pensive look on her face.

"What?" I snapped. "Don't tell me you agree with her?"

Garrett would hound us until the end of our days. Yes, I was stupid to entertain my relationship with him—and for so damn long—but I knew what a relentless ass he could be.

"And the neighbors saw us," I pointed out. "We might have even been captured by their surveillance cameras."

Wynter shook her head. "He said he took care of all of it. Wiped it clean. Nobody has a shred of evidence."

I had no fucking idea what that meant. How could a person even do all that? Maybe he was a hacker. *A super brilliant hacker*, I thought dryly.

Suddenly, the kitchen seemed too crowded. It didn't help that I'd been on the edge of my seat since last night. Breathe the wrong way and I could snap. Say the wrong word and I teetered on the edge, ready to lose my shit. Every time my phone buzzed, I jumped.

Juliette's father... Mr. Brennan... Liam... Damn it, I didn't know what to call him. My orgasm man. He put a clause on keeping the money.

To be available. Whenever he wished. Wherever he wished.

I was too stunned to ask questions when he dropped me off at the dorm last night, but now, I had so many of them. Needed specifics.

Some clarifications. Longevity of our agreement. Did he expect me to just obey? I mean, it was okay as long as I enjoyed it, but what if—

God, I hoped he didn't expect backdoor activity.

Of course he'd already sent me a message, demanding to see me tonight. While my body hummed in eagerness to see him and experience more out-of-this-world orgasms again, I ignored his message, just as I had Garrett's. I'd just seen Liam last night. I needed time to process all the shit that happened, and I really did have to study.

At least enough so I could finish my four-year education on a high note.

But then a few hours later, another message came in from Liam.

> Miss Hayes, don't forget I still have a tape showing you stealing from my safe. I expect you to answer me, not ignore me. After all, a million bucks should buy me that much.

I instantly replied with a lie.

> I'm studying, Mr. Brennan.

Then I followed up with an eye-roll emoji.

> Don't be sassy.

I could almost picture him growling.

> Or I'll spank that gorgeous ass of yours.

I scoffed softly.

> Don't threaten me with a good time, sir.

I watched bubbles fill the text box and smiled smugly to myself. Until the next message came through.

> I'm going to gag that pretty mouth of yours. With my cock.

A choked sound escaped me, and everyone's eyes snapped to me.

"I was checking my grades," I mumbled, lying through my teeth. "Nothing yet."

Another text came through.

> Go back to studying, Davina. If you do well, I'll reward you. With nipple clamps and a butt plug.

With damn nipple clamps and a butt plug! What the hell? My insides quivered at the possibility. The man was corrupting me.

I let out a slow breath, calming my wildly beating heart. He let me off the hook. I should focus on that, not a butt plug and nipple clamps.

Just because I couldn't let him think he rattled me so easily, I followed up with an emoji of rolling eyes and an old man GIF reply.

A million dollars in cash sat in our dorm room now.

Wynter shut her book loudly, and I startled as if I'd heard a gunshot. She slid down onto the floor. The three of us followed. So there we were, the four of us crammed on the floor, facing each other. Four college-aged criminals. We were graduating, finishing our finals, and hadn't even given our lives a fair chance. We went straight to crime.

Silence lingered as we sat on the dingy little kitchen floor, the boxes and tape all around us. It was probably the most time we'd spent in this kitchenette since we moved in.

"You know, Juliette might have a point," Wynter muttered, as if she was talking to herself.

"Garrett will nag us all to death," I protested. "And he might go to the police! Evidence or no evidence."

"Garrett has a big mouth," Juliette spat out. "I never liked him."

I groaned. That was so not the point right now.

"Maybe we should kill him," Ivy suggested, and I rolled my eyes. We couldn't even properly rob someone; how could we possibly kill someone and get away with it?

Wynter's eyes traveled over the three of us. "Forget killing. Back to the money. If we pay him the ransom, it'll be an admission of guilt," she reasoned. "Now, he has no evidence, and giving him money might give him leverage."

Okay, as far as reasons went, that wasn't the craziest one I'd heard.

"Uncle always says to never admit guilt or give others a way to hold something over your head unless you absolutely trust the person," Wynter added.

Juliette and Ivy nodded their heads in agreement. I was focusing on the trust comment. Did I trust Liam?

"And we don't trust Garrett," I agreed. "Except we left him without a home."

"And I'm sure he has insurance, which will pay for damages and any items he lost," Juliette reasoned. "We should keep that money for ourselves. We earned it."

I scoffed softly and the three of them narrowed their eyes on me. "We didn't exactly earn it," I said. "We stole it."

I'm earning it. Sort of. So it was earned income, right? Just non-taxable. God, it would seem Juliette's odd logic was rubbing off on me.

Except, I didn't tell the girls we got caught. There was no way in hell I could admit to what happened yesterday, that I agreed to be available at Liam's beck and call.

"Same difference." Juliette shrugged her slim shoulders.

"What fucking school did you go to where they teach you that stealing money is okay?" I snapped.

Wynter chuckled. "Mafia school?"

I shook my head. "Maybe I should have gone there too," I muttered. "Though they didn't do that great of a job with Juliette. Or you, for that matter, being the niece of an Irish mobster. We must be the worst criminals on this damn planet."

The three of them grinned at the same time. "We can learn criminal ways and become good," Ivy chimed in.

"Back to the matter at hand," I shifted the topic. "We're not criminals. The sooner we put this behind us, the better for us all."

"We could be criminals. The badass women that rule the world... or underworld," Juliette retorted, and I scoffed at that notion. I should have known better, because Juliette liked challenges. She immediately narrowed her eyes. "Cut me some slack," Juliette protested. "Dad and Killian kept me out of it, and I spent more time with Aunt Aisling and Wynter. I just picked up bits and pieces here and there."

"Maybe we should start a school that would teach girls how to be the best criminals," I muttered, semi-joking.

Their heads snapped to me with multiple gasps. Wynter's green eyes. Ivy's hazel ones. Juliette's blue ones. And all three had the same exact expression. It matched my feeling, trying to determine whether it should be a joke or a real thing.

Years later, I'd realize it was this moment that started it all. The school. Our future. And our children's future.

CHAPTER 25
Davina

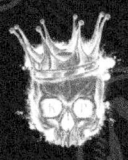

"That's not a bad idea," Wynter muttered, her fingers drumming against the cabinet. "Actually, it's a really good idea."

"I was joking." I snickered, though it wasn't entirely true. As I lay in bed last night, it dawned on me that if I ran into the two individuals of the Italian mafia last night on my own, I would have been helpless. And I didn't like it.

"But Wynter's not joking," Ivy replied, grinning like a fool. "I mean, why shouldn't women be just as badass as men or even better? Just look at my family in Ireland. They fucking sent me away so I wouldn't get wrapped up in their war. It never even occurred to them that maybe I could help." Her chest and cheeks blotched with frustration, and I could see her point. "We should vote," she suggested.

"Yes, let's vote," Juliette added. "About starting a school and not giving the money to that prick Garrett."

I exhaled. God, it was only three in the afternoon, and I was exhausted. The possibility of receiving a demanding text from Liam to be available to meet and perform some kinky shit had me both irritable and excited. It made no damn sense. My thighs clenched in anticipation, and I mentally cursed my body. Of all the men to find so devastatingly attractive, it had to be the head of the Irish mafia in New York.

"First, let's vote whether Garrett should get the money he's blackmailing us for," Juliette started, sounding like Judge Judy. Nobody raised their hands, including me. "Let the record show the vote is unanimous. Garrett the dickhead won't get our money."

The three of us rolled our eyes. Juliette was taking this to a whole new level, but she had a knack for theatrics.

"Okay, second vote," Ivy continued. "Should we start a school for badass women?"

"I hope that's not the name we'll use," I muttered.

"We'll worry about the name when the time comes," Juliette added. "Now, if you vote yes, raise your hand."

Ivy and Juliette instantly lifted their hands. Wynter and I shared a glance.

"I'm all for it," Wynter started, "but with my training schedule, I'm just not sure if I can fit it in until the Olympics are done. But after I get the gold medal in pair skating, I'm in."

"Well, it'll take us that long, if not longer, to set it up," I added. "Besides, we'll have to steal more money, because that million won't be enough."

That was another thing. In my guesstimation of how many stacks of money to take, I'd stolen double the amount we actually needed.

"Or we can seek investors," I suggested smartly. After all, I'd learned something at Yale. Suddenly everyone was shaking their heads. "No?" I asked. "Why?"

"Investors would have a claim on whatever we build," Juliette said.

"Yeah, I know how it works," I muttered. "Why would we object to it?"

"I have to agree with Juliette," Wynter chimed in. "If it's just ours, then nobody can tell us what to do. It will be just the four of us."

It made sense, but it would take us forever to gather those kinds of funds.

"And we can't ask any criminals," Wynter continued. "Even if they didn't put a claim on the school, there'll always be something they'll want. This will be built all by ourselves and our own hard-earned..." Her voice trailed off, realizing it wasn't exactly hard-earned, so she added, "Okay, stolen money."

"Yeah." All three cheered and I shrugged my shoulders and joined in. What are friends for, if not to dream with and support each other?

"I vote we steal from the Italians." Juliette grinned. "And then the Russians. Maybe even the cartel."

Great, Ivy and Juliette were getting all fucking excited for our brilliant future as criminals. We all should have studied criminology. By the time we were done stealing, the entire criminal world would be after us. At least my business degree might come in handy once we actually had the school established. Assuming we were still breathing and not at the bottom of a lake somewhere.

"Well, I did my part last night," I muttered. "It's someone else's turn to steal."

Juliette and Ivy exclaimed at the same time, "I volunteer. I volunteer as tribute."

Wynter and I snickered.

"You two are crazy," Wynter proclaimed, but then we all knew that. It was the reason we paired Ivy with Wynter and Juliette with me when we went out. Otherwise, we'd end up in jail. "If we do this, Davina and I are making decisions on who will steal from whom."

"So you're in?" Juliette asked, her voice full of hope and her eyes ping-ponging between the two of us.

And just like that, we were on board—either because we were insane, or we were just as good at making trouble as our two best friends.

"Hell yeah," we both answered at the same time, grinning mischievously. A round of high-fives followed.

"Where else would I use my Yale business degree?" I remarked sarcastically, smiling like a fool.

"Or my ice skating championship skills," Wynter added. When the three of us gave her blank looks, she continued, "Or my mathematics and physics?" No comment. "Okay, I'll hustle and learn something useful."

"Seems Davina is currently the only one with a useful skill," Juliette proclaimed. "My theater and performance studies are useless. And I discovered that right on the day of my very last exam of my four-year college experience," she added exasperatedly. "What a damn waste!"

"Actually, theater and performing is a great skillset for a con artist," I told Juliette. "You'd probably be able to sell whatever we decide to do."

Juliette's eyes lit up. "I never thought of it that way."

"I'm doomed with photography and arts," Ivy muttered dryly. "I guess I could be the photographer for our new school. Make it sexy and all."

"Because parents want to send their kids to a sexy school." Wynter snickered, and we threw our heads back, laughing wildly.

"Actually, I think we can use your skillset too, Ivy," I announced. "Whatever we end up doing, we'll have you deep dive into learning the ins and outs of the building. Spot where the cameras are, the routes the personnel take."

"That's brilliant," Wynter announced. "Ivy can take pictures of everything so we can get oriented before we even get there. Ivy would have the best knowledge on how to get good shots in order to make sure all potential problem areas are laid out."

"Holy crap," I murmured. "We're really doing this."

This whole thing seemed unreal.

"Okay, if we're doing this," Juliette commented, her eyes shining excitedly, "I think we should rob the Italians."

I frowned. "Why the Italians?"

She shrugged. "Well, if we steal from the Irish again, they might blame the Italians." *No, they won't.* "So, we'll steal from the Italians. You know, spread the wealth."

Wynter scoffed. "More like steal the wealth." The three of us turned to face her, and she smiled her innocent smile. "Not that I'm complaining. I'm just being technically correct, you know."

"Won't they blame the Irish if they see you two?" I questioned. After all, Juliette and Wynter were family members of the highest-ranking Irish mafia man.

"There aren't too many people in the mafia who know our faces," Wynter explained. "My mother didn't want to be part of the underworld. She moved to L.A. and cut all ties to the mafia world, with the exception of Uncle Liam, Killian, and Juliette."

CORRUPTED PLEASURE

Their family relationships were complicated for sure. Just like mine was.

"So, where do we rob the Italians?" I asked, my tone slightly exasperated. I couldn't even believe I was asking. The four of us were batshit crazy. Maybe four years of Yale got us certified diplomas in insanity.

"We shouldn't do it in New York," Wynter answered.

"Why not?" Juliette inquired. "We robbed the Irish in New York."

Ivy's and my eyes darted between the two cousins, anticipation building.

"Because we don't want to start a war," Wynter explained patiently.

"Nobody would know it was us," Juliette protested.

"It's safer if we do it somewhere else." Wynter had a point, I thought, in my non-expert criminal experience. "Too many robberies in one area will have people looking around here. And we want them looking anywhere but here."

"Then where do we *go* to rob the Italians?" I asked her.

"Not sure," Wynter murmured. "Philadelphia? New Jersey? Chicago?"

"Geez, Chicago would be a stretch," Ivy complained. "We'd have to fly, then rent a car."

"We can't fly and rent a car," Juliette said, pondering the choices. "It's traceable. We'd have to drive; it would be an in-and-out job." Gosh, maybe Juliette knew a bit more than she led on about criminal activities. "Chicago might be the best option if we're doing this."

"Why Chicago?" Ivy questioned her. "Chicago is so fucking far away." Especially if we had to drive there. "What about Philly?"

"Or Baltimore?" I added. "I read Nico Morrelli owns quite a few casinos there. We could rob one of his?" I suggested hopefully.

We've all been doing research on mobsters. Though, Google wasn't really a reliable or vast resource on the topic.

"Nico Morrelli, huh?" Ivy retorted. "You know they call him the Wolf. No, thank you. I'd rather go to Chicago."

I snickered. "I bet you there are different kinds of wolves there, too."

"Yeah, the Italian ones." Ivy smirked.

"In Chicago, it's mainly the Italians running the show," Juliette explained, ignoring our stupid discussion on wolves. "The syndicate. And they recently opened a super fancy casino."

"It's settled then," Wynter concluded. "We'll be robbing the Italians in Chicago. I have some studying to do. You three research the information on the casino they own. We don't want to accidentally rob an honest person."

"Oh my gosh, we're really doing this." Juliette and Ivy gasped with disbelief.

"Get the address and do the proper research. Building layout," Wynter demanded. "We want to know who owns it, their peak hours, what the maximum bets are at each table. We want to know it all."

"Don't be a control freak, Wyn," Juliette complained. "We'll do our homework."

"That'll be a first," I muttered under my breath.

Standing up, Wynter grabbed her book and sauntered into the other room.

We're really doing this.

CHAPTER 26
Liam

It was just past three in the afternoon.

I had a shipment coming tonight, so I'd have to be on my way soon. I had enough time to dial up Juliette and Wynter though. I hadn't heard from them in a few days.

Dialing Juliette's number, I waited as the line rang. Nothing. Then Wynter. Nothing. Davina. Again, nothing.

These women were exasperating. I had a feeling they were getting into trouble, though Cassio gave me a guy that was tailing them. He hadn't called, so I assumed they were within the designated area of New Haven, Connecticut.

But my gut feeling warned me otherwise, so I dialed Nico Morrelli.

"Twice in one week," he drawled. "This must be a record."

"I know you just sent me the hacker information," I told him. "I haven't had a chance to go through his background. However, I trust *you*, and I need a favor."

"What do you need?"

I recited the three phone numbers, although I was certain all three women were in the same location.

"I need you to tell me where the location pins these numbers."

It took him two seconds. "All three numbers are together. Looks like they're in Chicago."

"Fuck," I cursed. "These women will be the fucking death of me."

"Anything I can do?" he offered.

"No, thank you," I grumbled. "You have two daughters, right?"

"I do. Twins."

"You might want to consider starting to look for a high-security boarding school," I told him. "To keep them locked down to one spot."

He chuckled, but I was fucking serious.

CHAPTER 27
Davina

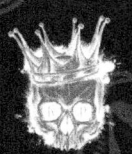

"This motel fucking sucks," Juliette complained for the tenth time. "They don't even have room service."

"Even if they did," Wynter spat back, "it wouldn't be open at fucking midnight."

Needless to say, Wynter was tired and cranky. She'd missed her workout today and refused to let Ivy or Juliette drive. The former couldn't get used to driving on the right side of the road and the latter was a bad driver, period. In order to make it to Chicago safely, Wynter and I alternated driving.

We stopped at McDonald's and ordered plenty of food before checking into the motel. Juliette complained about the calories going to her butt, Wynter was annoyed that she was using her once-a-week splurge on such a crappy choice, and Ivy just fucking hated fast food.

"Come on, everyone." I tried to pacify them, getting the food out of the McDonald's greasy paper bags. "Let's eat and recap what we all know."

Juliette and Wynter threw themselves on the couch while Ivy fell back on the bed.

"I really don't—" Juliette started, and I glared at her.

"Fucking eat," I ordered her, pacing around. "And listen."

Okay, so I was a tad bit cranky too. It has been a long day for all of us. A long week. I had used every spare moment over the last several days researching the casino, the owners, the working hours, even the people that worked there. I searched LinkedIn for anyone and everyone that had listed their employer as Royally Lucky.

The owner of the casino was listed under a corporation called Heathen Royals. Not much to go off there. But we asked one of the nerdy Yale boys to trace the corporation, and thank God for brilliant nerds. He traced the corporation to Franco DiLustro, who was a member of the syndicate.

"Okay, we know the owner," I started. "I was able to find the name and picture of the floor managers. This is the guy that manages the first floor. We want to stay clear of Mr. Grumpy." I lifted my laptop and showed all three of them the picture of a forty- or fifty-year-old, dark-haired, skinny dude with round glasses. "However, my research shows that sometimes the second-floor manager and first-floor manager swap floors. So, we need to make sure to stay clear of this dude too." I showed them a picture of a fifty-something bald man with a round belly and big grin on his face. "We'll call him Mr. Happy," I continued in a serious tone. "So, we have to keep an eye out for Mr. Happy and Mr. Grumpy. Keep both of them away from the poker table where we'll be playing."

Juliette bit into her Big Mac and chewed it like she wanted to murder it. I had half a mind to tell her the damn burger was already dead.

"Robbing a safe is so much easier than all this shit," she complained.

Of course she'd say that, because it wasn't her that got caught. And then bent over the desk to take some ass-spanking. I still hadn't shared it with them. I mean, how did you break that kind of news to your friends?

"How much money are we taking to the tables?" Wynter asked a reasonable question. "I was thinking five grand. We lose it, we just walk away."

"Well, that's just it," I told them all. "Each casino has limits on how much you can win at the table without raising a flag. I searched and searched this casino's site and all the gambling blog sites. None of them indicate what that limit is at this place."

CORRUPTED PLEASURE

"So if we're winning, how do we know when to stop?" Ivy asked. "I mean, we don't want to walk away too soon."

"I'd say we play it safe," I suggested. "Let's go with fifty grand and walk away."

"We're doing all this for fifty grand?" Juliette snickered. "What's the damn point? I'd never go through the anxiety of the card game just for fifty Gs."

Wynter's eyes flicked my way, but she said nothing. I knew what she was thinking. Juliette was bad at numbers. She shouldn't be the one playing. The problem was that each time either Wynter or I even hinted about it, Juliette dismissed it and changed the subject.

"Anyhow, I found some pictures of the grand opening of the hotel." I ignored Juliette's comment. After all, it was her damn idea to rob another place. "This old man cutting the ribbon is Franco DiLustro." I showed them all the pictures. "The papers say he's a brother to Gio DiLustro, the kingpin to the syndicate in New York."

A few gasps traveled around the room. I hoped the man wouldn't be in the casino today, because if he was anything like Gio DiLustro, it wouldn't be a pleasant encounter. The one from the club still bothered me.

"Are you sure?" Wynter asked. In this whole ordeal, she and Ivy had focused on researching the layout of the casino, though Wyn's time was limited.

I shrugged. "That's what the papers say. Why?"

"I just didn't realize there were DiLustros in Chicago too," she muttered. "I thought they were just in New York."

"Should we not do it?" I questioned.

Wynter's hesitancy hit me all wrong. "I just heard that the DiLustros are a force to be reckoned with." So was her uncle, but I kept those words to myself.

"We've done our homework," Juliette argued.

"That's right. We have a good plan," Ivy chimed in. "We know the layout of the parking lot and the casino. We stick to the poker table, and stop at our agreed cap. Then we clear."

"Don't forget about the backup plan," I reminded them all. "If we notice the managers or any suspicious person, we have to distract them. By any means necessary."

"If all else fails, I'll pull the handle on the fire alarm," Ivy joked around. "That'll cause panic and people will stumble out of there. It will be like a stampede."

"Let's not joke around about it. People get hurt in stampedes," I warned her.

"We should have a warning signal if all our other shit fails," Juliette suggested, and it was the best advice she'd come up with yet.

"That's an excellent idea," I agreed. "A whistle?"

"Yes," Juliette eagerly nodded. "*Hunger Games,* Rue's whistle."

"Are you for fucking real?" I objected. "Rue's whistle."

"Yeah," she answered nonchalantly, then quickly reached for her phone, scrolled through it, and pressed play. The whistle from the movie sounded through her speakers. "This one. See, easy peasy."

I stared at her blankly.

"Maybe we're taking this *Hunger Games* thing too far," Wynter said softly, though I could hear humor in her voice.

"So what?" Juliette sneered. "It's a good sound, and there are no chances anyone else would whistle it in a casino."

"Because nobody in the casino is childish like that," I muttered.

"Exactly," Ivy agreed, grinning.

"So there will be no way of confusing the whistle," Juliette reasoned.

I shook my head in disbelief. "So we're still going with the *Hunger Games* theme?" I asked incredulously. Juliette and Ivy grinned stupidly, despite the fatigue on their faces. Even Wynter's lips were curved into a smile. "Maybe I'm just cranky and tired," I muttered.

"You need some millions," Juliette explained. "Once we all get lots and lots of money, then we'll be swell. The Hunger Games continues, so may the odds be ever in our favor."

"Happy Hunger Games!" Ivy exclaimed.

A choked laugh escaped me. Here we were graduating from Yale, yet acting like the biggest idiots.

"Okay, Rue's whistle it is. I'll practice in the morning. I guess all of us will. Now, back to the preparation," I concluded that discussion. "Ivy, you'll be on the south side of the poker table." I showed her the floorplan and pointed to the area. "Here is the emergency exit door that will dump you right by the area we'll park the Jeep in. If something happens, just head out that way. Juliette, you'll be on the west side of the poker table." I pointed to the area where she'd be standing. "There is an exit right here." I tapped the circled door. "Something happens, run out that way."

"Hold on. I'll be at the poker table," Juliette corrected. Damn it, I wished she'd realize there was no chance in hell she'd win even one round of a poker game. She was usually the first one out.

"We all need to give another look to all the ways out of the casino," Wynter chimed in, saving me a response. "And the moment we walk in, we need to spot them so we can orient ourselves to them."

Juliette and Ivy nodded their heads.

"Okay then," I concluded. "We'll be robbing a casino tomorrow night."

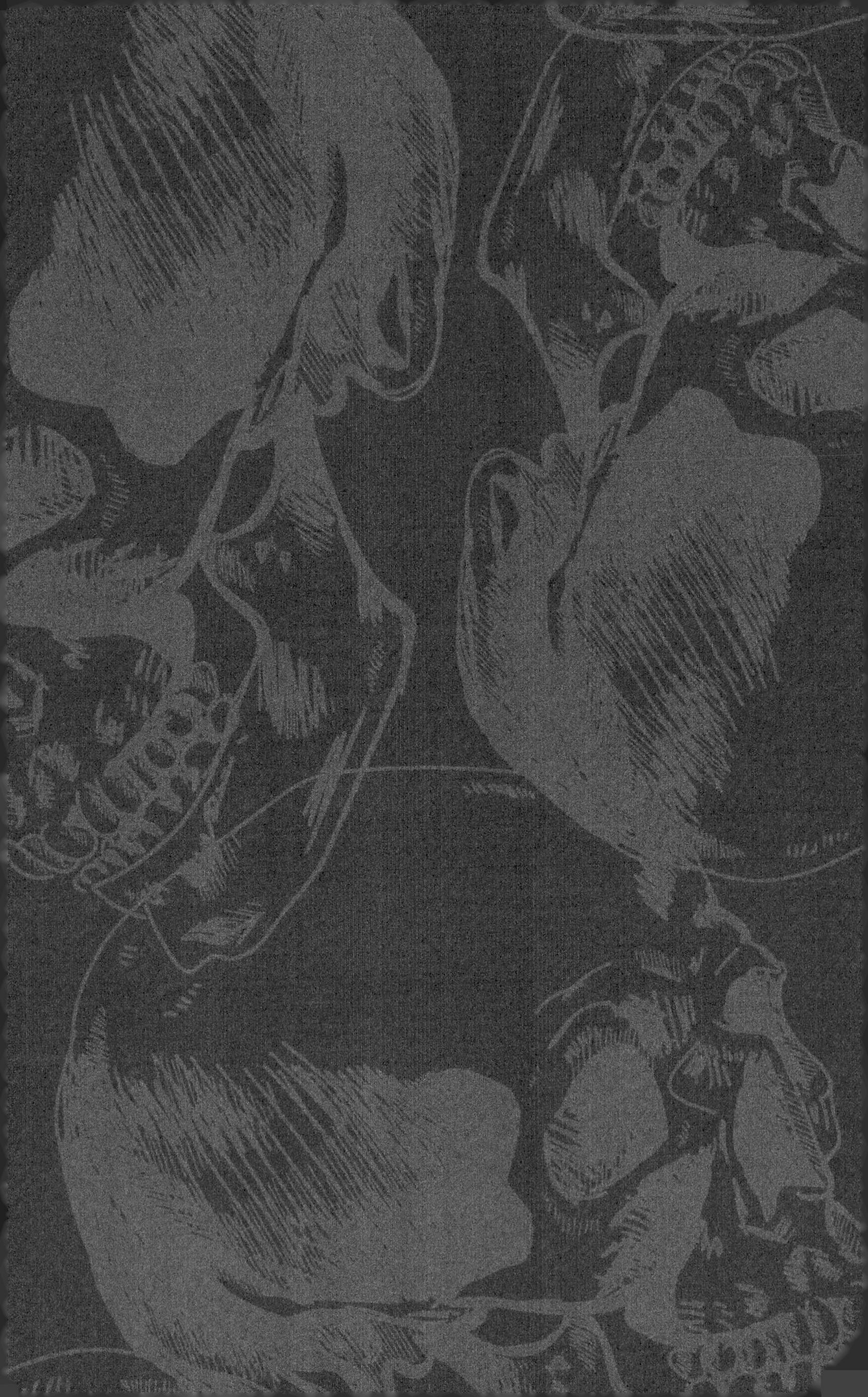

CHAPTER 28
Davina

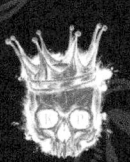

Royally Lucky.

More like royally fucked up.

Ivy and Juliette identified the blind spot of the parking lot not too far from the entrance. It was on the left corner of the building, right under a single large oak tree.

The casino steakhouse was more extravagant than anything I'd ever seen. Located on North Michigan Avenue in Chicago, the tall glass building glimmered like a castle of sin.

"Are we sure about this?" I asked, my eyes traveling to Wynter seated in the driver's seat and then to the backseat where Juliette and Ivy sat.

"Yes!" Juliette confirmed. "We've come too far to give up."

"Let's just get this over with," Wynter muttered. "Davina, can you share the layout of the casino again?"

Juliette and Ivy were treating this like a game. I wasn't. I had no desire to find myself or them in a similar situation as the one I had in the Eastside Club. Yes, the orgasms were great, but I had reached my limit on the number of men I had to be available to whenever and wherever they demanded. One was more than enough.

And Liam Brennan isn't the sharing type, I reminded myself.

"The high-stakes poker rooms are on the second floor, but we want to stay away from those." Wynter nodded in agreement. Juliette and Ivy preferred we go all-in, but that made it easier to get caught. Those rooms were secured and locked during the games, so it'd leave the person at the poker table vulnerable. "The first floor is where we want to be," I stated matter-of-factly. "We'll pass the slot machines. Then there are roulette tables behind them. The open poker tables are at the far end of the room on the first floor."

"Do you have the oil in your purse?" Juliette asked. "Are you sure they won't search our bags upon entrance?"

It was our escape method. If shit hit the fan, I'd dump the oil all over the floor and people would start sliding all around as we ran out of there.

"It's lavender oil," I reasoned. "They'll think it's for a massage or some shit like that."

"The special kind of massage." Ivy smirked.

I rolled my eyes. "Focus on the task at hand." I scolded her. "The important question is whether it's smart that Juliette sits at the poker table. She's the worst at math, and her memory sucks."

"She's an airhead," Ivy teased goodheartedly.

"Hey," Juliette protested. "I'm right here, you know."

"We have to play to our strengths," I comforted Juliette, patting her hand. "You'll lose the money we stole from your dad. We're trying to get more. Think about our plan. We came to win and increase our stash of money."

At least Juliette didn't outright disagree. She actually seemed to be considering my words.

"We should have Wynter sit at the poker table," I added firmly.

Wynter knew how to play poker really well. It was a game she grew up playing with her mother, uncle, and grandfather, and she had yet to lose a single game against anyone for as long as I'd known her. Nobody at the university ever wanted to play poker with her because she'd always win.

"I agree," Ivy chimed. "Wynter is great with numbers. Davina is good too, but I think Wynter would do better with it. Especially if it comes down to counting cards. She's basically unbeatable at Yale."

"Okay then. What do I do?" Juliette demanded.

Wynter and I shared glances. "We'll just swap your and Wynter's roles. She plays, and you keep an eye out."

"Like we talked about last night, the three of us will keep an eye out," I announced. "We'll distract any member of the staff that we notice approaching. By any means necessary."

"I'm a bit nervous," Ivy admitted.

"We just stick to the plan," I told her. "And we watch each other's backs and blend in."

"We're dressed appropriately for the casino," Juliette added. "There should be no issue blending in."

I thought we looked good. Wynter wore a long, sleeveless red dress with a deep neckline and slits that came up to her thighs on both sides. Her back was bare, giving people a glimpse of her ivory skin. Her bun made her look slightly older with her curly golden strands framing her face. Her fake ID identified her as a twenty-three-year-old, and with her current appearance, she looked it.

I wore a sheer black, long dress that showed my skin and undergarments when the light hit it just right. Ivy wore an off-white, short dress, claiming that a long dress would make her appear too short. I called bull, because I was the shortest one in the group. But it was Juliette that dressed the most provocatively. She wore a short, midnight-blue dress that barely covered her ass and hugged her curves just right. I caught her tugging the hemline down a couple times, so it was a perfect dress to distract.

"Don't forget about the inside cameras," Wynter warned. "Keep your faces low, and keep a keen eye."

A cell phone buzzed and all four of us reached for our phones. It was mine.

"Don't tell me it's Garrett again?" Juliette groaned.

Garrett had called me eighteen times and sent me way too many texts. He hadn't called me that much during the entire time we'd dated. I hadn't replied to a single message. He also went off on a rampage about the surveillance, accusing me of some voodoo shit. Then he threatened to go to the police and explain to them that the four of us had come into his home without permission. The truth was he had nothing on us, thanks to Wynter's friend. So, I kept ignoring him. A single word could be used against us, and I wouldn't give him that ammunition.

Thank God it wasn't Garrett this time. I slid open the message from Liam.

> Call me, or you'll earn yourself a punishment.

Instantly, my cheeks flamed and my heart stilled as a delightful shudder ghosted down my spine. God, was it bad that I kind of looked forward to it too? Each time I thought about him, my pulse drifted between my legs, invaded my senses, and made the corners of my mind fuzzy, lust overtaking all my reason.

I had been thinking about Liam a lot. He had been wanting to see me for the past three days. Except I was busy preparing for a heist... sort of. Of course, that was not a good excuse. The right excuse was that I had to study for my finals, and since he knew Juliette and Wynter were studying for their finals too, he bought it.

I had to admit, a smug satisfaction about being able to deceive the head of the Irish mafia grew inside me. Not exactly something to be proud of, but fuck it.

"Yes, it's Garrett," I lied.

The four of us sat in silence, our eyes watching a parade of rich men dressed in tuxedos and women in glittering dresses climb up the black marble front steps leading up to the lobby of the large casino.

"Okay, let's do this." I reached for the door handle. "Remember your positions. If we see someone from management circling the table, we need to distract them." My eyes locked on Ivy and Juliette. "In any way possible."

The two grinned dumbly. "As long as he's hot," they responded in unison.

God knew my distraction at the Eastside was hot. *Don't think about the Irish devil now*, I scolded myself.

"If we spot Franco DiLustro, we are postponing this mission," Wynter announced. I agreed with her, because if he was like his brother, there'd be hell to pay.

Juliette and Ivy just rolled their eyes. "Are we clear?" I chimed in sternly. Those two needed an ass whooping.

"Yes, yes, yes," the two muttered annoyingly.

Those two would land us in major shit one of these days. I had no room to talk since I'd gotten us into this shit to begin with and kick-started our criminal career.

Getting out of the Jeep, we sauntered through the parking lot, seemingly confident.

"What if we got this all wrong?" Wynter asked under her breath. "If Franco DiLustro owns this casino, we should stay clear. Uncle would fucking kill us if he knew that we purposely went into a building owned by a DiLustro."

"He'll never find out," Ivy replied. "So let's not stress over nonsense."

"It doesn't matter if it's DiLustro or another Italian that owns it," Juliette added.

"I don't like this," Wynter mumbled begrudgingly.

"The top dog owns it, so we fucking take it from him. And if we need to, we kill him," Juliette answered, self-satisfied. "One less DiLustro in the world. We'll do society a favor."

Wynter almost tripped.

"What is it with you and killing people lately?" she hissed, her eyes glaring at her cousin. "We are not killers, and you fucking know it."

"Yet," Juliette added coolly.

"We should find a casino that belongs to someone lower in the food chain," Wynter grumbled. "Definitely one that has no connections to DiLustro."

Juliette shrugged. "This guy would have the most money."

"DiLustros are lethal," Wynter snapped, then realizing what she said, she quickly added, "Their sons might be more lenient, but the older ones are dangerous. We know that much, Juliette."

"We covered all scenarios and prepared for this," Ivy chimed in, attempting to calm both of them down. "You focus on the poker game. We'll worry about security." Ivy's eyes traveled between us all.

Wynter didn't seem comforted by that notion.

"Should we stop?" I asked, adrenaline pumping through my veins. "It's not too late."

This idea of starting the school had taken root in all of us. The truth was that we'd need millions, and it'd take us years to be able to get it together, but it gave us a goal.

Was it the right way to go about it? Hell no. Did it stop us? Fuck no.

"I can't believe I work in the coffee shop by day and rob the mafia by night," I muttered under my breath. Although, two days ago was my last day. Most students left the campus for summer, so the coffee shop closed up. They'd reopen in late August, but I wouldn't be a Yale student anymore.

"And Wynter is an Olympic ice skating champion by day and thief by night," Juliette elaborated, her voice shuddering from laughter.

"What can I say?" Wynter retorted dryly. "I like to multitask. Though, after tonight, we'll take it easy. Maybe put together a business plan. I have to focus on my training. Nationals are coming up in six months, and with Derek being in California while I'm here, it's been hard to practice."

"Agreed."

And up those black marble steps we went.

CHAPTER 29
Davina

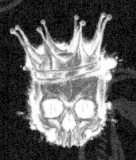

I took deep breaths in and then slowly exhaled. Wynter sat at the poker table, her back bare and looking like she knew what she was doing. The poker table out in the open in the back of the first floor was a good choice.

My five-inch heels clicked against the marble floor of the casino. I hadn't been in many casinos, in fact none, but I'd seen plenty of movies with them. I had to admit, this one was among the most luxurious ones I had ever seen. It even beat the pictures I'd seen of the Bellagio.

Gold decor everywhere, glittering crystal chandeliers and mirrored walls surrounded me. The center of the casino, where the poker tables were, had a high-rise domed ceiling, and I could see the windows of the offices that were clearly looking down on the casino floor. It was like an arena for the gladiators, except there were only gamblers here.

My stomach hadn't unclenched since we entered the building. My heart drummed and adrenaline pumped. I didn't know how much of this pressure I could take.

Wynter had bought five grand worth of chips, just as we agreed. Men sent hot glances her way. And just like her name, she graced them with her ice-cold glare that froze the air around her. She truly was an ice queen, on and off the ice, just as the media called her.

Except, I knew the warm side of her. She cared deeply and loved even deeper. I worried about her little arrangement with the mysterious, beautiful man in New York. I knew every time she received a text from him, because her face lit up with a look I'd never seen before.

I spotted Ivy in her position as we agreed, her eyes scouting the guards. Juliette did the same, pacing in a seemingly lazy circle. She was nervous though, her eyes darting to Wynter every two minutes.

We'd been at it for the past two hours. I was on the edge of suspense just like Juliette. Ivy too, except she'd started biting her nails. Cold sweat trickled down my back while my hands grew clammy holding on to the champagne flute I hadn't drunk.

A loud murmur and awed voices had me glancing at Wynter's table. She won another poker hand. She was at three hundred grand now.

Jesus, she was good. I caught her wiping her hands down her long dress. She was nervous too. It was odd. She netted fifty thousand within the first thirty minutes. Not bad, considering we brought only five thousand dollars' worth of chips to the table. Once we reached fifty grand, we fully expected someone to show up and send her packing. Yet, nothing.

And I was surprised Wynter continued playing. She wasn't the risk-taking type.

About thirty minutes ago, one of the managers showed up. The grinning one that usually worked the second floor. Just as in the pictures, he still smiled, looking happy as he observed Wynter playing.

When we spotted him, Juliette rushed to him and played a drunken young woman. She managed to distract him for all of thirty seconds. Figure that, she wasn't his type. Then he continued to Wynter's table.

I'd give Wynter credit though. She kept her cool. Maybe it was the reason she continued playing. It would have looked suspicious if she bolted when the floor manager showed up.

I watched him circle the table for the fifth time and stop two seats over from Wynter, his eyes on her. The old man might have a jolly personality, but he also had a keen eye. I feared he was catching on to us.

Fuck! Should I do Rue's whistle, or wait it out?

My eyes skimmed over the room, and I instantly went on alert. I couldn't quite see their faces, only their profiles. The two moved as one, like two panthers going for their prey. They moved across the floor, and I knew, just *knew*, they were part of the syndicate.

He glanced around, and I recognized him. Shit, it was the guy from Liam's club. Dante.

Fuck! Fuck! Fuck!

Taller than most of the people in this room, it was harder to ignore them. Not that you would, not with their faces. Both were gorgeous in their own way, one as dark as Wynter's devil and the other dirty blonde. Both had a scruff of a beard on their faces and an animal magnetism that made everyone look their way, and then do a double take.

These two were deadly, and they both knew it. The casino got a few notches quieter, or maybe the buzzing in my ears increased, drowning out all the noise.

Panic rose within me and my eyes darted to my friends. Both Ivy and Juliette gaped at the two men, their eyes wide. They must have sensed the danger too.

A knot moved up my throat and my mouth went dry. I scrambled for the phone, but before my trembling hands could unlock it, I noted Juliette moving toward them. I met Ivy's gaze across the room and her eyes widened. I wondered if she knew them. Or maybe she was just as mesmerized by them as the rest of the women in this room.

We were fucked. It was fucking whistle time.

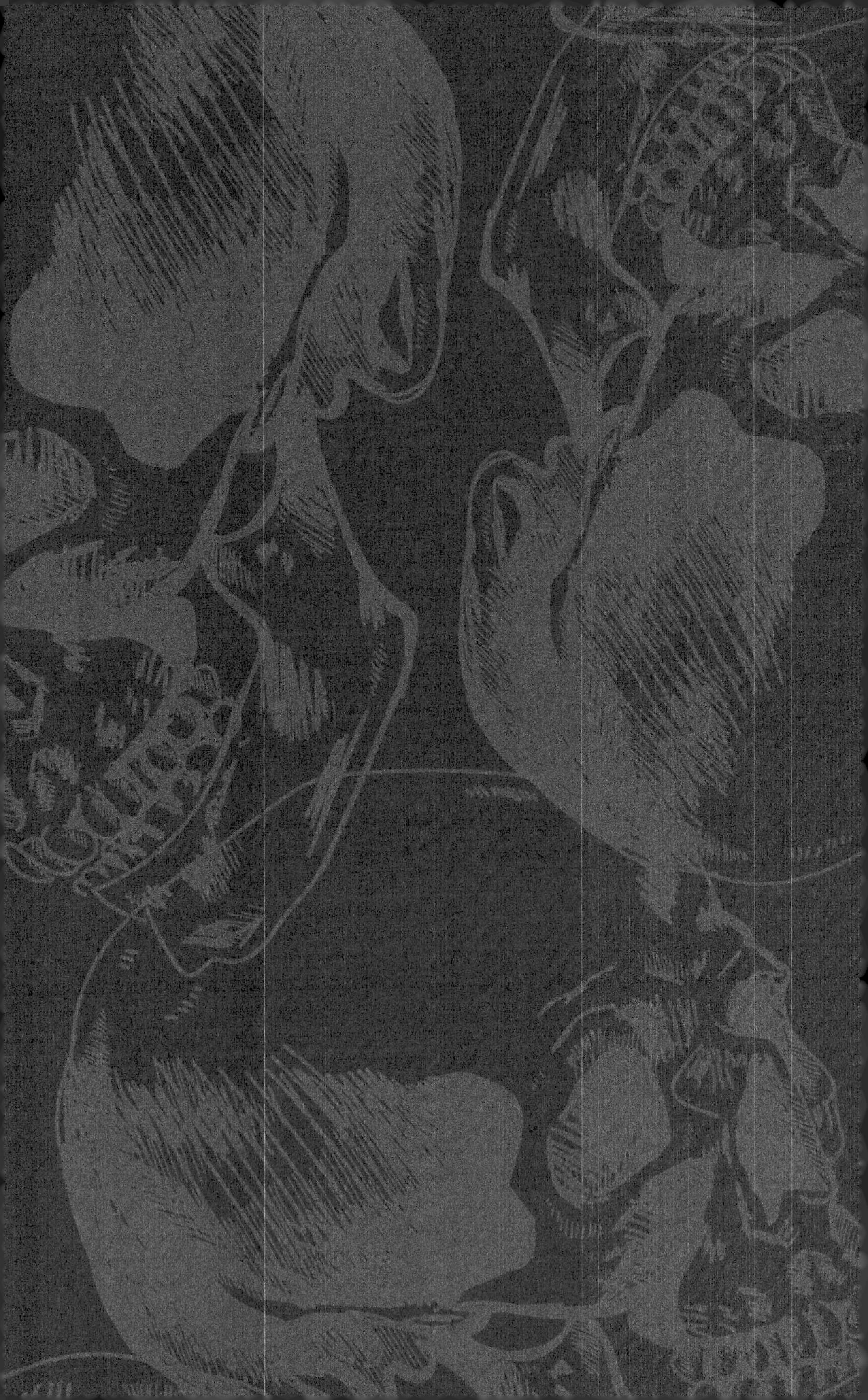

CHAPTER 30
Davina

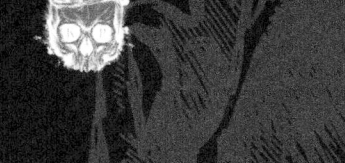

I watched in slow motion as Juliette stumbled over the smooth black marble floor and slammed right into one of the two men.

Dante caught her without any effort, and the usual, flirty Juliette blushed so hard, I could see it all the way from here.

My mouth just about dropped, because in all our four years of college, I had yet to see her blush. And we had done some stupid shit worth blushing over.

"Well played, Juliette," I muttered under my breath. Then, inhaling deeply, I whistled Rue's tune. Dante's eyes darted my way and recognition flickered in them, but before he could act, Juliette's palm pressed against his cheek and brought his attention back to her.

Time stilled as those two locked gazes. His movement was smooth, his one hand holding on to Juliette by her elbow while the other hung loose from his suit pant pocket. The man was built, a wall of muscle underneath his expensive, dark, three-piece suit clearly visible.

From the corner of my eye, I noted Ivy moving until she was by the fire alarm handle. My gaze shot to Wynter. She spotted the whole scene too. Tilting her head like a queen dismissing her subjects, she stood up from the table.

"Keep him busy, Juliette," I whispered to myself.

Wynter scooped up her chips and walked quickly away from the table, but not in a way to cause suspicion, making her way to the area where she'd cash them in. Juliette's mouth moved as she spoke to the strangers. She was rattled, all her focus on the dark-haired man. Her hands shook as she smoothed them against his chest, trying her best to appear like an experienced seductress.

The blonde one eyed her, almost amused, his beautiful lips twisted into a cruel smile. He said something, and Juliette's gaze darted to him. Her mouth parted as if whatever he said shocked her, but then she got herself together and nodded. But her attention quickly returned to Dante.

Her hand still pressed against his chest, she took his tie, then said something as her eyes traveled between the two men.

Jesus, she's really working on seducing both of them!

Whatever she said, it worked. Both of them stared at her, their dangerous aura and vibe entirely zeroed in on her. It was like waiting for a cobra to strike while Juliette poked at it.

I shifted nervously, eyeing Ivy. She was in place. Wynter glanced over her shoulder, her one foot tapping nervously underneath her long dress as she waited for her cash. Other than that small sign, she looked like the epitome of calm.

My heart thundered under my rib cage and a reluctant thought passed through my mind—my grandfather didn't exactly envision this for me when he sent me to Yale. But before I could ponder the error of my actions further, a loud whistle had my head snapping in its direction.

Wynter's signal. She was the only one that could whistle like a true New Yorker.

"Why in the fuck didn't she do Rue's whistle?" I grumbled under my breath as I pulled the big bottle of oil out of my oversized bag that totally didn't match my dress.

Everything else that happened after that whistle was a blur. Ivy pulled the alarm handle, and Juliette rammed her knee into the dark-devil's nuts before taking off. Before he and his friend could go after her, I swished the gallon bottle of lavender oil across the floor, emptying it, and then ran. It was pure luck that all their attention was on Juliette so they hadn't seen me dump the oil.

Seeing them slide across the slick marble floor and almost falling onto their gorgeous asses was a priceless sight. I wished I had recorded it.

Running off while the rest of the guests attempted to remain upright on their feet, I didn't stop to look back again.

"Don't stop," I muttered breathlessly as I ran. "Get to the Jeep."

Fuck, I should have considered getting up in the morning and going for those long-ass jogs with Wynter because I could barely breathe.

The alarm blasted throughout the large building. The yelling of people behind me was loud, screeches of women and commotion creating the exact clusterfuck we intended. My heels dug into the blacktop as I ran across the parking lot, and I prayed everyone was already there. I couldn't wait to get the fuck out of this city.

I rounded the corner to find all three of my friends already there. Wynter was already behind the wheel, Juliette and Ivy climbing into the back seat.

"Hurry," Wynter shouted.

I threw myself into the seat, breathing heavily. We could already see the police, ambulance, and fire engine lights approaching, the sirens blaring.

"How much did we get?" Juliette asked.

"Three hundred thousand," Wynter replied as she put the car into drive. She sped across the parking lot in the opposite direction from all the fire engines approaching.

"How come you didn't stop at fifty thousand?" I asked her curiously.

"Nobody came, so I pushed my luck. It wasn't until I was at over two hundred that the manager showed up," she explained.

There was a hint of pride to her voice. I was proud of her too. That was an amazing game.

"Holy shit," all four of us whispered at the same time.

If we could do this for a few months, maybe a year, we could have enough money to start a business. This school for female criminal masterminds, based on our own experiences.

"Let's get out of here," I breathed.

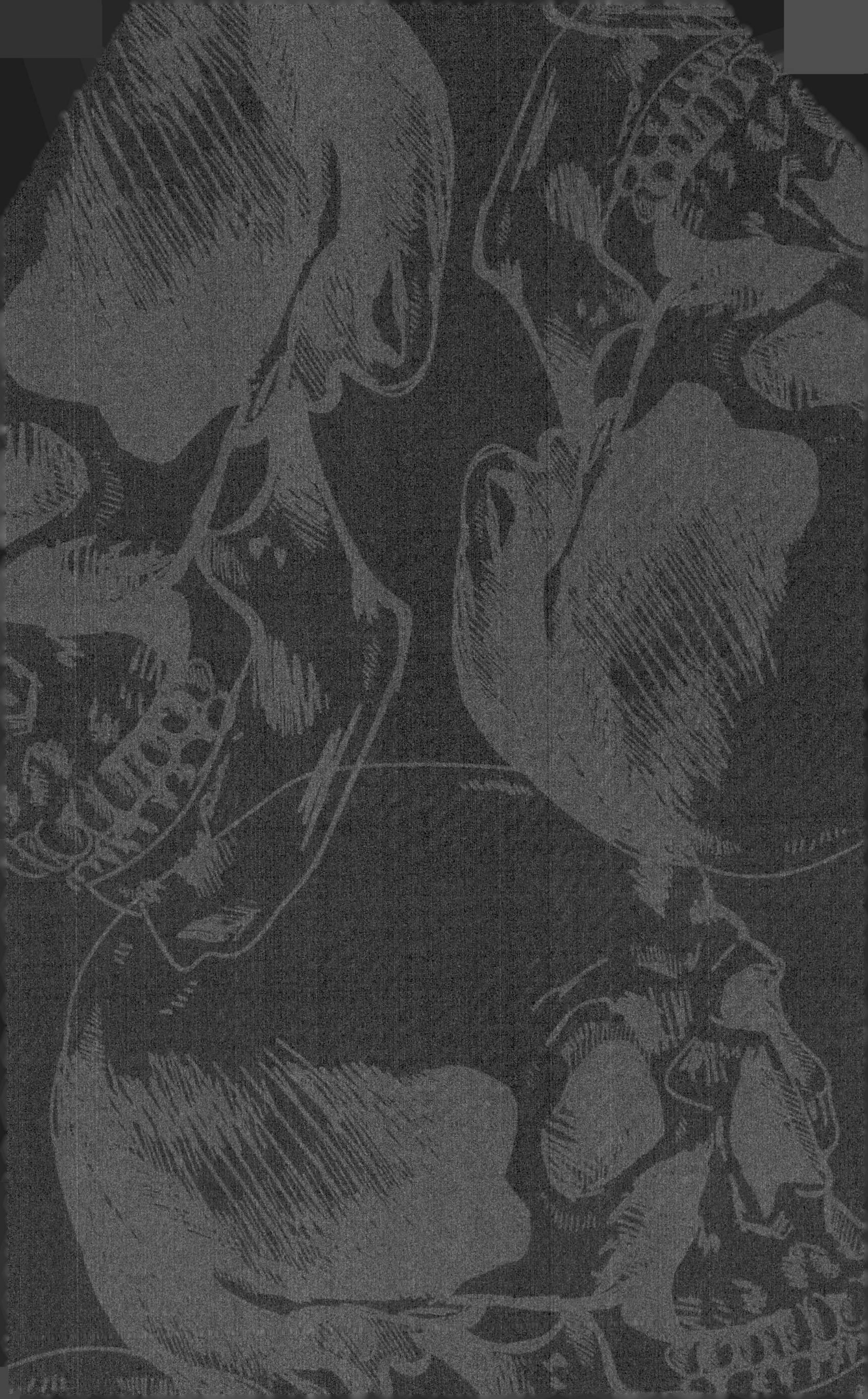

CHAPTER 31
Liam

A whole fucking shipment of guns, lost.

One of my trucks was hijacked on its way to my warehouse. The truck was approaching the George Washington Bridge from the New Jersey side.

I sat in the car with Quinn on my way to the location where the truck was parked, according to Nico's hacker. The guy was really good. I didn't trust him with my family, but business was different. Lucky for me, we were alerted of the hijacked shipment within five minutes, so locating it didn't take long.

The four women, on the other hand, were an entirely different story. I sent a message to Cassio thirty minutes ago, and I was anxiously waiting for a status update. I was worried, then furious, and then back to worried at the recklessness these women exhibited.

My phone rang. It was Cassio. Perfect timing.

"Why isn't your guy tailing the women?" I answered the call, my jaw clenched.

"My guy was shot dead while tailing them," he retorted dryly. "In goddamn broad daylight, at a Pennsylvania gas station. Who in the fuck are these women, Liam?"

Fuck!

Dread tightened my lungs. Did the Russians find them? If they got their hands on them, they'd kill Juliette, Davina, and Ivy without a second thought. War was coming, whether I liked it or not. The Russians had been attacking my warehouse systematically with the end goal of weakening me. It was the Russians who undoubtedly hijacked my shipment today.

It was a bad fucking day when you hoped it was the DiLustros, but they wouldn't have violated our agreement, or have been so obvious about it.

"They're important," I told him.

"I see," Cassio said. "I need to know how important they are, Liam."

I looked at Quinn and rasped, "Call Nico Morrelli and ask him to check the same phone numbers I gave him earlier." I didn't even finish my sentence before Quinn was on it.

"Very important," I answered Cassio's question, gritting my teeth. "If the Russians get their hands on them, they'll get access to all of my territory." *Because I'll give them all away just to keep the girls alive.*

"Russians?"

"Yes, fucking Russians," I spat out.

"You should really consider hiring Alexei Nikolaev," he tried again. "He's the best in the field."

Fuck! I knew it was true.

"Can you have him get in touch with me?" I gritted out. I was gambling here, but I knew one thing for certain: the women would be safe if Nikolaev tailed them.

"I will," Cassio agreed. "His wife just had a baby, so it might take him a few days."

I fucking hoped all this was a coincidence, but I feared it wasn't. When I didn't respond, Cassio continued, "Do you have a few days, Liam?"

My fist clenched. Quinn threw me a worried glance, but I ignored it.

"I don't fucking know," I answered, my jaw ticking. "I've been under attack for the past three months."

"The Kingpins?" he inquired. "Or the Russians again?"

"Russians." There was no sense in mentioning the attack from three months ago that the Italians and Russians coordinated at the same time.

"Have you considered locking the women in the compound?"

It was ironic that I had given similar advice to Nico earlier today. "They didn't exactly grow up locked up," I retorted dryly. "Listen, I'll owe you big time if you get me connected with Nikolaev. I have to go."

"If you need anything, just tell me," Cassio concluded. "My warehouses, anything."

"Appreciate it." It dawned on me that if I moved the shipment I was about to hijack back to my own warehouse, it'd be at risk of getting attacked. But if I stored it in one of Cassio's places, nobody would know it was there. "Actually, since you offered. I'm about to take my stolen shipment back. If you have a free warehouse, I'll pay you to store my goods there."

"You got it."

It was settled. Satisfied with at least one part of today, I ended the call and turned my attention to Quinn.

"Nico got them on the satellite," Quinn explained. "They are on the move, and it's just the girls. Nobody on their tail."

Thank fuck!

"Please ask him to tail them until they are safely back, and alert me immediately if something happens."

I knew Nico would have it covered. There was nobody better than him. Now, I had to focus on this attack.

"How many men do we have?" I demanded.

My driver sped through traffic, weaving through the lanes to get where we needed to be as soon as possible.

"Ten," Quinn answered. "Five following us and five meeting us there."

"We're going to throw a gas canister into that place before we walk in," I told him. "Warn everyone to have their masks ready." It was part of our standard attack gear. "Once we're inside, kill to defend. But no matter what, keep one guy alive for questioning."

I turned to look out the window. The skies were gray, and it reminded me of Davina's eyes. I'd hoped today would be a better day. I wasn't in the mood to deal with this shit. Maybe I was getting old, but this constant battle with the Russians was wearing me thin.

It took us thirty minutes to get to our location. First, I went over the plan with my men. We'd split and attack the west and east doors of the warehouse, then flush out whoever was in there.

Quinn led one group and I led the other. I lifted my hand and counted to three, then we threw the tear gas in. Another five seconds and we all charged in. Gunshots echoed, men were rolling on the ground, grunting and moaning.

There were only five men here, their guns scattered on the floor, my men's guns pointed at their heads.

"Who's in charge here?" I asked.

None of them answered.

"Who in the fuck is in charge here?"

"Nyet. Nyet." Fuck! Russians. It would have been so much easier if it were the Italians.

"Who's in charge?" I gritted. "I won't ask again. Next time, I'm shooting."

All fingers pointed to the man to the far left.

"Lovely," I drawled. "Tie them all up."

While my men worked on tying them up, I strode over to the supposed leader. He didn't look like much. He was older than me, with salt-and-pepper gray and a matching beard. He was probably approaching his sixties.

Too old to be in this kind of shit, which meant that he'd probably worked for Volkov for a long time. I was making an assumption though, so I'd need verbal confirmation. Assumptions got you killed.

"Who do you work for?" I demanded.

Nothing.

I pulled out my knife and gave him a sardonic smile. "Let's do this the hard way then, shall we?"

Quinn came behind him and grabbed his head, then gripped it tight.

I pushed the tip of the blade against his cheek and sliced it open. A bloodcurdling scream echoed through the warehouse. Blood dripped down his chin and onto his shirt.

"Next is your eye," I drawled, giving him a heads up with a menacing grin.

"Do the right eye," Quinn suggested. "He seems to favor his right side."

I pretended to seriously consider it.

"That's a good idea," I agreed. "But I think we should torture all of them at the same time. It's only fair. After all, this is a democracy. We aren't in Russia."

A round of snickering by my men followed.

"Wait," one of the men screamed. "We were just hired to get the truck and bring it here."

"By who?"

"A Russian."

I scoffed. "There are millions of Russians in this world. How about you narrow it down?"

"Will you let us go if we tell you?"

The guy with the beard spat something in Russian at the other guys.

"I'll set you free." *Lie.*

A brief shared glance among the Russians. "Pakhan Volkov."

Fuck! Couldn't it be any other Russian? But then, I'd already known the answer all along. I'd just hoped it was someone else.

"What does he want with my equipment?" I asked, but did it really matter? I already knew what his main goal was. Volkov would never stop, not until either he was dead or all the Brennans were. Plus anyone that worked for us.

"He wants his granddaughter."

"She's dead," I told him. To the world, Aisling Brennan died over twenty years ago. "And so are you."

I pulled out a gun from the back of my pants, lifted it, and fired. Their bodies slumped forward in their chairs, and I put my gun in the back of my pants.

"Clean this up," I told my men as Quinn and I turned to walk out the door.

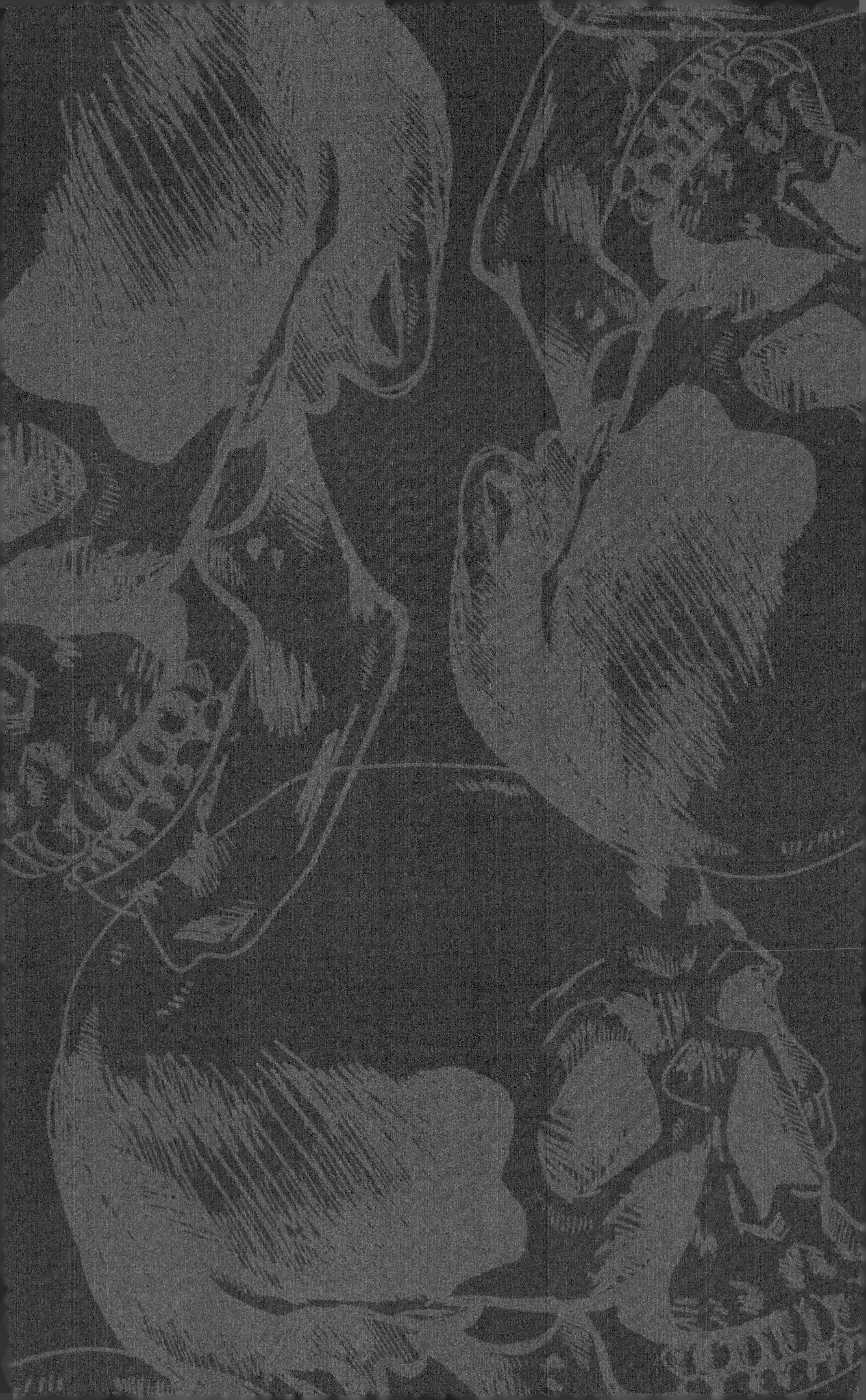

CHAPTER 32
Liam

"She what?" I barked at Dante and Basilio DiLustro on the other end of the call. I had yet to go to sleep after the whole warehouse fiasco. I retrieved the stolen shipment and stored it in Cassio's warehouse, and had been waiting for Nico's updates. "Are you fucking with me?"

Davina destroyed their casino? Cost them five hundred grand? That was what the women were doing in Chicago… Gambling!

"You're not my type," Basilio retorted dryly, the little prick was getting on my nerves.

"Nor mine. Though your girl on the other hand…" Dante left the sentence unfinished, and I clenched my fists.

"You arses approach Davina and I'll slice off both of your dicks," I growled.

"I'd like to see you try," Basilio said, his tone aloof even over the phone. He'd always been overconfident.

"I have a few years on you two." Twenty, to be exact. "You two were still shitting in your diapers while I dealt with the Colombians, Russians, and you, fucking Italians."

"Gosh, I'm feeling loved," Basilio drawled. "How about you, Dante?"

"So damn loved," Dante sneered. "Did you send your woman to my casino?"

"Tell me exactly what happened." I gritted my teeth, refusing to confirm or deny. Regardless of what the women were up to, they were under my protection.

"Well, she must have pulled the emergency handle, ruining the night's earnings, and then to top it off, she dumped lavender oil all over my marble floors. The fucking building smells like a spa," he grumbled. "Not exactly the atmosphere I was going for."

"Was she alone?" I asked. I knew she wasn't, but the two DiLustros hadn't mentioned anyone else.

"The casino was crowded, but she stood alone," Dante answered, his tone even. "Not to worry, old man, she didn't have another daddy there with her."

I gritted my teeth. For a few seconds, I debated going to Chicago myself and shooting the motherfucker. My age never bothered me, but for some goddamn reason, when it came to Davina, it did. I shouldn't fuck with her, yet a corrupted plan was forming in my mind. And making her pay me by bending to my will sexually was only a small part of it.

Yeah, there was no chance in hell I'd let her off the hook.

"I want to see proof," I growled. I wouldn't put it past the Italians to fucking lie.

"Thought you might ask," Dante drawled. "The footage is coming your way now."

My phone dinged the next second and I slid my phone open. A video started playing, and sure enough, there was Davina, looking hot as fuck in a long dress, swishing a bottle of oil and then running like the devil himself was chasing her. But there was no sign of Wynter, Juliette, or Ivy.

"I need other angles too," I demanded. "If she was at the casino, she had to have played slots or at least a game. Why would she show up there just to dump lavender oil on your precious marble floors?"

"Hold on a second," Basilio chimed in, then muted the line.

I didn't like this shit at all. I knew without a doubt those two shitheads were hiding something. But then, it was glaringly obvious that the damn girl squad under my protection was hiding something too.

The beep sounded and Basilio's voice came on. "Dante is sending you footage from the south and west cameras. The other cameras have confidential information, so you won't be getting those."

His comment struck me as odd, but my phone dinged and I checked the new footage. Just as I suspected, Juliette and Ivy were there. I watched as Juliette approached Dante and his blonde brother who ran Philadelphia. They exchanged a few words, and it sure looked like that little minx was flirting with both of them. Ivy pulled the emergency handle, and then Juliette kneed Dante into the balls.

Fucking highlight of the footage.

Though, it left the question of where Wynter was. She had to be the one playing the table. Wynter often played cards with my father, even me when I had time. As she'd gotten older, she'd become a strong player.

"What's the goddamn damage?" I asked, reining in my temper. I couldn't ask about Wynter and bring attention to her, and I certainly wouldn't point out Juliette and Ivy. Neither Dante nor Basilio knew who they were. If I hadn't run into Dante and Gio with Davina, they wouldn't have known her either.

Goddamn girl squad.

The studies at Yale seemed to have been a waste of money if the girls had turned to fucking crime. The question was why. Did they just wake up one day and decide to start robbing people?

It was time I taught my little thief a lesson. Whatever the fuck Davina had going on, I'd put an end to it before she got herself killed. Before any of them got themselves killed. But Davina was in a peculiar situation because they knew she was connected to me, and that made her more vulnerable.

Five minutes later, I was half a million dollars lighter. Lost earnings for two nights and cleaning service for lavender oil.

"No more fucking around," I muttered to myself as I picked up my cell phone and sent off the message.

> Tomorrow. My place. I'll send the address ahead of time.

The girl needed a major intervention.

CHAPTER 33
Liam

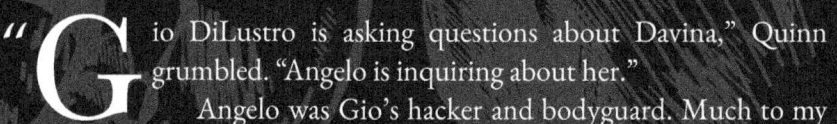

"Gio DiLustro is asking questions about Davina," Quinn grumbled. "Angelo is inquiring about her."

Angelo was Gio's hacker and bodyguard. Much to my dismay, he was very competent.

We sat in my home office at the penthouse. I had another two hours before Davina would arrive. And this latest development of Gio DiLustro's interest in Davina was the most disturbing. What was that saying... when it rains, it pours.

It certainly did. Russians that kept attacking, the girl squad shit, and now this.

"Fucking DiLustro," I cursed. If he started sniffing around Davina, it would lead him to my niece and Juliette too. "What did he find out so far?"

"Not much," Quinn grumbled. "Just the basics. Her name, place of birth, her ex-boyfriend. Morrelli was able to divert most of the search to insignificant details."

"Good. Let's keep it that way."

"You should know he went to see him." When I raised my eyebrow curiously, he clarified, "Her ex-boyfriend."

"If her ex-boyfriend is idiotic enough to entertain a DiLustro, fuck him." I gave zero fucks about him.

He wasn't my problem. Davina and my family were my only concern.

My desk phone rang and I answered, "Yes."

"Liam Brennan." A cold, Russian accent came through the speaker. It was either Pakhan or Alexei Nikolaev.

"Yes."

"Alexei Nikolaev."

Thank fuck!

"Thank you for getting in touch," I said. "Cassio mentioned you just had a baby, so I'm sure it's not a good time."

"No."

Okay then. "I hear you're the best at tailing people. I need someone watching four women and keeping them safe until I get the threat neutralized."

However fucking long that takes.

"Why?"

"How much has Cassio told you?" I inquired.

"Nothing."

There was a reason Cassio was trustworthy. "My niece is related to the Pakhan. Officially, she and her mother died twenty-one years ago. Unofficially, they're still alive."

A heartbeat of silence. "Their names," he demanded in a hoarse voice.

This man really didn't like to talk. "Wynter Flemming, Juliette Brennan, Ivy Murphy."

"Fourth name."

Fuck. "Davina Hayes."

Two heartbeats of silence. "I'll start tomorrow."

Click.

It was the right move. I knew the women would be safe. I wasn't so sure I did right by Davina though. I felt directly responsible for getting her wrapped up in this shit. First the DiLustros, and now the Russians. And to put the icing on the cake, I'd inadvertently put her on her own family's radar. The Ashford family.

Goddamn it!

Gio's curiosity about Davina was bad news. Everyone knew that DiLustro liked to exploit weaknesses in his enemies. And despite our uneasy truce, we were enemies.

I was worried that the girls had gotten themselves in trouble, and if I didn't get to the bottom of it, they'd end up in even more trouble. I had to figure out what those girls were up to.

Both Juliette and Wynter were avoiding me. My niece even went so far as to send me a message stating I was imagining things in my old age. And then sent an emoji of an old man with a cane. A goddamn cane!

Those girls needed a good timeout, except I'd have to tie them to a chair to ensure that they didn't bolt instead. And only the fucking saints knew when Wynter and Juliette ganged up on me, all hell broke loose. Unfortunately, I had a feeling they had expanded their forces. Now it included a raven-haired beauty and a red-haired hellion.

"They'll be safe with him tailing them," Quinn commented.

"Yes," I agreed. "Keep throwing breadcrumbs to divert Gio and Angelo elsewhere," I told Quinn. "Work with Nico if you have to. Wynter will be flying back to California once she's done with her last final at Yale. Juliette will follow her."

"And Davina?" he asked.

"I'll keep her safe." Because she was mine.

I turned my attention to my laptop and started reviewing the spreadsheet. Quinn still hadn't moved.

"What is it, Quinn?" I asked, exasperated, never peeling my eyes off the screen. I wanted to be done with the damn spreadsheet. Reviewing numbers and books was my least favorite part of the job, but it needed to be done.

"I'm glad to see you found an interest," he said, the meaning behind his words didn't escape me.

"And?" I smirked. I didn't have to look up to know his next words would be full of smug satisfaction.

"And I'm surprised you still know how to work your dick. It hasn't shriveled up and fallen off, eh?"

I flipped him the bird. "Considering you're older, fucker, it must mean yours is long gone."

"Nah, mine works just fine, you old arse."
"Get out, Quinn."
His chuckle rang in the room long after he left.

CHAPTER 34
Davina

I parked Wynter's Jeep in the underground garage, a row of luxury vehicles lining the entire wall. Wyn's bright red Jeep was by no means lame, but compared to these cars, it looked ancient. My Honda would look like a pile of junk. The damn thing might be out of commission for the foreseeable future. The repair would cost way more than the car was even worth.

I was dropping Wynter off at her ballet class with Madame Sylvie, which was right outside the city. I'd bet her plans encompassed more than just a dance class. She didn't wear her casual leggings and oversized T-shirt. Instead, she actually blow-dried her hair and pulled it up into a high ponytail, put cropped jeans on, and wore a shimmering pink blouse that offered a glimpse of her bra.

Juliette and Ivy were too lost in their scheming to take over the world by starting a school for mafiosos and the next casino we should rob to notice Wynter got dolled up.

When I dropped her off, there was a slick McLaren sitting in the parking lot with a guy in a three-piece-suit leaning against it. It was the same guy that she asked to wipe out the surveillance. His hands casually in the pockets of his suit, he looked like a gangster from the *Peaky Blinders* series, except Italian. And super gorgeous.

He spotted us even before we spotted him, his eyes already on Wynter.

The man had so much sex appeal I could practically taste it. And he only had eyes for Wynter, who fucking glowed in the seat next to me. Her smile was so bright, I searched for my sunglasses so I wouldn't lose my sight.

After four years, Wynter might have finally developed a major crush. I just hoped it wasn't with the wrong guy.

My eyes locked on the object of her crush.

Expensive suit. Fast car. Confident smile, and something hot flaring in his eyes. It was all aimed at the woman next to me.

"Call me if you need me," I whispered.

She leaned over, pressed a smooch onto my cheek, then grabbed her bag from the back seat and shut the door. She rushed toward him in her pink ballet flats and a big smile on her face. He didn't move an inch, but the intensity of his stare took my breath away. The heat of his gaze felt like a blazing furnace, and I wasn't even the object of it. It was so strong, time seemed to slow, and his entire attention was on my golden-haired friend.

I wondered if Wynter could feel it. She had to. I couldn't help but think that those two would either make the greatest love story or the most tragic one.

By the time I made it to Liam's building, I wasn't quite sure if I wanted to be the object of the look Wynter had gotten from her man or not. I didn't exactly believe in love. Desire, lust, temporary fixation... yes. But not love. Just look at my non-existent relationship with my parents. I never even knew them.

On the elevator ride up to his penthouse, Liam's eyes flashed through my mind. I'd never felt anything like this before. The way he made me feel was only read about in books or seen in movies. Maybe it was the same for Wynter.

My phone dinged and I pulled it out of my purse. It was our group chat.

> We could call the school Badass Females.

Of course, that was Juliette's suggestion.
I quickly typed my response.

> We'd be cutting ourselves short if we only opened the school for girls. We could have an enhanced program for girls, but the school should be for both genders.

Ivy chimed in.

> I agree with Davina. She has the best business sense among us.

My lips curved into a smile. That was a first.

> The Kingmakers?

I suggested, though I wasn't serious.
Bubbles instantly showed up, and I could already picture Juliette typing vigorously.

> Fuck that. We are making queens, not kings.

Ivy's response came in.

> Scratch that one. Diamond?

> Ladies, I'm busy. Can we do this another time?

It was Wynter, and it didn't escape me that she didn't say she was in the middle of her ballet class.

> How about St. Jean d'Arc? She was a badass female, and it would be a good cover for the exclusive school. To any outsiders, it would seem like just another Catholic school.

> Yes.

Juliette confirmed.

> Though there will be nothing saintly going on in there.

An emoji of a devil followed.
Then Ivy's confirmation.

> Yes.

That was settled then. I didn't expect a reply from Wynter, but I had a feeling she'd agree.

The elevator opened to the impressive foyer with Liam standing there.

My breath stuttered to a halt.

He was waiting for me, like my own knight. Liam Brennan was the type of man that swallowed the room and made your heart flutter. He certainly made mine dance in the most unusual way.

His wide shoulders looked like they could take the weight of all the world's problems and keep you protected. The muscles that I felt first-hand a few nights ago were strong and bulky. My ass burned with the memory of his palm smacking against my flesh.

Good God!

I never thought I'd allow a man to spank me, much less enjoy it. But I did. So much that just thinking about it made me achy and wet.

"Davina," he greeted.

His voice did things to me. It was husky and raspy, pure sex. Maybe I could ask him to just talk and I'd touch myself. It wouldn't take me long to orgasm. Especially after experiencing his mouth against my thighs. It had to be that scruff of a beard.

"Mr..." My words faltered when he narrowed his eyes on me. "Liam."

Satisfaction flashed in his eyes and his lips curved into a smile. My insides instantly melted, knowing I'd pleased him.

He extended his hand, and I slipped mine into his. I felt the electric shocks down to my core and my eyes flashed to his. He was so much taller that I had to crane my neck to meet his gaze. It was hard to tell by his expression whether he felt the same attraction.

Please don't let it be one-sided, I prayed silently.

The irony didn't escape me. Only a few minutes ago, I claimed I didn't believe in anything but lust and desire. And here I stood with a fluttering heart, choking on my own words.

"You look beautiful," he said, his eyes roaming over me. I didn't get dressed up because I didn't want it to seem like I was trying too hard. I just wore a simple yellow dress and sandals.

"Thanks," I murmured, feeling the blush rising up my chest and neck.

He led me through his penthouse, the space wide open with marble floors, indicating nothing but the best for the head of the Irish mafia.

My eyes trailed over the decor. Everything in this place was pristine and expensive, like it belonged in a magazine. Elaborate foyer. Gorgeous salon. Formal dining room with views of New York City's glittering lights. For a fleeting second, I caught a glimpse of a king-sized bed through the cracked door of what must be a bedroom.

Holy crap!

I had never seen a bed so large and with so many pillows. A fluffy, dark blue duvet over the large bed was inviting, promising corrupted pleasure that we'd both enjoy. A shiver ran down my spine, immediately followed by a blast of heat.

Liam's gaze flicked to me, something dark in his eyes.

"I thought we'd have dinner first." Liam's voice filled the sexual tension sizzling between us. This man read me like an open book. Just wonderful.

"Ummm, okay."

He chuckled as if I said something funny. "Unless you're eager to go straight to fucking."

I glared at him, though a delightful shudder ran down my spine at his filthy words. Butterflies in my stomach took flight as expectation vibrated under every inch of my skin. God, I wanted him so much, I wouldn't mind going straight to fucking.

Jesus, Mary, and Joseph! I had lost my mind.

It was best not to comment. I didn't trust my voice or words not to betray me.

The minute we entered the dining room, my steps halted and my breath hitched. The fear of heights kicked in as I looked through the large floor-to-ceiling windows. I was so nervous earlier that I didn't think much about how high we were, so my fear had a delayed reaction and now, it was in overdrive.

Liam's eyes burned my cheek, waiting for me to say something, but I couldn't find my voice.

"Is everything okay?"

Fuck, the dining table was too close to the windows. I'd never be able to take the steps to get close to the windows. My eyes darted to Liam.

I swallowed hard. "I-I'm scared of heights," I muttered. "Too close to the windows."

His eyes traveled over the dining room then back to me, a look of concern dominating his features. "If I bring the table closer to the wall on this side, will that work?"

I licked my lips, my pounding heart and rapid breathing making my mouth dry. I couldn't believe he was even contemplating a solution for me.

"Or I could tear off the thick curtains from my bedroom and try installing them here, though that might take a while," he suggested in a pensive tone.

A choked laugh escaped me while I envisioned the head of the Irish mafia in New York installing curtains. That would be an unforgettable sight.

"I think the table away from the window will work," I told him, my smile slightly shaky. It was a miracle I could even smile. "I'm sorry."

"Don't be," he assured me, squeezing my hand. "Stay here, or if you feel safer in the hallway, that's fine too." His eyes locked on me, searching my face. I nodded, and then the corner of his lip tugged up. "Or you can always go to my bedroom," he teased, trying to distract me.

"Dinner in bed?" I joked, though my voice was shaky.

"Now there's an idea."

He moved toward the table while I remained plastered against the opposite wall.

It took him no time to drag the large dining room table away from the window. I watched his muscles bulge and flex. God, he really had nice muscles. The nicest ones I had ever seen on a man.

Talk about extremes. From burning lust to fear and back to lust.

"Good?" he asked. I couldn't help but compare his behavior to every other man I had dated in the past. When my fear of heights came to the surface, they liked to taunt me about it, thinking they were being cute. They'd startle me and nudge me too close to the balcony. They'd chuckle and promise they'd save me. I didn't believe them.

Until Liam.

I'd stake my life that he'd never do something so immature. And something told me he'd catch me if I was about to fall. Bizarre, really, since I didn't know him well at all. And he caught me stealing from him then blackmailed me to give him what he wanted.

Yeah, conflicting signals there for sure.

Finally satisfied that the table was far enough from the window, Liam came over to me and led me to it. Food already awaited us, spread over the table set for two. Though, when he moved the table, the perfect set-up was now slightly rattled.

"Thank you," I told him, my heart warming with such a simple gesture.

The scent of cooked meat and vegetables filled the air and my stomach growled. I hadn't eaten since breakfast, busy with packing and scheming on how to rob a few more places.

Yeah, my best friends and I were nut jobs.

Liam pulled out a seat for me and, like a true gentleman, made sure my back was to the window as I sat down. I was touched by his concern. I guess he deserved extra points for not taking me straight into his bedroom, spanking me, and then fucking me. My pussy quivered, liking the idea of being spanked and then fucked.

God, I needed to get my head out of the gutter. At this rate, I might be throwing myself at this man. It was like someone slipped me an aphrodisiac that kept going and going, but only around him.

He sat himself to my right, and he lifted the lid.

"I wasn't sure what you liked," he started. "So we have some seafood, chicken, and lamb."

I smiled at his thoughtfulness. Though, it wasn't as if I had a choice in coming here. His text was clear. Come, *or else*.

"I'll have chicken, please."

He made up my plate and then proceeded to make his own. I tried not to show my surprise, but the man could eat. I guessed as much, considering his size, but he seriously had an appetite.

"So how do you stay in shape?" I asked curiously.

I was one of those women that gained weight after the first slice of cake I ate. At five foot four, I was the shortest of the four of us, so that weight went straight to my ass.

"I work out every morning." Yeah, fuck that. I liked to sleep in whenever I could.

I bit into my chicken and chewed slowly, then waited until his mouth was full. Swallowing my food, I took a sip of water, then commented, "So how long do I have to do this for?"

"For as long as I demand."

"That's not right," I protested.

"It's not right that I caught you stealing from me," he drawled. Yes, he had a point, but I couldn't possibly agree with him.

"Well, there has to be a payment plan that I could track against. A timeline," I said weakly. "Otherwise, this could be a life sentence."

"You didn't seem to be complaining when you were riding my face."

My cheeks singed. I knew they were as red as tomatoes, and it wasn't attractive at all.

"There's no need to be crude."

He smiled, clearly smug with himself. "But you enjoy it. And I bet if I touched your panties right now, they'd be soaked." I shook my head feebly. "Should we test it? And then I get to keep your panties."

I smothered a sigh. The man was an Irish devil, a handsome one at that. It was pointless to deny it, or him. I *was* soaked, and he still had my panties from our first endeavor. I happened to love my undergarments and didn't have money to spend on new ones. Well, except the million I stole from him, but it felt wrong to spend that money on panties and other frivolous things.

"How are your exams coming along?" he drawled. Something about the way he said it had my instincts flaring, but his face didn't portray any smugness, so I attributed it to my paranoia.

"Good. Studying for my finals is taking up all my time."

His beautiful lips curved into a smile, like he knew something I didn't.

"I bet," he said.

I'd become a criminal and a liar. Career goals piling up. How lovely!

"Yeah, it's been stressful." Theoretically, not a lie. It had been super stressful planning our heist. For the past twenty-four hours, the girls and I had been on pins and needles, expecting the police to show up at our dorm door. Or the fucking Kingpins. I wouldn't recommend looking them up or paranoia would hit tenfold.

"But now it's over," he concluded.

"What do you mean?" I breathed.

"You're all done with tests, Davina. You've been done with your last final for quite a few days now." Shit, he knew. "Now, we're going to discuss the terms of our arrangement and why you ignored my text."

Silence stretched and I swallowed hard.

Everything spiraled out of control, and it had happened so fast I barely had time to breathe. I had a boyfriend, caught him cheating before I had fully moved in, accidently burned a house down, planned and failed at a heist, planned and succeeded at another heist, and now, here I was in this penthouse with this gorgeous man that had my insides quivering with need. The heaviness between my legs was becoming a familiar feeling around this man.

"Did you always want to go to Yale?" Liam's question caught me by surprise. I fully expected him to grill me about not answering his message.

"Yes. My grandfather went to Yale before joining the military." Thinking about Grandpa always made me smile. "He said those were some of the best years of his life. He met Grandma at Yale too. So when it came time to decide where to go, it was a no-brainer."

"Have the last four years been the best years of your life?" he asked.

I chuckled. "Yes, for the most part."

"What parts didn't you like?" Liam seemed genuinely interested.

"Umm, I..." Truthfully, Garrett was the only part of my four years at Yale that I didn't like. Although, if I hadn't bothered wasting time with him, we wouldn't have ventured into our criminal endeavor. Yet somehow, it felt like I was exactly where I was meant to be. Maybe I was officially a criminal.

"Just say it, Davina," he encouraged.

"My ex-boyfriend," I started, and Liam growled. Actually growled. "He turned out to be an ass, and I'm not too happy that I wasted my time on him."

"What did he do?" he inquired, looking like he was ready to go into attack mode. Something about it made my heart palpitate.

"Uh, he cheated." I shrugged. "I guess he was being a boy."

"He was being a dumbass," Liam drawled. "His loss is my gain."

My cheeks heated up. Fuck, he could be so hot and sweet.

"What about you?" I steered the conversation away from myself.

He ran a hand across his mouth, as if he was debating what he should tell me.

"Well, I don't see a point in cheating," he said, and I believed him. "It's too messy."

Isn't that the truth? Just look at the mess my friends and I had gotten into it.

"You don't have to worry about me cheating on you, Davina," he said. "You are more than enough for me. The way you pant for my cock. The way your greedy pussy clenches around my dick. It's heaven. Nothing will tear me away from you. Not heaven, not hell. And certainly not another woman."

For some reason, his words pleased me. A lot. His arm brushed against mine and his body heat overwhelmed me. And his scent. Deep and masculine. It made my head dizzy and my skin buzz like a live wire.

"Do you have any hobbies?" I asked, trying to change the subject.

"Apart from eating your pussy?" he retorted. Failed attempt at diversion. I rolled my eyes, ready to offer him an insolent comeback, but he beat me to it. "I believe you sucking my cock will be another favorite hobby."

I blew out an exasperated breath. "Any *non-sexual* hobbies?"

He chuckled, amusement flashing in his eyes. "Boating."

"Boating?" I scoffed. "That gigantic boat cannot be called boating. It's a goddamn house on the water. You could barely feel the waves while on it."

He cocked an eyebrow. "Luxury boating?"

"I guess so," I mused. Maybe we have a bit in common. I loved boating too, though I never had the luxury of spending time on a yacht. Not until the other night. "I like boating too," I admitted.

His eyebrow shot up. "Really?"

I nodded. "Yes, I grew up in this little beach town where there was nothing to do but fish, boat, or lounge around on the beach."

"It actually sounds pretty relaxing."

I smiled. "It was, but it could get boring. My grandfather made it exciting."

"You're close with your grandfather." It was a statement, but I still nodded.

"Yes, very much so. My parents..." I paused for a second but then decided to just spit it out. "My parents didn't want a kid, didn't want me, so he was all I had. I was very lucky, because he's amazing."

"Your parents are probably regretting it," he said softly. "You are pretty amazing yourself."

I wasn't quite sure I'd qualify as amazing. The girls and I had done some not-so-amazing things.

I tilted my head, observing him. "How about you? Any childhood memories you miss?"

"I'd say spending my summers in Ireland. For a few years, we lived there exclusively, but then I came back and had to work on getting back what my father lost. But whenever I could, I'd go back in the summers and spend a few weeks there."

"I read that the best time to visit Ireland is in July."

He shook his head, amusement passing his expression. "Actually, I'd recommend September. Less tourists."

"Those damn tourists." I chuckled. "Are you close with your father or grandfather?" I asked him curiously.

"My grandfather was killed before I was born," he answered, his expression tight. "When I was a little boy, my father was my hero. Then things happened, and we drifted apart. But I am close to my sister."

I sensed a long and bad story there.

"I'm sorry," I muttered and returned my attention to my food.

We ate the rest of our dinner in silence. Truthfully, I'd been done with my food for a while, but I kept moving it around my plate so it looked like I was still eating. Something about this whole dinner had me on edge. I felt like a prey that had already been caught.

Even worse, I behaved like I wanted to be caught. By him.

Liam leaned back against his seat, his gaze burning my cheek. Analytical. Studious. Lustful. And my heart tripped over its next beat.

I ached for him. My pulse was shaky and so were my hands, so I gripped my fork as if my life depended on it, hiding the impact this man had on me. He was too much, though at the same time, it wasn't enough. Not until I could feel his skin against mine. His hands on my aching core.

"Wine?" he offered, leaning back in his chair. I shook my head, placing my fork down. "Or would you prefer my most expensive cognac?"

Why wasn't I surprised? Every single crime we had committed so far, we had gotten caught. One way or another. Well, except Chicago.

"I want your most expensive cognac," I told him.

"I expected nothing less," he acknowledged with a smile, then stood up and strode to a small minibar in the corner of the room, right by the window. My heart stammered at his proximity to the window.

"Aren't you scared someone might shoot you through the windows?" I asked him. "I'm sure you have a buttload of enemies, being a criminal and all."

He glanced over his shoulder. "The windows are bulletproof."

"Oh." I guess it was safe then. If a bullet couldn't pierce through the window, a body certainly couldn't fly out of it.

"And you're right," he continued. "I have a buttload of enemies. Are those the words they taught you at Yale?"

"That and fuck," I retorted sarcastically. "You shouldn't hang around the windows too much if you have a buttload of enemies," I added, watching him pour two glasses.

He came back and handed one glass to me. I'd had enough alcohol to last me a lifetime, but I took it anyway. The cognac barely touched my lips when he spoke again.

"Worried about me?" he joked.

"Nope."

He chuckled, like he didn't believe me. He lowered his big frame down onto his chair next to me.

"I have a proposition for you," he said, his voice deep and firm.

"I'm scared to hear it," I retorted dryly.

He chuckled. "I doubt it. A woman that is brave enough to steal from the mafia should be able to handle this proposition like a piece of cake." He arched an eyebrow at me to punctuate the point. "A walk in the park," he added.

Sirens blasted in my brain, but I couldn't do anything but wait for him to reveal whatever it was he needed to say.

"Don't keep me in suspense then," I said, hiding my nervousness behind my sarcastic tone. I took a sip of my drink as Liam watched me like a hungry wolf.

His eyes darkened and locked on my mouth. "I'm going to enjoy fucking that sassy mouth of yours."

I choked on the cognac and started coughing loudly. Unlike anyone I had ever met, Liam could go from business to flirtatious to pure filth in the same second. He knew exactly what he was doing to me, I had no doubt.

"You'd let me deepthroat you, wouldn't you?"

Fuck!

I had to fight the urge to nod my head. His tone was dark, pure sex, and my thighs clenched with need. God, his filthy words would be my doom. They set me aflame, and my pussy throbbed in response. If another man would have said those words, I would have punched him in the eye. With this man, I wanted to ask *when* he'd fuck my mouth.

To ensure I did no such thing, I took a sip of the cognac.

"My proposition is that you marry me." I choked on my drink again and spit it all over the table. I eyed him through my coughing fit, expecting him to laugh. Anything. All I could see through my watering eyes was his serious face.

Juliette never told me her father was crazy.

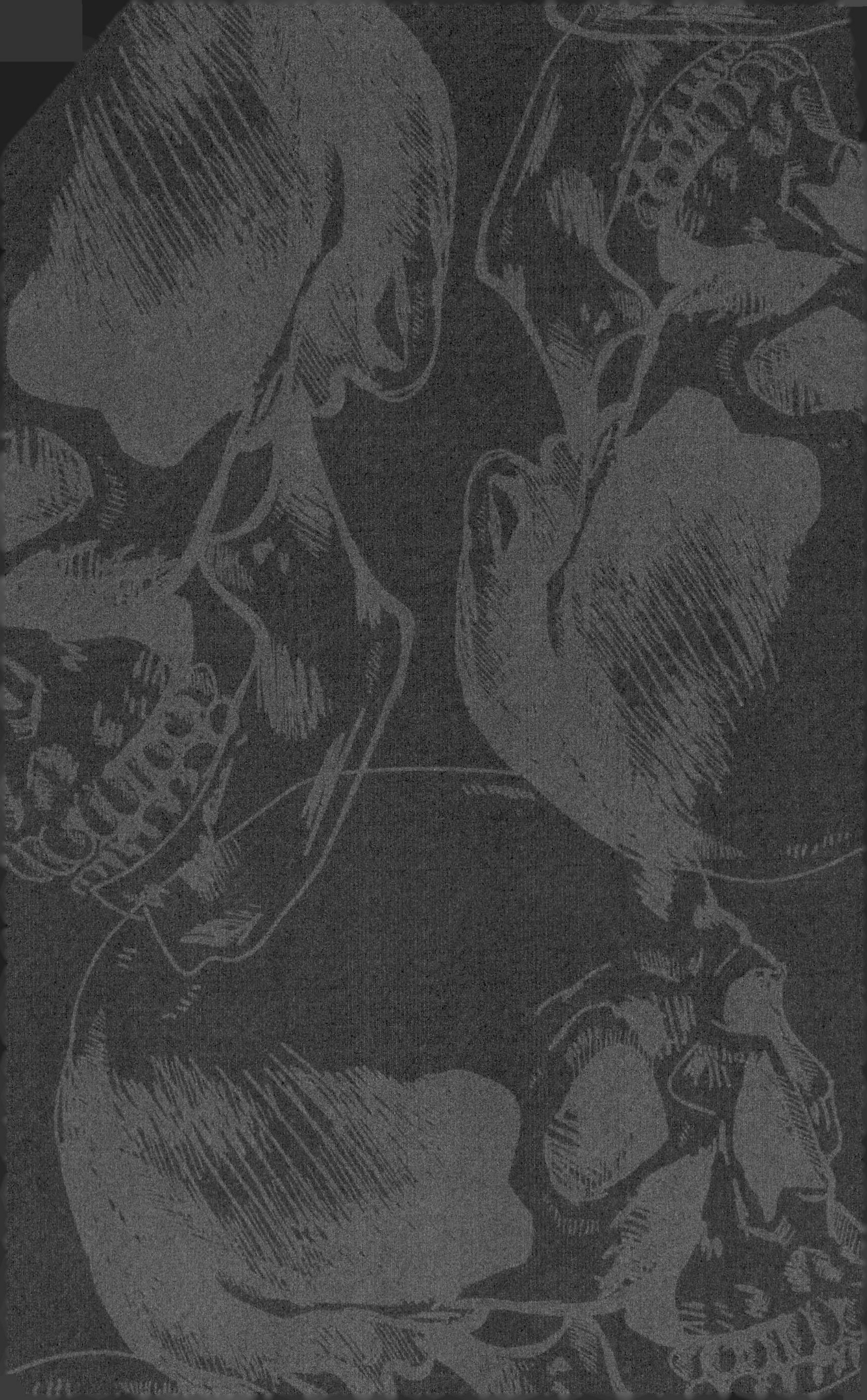

CHAPTER 35
Liam

All things considered, she took the news well. She hadn't walked away. Or slapped me. Not that she'd ever succeed. I watched millions of emotions flicker across her expression. It wasn't the brightest idea I'd ever had, but it was the most effective one to keep her and my family protected.

With their endeavor in Chicago, they had brought on more shit. I should lock all four of them up in a room and feed them twice a day.

"I'm not marrying you," she hissed, her eyes like two thunderbolts ready to strike me at any moment.

"It's either that, or you go to jail." Her eyes widened with disbelief. "Don't think I won't hesitate to turn you in. I have the tape, and I intend to use it if you don't cooperate."

I'd never do it, but she didn't need to know that. Besides, she got lucky that night in my club, and no such recording existed. She wasn't that lucky in Chicago, but I'd keep that to myself. For now.

I watched the delicate skin of her throat bob with her swallow. I could already picture thrusting into her throat.

"B-but..." She took a deep breath, her chest rising and falling. An attractive blush crept up her neck.

I took advantage of her loss for words. "We will make our arrangement legal," I said. "We've already established that you will submit to me. Whenever I say. Wherever I say. Now, I legally want to make you—and your pussy—mine."

"That is the craziest fucking thing I've ever heard," she snapped. "My pussy is mine. Just as your cock is yours. You can't claim shit like that."

"Oh no, Davina. That's where you're wrong," I purred. "My cock is yours. It belongs in your pussy." Then I grinned. "Correction, my pussy."

"This is ridiculous." She scoffed and her mouth pursed, feigning indignation.

A shiver that worked its way down her spine didn't escape me. I fucking loved how she got aroused with my filthy words. Corrupting her would be the highlight of my life. And I didn't lie. She was my manna. My fucking heaven.

"You fighting me and our attraction is ridiculous," I told her.

Davina's grandfather was in a facility, and the only reason I could think she needed money was for him, but it didn't fit the bill. The million she stole from me should be adequate enough to settle any kind of bills she had. Maybe the four girls had some crazy idea and when splitting it four ways, it didn't cover their needs.

Whatever the fuck it could be, I couldn't even fathom. But I would uncover it, one way or another.

She straightened her shoulders and met my gaze head on. "I guess jail it is," she said stubbornly, her voice shaking, "because I'm not marrying you. I will miss the sex though."

The girl had some balls, I'd give her that.

"I might just let you go to jail to serve your time, baby," I drawled, locking eyes with her and watching her like a hawk. "But the Italians won't."

Game. Set. Match.

My little thief didn't realize I never gave up.

Surprise flashed in her eyes. Yes, this girl was an open book.

"Italians?" she asked in a tentative voice.

"I know the four of you were in Chicago." Her soft gasp filled the room. "Tell me, was it you or Wynter who played poker? I know it wasn't Juliette. She's lousy at math. And from what I understand, Ivy is not much better at games."

Davina's lips thinned. Her cheeks heated, and the guilt in her eyes was admission enough.

"You're not a good liar," I mused.

"I didn't say anything," she gritted.

"You don't have to," I drawled. "Just remember this, Davina. They recognized you. They'll go after your family." The Italians had no scruples. While we stuck to a code in my organization, the Italians under Gio and Franco DiLustro would go after anyone and everyone connected to Davina. "They'll go after your grandfather, no matter his age." She stiffened. Good, finally I was getting somewhere with her. "Your parents."

A vulnerability flashed in her eyes, and she bit into her bottom lip. Fuck, I didn't like seeing her upset. The reasonable part of me knew I didn't need more trouble. But for the first time in my life, reason didn't do shit for me. It zeroed in on her and wouldn't let go. And the idea of her hurt or under the Italians made me crazy.

Besides, I had decided she was mine already.

My father had been nagging me about it for decades. Fuck it, I'd finally make him happy, though for completely selfish reasons. To own her and to keep my family protected.

"I'll protect you and your grandfather," I promised her. "One way to ensure I can do that is to put a ring on your finger."

Well, my father would be proud. Entrapping my wife by any means necessary. The thing was that for me, it was her or nobody else. She was the one for me. The added benefit was keeping my family safe. Appeasing my father was just an afterthought.

"What am I supposed to tell Juliette?" she challenged, her voice shaking, sounding bitter. "About marrying you. She won't like it."

"Lie to her," I told her with a shrug. "You have no qualms about lying to me."

"That's not fair," she protested. "I've known her for a lot longer. Besides, she's my friend."

My lips curved into a smile. "Have you told her about me eating your pussy?" Her ivory cheeks flamed crimson and I got my answer. I chuckled. "Then this should be no problem."

"Getting married is a mistake," she insisted. "You insist I marry you, fine. Just to keep my grandfather safe." She didn't say parents. She didn't know anything about them. "But I won't tell my friends if we get married. It won't last, anyhow."

I shrugged my shoulders, though something about that statement bothered me. I didn't care to evaluate it. I shouldn't care, but fuck if I'd start caring about the morality of my actions now. And contrary to her belief, our marriage would last.

Till death do us part.

"I don't care about the particulars, Davina," I said coolly. "But you'll be my wife, and you'll find yourself in my bed every night. And you'll get the girls to leave the dorms and stay at my house."

"Here?"

"No, not the penthouse. My house in the city. The same one where you spied on me jacking off in the shower."

And just like that, her cheeks flamed again. Fuck, I loved riling her up.

"All three of them?" she breathed, her voice hoarse.

"Yes."

I'd feel better with those hellions under my roof until they left for California. Alexei would be shadowing them starting tomorrow. It was the safest thing to do for now.

"But finals are still going on," she argued.

"They are not." I confirmed that with the school. "Wynter's working on a project. She can remain in her dorm until then, since she's training there anyhow." It would be only a couple more weeks. Besides, as close as the four of the women were, I was certain she'd stay at my city house more than the dorms.

"Is this some feeble attempt to control us?" she questioned, her eyes narrowing on me.

"Take it as you will, but you ladies will stay at my house." I leaned over and was so close to her, I could see faint sun freckles on her nose. "And you, my soon-to-be wife, will be coming with me to the penthouse. Here, I don't have to worry about anyone hearing your screams as I fuck you." Her eyes hazed and I realized this girl liked my dirty talking. "Or spank you," I added smugly.

A sharp exhale slipped through her lush, parted lips.

"You're nuts," she replied, though her voice was too breathless. "Honestly, the idea of marriage repels me." Well, at least she didn't say the idea of marriage to *me* repelled her. It was a general statement. "You'll make sure my grandfather is safe? No matter what."

"I promise," I vowed. "No matter what."

Truthfully, I never planned on getting married myself, but considering the shit Davina and her friends had found themselves in, it was either that or let Davina pay for associating with us.

And I couldn't let that happen. She was mine to protect, just like Wynter and Juliette.

"We'll go to City Hall tomorrow, Davina," I told her. "You'll spend the night here so we can ensure there are no creative attempts made by you to get out of this."

She swallowed hard and her eyes darted away from me, guilt written all over her expression.

"Another thing, Davina," I warned, and her eyes returned to me, narrowing in displeasure.

"What?"

"No more heists," I warned her. "And don't think I've forgotten that you ignored my message."

"God, you're demanding," she complained, rolling her eyes.

"You bet your ass," I growled. "You like it though. It makes your pussy wet."

Another eye roll. "You're too cocky, Liam."

"Maybe, but your pussy likes it." I grinned at her scandalized look. "Now stop sassing me, or I'll punish you."

Her gaze flicked down to my lips, and I knew instantly she was aroused. It didn't take much for her. Just some filthy talk and bossing her around.

"Stand up and bend over the table."

"Not this shit again," she grumbled, though her voice was breathless.

"That's two. Bend over."

Her breathing became harder. "I'm not doing this, Liam. You can't make me."

"Three," I purred. "Don't worry, Davina. I'll spank that beautiful ass of yours and then I'll make you come all night long. But only if you listen."

She turned crimson. Such a fucking turn-on. I stood up and patted a spot on the table next to me. "Five seconds, Davina. Otherwise, I won't let you come at all. I'll bring you to the verge of orgasm, just to withdraw it. Over and over again."

She scoffed but did as ordered. She bent over, her elbows resting on the dining room table, and I'd never again be able to eat off it without thinking about her sweet pussy after tonight.

Fuck, I could smell her arousal. It made my mouth water.

"Good girl," I praised her, placing my palm on her ass cheek. "You look so beautiful like this. Arse pushed up and ready for your punishment."

"Freak," she muttered, though whether she knew it or not, she pushed her arse into my palm.

"What was that?" I challenged. I could see a flush creeping up her neck.

"Nothing."

Placing my palm on the soft skin of her outer thigh, I trailed my hand higher and higher until I reached her panties, then hooked my fingers into them and ripped them in one move.

Her sharp gasp broke the silence of the penthouse. My balls were tight and ready to explode. But first I'd teach her a lesson.

"We won't be needing these." I discarded her panties and put the palm of my hand on her gorgeous arse.

Smack.

She arched her back and cried out. "Oh God!"

I chuckled. "God can't help you here."

She didn't want God's help anyhow. She wiggled her ass again and glanced over her shoulder. Holding her gaze, I brought my hand down.

Smack.

"Liam." Her moan vibrated through the room. The little mewling noises she made were fucking music to my ears.

"Should we smack your pussy too?" Her thighs were glossy from her arousal, and it didn't escape me how she was clenching her thighs together.

"Ask me nicely to smack your pussy," I demanded. I wanted to hear her say it.

She panted, her mouth parted, her eyes still on me. I was so fucking hard, I feared that for the first time in my forty-seven years, I might actually spill before I was ready.

"Ask me," I gritted.

"Liam, please spank my pussy," she pleaded, spreading her thighs open to give me better access.

"Please, Liam, I—"

Her words faltered as my hand slapped against the tender flesh of her pussy. She cried out and my cock jerked. She looked like pure temptation, watching me with those lust-filled eyes and her parted red mouth.

Adjusting myself, I decided that next time, we'd do this while both of us were naked. This was torture for me too.

"Let's finish our food," I told her. Truthfully, we were both done, but I'd need a stiff drink to get myself together.

"You want me to sit and eat now?" she shrieked, her eyes wild and her breathing labored. My little thief was turned on just as much as I was.

I ignored her smart-ass comment. It was for the best, otherwise she'd come back with another sassy remark. Then I'd have to bend her over this table and spank her beautiful ass red and she wouldn't be able to sit tomorrow.

We can't have that on her wedding day, I mused silently.

Fuck, heat raced straight to my groin thinking about her beautiful, red ass and the way she'd pushed it against my palm like a cat.

"I can find someone who won't leave me all hot and bothered," she fumed, her eyes flashing like lightning bolts.

"There will be no other men for you," I growled at her. "You're mine now. *All* of you is mine. If you let any other man touch what's mine, you cut their lives short." I leaned forward, inhaling her scent deep into my lungs. "And they'll suffer first." I reached out and rubbed my thumb over her bottom lip. Her tongue darted out and licked it. "Good girl," I purred, and she followed up with a gentle nip of her teeth. "Your mouth is mine. Your breasts are mine. Your pussy is mine. Your ass is mine."

I trailed my hand down her chest, over her breasts, pinching her nipples through her little yellow spring dress, her arms bare and tempting me. She moaned, her eyelids half-closed.

"Every inch of your body belongs to me now, Davina."

A soft whimper left her lips and I'd bet my life she was drenched. I stood up from my spot, and without prompting, she did the same. Her eyes darkened with lust and she took a small step, bringing herself chest-to-chest with me.

She might have hated the idea of marrying me, but she couldn't deny she wanted me. If nothing else, we'd have a good time fucking. And she'd be safe from the Italians and Russians and anyone else who dared threaten my wife.

Her arms came up and she wrapped them around my neck. I needed to bury myself inside her. Pulling her up by her thighs, she wrapped her legs around me.

Right now, it was just us. Nobody else. Not her friends. Not the Italians. Not the Russians.

I captured her mouth in a kiss, possessive and demanding. During our first kiss, I'd realized I was fucked. She tasted like heaven. A sweet addiction.

She tasted like *mine*.

She parted her lips, letting me in. Her tongue brushed against mine and I wanted more. No woman had ever tasted like her. If I thought her pussy tasted addicting, it was nothing to her lips. She gave my top lip a gentle lick, stealing my breath away. God, if there was a blissful way to go, this had to be it.

I nipped her bottom lip, then carried her to my bedroom. I'd fuck her senseless until I put that ring on her finger. Then I'd fuck her some more, until she screamed my name. Until she couldn't remember anyone else's name but mine.

I put her on the bed, her fingers clutching at my hair, unwilling to let go. Her legs remained locked behind me as if she were scared I'd leave her.

As if. Nobody and nothing would pull me away from her right now.

"I-I need..." she breathed, her breath hot against me and clawing at my shirt. The bedroom was dark except for the bathroom light shining over her pale skin.

"Me too," I admitted. "I need to taste your pussy." She visibly shuddered underneath me. "I need to bury my cock inside you."

She moaned, her skin blushing attractively.

Sitting up, I pulled off my shirt and worked on my pants next while she got out of her dress. I stared at her curvy body in a strapless bra. She had curves in all the right places, just the way I loved it. I never liked women to be just skin and bones. I wanted to feel their flesh, hold on to their hips as I pounded into them.

She was perfect.

Arching her back, she gave me access to reach behind and unclip her bra. Then I discarded it onto the hardwood floor with the softest rustle.

"Fucking goddess," I rasped, more to myself than her.

Her legs parted and I could see her slick desire glistening on her inner thighs. Fuck! It made my mouth water. I draped my body over hers, my mouth ravaging every inch of her pale skin, nibbling and kissing. She writhed against me, rubbing like a cat, begging for more.

I grabbed her waist and flipped us over, sitting her on top of me. She squealed in surprise, not expecting the move.

Grabbing her by the back of her neck, I pulled her in for a possessive, bruising kiss.

"I want you riding my face," I whispered against her lips. "Just like our first time." Her lips parted and her panting got harder. "Show me what a good girl you are."

Hoisting her up by the hips, I positioned her over my face and latched on to her pussy. A growl of satisfaction crawled up my throat at the same time that she cried out in delight, my tongue slid deep inside her entrance.

I locked my eyes on her face as she started to grind herself against my lips. Her gaze locked with mine and I felt fucking consumed.

A girl half my age was corrupting me as much as I was corrupting her. She ground herself harder against me, her expression and words mirrored the pleasure consuming her. I had to be a fucking bastard, but I didn't give a damn. She'd be mine, and I'd ruin her with my cock and my mouth.

She'd scream *my* name every night. Warm *my* bed every night.

Forty-seven-years-old, and I'd finally lost my goddamn mind.

I sucked hungrily at her clit, nipping at it gently, and she screamed out my name. "Oh, fuck… God, Liam," she cried out. "Oh, Liam… Don't fucking stop."

Her pussy pulsed against my lips, her soft thighs clenching around my head as her spine curved inward and she came all over my tongue. I lapped up every drop of her, eating her up like my life depended on it. I devoured her like the delicacy that she was. She quivered, her muscles slowly relaxing, but I gave her no reprieve.

She could take all of me. She *would* take all of me.

My cock was marble hard, aching for her. She'd be my heaven after shitty days. The mother of my children. A partner to talk to and trust… eventually. My hands on her hips, I shifted her down my body and slammed into her soaking core in one brutal move.

"Fuck," I groaned, grasping her hair at the scalp to pull her down to my lips. I fucking shuddered with how good she felt, clenching around my cock. "Now fuck me, baby. Show me you want me as much as I want you. After tomorrow, you'll be mine, and I'm never letting you go. Never."

I dragged her lips to mine, nipping at her gently, and our tongues danced to an ancient dance. She moaned into my mouth, greedily sucking on my tongue. She was just as hungry for me as I was for her. Maybe it was the reason we felt this sizzling attraction. Both of us were just as greedy.

"Ride me," I ordered her.

Her beautiful stormy eyes focused on me, she gripped my shoulders, using them for balance as she started to ride me. She bounced herself on my hard cock, her pussy clenching around my shaft in a glorious chokehold.

My cock buried deep in her pussy, she ground herself on it hard and fast. Just the way I liked it.

"Liam, Liam, Liam," she chanted my name like she was praying at the altar as she chased her pleasure.

I grabbed her hips tightly, my fingers digging into her flesh, and I slammed her down onto my cock harder and faster. Her moans of ecstasy vibrated against the bedroom walls.

"That's right, baby," I grunted. "Take it all."

This woman was made for my cock. I moved her faster, thrusting from underneath her.

Harder. Deeper.

Her whimpers and moans were like manna from heaven. She clamped down around me so tightly that I felt sweat beading on my forehead. She hung her head back, filling the room with her pants.

"I'm going to come inside you," I ground out.

I thrusted like a madman, all my control slipped away, and at this moment, I was like a beast fucking its mate. I pushed into her from below, hard and deep, and her screams were music to my ears.

"Say yes," I demanded. "Give it to me."

"W-what?" she breathed, her hips moving up and down against my shaft.

"Tell me to come inside you," I grated the words, barely holding on to my sanity. "Because you're mine."

"Yes. P-please, Liam," she moaned.

Two more bounces of her on my cock and I grunted my own release, my cock pumping into her.

"Mine," I vowed on a grunt as my heart thundered violently in my chest. God, this was the most intense orgasm I had ever had, and I was certain it was because it was with her.

I kissed the soft spot on her neck, her pulse pounding hard under my lips. My hand rubbed down her back, a sheen of sweat across her back. I was still buried inside her and I already wanted her again. Again and again.

What the fuck was this woman doing to me?

Davina's silky hair covered my chest like a dark curtain as she laid there, spent and beautiful.

So fucking beautiful that something in my chest actually ached. I had never wished for a wife. I took Juliette and Killian as my own, but I had seen what love could do to people. With my father. With my own sister. It fucking ruined you.

Yet, I wanted this young woman. I wanted to consume her, not only her body but her heart and soul too.

The question was whether I was willing to give her my own.

CHAPTER 36
Davina

"Well, that went great," Quinn drawled. He was our witness at the courthouse, where people got married like it was a fast-food drive-thru. "I'm surprised the judge didn't call the police while you were reciting your vows."

Liam had secured a beautiful, simple white Chanel dress and white pumps with a red button that matched the red roses braided into my hair by the hairdresser he'd hired. He even bought me fancy undergarments from La Perla. It was like he knew I loved luxurious lingerie.

Despite the circumstances, I felt beautiful.

"You behaved like we had a gun to your head," Quinn added dryly.

He was getting on my nerves. "The judge *should* have called the police," I snapped. "Because Liam's forcing me into this shit."

Liam grabbed my clammy hand and pulled me along, proclaiming, "It's done and behind us now."

It certainly was.

It took us all of ten minutes from the time we arrived before we were proclaimed husband and wife. Until death do us part, the judge said. *Or we get a divorce*, I added silently. Though, something about that thought didn't sit well with me.

A man had been waiting for us as soon as we arrived at the courthouse. He fussed over us from the minute he met us until he delivered us to the judge who would perform the ceremony.

Liam Brennan must have had connections to be able to secure such speedy service on such short notice. But then again, I knew that. He had connections in the criminal world as well as the political one.

And I got my confirmation of those connections right before the judge commenced the service.

"Thank you for your generous donation, Mr. Brennan." The judge beamed like a hundred-watt light bulb. "Mr. Byron Ashford insisted I don't mention it, but I couldn't not thank you."

Holy shit! Did he mean Byron Ashford, one of the Billionaire Kings? His father, Senator George Ashford, had been eyeing the presidency.

Even I, with my limited knowledge of the political world, had seen the papers mentioning Byron's sister, Aurora Ashford, who married a Russian mobster last year. Alexei Nikolaev. Some scary, tatted-up dude, if pictures were anything to go by. Reporters were having a field day with that little connection. It was a smear on Senator Ashford's political career for sure, but his daughter didn't bother hiding it. Not that she should.

But all that had faded into the back of my mind as soon as the ceremony started.

My thoughts scattered, aware only of Liam's hand on the small of my back and his body next to mine. I couldn't remember all of the words we spoke, I just felt *him*.

The whole ceremony was a blur, with the exception of the vows Liam uttered as he held my gaze.

You are blood of my blood, bone of my bone.
I give you my body, that we might be one.
I give you my spirit, until our life is done.

The words were beautiful, and my heart shuddered with all the possibilities of love with this man. The heat in his eyes could fuel the world and it seeped into my bloodstream, feeding this addiction that had formed while I was too busy making other plans.

The moment he slid an expensive diamond wedding band onto my hand, he stole my breath and my heart. To my amazement, my hand didn't shake at all. As if this was what I had waited for my entire life.

As he promised to love, honor, cherish, and protect me for the rest of our lives, his gaze met mine, burning into my skin, and my heart flipped. For being forced into this arrangement, I behaved strangely, fluttery and jittery. Like I was a real blushing bride, and something inside me glowed under the city's warm breeze.

When we stepped back outside, the New York sun shone bright and held promises of a future. I had no idea where the thought came from, but it held steady in my heart.

Liam stepped in front of me and took my chin gently in his grip. The city buzzed around us, but the only thing I was aware of was this larger-than-life man in front of me. Our eyes met and every single cell in my body vibrated with hope and something that had my heart flipping in the most concerning way.

A large shadow came behind me, and Liam lifted his gaze above my head.

"Brennan," a cold, accented voice echoed, and I followed Liam's gaze.

I gasped, recognizing the man. *Alexei Nikolaev.* For a moment, all thoughts left me, and I just stared at him. The man was even scarier in person than in pictures. The scar on his lip made him look menacing, and the abundance of tattoos didn't make it better.

Instinctively, I took a step closer to my husband and Liam's hand wrapped protectively around me. It was the wrong move, because until that moment, his focus was on Liam. Now it was on me. The palest blue eyes I had ever seen reminded me of arctic waters as they locked on me.

"Hello," I choked out. Something flickered in his gaze, and it was that small expression that turned him from completely unapproachable to slightly less frosty. I couldn't tear my gaze away from him, so I kept staring. The man was beautiful in a shit-your-pants kind of way. Though it was his eyes that kept you staring. Like there were ghosts lurking in them, threatening to come out and swallow you whole.

He tilted his head at me, then his eyes returned to Liam. "Brennan. A word."

Liam's eyes darted to Quinn, and without a word, the latter came up to me, his hand ready on the gun.

Jesus Christ, what have I gotten myself into?

CHAPTER 37
Liam

"I don't remember calling you to my wedding," I said dryly.

Alexei's jaw barely flickered, his expression remaining stoic. "She's family."

I'd hoped that neither Nikolaev nor the Ashfords knew about Davina's existence. This was a clear confirmation that they did. And fuck if that didn't piss me off even more. They knew about her and didn't even fucking bother to reach out to her.

My jaw tightened. "She's mine now," I told him. "You didn't bother with her before. Why now?"

He held my gaze. "Davina wasn't ready."

"And how in the fuck would you know?" My voice was dark. "She's a grown-ass woman that knows what she wants."

Alexei didn't move a single muscle. "Did you force her to marry you?"

Ah, there it was.

"What do you want, Nikolaev?" I gritted, ready to reach for my own weapon and shoot the motherfucker if he tried to take my wife from me.

"I want my sister-in-law to be happy." Alexei's voice was apathetic. "It's my wife's wish."

My eyes darted to Davina who stood next to Quinn, her eyes full of worry and fear on the two of us.

"I'll make her happy." It was my vow to her, but if it'd get this motherfucker to stop scaring my wife, I'd vow it to him too. To the whole goddamn world.

"See to it that you do." I shook my head, sardonic amusement filling me. This fucker was something.

"When my wife is with me, watch the other three women," I told him. "I've got her back."

Nikolaev's lips actually tilted up. "Don't worry, the other three women are being watched."

"You're missing the point."

"I get it. You don't want me around your wife."

I worried if Davina found out about her extended family, she'd be even more upset and feel like they didn't want her either. Just like her parents.

"She knows her mom and dad abandoned her," I told him, my eyes darting back to my wife who was now chewing on her lip. "It leaves a mark on a kid. If she learns her brothers and sister knew about her, which they obviously did, and never bothered to reach out, she'll think they didn't want her either."

It was at that very moment I realized I had fallen way too deep for my wife. I wanted to protect her not only from physical harm but also any heartache.

"They want her," Alexei concluded. "They always have."

That was good.

"Then tell them to let Davina decide if she wants them in her life."

It would be up to my wife and nobody else.

CHAPTER 38
Davina

I watched the two men exchange words, and every so often, their attention would come back to me.

It had to be a sign they were discussing me. The question was why. It couldn't be about the heist in Chicago. Those men were Italians, not Russians. Though, if all Russians looked like this dude, we had to seriously reconsider staying away from those men!

"They're not going to kill each other, right?" I asked Quinn, suddenly very worried I'd become a widow after just becoming a bride.

"Don't worry, lass. This is normal." Quinn was feeding me shit, I knew it. "Ah, here he comes."

Both men walked over to us, both dominating the sidewalk. Passengers threw wary glances at them, and I couldn't blame them. They both looked formidable.

"All good?" I asked, my eyes ping-ponging between the two men.

"Yes," Liam assured me, taking my hand.

Alexei Nikolaev just tilted his head. "I look forward to seeing you again, Mrs. Brennan."

A choked laugh escaped me. I wasn't sure seeing him again would mean survival for me. The man looked like a killer, unlike anyone I had ever met before.

"Call me Davina," I said. Why? I had no freaking clue. "Umm, congrats on your recent marriage." A blank look by him, and I mentally slapped my forehead. I swallowed again. "I-I just happened to see it somewhere in the paper," I added, clarifying I wasn't a stalker.

"I'll be in touch, Nikolaev." Liam concluded the meeting, though Alexei didn't remove his eyes from me. So fucking uncomfortable.

Liam urged me to the car that waited for us, and I slid into the back of his Rolls Royce. A sigh left me.

"That went swell," I muttered.

Liam chuckled. "You did great. He's actually a good guy."

"He looks like a killer," I rasped, gaping and wide-eyed.

"Maybe, but he's still a good man." Liam would know, I guess. "Now, let's go celebrate our marriage, wife."

He insisted on making this a fancy affair. I'd rather he didn't make it an affair at all, though deep down, I liked it. Maybe it was that which scared me the most. Liking him way too much.

For some dumb reason, my mood instantly soured. Not because I liked him too much, but because I was certain he didn't like me as much as I liked him.

"What displeases you?" Liam asked.

"You really have to ask?" I bit out, more irritated with myself than him. "I got married to an old ass man without being asked. Not to mention he's a criminal."

It was the only ammunition I had, and I used it shamelessly. I didn't want to fall for this man. Each orgasm he gave me had me spiraling deeper into an abyss. And when he was thoughtful and sweet, I feared I'd go anywhere with him.

Like this morning, when he brought me breakfast in bed. To freaking bed. And then he fed me, claiming he wanted to ensure I kept my curves. The same curves Garrett made fun of.

"You didn't complain about my old ass last night." Liam didn't miss a beat. "If I remember correctly, you begged me for a reprieve." He was right. The man was a beast in bed. I lost count of the orgasms he gave me until I had to beg him to let me rest. "And about the criminal comment, we are two peas in a pod, Davina."

Quinn snickered in the front seat as he started the car.

What. A. Fucking. Asshole.

"How do you like the cake?" Liam asked me as the silence stretched between us at the fancy restaurant, which I just learned he owned. It was just the two of us, the entire restaurant closed to the public so we could enjoy our wedding lunch. Quinn had left once we arrived, leaving the keys with Liam. My husband.

Jesus, Mary, and Joseph.

I got married today. At twenty-one. I burned down a house, robbed the head of the Irish mafia, robbed a casino, and got married. All in less than a month. I'd been busy for sure.

I lifted my gaze to meet Liam's dark blue eyes on me.

"It's delicious." It was true, the cake melted in my mouth. It was the most delicious dessert I had ever eaten. "It will probably go straight to my hips."

His eyes traveled over me, like a warm caress on my skin. "I love your hips," he drawled. "Gives me something to hold on to."

Heat bloomed in my lower belly and I clenched my thighs. God, the words he uttered did things to me. And the way he watched me. His gaze burned like a lit match, consuming me until there was nothing left of me.

He had never said it, but I got a sense this man always demanded everything. He wouldn't be satisfied with just fractions of me. He'd want it all. My every thought, every heartbeat, every breath. Every goddamn thing.

"I have to go back to the dorm," I told him as I stabbed a fork into my cake. It would be easier if my reaction to him was purely physical and fleeting. I'd prefer that to this and the fluttering of my heart. Maybe I should have my chest checked, it could be a sign of a heart attack. *Great, now I'm a doctor and a criminal.* "I have Wynter's car and have to give it back," I said, a bit too harshly, but it was aimed more at myself.

"Absolutely not," Liam objected. "It's our wedding night, and I'm looking forward to being balls deep in my wife."

My cheeks burned and I snuck a glance around us, praying none of his staff heard him.

"Jesus, keep your voice down."

My phone buzzed for the hundredth time today. My group chat with the girls speculated about where both Wynter and I were all night. Interesting that Wynter spent the night out too.

And Garrett sent another few dozen threatening messages. I was hoping he'd eventually get the memo and just move on. Wynter's friend said Garrett's insurance claim was already in process, so he'd be fine.

"Go ahead and answer that," Liam urged. "Tell the girls you'll get back to the dorm tomorrow and fetch them back to the city. I'll have one of my men take the Jeep back to Yale today."

"I don't like this," I muttered. "You're overtaking my life. You can't tell me what to do. I'm a grown woman."

"Thank God for that." He grinned, his gaze turning soft, and I had to remind myself to breathe.

It made him look so much younger. I inhaled deeply, his unique scent had quickly become intimately familiar.

He trailed his gaze down my body and his eyes darkened. Just like they did every time he wanted me. A bottomless blue ocean. *Mesmerizing*. The way he watched me with blazing desire made me hotter than fire.

I rolled my eyes, hiding the impact he had on me. Just the way he looked at me overwhelmed all my senses.

"How am I supposed to *fetch* them?" I breathed.

"I bought you a car," he explained. "It's my wedding present to you."

My eyes widened in shock. He got me a wedding present? I opened my mouth, then closed it and opened it again.

"That's not what I meant," I explained. "I mean how do I convince them to come to your city house?" Then I realized how rude I was and quickly added, "Thank you for the wedding present, but that's not necessary. I'll buy my own car when it's time."

My Honda was a goner. Not worth saving that hunk of metal.

"No, you'll take the car I got you or take one of mine in the garage." God, he was really too much. "I'll arrange for you three to receive a letter stating you have to vacate the dorm immediately. I'll send a note to Juliette to use the city house."

"How manipulative," I noted snarkily. Truthfully, I liked the way he took charge of seemingly every situation. But it scared me to show him how much I liked him taking care of me when there was always the possibility I could lose him.

As a kid that grew up without parents, I loved protection and attention. I didn't particularly like that quality in myself, but it was ingrained in me. My grandfather was the only family I'd ever had and who always put me above himself.

"I keep my family safe," he replied, unperturbed by my snarkiness. It was as if he'd read my thoughts. "At all costs. And you are mine now too."

Then he stood up, extending his hand.

"Let's go home," he murmured softly.

It was then that I realized I was already a goner for this man. Because as I put my hand in his, a startling realization settled in the pit of my stomach.

Anywhere he'd go, I'd follow. Anywhere he'd be would feel like home.

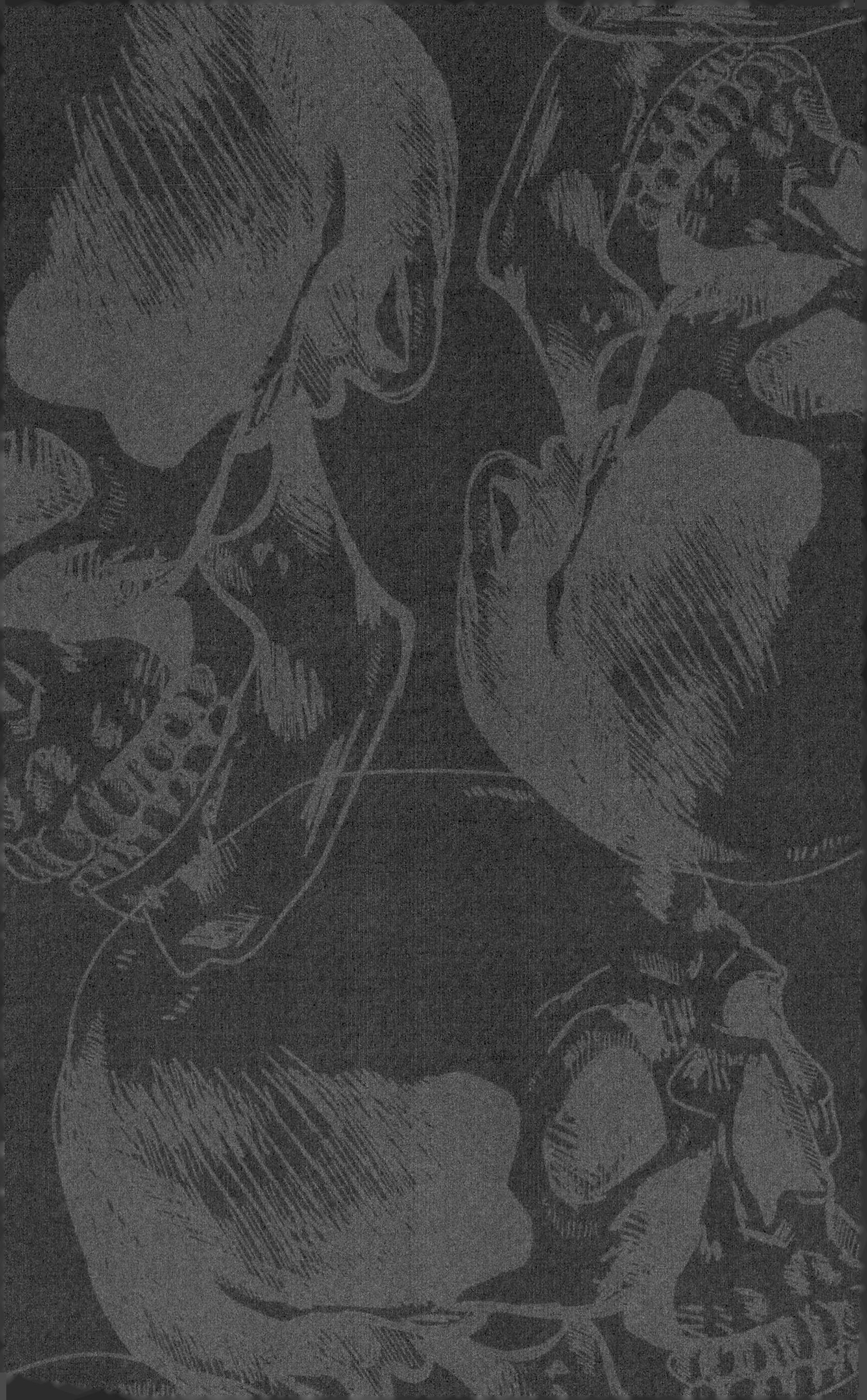

CHAPTER 39
Davina

The moment we entered his penthouse, I slipped off my heels and sighed in relief.

Liam headed for the minibar. He was dressed in a black three-piece-suit, and I had to admit, being the first time I'd seen him in a suit, he looked handsome. Now I couldn't decide whether I liked him in a suit or jeans better. The man was smoking hot.

From my spot at the doorway, I leaned against the door and watched him twist the top off a bottle of Cognac Brugerolle. Another bottle that cost over one hundred and fifty thousand dollars.

"Jesus," I muttered. "How much money do you spend on cognac?"

He turned around and raised the bottle with his one hand, while he held two glasses in his other.

"My most expensive cognac," he announced. "Today is the perfect day to open it."

"Are you sure?" I asked. "That bottle is worth one hundred and fifty grand."

A smile pulled on his lips. "How is it that you know so much about brands of alcohol?"

I shrugged. "My grandpa owned a liquor store." He didn't seem surprised. "But you knew that already."

"He taught you brands of alcohol?"

"Sometimes when I'd help him out in the store after hours." The truth was that my grandfather should have retired a long time ago, but he kept working so he could support me. "He was too old to keep working, and I liked to help him and be around him as much as I could."

"What do you know about your parents?" he asked.

I had a feeling Liam might already know my story, and somehow, I resented it. I didn't like anyone knowing my parents abandoned me. It always made me feel unworthy. Inadequate. Even before I learned how to talk, they found me unworthy to stick around for.

"It was just my grandfather and me," I told him quietly. "I know my mother's name and absolutely nothing about my father."

I refused to lower my eyes. My brain knew it wasn't my fault, but emotionally, it was hard not to look for a deficiency in myself.

"It's their loss," he said, his eyes seeing too much of what I'd hidden for so long that it became a part of me.

"Your mother or father didn't abandon you," I retorted, and to my horror, my voice sounded slightly bitter.

"They didn't," he agreed. "But my mother fell ill when I was very young, so I barely remember her. And my father was very absent for a long time after losing the love of his life. He wasn't much of a father to my sister and me once my stepmother died. So I was left to care for my much younger sister."

"I'm sorry," I muttered. I couldn't even imagine loving someone so much that you couldn't continue living without them. Not even for the sake of your children.

I shifted, eyeing the windows. It was better to stare outside, no matter how scared I was, than into his eyes, letting him see the insecurities that had always plagued me when it came to my parents.

He returned to the task at hand and placed two glasses onto the bar table, then poured cognac into them. He strode to me and handed me a glass.

"I'll put something on these windows," he mused. "I can't have my wife lingering in the doorway."

His wife. It still struck me as surreal. I'd jumped on a speeding train and there was no safe way to jump off anymore. Not that I wanted to, which was even scarier.

I reached for the glass and took a sip of my cognac. His gaze tracked my every movement, locking on my mouth as I licked a drop of the liquor off my bottom lip.

"How come you've never been married before?" I asked bravely.

"I got myself a curious wife, I see." He chuckled, amusement coloring his voice.

A tense yet almost comfortable silence filled the room. It was deceitful, because I could practically sense secrets dancing around us in the air.

"I never wanted to get married because I saw firsthand the way it destroys lives." His admission sent shock waves through my body. I wasn't even sure why.

"What do you mean?" I whispered.

"I didn't believe in getting married just to get married, but I also saw how much it changed my father and my sister. So, I never bothered with it," he explained. "And truthfully, no woman really made me want to take that step."

I frowned, confused. "So why now?"

"From the moment I laid eyes on you, Davina, my cock stirred to life. Yes, it was physical, but it's really more than that. Obsession, passion, admiration, fixation, affection. Call it what you will, but I'm keeping you. Life keeps throwing you my way because you belong to me. I want all of you. Forever you and me. Every day for the rest of our lives."

I stilled at his admission. His voice was so full of reverence that my chest grew twice its size with feelings I refused to acknowledge, and a flutter of butterflies danced in my lower belly.

"We barely know each other," I rasped, voicing my worries. My heart knew it was too late, but my brain refused to fall in line. It insisted on reason and barriers so I wouldn't be discarded by another person in my life.

"Davina, you can trust me." The statement was unexpected. As if he read me like an open book, the timing of it was frightening. Sex was one thing, giving up your heart and trusting someone to handle it gently was entirely another.

The only man I had ever fully trusted was my grandfather. Even with the girls, I could never quite bring myself to reveal certain things. And I trusted them, I really did. They had been there for me over the last four years, and I'd been there for them. We did some fun stuff and some dumb things.

"Okay." It wasn't until I voiced my agreement that I realized, to my shock, that I *wanted* to trust him. My grandfather had told me so many times that one day I'd find what he had with my grandmother, but I'd never believed it.

Nevertheless, right now, every fiber of me wanted to rely on Liam and his strength. Except, my secrets weren't only mine to reveal now. They protected my friends too.

"How would you feel if we moved your grandfather?"

I blinked. Then blinked again.

"What do you mean?" I questioned him, confused.

"We're married now," he explained. "We could move your grandfather to a private facility closer to us."

Was he saying what I thought he was?

"Y-you mean here in New York?" I asked, holding my breath.

"Yes."

There was nothing I would like more, but the prices here were exorbitant, and I'd never be able to afford it.

"Assisted-living homes are too expensive here," I told him, resigned.

"I'll pay for it."

"It's way too much," I protested, though my heart wasn't in it.

"No, it's not," he objected. "We can afford it."

"We?" I whispered.

"Yes, Davina. We." He took a sip of his drink. "You're my wife now. And my responsibility. We'll ensure your grandfather is close to us so you can visit him anytime you want."

"But—"

"My money is yours, Davina."

I snickered softly. "Oh, in that case," I teased. "Hand over the checkbook. I'll move all the money into my account."

He didn't miss a beat. "Your money is mine, and my money is yours. It doesn't matter what account it's in."

I chuckled. "I bet people going through a divorce would disagree." Our eyes locked. Liam was dead serious. "It's just so much money," I muttered seriously.

He ran a hand across his jaw. "I'm doing this for a selfish reason, wife. I don't want you traveling to Texas to visit him, and I certainly can't be such a bastard to forbid you from visiting him. I have a list of the best facilities, and you can decide which one is the best for him."

A smile pulled on his lips and my insides melted while tears pricked the back of my eyes.

"Thank you," I choked out.

This man, who barely knew me and had never met my grandfather, cared about my grandfather's well-being like it was the most natural thing in the world. Regardless of if he was doing it for me or himself, something warm spread through my chest, feelings blooming like the first spring flowers.

It both terrified me and thrilled me at the same time.

I placed the glass on the table and closed the space between us. Reaching out to him, my fingers gripped the end of his tie. God, he was like a furnace on a cold winter day.

Rising to my tiptoes, I reached for his mouth.

"This means so much to me," I murmured against his lips, my voice shaking. My grandfather was the most important person in my life. My girlfriends were important to me too, but my grandfather had been there for me my entire life. I wanted to repay him for all of his sacrifices. If it weren't for him, who knew where I'd have ended up.

I pressed my lips to Liam's strong jawline, his scruff rough under my lips. Kissing a line down his throat, I ran my tongue up his neck, tasting his pulse. He set his glass down, grabbed the back of my neck, and took my mouth for a deep kiss.

Somehow it didn't surprise me that he wasn't gentle. He liked dominating, possessive, and hard. And apparently so did I.

The taste of him made me drunk. Dizzy with desire and something else I didn't care to evaluate.

"Bedroom?" I breathed against his lips.

"Fuck," he groaned, then grabbed my hips and lifted me. My legs wrapped around his waist as his mouth consumed me. He kissed like he was starved for me, just as I was for him.

He walked us to his bedroom, never breaking the kiss. He kissed me like I was all he ever wanted, like he would eat me alive. His kiss was controlling, consuming, and everything that made my thighs clench with need and burning desire.

Once in the bedroom, I slid off his body. Every single light in the penthouse was on, like he wanted to ensure he could devour every inch of me. He trailed his mouth down my neck, nipping my skin, marking it as his.

He yanked on my dress, and a rip sounded as it slid off my body. He pulled down my bra, then bent his head to suck my breasts. My hands buried in his hair, and I sighed as he bit my nipple gently.

"P-please," I breathed as his hands gripped my ass. A lungful of air escaped me as he bit the sensitive skin on my left breast. "I want to see you naked. Please."

I had yet to touch all of him while he was naked, and like a greedy wife, I demanded to see him. I'd enjoy all this for as long as it lasted. I'd give him everything, because he was giving me everything.

He straightened and our eyes locked. The only sound in the bedroom was our heavy breaths and the thundering of my own heart.

He took a step backward, and as I watched him remove his clothing, my mouth watered. The orgasms he had given me last night had me quivering with anticipation.

I admired his strong body. I called him an old man, but his body was that of a thirty-year-old that spent a lot of time in the gym. His chest was sculpted and broad, and my fingers itched with the need to explore him. Every single inch of him.

His pants followed, leaving him only in his briefs, and the outline of his cock mesmerized me. A loud gulp sounded in the room. I wanted to taste him, let him deepthroat me. For the first time in my life, I was willing to get down on my knees and offer a blowjob.

"Your eyes," he murmured, and I lifted my head to meet his gaze. "They become darker when you're turned on."

"Must be all the time when I'm around you then." The words slipped out before I thought better of it.

CORRUPTED PLEASURE

He didn't seem to mind though because his deep chuckle followed. His chest rose and fell rapidly, his eyes greedy on me. *Good*, I thought smugly. I wanted him to crave me as much as I craved him.

He kicked off his briefs and my eyes widened. Liam was *very* well-equipped. Definitely bigger than an average man, but then there was nothing average about this man in front of me.

"Want my cock in your mouth?" I shuddered with anticipation at his question.

I lowered to my knees slowly, my eyes locked on his gaze. The muscle in his jaw ticked, as if he was hanging by a thread, reining in his control. I wanted him to lose it.

I slid my hands up his thighs and opened my mouth, my gaze never breaking our eye contact. He put his hand on my head and thrust inside, the warm salty taste of him delicious. I shuddered with delight as he glided across my tongue.

I was getting drunk off the taste of him.

My eyes fluttered shut, but he snapped, "Eyes on me, my céile."

I blinked my confusion, and he translated, "My *wife*." I grew hotter. The way he uttered those words sounded possessive, endearing, worshiping. "Now suck me off."

My clit pulsed, every fiber of my being completely turned on by his dominance. I held his gaze and held on to his thick, strong thighs as he thrust in and out of my mouth.

"So fucking beautiful," he praised. "Let me all the way in." I relaxed my jaw and throat, and Liam thrust deeper until I gagged. "So perfect," he purred.

I moaned and my nails dug into his thighs. I let him deep throat me, gagging on his length.

Yet, I had never felt more powerful. His eyes grew dark and hazy, and heat bloomed in my stomach then moved lower. My pussy throbbed with the need to feel him inside me, and I squeezed my thighs together to ease the ache. This was for him, to see him unravel just as he unraveled me.

He grasped my face between his two rough palms, gently caressing my cheek with a thumb.

"That's right, wife," he said. "Take every inch of me."

God, I had no idea it was possible to fall for someone so quickly. The startling revelation hit while I was on my knees, giving him a blowjob. Yet, the expression on his face, the way he was coming undone because of me, was the best kind of aphrodisiac. He was teetering on the edge of control, and I had the power to take him over.

I relaxed and breathed through my nose, taking him deeper. He pushed, then stilled. I swallowed and he slipped in deeper. His hips pumped him all the way into my throat while he held my head. He murmured soft words I couldn't recognize, but I thought maybe they were Gaelic. He drew back, I took a breath, and he pushed back in.

He swelled in my mouth and I sucked him, my tongue swirling around his shaft, and I could feel him pulse. His groan rumbled from low in his throat, turning hoarse, as he came down the back of my throat. I swallowed his cum and licked my lips, my skin growing hot under his stare.

He pulled out of my mouth with a soft pop, our eyes locked as he ran a thumb across my bottom lip. I was in heaven, the taste of him still in my mouth.

"So gorgeous," he breathed. "My wife can obey when she wants to, huh?"

CHAPTER 40
Liam

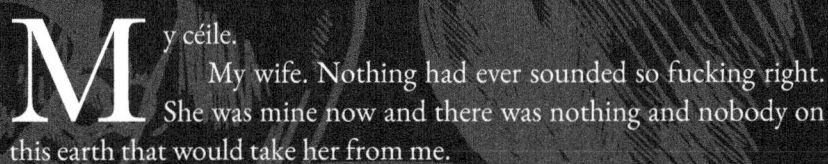

My céile. My wife. Nothing had ever sounded so fucking right. She was mine now and there was nothing and nobody on this earth that would take her from me.

I swept my thumb over her luscious lips curved into a triumphant smile. She was smugly satisfied with herself, still on her knees. And she had every right to be. I had never come so hard in my whole goddamn life.

Heavens, she was perfect. She had the most beautiful, luscious body, with generous curves. And the lust and hunger lurking in her eyes matched my own.

"You'll be the death of me," I muttered more to myself. I was too old for her, but fuck if I cared. She was mine, and anyone that dared to touch her would find a painful end.

"I'm sorry." She bit her bottom lip, lust lingering in her stunning eyes. She didn't look sorry at all.

"I don't think you are."

A smile spread across her face and she tilted her head, as if contemplating the way she wanted this thing between us to go. As if there was a choice. There was only one way it could go.

"You know, I think you're right." She lifted her chin a few inches, showing me her little flare of defiance that I'd come to know so well. "I'm not sorry. Maybe you ought to spank me and make me sorry."

Little minx.

"Do not tempt me, céile," I warned in a low, dark voice. Her cheeks flushed and her eyes lowered to the floor. I grasped her chin between my fingers, forcing her to hold my stare. "You're playing with fire."

Something flashed in her eyes, but it was gone so fast, I couldn't quite hone in on it.

"Then spank me," she whispered huskily, a visible shudder traveling down her beautiful body. "I dare you." The challenge coloring her voice and shining in her eyes.

"I shouldn't give it to you because you want it," I drawled, even though there was no chance in hell I wouldn't give her pleasure. I wanted to see her body burn with anticipation, her cheeks flush crimson, as well as her ass.

"It makes no difference to me."

I traced her soft skin with my fingers, the curve of her neck and collarbone. I laughed gruffly. "I bet it makes a difference, céile. I'd bet all the money you stole you're already soaking wet."

She refused to look away or comment. She was the perfect mixture of stubbornness and submission.

It was like this woman complemented all my darker desires with perfection. I thrived on control, and my young wife found ways to shatter it with every look she gave me. Every word she uttered.

"We need a safe word," I finally concluded.

Surprise flashed in her eyes and her mouth parted with shock. She must have not thought I'd follow through. My wife had yet to learn I thrived on challenges.

"Scared?" I teased her softly.

She shook her head, her silky black hair bouncing with her every movement.

"Give me a safe word, my céile," I demanded.

Her delicate neck bobbed as she swallowed, and images of her sucking me off mere minutes ago had me instantly hard. I watched her like a sinner waiting for his absolution as she pondered through God knew what word choices.

Her eyes met mine and her fingers tightened in her lap. Just as I thought she'd back out, her soft voice came through.

"Cognac."

My mouth twisted with amusement. "Very appropriate."

"I thought so too," she agreed, smiling. I reached for my tie that laid discarded on the floor. She traced my every move with her hooded eyes.

"Stand up," I ordered her. She scrambled to obey, her movements too eager. My lips curved into a sinful smile. Davina wasn't a woman to follow orders. It spoke volumes about how much she wanted this. Probably as much as I did.

Excitement practically vibrated from her every pore, her chest rising and falling with each breath. My eyes roamed around until I found the belt. I grabbed it and smacked it against my palm, testing the strength and weight of the sting.

Her sharp inhale filled the room. "Want to stop, wife?" I asked her in a soft tone.

Her dark stormy gaze met mine and she swallowed.

"Fat chance," she muttered breathlessly. "You scared?" God, that mouth of hers would get her into trouble one day. Part of me was too eager to use the belt on her tender, untried ass, and then reward her. Her courage fucking pleased me immensely.

She was excited, maybe even more than I was. The scent of her arousal fragranced our bedroom. Her full breasts rose with each breath. Her hardened nipples tempted me.

"Bend over the bed," I ordered in a growl.

She followed the demand, her ass on full display and tempting me. I had a feeling my young wife would obey me in the bedroom, and only in the bedroom. It was fine though, because if I'd wanted a doormat, I would have married a long time ago.

"I'm about to ruin your pussy and your ass," I growled, palming her ass with my free hand. I couldn't resist tracing my fingers in between her thighs and gliding them over her slick folds.

She wiggled into my hand, a soft muffled moan traveling through the air. I brushed her hair to the side and my lips found her ear. Her scent was intoxicating. I'd never need alcohol or drugs, her scent would be enough to ease me down. I knew it deep down in my black Irish heart.

Maybe I had something in common with my father after all. Didn't he say the moment he spotted Aisling's mother, all his senses could only be eased by that woman? He couldn't walk away. It physically pained him.

"Promises, promises," she whispered, attempting to taunt, but her voice was too hoarse.

I slapped her ass playfully, then straightened and reached next to me to grab my phone.

"Oh my wife, I promise and deliver," I told her as I opened the camera and turned it to video.

She looked at me over her shoulder, her dark hair in such a contrast to her ivory skin.

"Are you going to record us?" she asked, her eyes darting to my phone that I propped against the nightstand.

"I am." She didn't argue, and for that alone, I would reward her. God, I couldn't wait to feel her clench around me. But I'd take it slow. We had all the time in the world. So, I admired her naked body, tormenting myself with the beautiful sight.

Returning to her, I trailed my hand down her graceful back, then slid my hand over her round ass and reached between her thighs.

"Your body is burning with anticipation," I purred with satisfaction. "For your punishment. To feel my cock inside your tight cunt. To feel my cum leak down your thighs."

"Fuck," she moaned as my finger slid between her folds and she eagerly rocked her hips against it.

I retracted my fingers. "Not so fast."

A frustrated noise left her throat. "Don't be an ass," she complained, turning her head to glare at me. "Just give it to me."

I chuckled darkly. She was greedy. It pleased me immensely because I'd be a greedy motherfucker when it came to her. I'd own her every hole, her every thought, her every smile.

"Face down on the comforter and ass up," I ordered her, slapping her ass gently.

She moved forward and got into the position, wiggling her ass and tempting me. Holy fuck, that ass was magnificent.

"Hands behind your back." She obeyed without hesitation, her curiosity pushing her forward. My hand at the small of her back, I looped my silk tie around her wrists a few times, then tied it off in a loose knot.

I felt her tense when I picked up the belt, peeking over her shoulder.

"Remember the safe word?" I asked, leaning over her back and placing a small kiss on her creamy shoulder.

"Cognac," she murmured, her face still turned and her eyes watching me. I couldn't resist her mouth. I brushed my lips against hers and I licked them, nibbling on her plump lower lip, reveling in her shudders.

She moaned, and I took advantage of it, thrusting my tongue into her mouth. She tilted her head back, my cock pushing against the sweet curve of her ass. Our tongues hungry, I ravished her mouth, my teeth biting her and swallowing her whimpers. This woman, my wife, didn't seem to mind the pain with the pleasure. In fact, she thrived on it, just as I did.

At this point, I was painfully hard. And she had just sucked me off. Before I lost my head, I pulled away.

"That's right, baby. Cognac."

I shifted slightly away and stroked the strap of the belt along the curve of her bottom, teasing her with the possibilities.

"Relax," I instructed softly. "You're in control."

I wrapped the strap around her upper thighs and buckled the belt, having it secured so she couldn't move her legs apart. I heard her sharp inhale of surprise. It wasn't what she'd been expecting.

With both her arms and legs bound, it seemed I had all the control. But it was important to me that she knew she was in control of this.

"Remember, you're in control," I purred as I glided my free hand down the slope of her spine and my other hand caressed her ass. I sensed her relaxing with each second, pushing into my touch. She was pure perfection.

Her body was soft and yielding, craving dominance. Just waiting for it.

Smack.

She gasped in shock, and I soothed her pain with the caress of my palm. Then as I sensed her relaxing it into my hand, I slapped her other ass cheek. The savage need for her twisted in the base of my spine.

"Count, céile."

Her body ground against the sheets, and it was erotic as fuck. She wanted to get off, but there'd be none of that. Only I would get her off. Not her toys, not her hands, not my fucking sheets.

I lifted my hand and put a bit more force behind my next spank on her ass.

Smack.

Her scream vibrated against the bedroom walls. "Count," I ordered.

"One." Her voice was too throaty. I fucking liked it.

I repeated it again, my greedy wife pushing her ass into my hands.

"Fuck," she groaned, the scent of her arousal all around me. I chuckled darkly, but before I got to correct her, she rasped, "Two."

I traced my fingers down the crack of her ass and all the way down between her legs. Pushing my fingers between her thighs, her arousal drenched my fingers. This woman was an addiction I never saw coming. From her first words to me, she had slowly and continuously flowed into my bloodstream.

Another smack on her plump ass. Goddamnit, I wanted to bite that ass.

"Three," she breathed.

Smack.

"Four." A needy sound slipped from her mouth. And then, as if she couldn't hold off anymore, she glanced over her shoulder, her eyes hazy with lust.

"Please, Liam. I need you," she begged. I was hard as steel and couldn't wait to bury myself in her. Her thighs clenched as she attempted to rub her legs together and a frustrated whimper slipped through her lips at being constricted.

A low, possessive growl escaped me as I pushed two fingers through her clenching thighs and deep into her entrance. She trembled, her body pushing against me.

CORRUPTED PLEASURE

"You'll scream my name," I rasped as I wedged my fingers deeper into her, hitting her sweet spot.

Her moans and whimpers were an aphrodisiac to my ears. I wanted so much from her. Her everything. My other hand curled around her slim throat.

"Yes, yes, yes," she cried out, pushing her ass against me. "Liam, please. Give it to me."

I begrudgingly released her throat and slapped her ass. "I say when you get it."

She whimpered. "O-okay."

Her insides clenched around my fingers, and fuck, I wanted to feel her pussy squeeze my cock. Her juices coated my fingers and dripped down her thighs. I curled my fingers inside her pussy, exploring and stroking her swollen flesh.

Her moans increased in volume, her walls clenched around my fingers, and her body rocked against me. She was on the verge of climaxing, her slickness trickling down my fingers. She continued pushing against them, grinding against them.

"So fucking beautiful," I praised, then spanked her ass again.

"Fuck," she cried out. "Please."

She squirmed under my touch. I kneaded her red butt cheeks, then as if I couldn't stay away from her pussy, my hands gripped low on her ass. My fingers slid down to her clit, teasing her and then smearing her wetness around her asshole.

"Has anyone fucked you here?" I asked her, pushing one finger into her ass. She writhed against the sheets, her pleas muffled, her body begging for me.

"N-no," she breathed, her voice hoarse. She was so delicate to my roughness, it had the hairs at the back of my neck standing on end. A good man wouldn't corrupt her, but I'd never claimed to be a good man.

"My ass," I grunted, pulling my finger out and smacking her ass one last time. I didn't have enough control to take it slow today. In one swift move, I loosened the belt and spread her thighs wide open, her juices dripping down her inner thigh. "Say it's my ass."

"Yours," she panted, her wrists still locked at the small of her back.

My hand grabbed her nape as I thrust into her tight pussy in one ruthless move.

Fuck.

Her scream shattered the air. "Liam."

I pulled out of her tight pussy, then drove in harder and deeper this time.

"Fuck," I grunted. She was heaven on Earth. My fingers tightened on the nape of her neck, gripping her silky strands, and I thrust in and out of her with speed and obsession. The sloppy sounds of flesh against flesh, her wet arousal, and her loud moans reverberated around us.

I wanted to be inside her forever. Die this way. I'd always liked it rough, but this was so much more. So different. Raw. Consuming. Primal and wild.

"Don't you fucking stop," she screamed.

I pounded into her faster and harder, her body slid against the bed, her ebony hair covering her face, and I had to see it. See her as she orgasmed.

Pushing her hair out of her face, I rasped, "Turn your face."

She did it without question, her lustful stormy eyes connecting with mine.

One of my hands wrapped around her waist, my thrusts wild and hard.

"You belong to me." I picked up my pace, ramming into her fast.

"Fuck," she cursed, her walls tightening around me. "Fuck... please, Liam... oh, I need... please..."

A maddening possessiveness spread through my veins, each thrust into her tight cunt taking me spiraling out of control. I hit deeper inside her and that made her screams turn high-pitched.

"Yes... yes... Liam, please..."

I felt her clenching tighter so I rolled my hips, driving deeper and harder into her until I felt her shattering around my cock.

"Liam!" she screamed, chanting unrecognizable words over and over again as she came undone. My pace turned frantic as I fucked her through her orgasm. She clamped around me, milking me and pushing me over the edge. My cum spilled inside her with such sheer force, I thought I'd died and gone to heaven.

I covered her body with mine, her wrists still bound behind her. I had lost my goddamn mind. I fucked her as if I wanted to consume every living fiber of her and claim it for my own. I slowly pulled out of her, then unbound her wrists. My gaze locked on my cum dripping out of her pussy, smearing her inner thighs.

Dark obsession unlike any I had ever felt before bulldozed to the forefront of my mind and sunk deep into my bones.

I wanted to brand her, see her swell with my babies, and bind her to me forever.

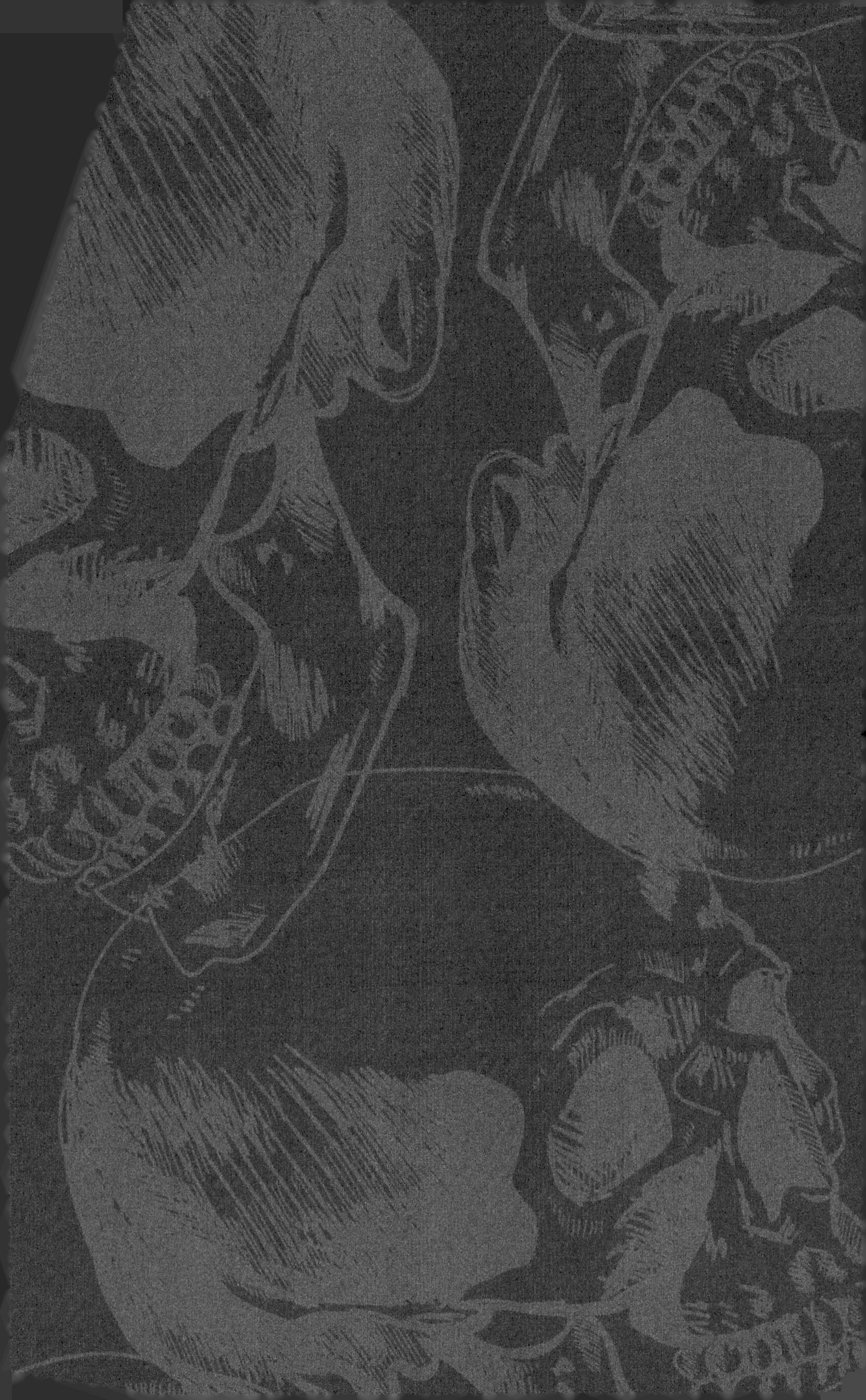

CHAPTER 41
Davina

"This is good," I told Liam's driver. He didn't stop. "Hey, I said this is good. Just stop here."

My new husband insisted I be driven back to Yale. Truthfully, I was certain he hoped that somehow the girls would figure out that I was sleeping with him. And his driver bringing me back to campus was a sure way to be caught.

I pulled on the handle of the door, regardless of the fact that the driver hadn't stopped.

"Mr. Brennan insisted I drive you to the door," he complained.

"Well, you can watch me walk to the door," I protested. "Either stop, or I'm jumping out of the car."

I barely tugged on the handle when he slammed on the brakes, and good thing I had a seatbelt on, otherwise my face would be smashed against the dashboard. I glared at the head full of red hair next to me. Liam said he was his driver, but he looked more like his killer.

Fucker.

We'd rob him next if he didn't start driving better.

"Far enough, lass?" he snapped. I opened the door and flipped him a bird.

"Actually, no," I told him. "You in New Jersey would be far enough."

I slammed the door of his fancy, expensive car and rushed away from him before he decided to run me over. Or worse, follow me into the dorm.

I wasn't ready to tell the girls I fucked up big time during our first robbery and then slept with Juliette's father. Oh, but that wasn't all. I married him too.

Jesus Christ!

Talk about a freight train coming at you a hundred miles an hour. But that sex last night... Shit, if he would have asked me to marry him again while he fucked me, I totally would have screamed my acceptance of his proposal.

It's more than that, my heart whispered. I exhaled and ignored it, then continued walking. Awareness pricked at the side of my cheek and I turned my head to the right. It was all empty. I swore someone was watching me, and it wasn't the crazy red-headed driver still sitting in his car.

But no matter where I looked, there was nobody there.

Shaking off the obvious paranoia, I continued toward the building. At the entrance, I glanced over my shoulder and the driver was still there. I swatted my hand in the air, shooing him away. I didn't need a nanny to walk me to the door.

Slamming the door behind me, I rushed up the stairs. The hallways were emptier than usual, many students having already returned to their homes or on to whatever jobs they had found.

Unlike the four of us, most students found regular jobs.

The moment I entered the little dorm room, three pairs of eyes turned my way.

"Fucking finally," Juliette exclaimed. "Where in the fucking hell have you been?"

"Out," I muttered.

"For two fucking days?" she screeched. God, she behaved like she was my mother, not my friend. It was kind of comical.

"Yes."

"Was Wynter with you?" Ivy snapped, narrowing her eyes on me.

Dropping my purse onto the table, I threw myself onto the little couch where Wynter already sat, her face hidden behind the book.

"Hmmm." I didn't want to rat her out if she used me for an excuse while she was out. Admittedly, I was also curious to know where she was. It wasn't like her to go out and stay out. Not with her regimented training schedule.

Wynter peeked my way from the corner of her book and rolled her eyes, though she had a big smile on her lips.

"This is bullshit," Ivy and Juliette announced at the same time. Something was definitely up Juliette's and Ivy's asses.

"Suddenly you and Wynter are roaming the streets at night with God knows who, while Ivy and I are trying to figure out the next place to steal from." Juliette was serious too. She pulled Wynter's book down so she could see her face. "That's not fair, we can't do all the damn work."

Jesus, I had never seen Juliette or Ivy so determined. If they applied half of that passion to our business once it kicked off, we'd be golden. Though, I suspected it might be the adrenaline rush of the criminal life that appealed to them.

"I already have a place to rob," Wynter announced, placing her physics book in her lap while our heads whipped to her.

"How?" Ivy asked her suspiciously. "You've been gone for two nights."

God, I just got home and we were already planning a new heist.

Ivy's eyes ping-ponged between Wynter and me.

"Both of you have been gone for two nights," Ivy said suspiciously. "Did you go scouting for places we could rob?" Ivy continued, almost sounding disappointed we went without her.

"Without us?" Juliette added accusingly.

Wynter and I shared a look. As a rule of thumb, we didn't lie to each other. None of us. Except, ever since I was caught by Liam, I had withheld information. It seemed Wynter held some secrets too.

"No, we didn't go together," Wynter mumbled her admission, as if she was disappointed she had to tell the truth. "I just happened to be there."

"Just happened to be there," Juliette repeated, blinking as if trying to process the words.

"Probably her date," Ivy mused mischievously. "If spending days with a man can be considered a date. Did you sleep with your three-piece-suit guy?"

Wynter flipped her off, her cheeks turning pink. Her sundress left her chest exposed and gave us all a view of the blush on it as well. Juliette and Ivy giggled, eager for the details.

As wrong as it was, I was glad they had zeroed in on her rather than me. And the horrible friend that I was, I didn't attempt to rescue her. Because really, the details that happened between Juliette's father and me were non-disclosable. X-rated and all that.

"Was he good?" Juliette asked, grinning widely, the criminal activity temporarily forgotten. "I bet he fucked you six ways to Sunday."

Her eyes lowered to the book in her lap and she bit her lip. Wynter's fair skin turned crimson and her blonde curls couldn't hide it. Whatever happened, there was one thing for sure. Wynter had a wild night, possibly two, with her mysterious stranger.

"Do you want to hear about this place or not?" Wynter snapped. "Because it's a really good one, and we could probably get millions out of them."

But Ivy was focused on getting the details out of Wynter's sexual encounter.

"You're not going to share?" Ivy asked, disappointed.

"Fuck no," Wynter retorted dryly.

I wasn't surprised to hear her push back on Ivy, but it worried me. She was never the secretive type, and when it came to this guy, she was keeping it all in. I wasn't much better, but I had more experience with boys than her. Wynter had kept it all platonic in her past, partially because she was too busy, but I thought she also didn't want to take a chance at heartache.

"At least tell us whether he was good. Was his cock big? Did he split you in half?" Ivy complained.

"Ivy," Wynter scolded.

"What?" She fluttered her eyes innocently. "I need details. How did it feel as he thrust into your—"

"Ivy!" Wynter exclaimed, horrified.

"Did he eat your pussy?" Juliette asked curiously. "Fuck your ass? Did you suck him off? Tell us *something*, for Pete's sake!"

"Both of you just shut up," Wynter breathed out, her face flaming hot. I watched her, mesmerized, her big green eyes glaring at us. I'd seen Wynter run ten miles *and* speed skate, and she had never been this red.

"At least tell us who he is," Juliette tried to reason with her. "Give us his name so if he upsets you, we know who to kill."

Wynter sighed heavily. "I can't tell you details about it. If it gets back to Uncle Liam, I don't want you in trouble. It's best if you don't know."

Alarm shot through me and the three of us stared at our best friend, momentarily dumbstruck.

"Are you in trouble?" Juliette asked, concern lacing her voice as her brows furrowed.

"We can help you, Wyn," I offered. "Just tell us what we need to do."

"I'm not in trouble." It didn't sound convincing. "It's just..." Her voice trailed off and she looked out the window, lost in thought. "It's just that Mom and Uncle wouldn't approve."

"Of the three-piece suit?" Ivy asked. "They might. He seems rather charming." Ivy's eyes darted to all of us, encouraging us to chime in.

"Yeah, he definitely seems charming from afar," Juliette added, though I wasn't sure if it was helpful.

Wynter let out another heavy sigh. "It won't matter," she muttered. "My mom would never approve."

"She will," Juliette argued. "I know she always demands all your attention be focused on ice skating, but that's not feasible. Your whole life has always been just ice skating. There should be a balance, and she knows that. She freaking had you when she was your age!"

"You can still do both," I chimed in. "You can ice skate and have a relationship."

Wynter forced a smile on. "Yeah, I'm probably thinking too much into it," she mumbled. "I just know how much she dislikes the East Coast and Uncle's world full of criminal activities." She pushed her hand through her curls and tried to ease the tension in her shoulders.

"Do you ever feel like you're missing parts of the story?" Juliette asked out of nowhere.

All our eyes snapped to her, and for several heartbeats, none of us moved or said a word.

"I do," I admitted. "The story about my parents. I feel like I'm missing all of it. There had to be a reason they didn't want me. And I think Grandpa is keeping it from me to spare me the pain."

"Same," Juliette muttered. "I'm not even sure who I am anymore. Brennan, Cullen... or what?"

"You are Juliette," I told her. "I don't care what last name you carry. You're my friend regardless."

"Agreed," Ivy announced. "This is the reason we need to build this school. So other kids like us always have somewhere to go and ask questions. The four of us are sitting here clueless, and obviously there are things in our lives that we should know."

"Yet we don't," Wynter muttered. "I get a sense that everyone but us knows it. Even worse, we're left defenseless. We don't know how to fight, how to hack. We are thieves... barely. It makes it even worse that we *are* actually members of criminal families, yet we're still clueless as fuck."

"You're right," Juliette agreed. "It's sad, really. We're part of some of the most powerful criminal families in the world and we're totally in the dark. It makes us vulnerable."

"Agreed," all three of us murmured.

"By the way, I overheard that the Eastside Club was turned over to the Italians," I mumbled and my cheeks grew hot. I had never been good at lying.

A round of gasps. "What? Are you sure?"

I nodded.

"Why?"

I shrugged.

"That's odd," Juliette grumbled. "I thought it was my dad's most cherished club."

"Who in the hell knows how those men think?" Ivy muttered.

"Okay, let's get back to our next heist," Wynter announced.

I turned to Wynter before we switched subjects completely. "You'll

CORRUPTED PLEASURE

tell us if you need us, right?" Wynter threw me a grateful look and nodded her head. "Now tell us about this potential location."

Her face lit up in relief at the change of topic and she smiled. It was that expression that always had the audience captivated. Usually, I only saw it when she was on the ice. I'd recorded her plenty of times to have seen it. But now, I'd seen it two or three times in the same week and only when she was around her mysterious stranger. I had a feeling that Wynter had it bad for this guy.

"It's a casino in Philadelphia," she announced in a low voice. "An armored truck collects all the cash from the casino every Saturday night. If we hijack the truck, we might have enough to get us going on the business."

I blinked. Confusion on Juliette's and Ivy's faces told me they weren't expecting it either.

"Hijack?" Juliette repeated. "Like steal the truck?"

Wynter shrugged. "Well, I haven't worked out all the details. I've been busy." Ivy scoffed, and I knew exactly what she was thinking. Wynter was busy with her man. Thankfully, Wynter ignored it. After all, she was good at ignoring what she didn't want to acknowledge. "But yeah, something like that. Just so we can take all the cash they're transporting and then we dump the truck." She grinned like she was suddenly very proud of herself. "Like the women in the *Good Girls* series."

I sat up straight. "You watched it?"

She nodded her head, her curls bouncing down her shoulders. Wynter never watched TV. Ever. She always had a competition to train for, choreography, ballet, or simply college classes to attend. She frequented some parties, but unlike us, she was never super excited for them. She loved ice skating, and to her, it was the best way to spend her time. Ivy asked her once if she felt like she was missing out, but she said she didn't. Ice skating mattered to her, while all those other things didn't.

"Yeah, it was *so* good." She beamed. "We could mimic the part where they push the stolen vehicle into the lake or whatever."

Juliette and Ivy chuckled. "Wynter Star Flemming has been corrupted! It only took four years of college."

The four of us burst into a fit of giggles when a knock sounded on the door. Juliette went to open the door and my stomach dropped knowing what would follow. It took just a minute until she was back with four letters.

I swallowed hard and ripped it open. God, Juliette's father must have had some serious pull. Just as he'd promised, the letter requesting we vacate the dorm within twenty-four hours had come. I knew Juliette's and Ivy's letters said the same thing.

"What the fuck..." Juliette muttered under her breath, then raised her eyes. "They want us out. The university."

"My letter says the same thing," Ivy confirmed. Ivy was sprawled over the floor while Juliette sat down with her legs crisscrossed. Wynter and I still sat on the couch.

"Mine too," I mumbled, feeling like shit. I should say something, admit to them what had happened between Liam and me. That I'd married him. Yet, words failed me, and I just remained watching, knowing I was doing wrong by my friends by not trusting them enough to tell them.

Wynter took a deep breath. "Mine says I can stay another two weeks."

"Shit," Juliette and Ivy cursed at the same time.

"Maybe you stay here and hide," Wynter recommended. "It's not like they check the dorms."

"Or we could stay at your dad's?" I suggested lamely. "M-maybe he'd let us all stay there."

"I don't want to go to Uncle Liam's before I have to," Wynter protested. If she finally got involved with someone, I'd understand that. This place gave us all more freedom. Though I hadn't expected the first protest to come from her.

"What if Ivy and I came along?" I tried, feeling like the biggest cheat. "I don't have a place lined up, considering... ummm..." I cleared my throat uncomfortably. "Well, considering recent events."

A heartbeat of silence, and then the girls nodded their heads in agreement.

"That's actually a good idea," Ivy chimed in, and I silently sighed in relief. "You think your dad would let us all stay there?"

"I'm going to wait before I join you," Wynter chimed in. "It's easier for me to practice and train here."

Juliette snorted. "Yeah, you're training alright, but it ain't ice skating."

Ivy burst into a loud laugh, falling over onto the floor. Juliette's eyes gleamed with laughter, but she managed to keep a straight face.

"It's probably good that you can stay here longer, Wynter." I returned the topic to the matter at hand. Their eyes snapped to me. "So we have an excuse to leave when we go rob the next place. We need to get it done before you move out of here and we have to figure out what to do with all the cash we've stolen."

"Look at you, woman." Juliette beamed. "Finally coming to the dark side. I'm so proud of our newly minted little criminal."

I rolled my eyes, but a stupid grin played around my lips.

"We definitely don't want to take the money back to Uncle's house," Wynter mused. "Besides, we have a bit extra in that bag now. He'd consider it his interest and take it back as his repayment."

Juliette snickered. "We can't let that happen. It's our money."

"Well, technically—" I started, but everyone groaned. "Fine, it's ours. All of it!"

Now we just had to hide it until we could figure out how to go about starting this business.

Assuming we managed to stay alive.

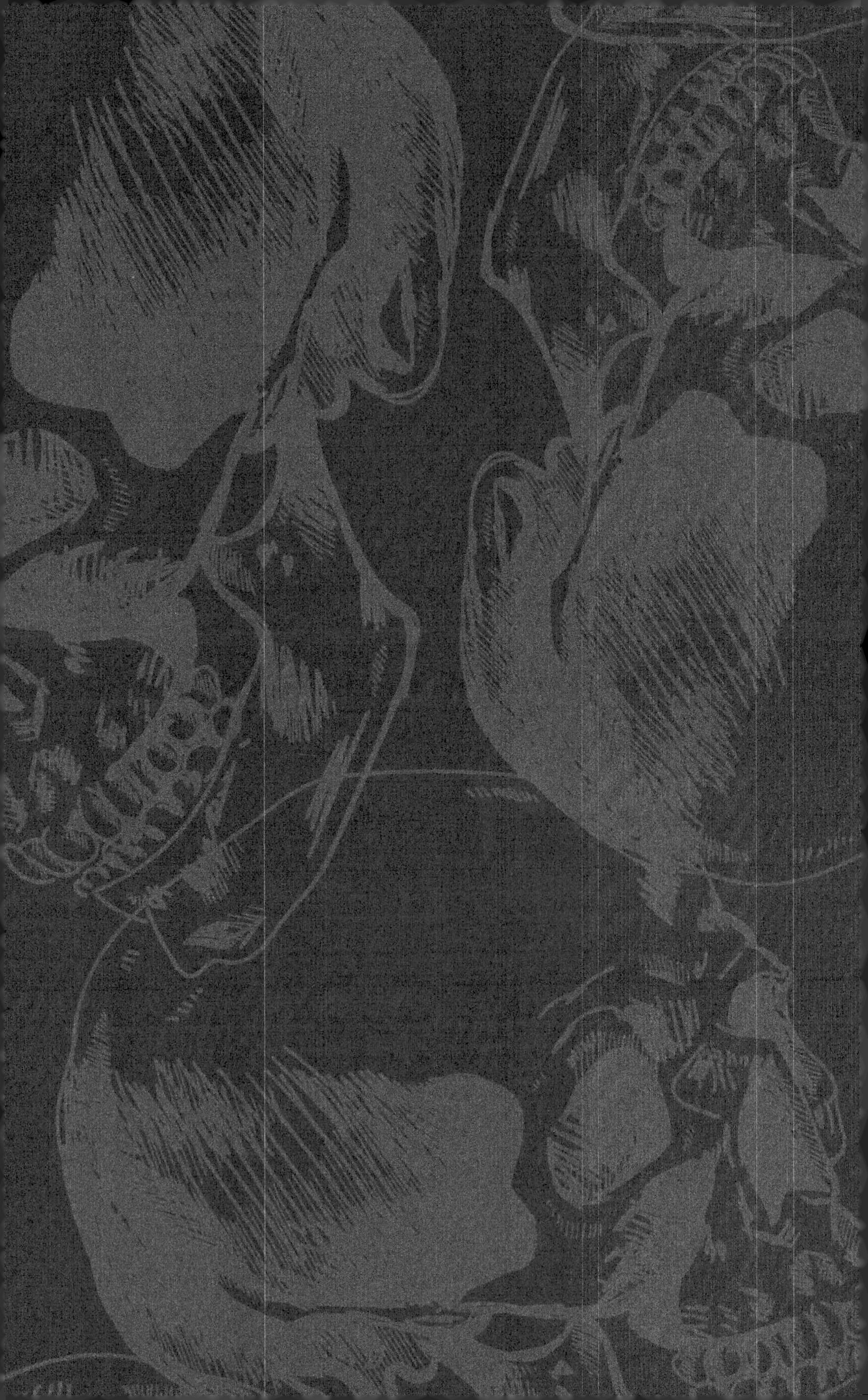

CHAPTER 42
Davina

Packing is a bitch.
    Packing while cranky and listening to Juliette's moaning about having to go live in Liam's luxurious home was a double bitch.

"What is your problem?" Wynter finally snapped, narrowing her eyes on Juliette. "You haven't stopped complaining since we got that notice."

Juliette glared back at her cousin. "Easy for you to say," she sneered. "You have another few weeks here."

"As soon as I'm done, I'll join you," she told her. "Besides, you already said you'll come to California with me, if that's what you're worried about. There's plenty of room for all of us there."

"I'm coming too then," Ivy announced. "It's better than going back to Ireland. Besides, you need my help with the next heist."

Juliette nodded eagerly. There'd be no going to California for me. I was married now, and my grandfather would be here.

"I'll visit," I promised.

"I wish you were coming with us too," Wynter and Juliette complained, "so we could all stay together."

"I wish," I told them. "But I found a way for my grandfather to be put in a facility here. So I want to stay here, close to him. And before you ask, I'm not moving him to California. I don't want to move him twice. This time will be hard enough on him."

All their eyes widened. "What?" Ivy exclaimed. "Grandpa Hayes is coming to the Big Apple?"

"How?" Juliette asked.

"When?" Wynter wondered.

"Tonight," I admitted, smiling. Despite all the shit that had gone down since we burned down Garrett's house, I was happy. Liam managed to not only give me multiple orgasms, but also showed how much he cared by securing a place for my grandfather in less than twenty-four hours. "I'd like to go see him after we're done tonight." I glanced at Wynter. "Could I borrow your Jeep? My car's out of commission for good."

And I didn't want to use Liam's wedding present. There weren't enough lies to explain how I had a Land Rover.

"Yes, of course." She grinned. "Can we come with you?"

"Damn, for Grandpa Hayes I'd consider staying here," Juliette mused.

"Me too," Ivy agreed.

I grinned. "It'd make him happy. But"—I locked my gaze on Juliette and pointed a finger at her—"you need to tell us what's bothering you. I can feel something is off, and I don't like to see you like this, Juliette."

Guilt washed over her face, but there was something else there too. Her blue eyes that were a completely different shade from her father's shimmered like sapphires while her bottom lip quivered.

Startled, I realized she was holding back tears. "Is this about the birth certificates?" I asked her. It was the only thing I'd ever seen upset her.

The next moment, tears were streaming down her face. I strode to her at the same time as Wynter and Ivy, and all three of us wrapped our arms around her. We'd smother her with love to make it all better.

"What happened?" I questioned. By Wynter's and Ivy's looks, they were just as puzzled. "Want to burn down another house?" I teased softly.

A choked sob mixed with a strangled laugh escaped her, and it was like she'd let loose. Her sobs shook her body as she cried in our arms. We didn't say anything, just held her as she let it all out.

"Shhh," I comforted her. I met Wynter's eyes and she looked at a loss for words. "Whatever it is, we'll get through it together," I vowed. And we would. We were family. I'd do anything for the three of them. They were my ride or die, right along with my grandfather.

And Liam, my mind whispered. But I wasn't ready to admit that to them just yet.

"Tell us what's wrong, Jules," Wynter urged her softly. "Tell us who we have to kill."

"Dad," she choked out and another wave of sobs followed. "He's not my dad."

"What do you mean?" Wynter rasped. "I thought those birth certificates were fake."

My heart clenched in my chest, and I immediately feared that things were too good to be true. Something big was about to ruin the little happiness that had started to form in my chest.

"He's not my dad," Juliette repeated, her voice trembling. "I've been doing research and found information on Aiden and Ava Cullen."

"What did you find out?" the three of us asked in a whisper.

"They had two children, born on the exact days as Killian and me," she said. "I found their obituary pictures." A soft round of gasps followed. "Want to see?"

"Yes," I answered when Wynter and Ivy remained quiet.

Juliette pulled out her phone and scrolled through her pictures, then showed us all a photo.

"Holy shit," Wynter muttered. "Killian and you look just like them."

"Right?" Juliette agreed. "I mean, there is no more evidence needed."

"What else did you find out?" Ivy asked her.

The anguish on Juliette's face was clear. Whatever she found, it wasn't good.

"My biological parents were killed and burned in their home in Ireland. They were hiding from the Russians."

"Russians?" Wynter asked. "That doesn't make any sense. I thought your dad..." Wynter paused, as if unsure whether she could still call her uncle Juliette's dad. "I thought the Irish never dealt with the Russians."

"It is one hard rule I've heard my father repeat," Ivy added. "No business dealings with the Russians."

I swallowed hard. "Maybe it's because of what happened to the Cullens?"

"I don't know," Juliette whispered. "All I know is that Ava and Aiden Cullen had two children, presumed dead. Dad... Liam was Aiden Cullen's best friend. Those coincidences are too big to be swept under the rug. Even if Killian and I didn't look like them."

"So he's hiding you?" Wynter breathed. "You and Killian."

The shock coloring Wynter's face matched my own. Ivy's eyes kept darting around, trying to make sense out of all of it too.

Juliette nodded.

"It makes perfect sense now that I never had a mother," Juliette continued on a whimper. "He never married, despite having two kids. You know if we were his, he'd have dragged our mother to the altar."

"How did you suddenly get your hands on those birth certificates?" Ivy asked the question I'd been wondering.

"When I went to see Dad in the penthouse after our holiday trip to Texas," she explained. "Remember that attack on the club on the west side of New York? He was held up because of it, so I waited for him. I went in search of a blanket." I remembered a similar blanket hunt three months ago in her family home. "He keeps that penthouse for his private use, so I wasn't familiar with where he kept stuff. I found myself in his office, and the birth certificates were just sitting there on his desk. They caught my eye because I saw my first name."

I wondered what I would do if I happened to find out the name of my father. I knew who my mother was, but my knowledge about her stopped there. I knew her name, what Grandpa had told me of her childhood, and that was it. Grandpa didn't like to talk about it.

"Did you ask Killian?" Wynter whispered, as if she worried the tone of her voice would upset her.

Juliette shook her head in response. "I just couldn't," she rasped.

Silence filled the room upon this discovery. The only thing disturbing it were Juliette's sniffles. It was a startling finding.

"How long have you known those birth certificates weren't fakes?" Wynter asked her.

"I've been looking up information and researching for months," she admitted. "So I've known for a while now."

"And you kept quiet about it?" Wynter whispered.

"I-I didn't want you to think I wasn't your family anymore," Juliette admitted, the vulnerability in her voice matching the one lingering in her eyes. "The way Irish view family only as blood kin had me scared," she added with a hoarse whisper.

"Juliette, we're family," I reprimanded her softly. "Maybe not blood-related, but you've done more for me than my own parents."

"That's right," Wynter agreed. "Nothing and nobody could take this away."

"Nobody. Not a man, not parents, not brothers. We're a ride or die kind of girl squad," Ivy stated. "For Christ's sake, we convinced Davina to whistle Rue's song. I mean, who else would ever do that?"

"Or burn down a house," I added dryly, a smile playing around my lips.

"I don't know a single member of our entire family, blood or not, that would ever stand by me like you three have," Wynter continued softly. "We are here for each other. This isn't just friendship. We're family, we're friends, we're everything. And we're stuck with each other forever. Regardless of what happens. I don't care what continent we live on, we'll always be there for each other." Wynter's eyes traveled over all of us as if she wanted to show us all that she meant it.

All of us agreed, nodding our heads with smiles on our faces. We had so much connecting us to each other. "Our kids will be family and our husband's better like each other, or they'll get the boot," she added teasingly.

And suddenly everything was better. So much better.

"Grandpa!" I ran toward the private clinic ambulance, uncaring that I probably looked like a little kid who hadn't seen her parents in years.

The girls were right behind me. "Grandpa Hayes," they exclaimed in unison.

Two paramedics had just sat Grandpa in the wheelchair, and I fell down to my knees and hugged him around his waist. His wrinkled hand came to my head, his palm gentle and frail as he patted my head like he always did.

"There's my little girl," he said, his voice gruff. "How did you make this happen?"

I grinned up at him. There was so much I wanted to tell him, but we had time. We'd go slow. The main thing was that he was close now.

"I wanted you close to me," I whispered softly. "It's my turn to take care of you."

"Besides, we know you missed us, Grandpa Hayes," Juliette said, her voice musical and playful. "And we totally missed you."

Grandpa chuckled. "Ah, Juliette. You always know what to say to make an old man feel better."

"What?" Wynter's eyes darted around, twinkling. "Where is an old man? I don't see one."

"I only see a badass grandpa," Ivy added. "I can't wait to hear your stories. We've missed them."

My lips curved up. This right here was priceless. No amount of money could replace it.

"Can I?" I asked the paramedic, tilting my chin toward the handles of the wheelchair. "You guys have done so much. We can show him to his room. The nurse already showed us everything, and we decorated it a bit."

The paramedic nodded with a smile, and I stood up to my full height.

"Come on, Grandpa." I took the handles and started pushing. "The girls and I have a little surprise for you."

"What is it?" he asked eagerly. He liked surprises.

"Ah, if we tell you, then it won't be a surprise," I said mischievously. "We don't want to spoil it. Do we girls?"

"Heck no," Ivy sang like a bird. "Though I can't wait to delve into those chocolates." Her eyes twinkled. "Oops, I let one surprise out of the bag."

Grandpa's chuckle made my heart warm.

"We'll all share them," he said, grinning. "But you have to tell me the rest of the surprises, Ivy."

Wynter put her hand around Ivy's mouth while the others pretended to be talking, her voice muffled.

"Ivy will keep a secret," Wynter stated matter-of-factly, though her shining eyes ruined her seriousness. "Otherwise, we'll torture her."

We all grinned.

"I am so happy my Davina found such great friends," Grandpa said, his voice caring and emotional. "I know she'll be in good hands when the good Lord takes me."

"We're all family," Wynter assured him softly, her hand falling away from Ivy's mouth.

"Forever," Ivy and Juliette sang.

"We're all family forever. But you're not going anywhere, Grandpa Hayes. Now you have to become a true New Yorker, and that takes at least twenty years," Juliette told him seriously.

"That's right," I agreed with her. "You just got here. The good Lord will have to wait."

"Besides, Grandpa Hayes," Wynter continued, "we want you around so you can meet your great-grandchildren. So hang in there. We'll need at least another twenty years."

"And another gold medal," Grandpa added.

Yes, this was family.

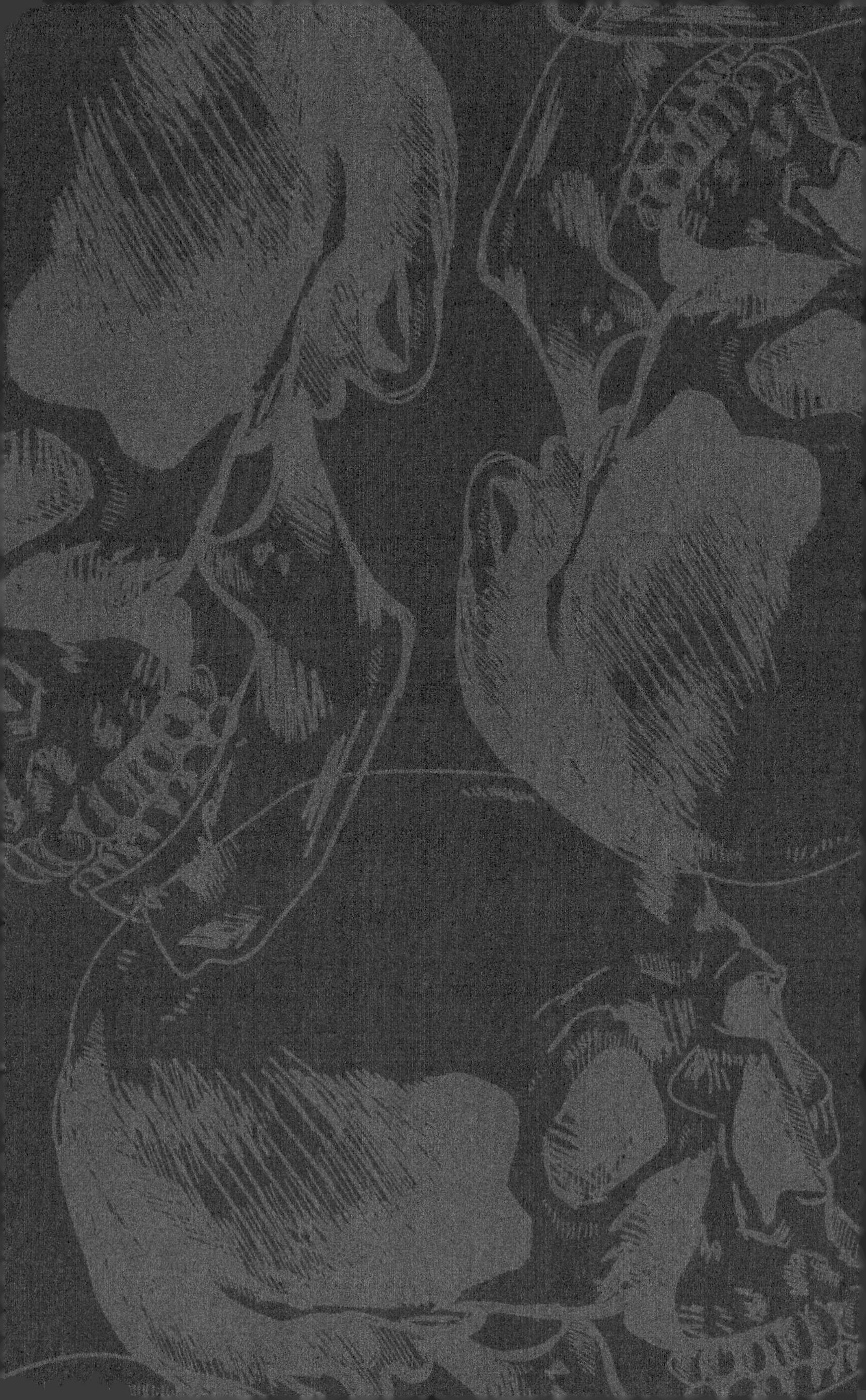

CHAPTER 43
Liam

"Where are you taking me?" Davina asked again.

It was meant to be a surprise date night. The first one with my wife, outside our home. But it turned out my wife was impatient and curious to a fault. It was cute as fuck as she kept trying to guess it.

"Don't you like surprises?"

"I do," she proclaimed, giddy. Her eyes shone with excitement, and I couldn't tear my gaze away from her.

"Then stop questioning me," I told her, amused.

My driver, the red-haired devil as Davina called him, drove smoothly through the traffic of New York City. It was only seven in the evening, and we had the entire night ahead of us.

"Well, it can't be dinner," she mused. "We already ate."

"We had a small dinner," I reminded her. "We could certainly have another one."

"Aha," she exclaimed. "So dinner and a movie?"

I made sure I memorized every single guess she made, because I vowed I'd give her every single one of those dates.

"Not today."

She looked stunning in a light-blue, off-the-shoulder dress that came to her knees.

"But another day?"

"Whatever you want." And I meant it. I'd give her whatever she wanted, just to see that happy smile on her face and her eyes shining like diamonds. "Did you see your grandfather today?"

Her face lit up and her eyes shimmered.

"I did. The girls went with me." She beamed, taking my hand and squeezing gently. "He's so happy and already looks five years younger."

"Do we need any upgrades to his room?" I wanted him to be perfectly happy here because I knew if her grandfather didn't like it here, neither would Davina. She'd follow him anywhere.

She scoffed softly. "You got him the best room. He loves it and I love —" An emotion flickered on her face, and she lowered her gaze, smoothing her dress while examining me under a thick curtain of her dark lashes. "I love it too."

"Good. If there's anything we need to do for him, we'll do it."

"We?" she asked, hesitation in her eyes.

I cupped her face and our gazes connected. "Yes, we. Your family is mine." I closed the space between us and pressed my mouth to hers. "*We* are family now, céile. We'll let him adjust, and then we can visit him together."

She nodded, and satisfaction hummed in my veins.

The car came to a stop and our conversation ended for now. I got out of the car, something warm rattling in my chest as I extended my hand to her and helped her out of the car.

"Sailboat?" she exclaimed.

"You said you had yet to take the boat to the Statue of Liberty. So, our first date will be sunset sailing with the view of the city that is now your home."

"What happened to your gigantic yacht?" she asked curiously while a sweet smile played around her lips.

"It's docked in another marina," I told her. "This is new."

She cocked her eyebrow. "New?"

I wrapped my hand around her shoulder as we walked toward the dock. "Yes, it's our boat. And I named her after you."

Her eyes widened. "No, you didn't!"

"Of course I did." I shifted her toward the end of the boat where the name proudly stared at us. *For my céile, Davina.*

She stared at it quietly while seconds ticked on. There was nothing in the world that could make me change that name.

"My grandpa named his boat after Grandma," she whispered. "I always thought it was the most beautiful thing."

We faced each other and she tilted her head to meet my eyes. It felt like stars were stolen from the skies and now they shone in her eyes. Just for me.

"Do you want me to change it?"

"Fuck no," she exclaimed and wrapped her arms around my neck. "I love it. Absolutely love it. Thank you!"

She dazzled when she smiled up at me. If I was smart, I'd look away. Instead, I soaked in her beauty and warmth as if my life depended on it.

"Well, lead the way, captain," she announced happily. "This will be the best date ever!"

I chuckled. "Even better than stealing from me?"

Her cheeks flushed. "Definitely better than stealing from you." Then she peered at me from under her lashes. "Except what happened after I emptied your safe. That was pretty..." Her chest heaved slightly. "That was very memorable."

I gently slapped her ass and urged her forward. "Come on, mate. Time to get our sea legs."

For the first time in my life, I felt lighter. Happier. Everything had always been about responsibility and keeping my family safe. But with Davina, it was just about us.

Her and me.

We launched the sailboat and cruised into the bay. It was calm today and Davina's eyes roamed the bay excitedly. She tilted her face toward the setting sun.

Her body pressed against me as I steered us across the water. I tightened my grip around her waist, steering with my right hand. It was just the two of us, which was the reason I preferred the sailboat to the yacht. I needed a crew for the yacht. This would be just for our own getaway trips.

"You hungry?" I asked her.

She was eager to get going, knowing there was a surprise waiting for her.

"No." She turned her face to look over her shoulder. "Are you hungry?"

"I could eat." *Your pussy. Right now. On the deck. All night long.*

"Want me to go and see if there is anything below deck?" she asked, and I chuckled. If she only knew what was on my mind.

"No. This kind of hunger only you can sate." The meaning came through and her cheeks flamed. I lowered my head and pressed my lips to hers. The kiss was gentle at first, but it quickly turned hungry. Heated. She always overwhelmed all my senses. Nothing had ever impacted me like this woman.

I forced myself to pull back before I lost my control and said to hell with the date plan.

She turned her attention to the horizon, her eyes on the Statue of Liberty.

"It's quite a view," she murmured. "Somehow it looks more mesmerizing and magnificent from this spot."

"I agree," I murmured. Though I wasn't talking about the Statue of Liberty. It was my wife that looked mesmerizing. She took my breath away, and all my control.

Once at the spot, I let her hold the wheel while I went to throw the anchor, then I grabbed the picnic basket I knew was waiting. You'd think I was some romantic schmuck. I wasn't. At least not until now. Suddenly, I was into wooing my wife to ensure her happiness.

I laid it all out, all the while Davina watched with a peculiar look on her face. As if she couldn't believe it. *Join the club*, I mused. It was a novelty for me too.

Once the picnic was set up, I patted the plush seat next to me. "Now come here, wife," I purred.

She smiled as she strolled over to me. "I have to say, I quite enjoyed seeing you so expertly set up the picnic."

I pulled her down to me so she landed in my lap. "And I'll quite enjoy expertly doing many other things to you and for you."

She snorted softly. "That sounded filthy."

"There is nothing clean about my intentions, wife."

She rolled her eyes cutely, and I couldn't resist pressing a light kiss on her mouth.

"Now eat," I ordered. "We want to feed those curves. We'll burn off the calories when we get home. With you bent over our bed."

She gasped, her lips parting lightly.

I picked up a bite-sized, heart-shaped sandwich that looked ridiculously tiny in my large hand. I'd give it to my cook, he had an imagination. But when I saw Davina gushing over it, I decided to give him a fucking big-ass raise.

"Open wider," I demanded.

"That sounds so dirty when you say it with that look in your eyes," she complained but opened her mouth nonetheless.

I put the piece in, all the while chuckling.

"You seem relaxed out at sea," she noted after finishing a bite and reaching for another. But rather than feeding herself, she offered it to me. "Heart for you and heart for me," she teased.

"I am relaxed at sea," I admitted. "Less people around. And less chances of someone killing me."

I opened my mouth and she fed me the heart-shaped sandwich.

"I love the sea too," she replied softly. "For different reasons. Obviously." Then she tilted her head, watching me, and I wondered what she saw. "You won't get killed, will you? I kind of want more dates before our time is up."

"Baby, death won't stop me from taking you on more dates," I told her. "Or from enjoying your mouth, your body, and most of all, your company for the rest of our days in our long life."

She chuckled. "Then we won't have a problem."

"My wife wants to keep me around, huh?" I teased her.

"I do." She bumped her shoulder gently against mine. "You created a greedy beast. Now I want sex all the damn time."

I threw my head back and laughed loudly. "You were a beast all along, Davina. You were just waiting for me."

She rolled her eyes again, though an affectionate smile played around her lips.

The sun had set and the sky had darkened. The lights on the boat were dimmed and it almost felt like we were the only two humans in this world.

"This is so damn romantic," she murmured. "You're earning some points."

"That's the goal," I whispered, skimming my mouth over her cheek. "Earn enough points to make sure you're happy."

And to keep that soft glow in her eyes.

"Your eyes are shining so beautifully," I murmured. "The stars are no match for you."

At that very moment, the sky lit up.

"Fireworks," she gasped. Her awed gaze held to the sky as the colors lit up the quickly darkening night. I sat back, watching her. I had secured it just for us. Colors danced across the dark skies, dazzling and captivating, but to me, nothing shone brighter than my wife.

Then a deep exhale left her lips and her eyes snapped to me.

"Liam, did you..." She left it unspoken, then her eyes returned to the sky, sparkling with 'Will you marry me?' "Is that..."

I never thought I'd see that sassy mouth at a loss for words.

"It's a yes or no question, céile," I murmured, brushing my lips over her earlobe.

"But we're already married," she rasped, her voice trembling.

"Aye, but this is the way I should have done it," I told her. It was true. Would I have still forced her to marry me? Yes. But she deserved the wooing, and I wanted to give it to her. This attraction between us was unique, and I was certain that we would have ended up exactly where I fast-forwarded us to.

"My answer is yes, Liam," she whispered, her eyes sparkling like diamonds. The fireworks paled in comparison to her shine.

"We'll be good together. I promise you, Davina."

CHAPTER 44
Davina

"Hurry up, you two," I rushed Juliette and Ivy. "We still have to drive two hours to get to Yale."

It took us four days to move into Liam's city house. The very same one I saw him in that first night. Yep, I'd come full circle. One of his men had most of my clothes taken from my room and to his penthouse. Without talking to me.

But what-the-fuck-ever.

I was floating on a cloud. Liam was amazing. Sweet, kind, and so damn thoughtful that I melted on the inside. In more ways than one. I loved talking to him. I loved doing things with him.

Besides, it was the least I could do after the amazingly romantic proposal. We had the attraction, but it was so much more than that. I had never met a more thoughtful man aside from my grandfather. It was hard to contain the happiness at having my grandpa so close and being able to visit him every day. Most of the time, the girls came along. Grandpa felt like he'd gained more granddaughters and was tickled about it.

The only thing that somewhat hindered my happiness was that I hadn't told my friends about my marriage to Liam and that he was the one that paid for Grandpa to be moved here. I gave them some story about an anonymous donor paying for it.

"We have all night," Juliette complained. "Stop rushing us."

All the lying was taking a toll on me. I hated it.

But Liam expected me in the penthouse every night. Which meant we had to be home. I'd pretend to go to bed or have an errand to run, and then sneak out the door. Unlike Wynter, I wasn't able to climb out the window.

The worst part was that at this point, I couldn't sleep without Liam's body pressed against me. Or at least feeling his hands on me. Trust me, I'd fucking tried.

One night, Ivy and Juliette decided to have a heist research party in the fucking foyer. A foyer! A huge-ass house, and they parked themselves in the foyer, blocking my way out. The back door would have been an option if the bottom of the stairs didn't lead to the foyer too, so there was no way to sneak around them.

So, I gave up and just went to bed. I ended up tossing and turning half the night until a body shifted the entire mattress and scared the living daylights out of me.

"What the fuck?" I hissed, his dark outline shifting closer to me as he climbed into the bed.

"I thought I told you I want you in my bed every night," he growled low in my ear, his chest pressed against my back. "Remember my condition, wife. You're to submit to me. Whenever I say. Wherever I say."

"Freak," I muttered, though my body already leaned back into him, relishing in his muscles. His hand came to my hip, his strong fingers pressing me hard against him. Goosebumps broke out on my skin, feeling his mouth on the base of my neck.

"For the record, I tried to come," I whispered, my voice a throaty moan. "But your daughter decided to have a party in the foyer."

"No excuses," he rasped, biting my earlobe. His voice, deep and low, vibrated with power. He was intoxicating. "Now I have to punish you. And I better not hear a peep out of your mouth."

God, the way he said it, I knew it'd be good. Everything with Liam felt good. I knew I wouldn't be able to remain silent.

His hand reached between my legs to find me soaking wet. "Mmmm,

I got myself an insatiable wife." Shivers ghosted down my spine hearing his deep voice in my ear. His fingers found my folds and smeared wetness over my clit. *"You're a wet mess between your legs."*

A throaty moan filled the dark room. The light slap between my legs was unexpected and I jerked against his hand.

"I said not a sound."

My ragged breathing was the only response. My furious heartbeat thundered in sync with my aching pussy. I sucked in a breath but remained silent.

"Good wife," he drawled. "I have to taste my wife's pussy."

In one swift move, he shifted his body on top of mine, his gaze dark and hungry. His finger pushed inside me, and I couldn't help but whimper with need.

With his free hand, he gripped my hip and bowed his head. My insides shuddered with anticipation of him going down on me. I was getting addicted to it. But instead, his mouth captured my nipple through the thin material of my shirt and he bit, making me cry out.

His hand still on my pussy, his voice went hard. "Ride my hand. Show me how you come, wife."

Our eyes locked and I began to move, grinding against his palm. His fingers inside me felt good but were not enough. Through my half-lidded eyes, I watched his fingers pumping in and out of me and the sight was so erotic that I bit my bottom lip to stop another moan from forming.

His big body hovered over mine, shifting down my body lower and lower, until his face was in front of my open thighs. He spread my pussy with his free hand and then leaned closer to my entrance. He inhaled deeply and his eyes closed for a moment.

"Fuck, you smell good," he growled. I writhed mindlessly against his touch, my moans getting louder and louder. "My queen."

His mouth latched onto my clit and a loud moan vibrated through the air. "Fuck."

He stopped moving his fingers and his eyes lifted up to mine. "Didn't I tell you to keep quiet?"

"I want you inside me," I whimpered, my hips rocking against him. Couldn't he see I needed him? I was panting and trembling all over.

"First you'll come from my mouth," he rasped. "But you'll keep your voice down," he warned darkly.

I would have agreed to anything at this point.

"I won't make a sound," I panted. I'd promise him the world just to feel his mouth between my legs.

Those words had to be the right ones because in the next moment, his mouth ravaged my pussy. It was the most exquisite torture feeling his tongue on my most sensitive spot, sucking me enthusiastically.

His tongue slid back and forth over my swollen, sensitive clit. When he pushed his tongue inside my folds, my hips rocked back and forth wantonly against his face. A crest of pleasure burned higher and brighter until I reached a peak.

As my pulse thundered and I breathed hard, I flew high, somewhere between the clouds. Then, spreading my legs wider, he crawled up my body and settled himself over me, balancing his weight on his elbows.

My eyes lowered, watching his cock slide inside me, connecting our bodies.

"Look at this greedy pussy," he rasped. "Who is it for?"

"You," I whimpered. "Just you."

"Such a greedy wife." He chuckled darkly. "Desperate to milk my cock."

My response to his dirty words was a moan that he muffled with his mouth as he thrust deeply inside me. I arched my back, gasping and out of my mind, clenching around his length. I started to grind against him, desperate for the friction between our bodies.

"Beg for it," Liam demanded in a throaty voice.

"Fuck," I moaned, grinding against his pelvis. "Please fuck me with your cock." My fingers dug into his shoulders. "Please, Liam."

His hands reached around me and his one hand slid between my ass cheeks, his finger finding that forbidden hole. He stroked it, smearing the wetness around it and pushing inside. I felt so full with his cock and finger inside of me.

"That feels so good," I breathed hard, my chest heaving against his.

His mouth muffling my sounds and our tongues tangling together, he fucked me hard. I was swallowed by his dominance, his finger pushing in *and out of me from behind. And all the while, he increased speed, thrusting inside me and filling me to the hilt.*

Writhing underneath him, waves of pleasure crashed down on me until I was buckled underneath him, moaning into his mouth. My orgasm hit me like the explosion of a volcano, and I convulsed around him, losing myself in the intense pleasure.

And at this moment, he was all I cared about. This feeling that only he could give me. Liam felt right.

I had never felt so connected to another human being as I did Liam.

"Hey, Earth to Davina." Juliette snapped her fingers in my face, and I blinked, then she did it again. I smacked her hand out of my face.

"What?" I asked, agitated.

"Why are you rushing us?" she demanded. "I asked you three times and all you did was stare into space with a blissful look on your face. What's going on with you?"

I pushed my hand through my hair. All this lying really had to come to an end, but today wasn't the day.

"I want to visit my grandfather before visiting hours are up," I lied. Well, technically a half-lie. These damn lies were really starting to pile up. Wynter still kept busy with her training, studying for her exams, and seeing her man. I was busy with my grandfather, my husband, and scouting properties for the school's location.

Ivy and Juliette were busy studying all the organized crime affiliations since they decided it was only fair that we rob the Russians, Colombians, and the Mexican cartel too. It was an advance payment toward their kids getting the education they'd need to survive the underworld.

Yep, we've all gone *loca*.

"Ah, okay," Juliette commented about me visiting my grandfather. "That makes sense. Let's go. We can finish unpacking when we get back."

I exhaled a sigh of relief. Thank God.

We piled into Wynter's Jeep. I certainly wasn't going to drive the Rover that Liam bought me. No amount of lies could explain why I suddenly had a brand new car. Besides, Wynter assured me that she was mostly on campus, and when she went out, her *friend* came to pick her up.

Juliette sat in the passenger seat and Ivy sat in the back. I drove, since it was the only clause given by Wynter. She didn't want Juliette totaling her car, and Ivy struggled driving on the right side of the road. Though, she swore *we* drove on the wrong side of the road.

Opening the roof and turning on the stereo because I wasn't in the mood for conversation, I sped out of the city and toward New Haven.

As I neared the campus, a little bit of nostalgia hit me. Yale's residential college had been our home for the past four years. The stunning buildings centered on a green courtyard were our everyday scenery, and the end had come too quickly. A random assignment of our living space brought the four of us together. It made us best friends and a support system for each other. The four of us were so different but complemented each other perfectly. Sometimes, I wondered if someone that worked at the school knew us better than we knew ourselves.

Maybe we could make something like this happen in our school. Slightly different, of course. Because instead of academic knowledge, we'd be teaching skills required to survive the criminal underworld.

Once I parked the car, the three of us rushed through the door of our old building. I had sent a heads up to Wynter before we left the house so she wouldn't be caught unaware.

"We're home," I exclaimed as we entered through the door, not bothering with knocking.

The three of us stopped abruptly to find Wynter bent over the window, speaking in a hushed tone.

"What are you doing?" Juliette blurted out, scaring the living daylights out of Wynter. She bumped her head on the top of the window.

"Ouch," she muttered, then whirled around while rubbing her head.

"Who're you talking to?" Ivy asked, eyeing her dubiously. Her eyes darted around the room, as if she expected to find someone else here.

"Nobody," she muttered. "I was breathing some fresh air through the window."

CORRUPTED PLEASURE

I suspected we'd just missed whoever was here. My eyes traveled around the room. The sheets on Wynter's bed were tossed. A faint scent that I'd bet belonged to a man lingered in the room. And a man's watch sat on the little nightstand.

The same second I noticed it, so did Wynter. Our eyes connected and her cheeks blushed. Ah, the ice queen had found her king.

I winked.

She breathed a little sigh and smiled gratefully, then shifted her body to block the view of the watch before inconspicuously shoving it into the drawer.

"How are you holding up without us?" I asked her, though she seemed to be doing really well.

"Ah, you know," she muttered. "Been busy with ice skating and working on a project for Professor Hall."

Juliette's eyes narrowed. "There isn't a single book open," she remarked.

"Well, I'm done now," she replied. "I knew we'd be outlining our plans for the Philadelphia heist."

"Let's all sit down," I suggested. We lowered down onto the floor since most of the furniture was already out of the room. We formed a circle and Juliette dug through her shoulder bag, then laid out the paperwork. I skimmed the paperwork laid on the floor, and for the first time, I was floored by her.

I had honestly never seen her make such a detailed outline for *anything*. Not for her assignments. Not for her theater roles. Not for any goddamn thing.

And here she had a detailed building plan of the casino in Philadelphia, each exit marked, the best escape routes out of the city, rush hour times, events scheduled for the next week and their times that could possibly interrupt our escape.

"Jesus, you went all out, huh?" I muttered, eyeing all the details.

"Well, we want to get those millions," she claimed proudly.

Wynter reached under the bed and pulled a notebook out.

"I have the schedule and route that the truck takes," Wynter said, her eyes shining excitedly. "They alternate, but never mix it up. It's always the same. One week it's South Christopher Columbus Boulevard, next it's Market Street, then they take the Benjamin Franklin Bridge, next Delaware Ave, and then all over again. This Saturday, they're taking South Christopher Columbus Boulevard.

"The driver comes from one side, but he can't leave the same way since it's one way. We'll hang around in the club. When he has to leave, we'll be called from the club to vacate the spot so the truck can depart. We'll follow him and then... boom."

She left the meaning of it lingering.

"How do you know their schedule?" I questioned her.

She grinned smugly. "I snapped a picture of the schedule from a document one of the guys left lying around when he went to the bathroom. Idiot!"

All four of us snickered at such a rookie mistake. Gosh, we were moving up in the criminal world.

"Wow, he must be a worse criminal than us," Ivy mused.

"Fuck yeah," Juliette said. "At least we learn and get better. Someone should tell that fucker his skills are a joke at best. We, on the other hand, kick ass."

I winced at the self-praise. We'd got caught both times. Well, I did, since Dante recognized me and called Liam. But at least the Italians thought it was only me. Liam wasn't as dumb and knew all four of us were in on it, but he was letting me get away with it.

Because he likes me? I pondered.

Maybe that should be my goal. *Make him pussy-whipped so he'll let me get away with everything*, I smirked silently, suddenly feeling so smug and smart.

"What are you smirking at?" Juliette called me out, and immediately my smugness evaporated like dust in the wind.

"Oh, I was just congratulating ourselves on improving our criminal skills," I lied.

"Right?" she eagerly agreed. "We're getting good at this. Soon, we'll be able to buy the property for our school."

We've been searching for potential properties and gauging sale prices so we'd know how long our criminal careers would last.

"If we're going to do it, we need to do it this Saturday," Wynter concluded. "While I still have this place. I have to move out next week."

And we knew what that meant. She'd have to go back to California. Then her life would be ice skating, training, and more ice skating. Unless she convinced her skating partner to move to New York and train here since she'd found herself a boyfriend.

"This Saturday it is," I announced.

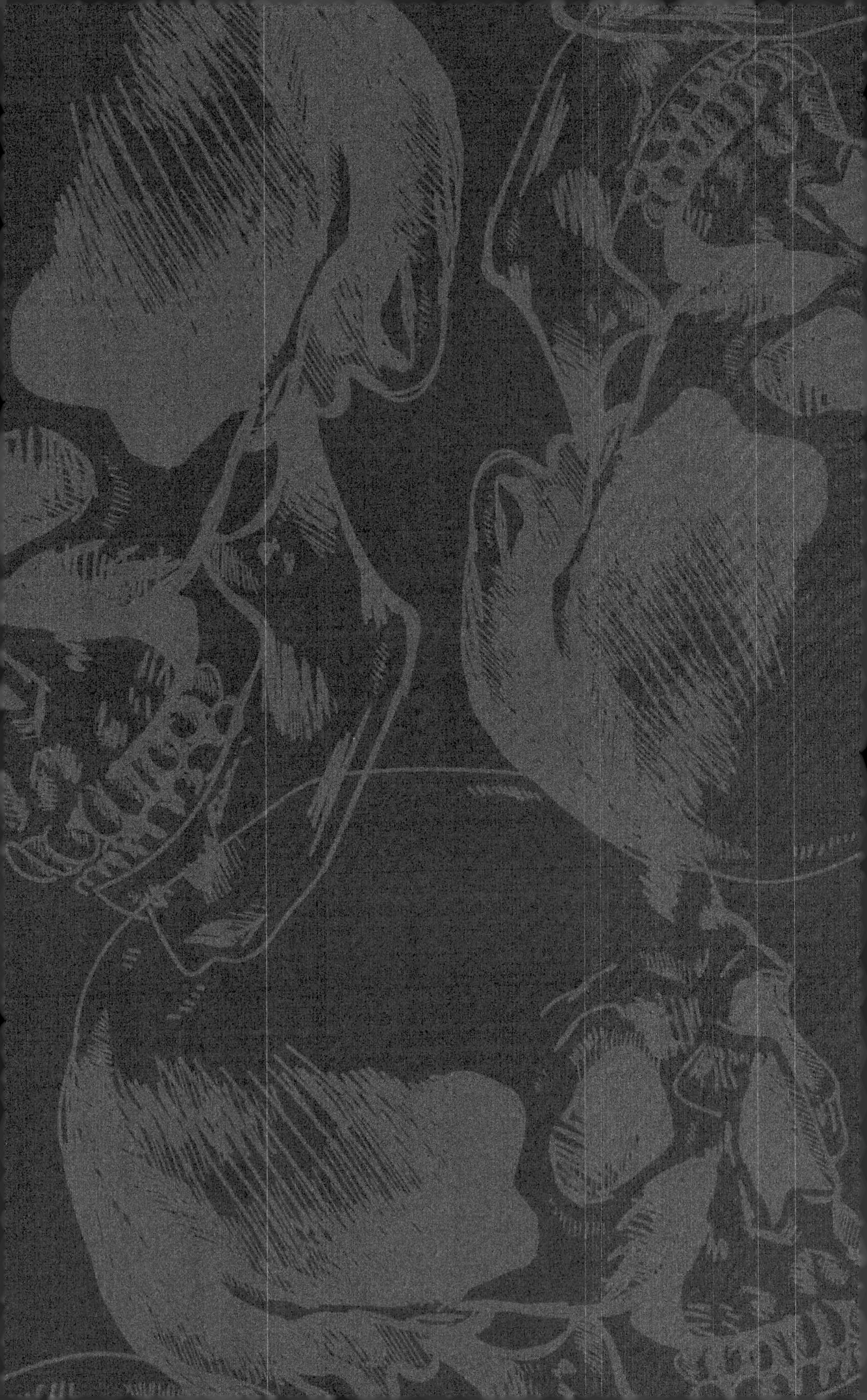

CHAPTER 45
Liam

Two weeks.

Two weeks of putting up with my wife sneaking around so she could spend evenings with me and nights in my bed so could fuck her senseless. I was all for standing by your friends, but this was bullshit and I'd put a stop to it, even if I had to break the fucking news to everyone myself.

She had become a need, absolute and unique, unlike anything I had ever experienced before. The need to have her near me was engraved in the very marrow of my bones. In the pit of my heart. With no chances o ever getting out.

She was naked underneath me, on her knees, her ass up in the ai and her head buried into the pillows. Her dark hair sprawled around a: my fingers dug into her ass cheek and my other hand wrapped around her waist, lifting her stomach the slightest bit. I wasn't sure anymore whether I was punishing her or pleasuring her.

I had taken her over and over again. Each time, I promised myself i. was the last time, that I'd let her rest. But then I'd succumb and take he again. Around this woman, I had no will to stop fucking her. The scen of her arousal fed my addiction. I wanted to eat her out. Pull her deep into my depraved desire so she'd never find her way out.

I thrust into her hard, sharp, and animalistic. Punishing her for not screaming at the top of her lungs that she was mine. I wanted to own every inch of her so she'd never go anywhere without me. Her body jerked underneath me. Her fingers fisted the rope I looped around her wrists and tied to the bed rails.

"*Fuck, fuck, fuck,*" she panted, sweat glistening on her beautiful skin.

"Who do you belong to?" I growled, one of my knees firmly planted between her open thighs, thrusting into her like a madman. She bit the pillow, muffling her sounds as I plowed in and out. Hard and fast. I leaned over so my chest covered her back. "Who?" I demanded, releasing her ass.

Her muscles melted into my touch and it was the only thing she couldn't control. She had a sharp brain and a sassy mouth, but her body betrayed her. I felt her craving as much as my own as her walls clenched around my cock.

I reached around and thrust two fingers into her mouth. She bit them, her teeth piercing my skin. Fuck, I loved her fire.

"Tell me." She glanced over her shoulder, her eyes met mine, defiant and lustful. Hazy and beautiful. I pounded in and out of her, eager to consume every fiber of her being.

"You," she screamed, her insides strangling me. She shuddered violently, milking my cock so perfectly. I clenched my teeth, ramming into her through her orgasm. She screamed my name, and I was certain the entire city heard her.

"Liam!" Her piercing scream vibrated against the walls of our penthouse.

I loved hearing my name on her lips, the way she breathed it when she panted. I followed her over the edge, spilling inside her, my balls aching with the intensity of my release as her own knees buckled and she collapsed onto the mattress.

Both of us breathing heavily, I fell on top of her. My forehead rested on the back of her shoulder, inhaling her sweet scent. I lifted off her and reached to the headboard to undo the rope from around her hands. There were faint red marks on her wrists. Shifting us over, I brought her closer to me and started to massage them.

She snuggled into me, her hands pressed against my chest as I rubbed her wrists.

"I like you too much," she murmured sleepily. "Way... too... much."

And she was out cold.

We'd fallen into a routine. We'd have dinner together. Date nights, because my wife loved those, so I made it a point to take her on as many as possible.

But she'd leave in the morning, and I didn't fucking like it. I'd allowed it for far too long. I wanted her with me, in the penthouse, all the time. I found myself no longer wanting my own space. Any space without her in it was bleak.

I brushed my hand against her forehead, pushing the hair out of her face. She leaned into my touch, even in her sleep she was attuned to me. I found that I really liked my wife too. *Way too much*, just like she claimed before falling asleep. Seeing how it ended for my father, I was certain it wasn't a good thing. Yet, I couldn't stop it any more than I could stop breathing.

I got out of bed, went to the bathroom, and returned with a wet towel to clean her up. She didn't even stir. Once I'd discarded the towel, I slid between the sheets and pulled her closer to me. She slept facing me, one smooth thigh hooked onto my own. Her lips were slightly parted, her breathing even, and the expression on her face so peaceful.

She looked so trusting, unscathed by my world, and I wanted to keep it that way. I wanted to keep her safe and happy. Fresh out of college, she and the girls had that invincible mentality, and it was my job to protect them all.

My thoughts traveled back to my father and the only woman he claimed he loved. The all-consuming kind that tore you apart.

Winter Volkov. I was seven years old when Father brought Winter Volkov into our home. She was beautiful and different. Her golden curly hair and green eyes mesmerized men all over Ireland. But just as my father only had eyes for her, Winter only had eyes for my father.

Their love was cut short by the birth of their first—and last—child. Father was so devastated that he refused to spend any time around the baby at first. It left me to be the only family to hold Aisling. For the first two years of her life, I was her mother, father, and brother. Nanny

Shelby fed her and changed her diapers, but I read her stories, held her when she woke up at night, soothed her, and promised I'd make sure she was always safe.

And I fucking failed. When she needed me, I wasn't there.

The guilt of what happened twenty-one years ago still haunted me every damn day and night. It was the reason I ensured nobody in the mafia could trace my sister, her daughter, or even Juliette. As far as the world was concerned, my sister was dead, and so was her baby.

Davina stirred in my arms and my eyes traveled over her. I married her to protect my family, but I feared she had bewitched me and found her way into my soul. My biggest fear became a reality when I looked at her.

She was so fragile and beautiful, it made my damn chest ache. It was too late to resist her now. That same all-consuming feeling I'd seen on my father around Aisling's mother had taken hold of me while I wasn't looking.

And it honestly scared the living daylights out of me because I saw firsthand what losing her would look like.

I had to protect my céile at all costs.

CHAPTER 46
Davina

I stood on the balcony. My best friends, my grandfather, and Liam were all inside, but I was too frozen with fear to call out to them. I remained glued to my spot, too scared to move and too scared to scream.

They were laughing and hugging. I missed them, but they didn't miss me.

"Grandpa?" I called out, but my voice was too small, too weak. Their happiness drowned it. "Liam?"

My lies turned everyone away. I lied to my best friends. My grandfather. Liam.

They didn't want me anymore. Just like my parents.

The feeling of loneliness swelled inside me until it threatened to choke me. The emptiness hurt my chest, making it hard to breathe. I wanted to run away and hide. Just like when I was a little girl.

This isn't just friendship. We're family, we're friends, we're everything, *Wynter's voice echoed through my dream.* We're stuck with each other forever. Regardless of what happens. I don't care what continent we live on, we'll always be there for each other.

I'd found my family. I would keep it, by any means necessary. My decision finally made, I decided it was time to come clean with the girls. I couldn't keep lying to them.

And a memory flashed through my dream. A memory long forgotten that shouldn't have been.

I ran and ran, as fast as my legs would carry me. I tripped, the sand breaking my fall. The beach was hot on my kneecaps. I slowly rose and watched over the horizon. The waves crashed against the sandy shore as the seagulls circled me, squawking. I wondered if they were greeting me or warning me. The large lighthouse rose above the sand dunes. It bore a black, white, and gray daymark, and I recognized it immediately.

My grandpa used to bring me here for our summer vacations. The Oak Island Lighthouse. Where turtles emerged from their nests and crawled into the sea, and we'd stay up all night watching them make their journey.

"Are you lost, little girl?" A woman's voice startled me, and I turned to face her. I didn't recognize her, but she looked just like I'd always imagined my mother would look.

I nodded my head, but I remembered Grandpa's rule. No talking to strangers.

"Looking for your grandpa?" She smiled sweetly, and I grinned happily. If she knew Grandpa, I could talk to her.

So, I nodded eagerly. "Grandpa and I are on vacation. He taught me how to swim. He doesn't want me to drown," I blabbed. "The saltwater tastes funny and there are sharks. Baby sharks. They don't bite, but they still scare me," I rumbled, my words tripping over each other, eager to leave my lips.

"You're brave," she commended. "Swimming with the sharks, huh?" I nodded my head with wide eyes. "And let me guess, you're six years old." She didn't ask. "Your grandpa talks about you."

I smiled with a toothless grin. I had just lost my two front teeth the week before.

She pointed to the lighthouse. "He's in there. He wanted to see the view from the top."

I gasped. He'd never leave me behind.

"Go ahead, go find him," she encouraged. "He really likes lighthouses, doesn't he?"

"He does," I agreed. "Thank you."

I really liked her. Her hair was dark like the night and her eyes were gray, watching me pensively. I wondered if she could be my mommy. Everybody had a mommy and daddy, except for me.

"Go ahead now." She nudged me toward it.

I shuffled my bare feet through the sand, making my way to the lighthouse. "I love the beach. I love Grandpa. I love turtles. I love our vacations," I repeated the words over and over again until I entered the lighthouse.

It was empty inside, but it felt cooler than outside in the scorching sun. I started climbing the steep stairs.

I can do it, the thought was loud in my head. Grandpa always said I was a good climber.

I was at the first landing. "Grandpa?" My voice traveled but nobody responded. The only voice I heard was my own.

"Keep going." The woman's voice sounded behind me, startling me. I didn't hear her. I thought she'd left, but her encouraging smile assured me it was okay.

I continued to the second landing, and that was when I saw Grandpa. He was all the way at the bottom.

"Hello, Grandpa," I yelled, grinning widely.

"Davina," Grandpa shouted. "Come down from there."

I smiled. "It's okay," I assured him. "The lady said you're here. I came for you. She's with me."

His eyes traveled behind me and sheer horror entered his gaze.

"Dalia, what are you doing?" he asked. "Get away from her."

Why? She was so nice.

A set of gray eyes that look like mine filled with concern. Grandpa's eyes darted all around, frantically searching. I didn't know what for. He was so far down, like a deep tunnel, but I wasn't scared.

He shuffled to the first set of stairs. "Stay right there, Davina," he ordered in his stern voice. "And you, Dalia, need to leave."

But I was too eager to get to him, and I didn't want him climbing so many stairs. I rushed down the steps. One step. Two steps. Three steps.

A hand on my back, then a push. I tried to lean back and regain my balance, but my foot tripped against the narrow step, and the next thing I *knew, the world tumbled. Falling through the air, I outstretched my hands, reaching for my grandpa, but I couldn't reach him.*

A scream tore through my lips as I flew through the air.

Grandpa's voice cried in my ear, "Wake up, my Davina. Wake up."

My eyes shot open.

I was face down on my stomach, sweat covering my skin as I hung on the edge of the bed, my fingers gripping the sheets. My heart raced, thundering so hard it hurt my chest.

My chest tightened, making it hard to breathe. I swallowed a lump in my throat. I occasionally had nightmares like this, but it had never been as vivid and clear as tonight. I forgot about that Oak Island Lighthouse, about that entire incident. And the woman. Somehow, I didn't think she was a stranger, yet I'd never seen her again.

No fucking wonder I was scared of heights.

Slowly shifting, I glanced to my right and found Liam asleep, his hand outstretched to me. Just like in my dream when I reached for my grandpa. As if to assure myself he was real, I reached out and touched Liam's hand. A feather-light touch, and instant comfort washed over me.

Liam's here.

A slow relieved breath swished through my lips and my heart's wild thundering eased. It made no sense why I cared that he was here. He forced me into this marriage.

After you stole from him, my reason whispered.

Yet, he felt safe. My instinct told me he'd protect me, no matter what. My eyes roamed over his naked body. He really was beautiful. Yes, he was in his forties, but he'd put twenty-year-olds' to shame with his fit, muscled body.

From the first moment I saw him three months ago, my attraction to him was instant. There was no doubt he was good-looking with that sculpted, tattooed body, but it was more than that.

It was like a pull. It would always draw you in.

I carefully got out of bed, my bare feet silent against the hardwood. I was completely naked, and I expected Liam's cum to run down my thighs since I fell asleep without cleaning up, but there was none. Did he clean me up? It was the only logical explanation.

My eyes had gotten used to the dark, so I searched for something to put on. I couldn't go around his penthouse naked. I found his shirt and bent over to pick it up. His unique scent of sandalwood, clean and crisp, hit me, and I was instantly aroused despite my aching muscles.

Ignoring my body's response, I pulled it over my head.

I padded across the room, the hardwood floors cool under my feet. It felt good against my hot skin. His bedroom was so much bigger than anything I was used to, especially after spending four years in a dorm room with four girls. Our combined dorm fit into his bedroom with plenty of room to spare.

I headed toward the bedroom door and out into the hallway. I was dying for a glass of water. The only problem was that the kitchen was an extension of the dining room and the large floor-to-ceiling window extended into it. Inhaling deeply and then slowly releasing my breath, I eyed the entrance to the dining room.

My heart skidded to a halt.

Large shutters covered the entire window. Liam had the entire window with the most magnificent view covered. *For me.*

Something fluttered in the pit of my stomach and my heart felt strangely... warm. Or something. Unlike anything I had ever felt.

I licked my lips and padded into the kitchen, then grabbed a glass. This place was so pristine and clean, I feared just pouring a glass of water would mess up the immaculate surface.

After finishing my water, I placed my glass into the dishwasher, careful not to make too much noise. Then I continued to wander around until I found Liam's office. Three monitors were on the large mahogany desk. Just like everything else this man owned, this room was large and decorated with taste and luxury. It exuded an intense, masculine vibe.

A black leather sofa and chairs placed on the farthest side of the large office gave it an approachable feel. A large chair sat empty behind the desk, and I could imagine him seated there.

I trailed my fingers over the smooth surfaces of the furniture. The leather couch, then the desk, the fancy handles. My fingers wrapped around the handle of the drawer and I tugged on it. I didn't expect it to open, but it did. To reveal a handgun.

"Well, he *is* a mobster," I muttered.

I tugged on the second drawer, which revealed documents. Curiously, I pulled them out and started reading. My eyes widened with each word I read.

It was a will made by the Cullen family, with birth certificates enclosed. Juliette's and her brother's. It had to be the birth certificates Juliette found.

Killian and Juliette Cullen.

I read the next document. It was a Brennan family tree. And sure as shit, Juliette and her brother weren't on it.

The next documents were about Aisling and Wynter and their legal name change. None of it made sense. Then the will of Liam's father, leaving it all to his son and his biological children. In the event he had no biological children, he was to get none of it.

Good God! How many secrets lurked in the dark?

"What are you doing?" I whirled around at hearing Liam's voice, all the documents in my hand flying through the air.

"I-It... it was open," I stammered, looking at him. He was in only his pajama pants, his chest and torso bare.

He took two steps and was right in front of me. He took in the chaos of the scattered paperwork on the floor. I knelt down, surrounded by his secrets, and rushed to collect them all and stuff them back into the drawer with haste.

"I'm sorry," I apologized. "I-I had a bad dream and then..." I trailed off, because what could I possibly say. I was snooping? It was clear that I was.

"What was the bad dream about?" he inquired, and I sighed. Maybe he'd let go of the snooping part.

"I remembered something," I rasped in a hoarse voice. "I think it's the reason I'm scared of heights."

Surprise flashed in his eyes. "What was it?"

I described my dream, the memory from my childhood. Every single part I remembered. I didn't expect to pour it all out.

"It's stupid, but I think that woman... I think she's my mother," I blurted out.

I didn't know what I expected from Liam, but it wasn't his next words.

"There's a file in the drawer about you. The last folder, right on the bottom."

"What?" I gasped in shock. "You had me investigated?"

He didn't move, holding my gaze. He was silent for too long, his shoulders visibly tense. My eyes flashed to the drawer.

"What does it say?" I whispered.

"Are you sure you want to know?"

My heart drummed against my chest wildly, like a bird in its cage. If he was asking me that, it must be bad. Right? Yet, I didn't want to be ignorant. I finally understood my fear of heights. It was time I knew it all.

"Yes."

"You're right. That was your mother that day on Oak Island." My heart sank with his confirmation. The little girl in my dream didn't understand it, but the adult me did. My mother purposely sent me into the lighthouse, knowing Grandpa wasn't there. "She pushed you down the stairs. Your grandfather wasn't the only witness. The lightkeeper saw it all too. She was convicted of attempted murder." A little hiccoughing sound escaped me. "Attempted murder of you. She had another daughter before you. The scenario was similar to yours, except that little girl didn't survive. They couldn't prove it, not until she attempted the same with you. She's still serving her sentence, scheduled for parole in another two years."

I blinked. A dull ache traveled through my system, but surprisingly, it didn't shatter me. It fucking sucked, but I never really had a mother anyway. You couldn't mourn something you never had.

"Why?" I choked out. "Why would she want to kill me? I was just a kid."

"She was crazy. Selfish. She thought if she eliminated you, your father would take her back."

The explanation didn't make me feel better.

His big palms cupped my cheeks, holding me captive. "Her loss."

I blinked. "It still kind of sucks."

He nodded. "It does. Sometimes life sucks, and people we love hurt us, but it makes us stronger."

I exhaled a shaky breath. "Is that supposed to make me feel better?"

He brushed his mouth against the tip of my nose. "Yes. I'll never let anyone hurt you. Family or not." The heat of his stare seeped into my bloodstream, filling my chest with warmth. "I'll never let you go, but I'll protect you with my every breath. You're part of me, Davina."

The pressure building in my lungs grew at the intensity of his words and promises that I was certain he'd keep. I met his gaze, possessiveness and darkness that kept pulling me in.

"Why?" I breathed.

"Because you're mine." Simple. Possessive. True.

"I am," I confirmed against his lips. And I didn't regret it.

"You want to know about your father?" he asked.

A choked laugh escaped me. "Did he try to kill me too?"

"No, he didn't."

I pushed my forehead into his chest. "That's good," I murmured. "I don't know, Liam. I want to know. I'm tired of being oblivious to it all. But he obviously doesn't care about me. Otherwise, he'd have at least met me. And I know he doesn't matter. Not really. I have all I need now."

I needed a father when I was a kid, and he wasn't there. There was nothing that learning his name could give me. He only had one thing over my own mother: he didn't try to kill me. But other than that, neither one of those two had any reason to be in my life.

So why did curiosity nudge me forward?

The lack of my parents in my life always made me feel like I was lacking something, but that was on them, not on me. Like Liam said: their loss.

"Davina, you should know one thing about your father." Liam's voice was soft but firm.

The next heartbeat drummed achingly inside my chest. "Okay, tell me."

It was probably time I learned who they both were. "He's a senator." My shoulders tensed, but I remained still. "Senator Ashford."

"No wonder he didn't want an illegitimate daughter," I said. "It would have ruined his career."

"You have five brothers and one sister, all older than you," Liam continued. "One of those brothers is illegitimate."

"Dear old Dad got around, huh?" I muttered bitterly.

"He did," he retorted dryly.

I recalled the day we got married, when the judge mentioned Byron Ashford.

"So you know the Ashford family?" I asked him.

"I do. Your father is a corrupt motherfucker, but your brothers and sister are good people. Your sister Aurora recently got married. Last year, in fact. She's an FBI profiler."

"That guy…" I paused. "Alexei Nikolaev. He's her husband."

Liam nodded. "He's your brother-in-law."

Unbeknownst to Senator Ashford, both of his daughters were now married to mobsters.

"How did her father take the news about his daughter marrying a mobster?" I asked, although it didn't really matter. That man would never accept me, even if I married a president.

"His daughter refused to end or hide her relationship and marriage to her husband, so he severed all connections with her."

I took a deep breath, then exhaled slowly. *I have brothers and a sister.* I had wanted siblings my whole life, and now that I learned it was a reality, I wasn't quite sure what to do with it. The Ashford men were known as the Billionaire Kings, among the crème-de-la-crème of elite society. Handsome. Rich as sin. And reclusive.

"Their mother is from this area, actually," Liam added. "My sister knew her. Mrs. Ashford was killed over twenty-some years ago. Drive-by shooting in D.C. by one of the syndicate rivals."

Approaching them would be pointless. Besides, they were strangers. Nobodies to me. I had everything I loved and wanted right here—my best friends and my husband.

Yet, I couldn't shake off the feeling of curiosity. I'd always wished for a big family, and this was my chance for it.

"Why was Alexei Nikolaev at City Hall?" I asked Liam.

He hesitated to answer for a heartbeat too long. "Your sister knows about you and wants you in her life."

Everything is happening too soon.

"I don't know." I hesitated. The girl scared of rejection was still deep down inside me. "I have everything I want right here." My voice was hoarse, but I meant it. They said blood was thicker than water and familial bonds would always be stronger, but in my case, that wasn't true. My grandfather was the only blood family that mattered to me, along with my girlfriends and my husband. It was all the family I needed for now.

"You have connections, don't you?" I asked, never lifting my head.

"Yes."

"Can you make sure that my mother never gets out of prison?" I didn't regret the words that came out. My grandfather taught me to be fair and forgiving, but only when a person deserves it. My mother didn't.

"Yes."

And that was that. I knew without a doubt he'd make it happen, and she'd never be able to hurt anyone again.

"Do you want to meet your father?"

I shook my head. "No, I don't." I didn't even have to think about it. Senator Ashford blew his chance. He knew about me and swept me under the rug. My grandfather never revealed the details of my birth or my father's identity, but he was honest. When I was old enough and asked a million questions about my parents, he finally sat me down and explained.

He told me just enough truth to understand my parents didn't want a baby, and then added how happy he was that *he* had me. He'd always said that Grandma and I were the best things that happened to him.

"Do you want to meet your brothers and sister?"

"Maybe one day." When I was braver and no longer planning heists with my best friends. "Thank you, Liam," I whispered. It was funny how the universe worked. Maybe I was meant to end up in his room three months ago or get caught by him in his office, so I could finally learn for myself what my grandfather had been saying all along. Family was more important than just blood. "A-are you mad about the other stuff?" I rasped.

His big palm rubbed my back. Maybe I was a coward, but I didn't dare look up to see his face. So I remained, my forehead pressed against his chest, and soaked up his strength and comfort.

"What have you seen, Davina?" he asked, his hand never pausing on my back.

"I saw a gun," I muttered. "Which wasn't surprising. You know, since you're a gangster and all."

"Gangster?" His chest rumbled with laughter.

"A kingpin of the underworld?"

A soft chuckle vibrated through his chest and straight to mine. My lips curved into a smile, feeling lighter. I liked him laughing.

"If you say pimp next, I'm going to have to smack your pretty little bottom."

"At least you think my bottom is pretty," I teased, and his hands lowered down to my ass, his fingers gently squeezing it. I felt his shaft harden, pressing against my belly, and instantly my body responded. My hands came around his waist and I rubbed myself against his erection. "I also saw your family tree, and your father's will with the clause about children. Then I read the will of Juliette's parents."

He tensed slightly, but his hands never stopped touching me. In such a short amount of time, this man's touch had become a necessity. I wanted his approval, his acceptance... his love. God, was it normal to want all that to happen this fast?

"I'm sorry," I choked out, emotion thick in my voice. His hands came to my shoulders and gently peeled me away from him. He took my chin in one hand, his fingers holding it firmly. Lifting my gaze, I met his dark blues. He didn't look angry. "I won't say anything," I added quietly. "About any of it."

Even though Juliette already saw the birth certificate, it wasn't my place to verify it. I couldn't betray her trust. I had to walk a delicate line here, staying loyal to both my husband and my friends.

Our eyes locked, and it was hard to know what Liam was thinking. Obviously, he wanted me. His erection pressed against me, straining for me, just the way I seemed to crave him.

"Get on the desk, my céile."

God, the fact that my insides combusted into flames at his command spoke volumes. I had never been so sex-crazed, and now I pretty much behaved like I was sexually deprived.

I wanted to please him. I wanted to be his everything. Because I loved him.

CHAPTER 47
Davina

The startling realization immobilized me as I stared at my husband while processing this latest revelation. It was scary. Terrifying. Thrilling. So damn thrilling that I forgot what he had asked me to do.

So when I didn't move fast enough for his liking, he looped his hands around my waist and sat me on the desk. Eye-to-eye with my husband, we stared at each other. His uncovered torso gave me a full view of his muscles and mouth-watering abs. He was so beautiful and strong, he stole my breath. But even more than his muscular body, I liked the way he cared about his family. Protected the ones he loved.

"Spread your legs," he ordered, his expression unreadable. I obeyed, regretting not putting some panties on and now being on display. "Lift your legs and put them on the desk."

I did as he said, tempted to fight him but too eager to know what he was about to do. After all, he was used to me being sassy. But right now, more than anything, I wanted to please him. I waited, anticipation building within me. My breathing slightly hitched, I remained silent, my heels planted on the edge of the desk and my legs spread wide open.

"Touch your pussy."

My soft gasp shattered the tense air at his demand. He cocked an eyebrow as if he waited for me to protest, and I bit into my lip, swallowing my words. Hesitantly, I snaked one hand between my legs and brushed my fingers over my clit.

A shudder rolled through my body, my folds already wet and achy. My fingers felt sticky as I kept rubbing, and a soft moan slipped through my lips. Satisfied I was doing what he commanded, Liam strode to the minibar I hadn't noticed.

I watched him fill a glass with ice and cognac, his eyes flicking my way to ensure I kept touching myself. By the time he returned to me, I shuddered with the need for release, my two fingers inside me, thrusting in and out. Except it wasn't enough. I needed him—his fingers, his cock.

He slid into his chair, watching me and sipping on his cognac. With heavy eyelids, I watched his lips on the rim of the glass, and suddenly I was dying for a taste of the alcohol. For the taste of him.

My fingers slid in and out of my wet folds, brushing against my clit faster and faster. Frustration crawled up my spine that he just sat there, watching me, instead of touching me.

"Are you going to make me do all the work?" I rasped, annoyed. It was scary how much I craved his touch. He had ruined me for anyone else. I only wanted him—his hands, his mouth, his cock. "Could have at least offered me a drink," I breathed.

He smiled darkly, then took another sip of his cognac. When he removed his lips from the glass, he rolled the ice in his mouth then leaned over and pressed his cold lips to my inner thigh.

"Ahhhh," I gasped, bracing myself on one hand. His mouth was my own brand of heaven. I rubbed my clit vigorously, hungry for release. I felt it at the base of my spine, now that his lips were trailing higher and higher to my sweet spot. He trailed kisses up my thigh, running the tip of the ice over my heated skin. The combination of hot and cold, along with his stubble against my soft skin created unbearable friction. My hips lifted off the desk, eager for his lips on my entrance. I was so damn close.

His hand wrapped around my wrist and stilled it, denying me pleasure. My gaze snapped to him.

"What—"

"Your pleasure will come from me," he proclaimed as he brought the glass halfway to his mouth with his other hand. A frustrated noise bubbled in my throat, but I said nothing. I knew the pleasure he alluded to would be so much better than anything I could do.

Liam brought the glass of cognac to his lips, the ice clanking with each movement. My tongue swept across my lower lip, my heart thundered against my rib cage. He took a sip of his drink and caught another cube of ice between his teeth. As if he was my magnetic opposite, I leaned over, unable to resist, and licked his cold lips. The ice dripped down his stubbled chin and I followed the trail of it.

This man was my alcohol, my drug, my aphrodisiac.

In one swift move, he leaned me back, and before I could protest, he disappeared between my legs. The ice against my hot, soaking folds had me jerking on the smooth surface of his desk. Fireworks exploded through every fiber of my being, and before I could scoot away, Liam grabbed hold of my thighs, keeping me in place as he thrust the ice cube against my clit.

The cube must have melted, because I felt his tongue against my clit.

"Oh, fuck," I moaned. His teeth nibbled on my clit at the same time that his fingers thrust deep inside me. The combination of ice and heat heightened all my senses on my entrance. His teeth on my clit sent shockwaves to my core as he mercilessly sucked and flicked his tongue against me.

Pleasure shot through me and my head hit the desk, my back arching as I came hard, shaking against his mouth. My legs slid off the desk, dangling from the edge, and I felt Liam's hands wrap around my ankles. He lifted his head from between my legs, licking his lips as his stare focused on me. The arrogance etched across his face told me he felt smug with himself.

He had every reason for it, not that I'd ever admit it. But holy smokes. Every time with him was earth-shattering. My legs on his thighs, he reached over beside me and lifted the glass of cognac to his lips.

Cognac. It always seemed to come down to cognac with him.

"My wife wants some cognac?" he asked nonchalantly.

I shrugged. "It's only polite to offer, you know."

He scoffed softly. "Polite?"

"Yes." I was feeling too relaxed after the orgasm he delivered and didn't realize the trap until it was too late.

"Was it polite to steal?" he drawled, taking another sip. He didn't seem mad, just slightly amused. I watched his Adam's apple move as he swallowed. Goddamnit, did he have to have a good-looking neck too? "Was it polite to go through my desk and read papers that weren't meant for you?"

He had me there. If there was a trend here, he seemed to always catch me committing a crime. But he should have locked the drawer if he didn't want any stranger's eyes on it.

"Do you want a baby?" I asked instead, unwilling to admit my wrongdoings.

Personally, I thought it was crappy that his father put a clause like that into his will, but to each their own. You couldn't control it. Though, without even knowing Liam's exact financial situation, I was certain that he didn't need his father's inheritance. But something about his father's will nagged at me.

"Do *you* want a baby, céile?" he retorted instead.

I tilted my head, watching him for any telltale signs.

"Liam, I'm twenty-one," I deadpanned. "A baby is the last thing on my mind."

He watched me in silence for three heartbeats before he asked, "What is on your mind?" I reached for his glass of cognac, but the fingers of his free hand wrapped around my wrist. "Tell me."

"Well, right at this moment, a drink is on my mind," I said.

"And robberies?" he inquired, and my heart skidded to a halt. "Are you planning any others?"

I laughed, though it sounded fake even to my own ears. "Should I?" I asked instead. "I thought you told me your money is my money."

Good thinking, I congratulated myself. *Turn it around.*

"Avoiding answering, huh?" he mused, as if I entertained him.

I remained silent because this man was too perceptive. He had a lot more years and experience of being a criminal over us, so I exercised my Fifth Amendment.

"What are you doing with all that money, Davina?" Jesus Christ, this man was relentless.

"I have no clue what you're talking about," I breathed out, my heart threatening to beat out of my chest.

Mental note: our school for raising criminals needed a class on swift interrogation avoidance. Ah, and distraction techniques.

Distraction!

I slid off the table and tugged on his pajama pants. He narrowed his eyes on me, probably aware of my diversion tactic, but he played along. Lifting his ass off the chair, I pulled his pants down his strong legs and discarded them onto the floor.

God, he was beautiful. Every single inch of him. Age played no factor.

For a moment, guilt gnawed at me. So many lies. To my girlfriends. To Liam. I didn't like it. I should have been upfront with Juliette and my friends about what happened in the club. But now it felt like I had dug myself deeper into this forbidden affair.

Does it still make it forbidden if he's my husband? I pondered, and immediately mentally slapped myself.

Nothing like finding justifications for my wrongdoings. But for now, I'd chosen to ignore my conscience and not ruin this. Whatever *this* was. I was his wife. Yes, my friends and I were doing something wrong, but we'd only rob criminals. So that made it alright. *Maybe?*

But I loved him. I wasn't sure exactly what kind of love it was, but I knew I wanted to make him happy. Please him. Give him everything and anything. Maybe after this heist, I'd just focus on my marriage. Come clean with the girls, and then focus on my husband.

My husband.

He was mine, and I'd keep him. Grandpa always said when you found something good, you fought for it. You kept it. Grandpa fought for me. I'd fight for my friends. For Liam. For my own happily ever after. I wasn't my parents' daughter. I was my grandpa's daughter.

My heartbeat fluttered. My chest felt lighter as I sat on his lap and determination settled in. A bulge poked at my ass, and it was my turn to smile smugly. I adjusted myself on his lap so I was facing him. I folded my legs so my knees cradled his lap, my arms wrapped around his neck.

Leaning into him, I showered his neck with small kisses while grinding against his hard cock, causing friction. I could taste his pulse, the addictive scent of him finding a permanent home in my lungs.

"I could be convinced to have a baby," I murmured against his skin. His cock was hard, thick, and so ready that my insides fluttered with a carnal need.

His hand gripped the back of my neck and pulled me away so he could see my face.

"Really?"

He didn't believe me. No surprise there.

"Yeah, really," I breathed out, leaning forward again and peppering his cheek with kisses.

Don't be a liar, my mind whispered, but I hushed it down. Eventually I wanted to have children. And I didn't tell him I could be convinced to have a baby *now*, but if he wanted or needed to have a baby, I'd do it. For him. When the timing was right.

"Let's not rush it," I added, wanting to be as honest as I could with him.

Feminism went out the penthouse window.

"We should practice," I rasped, licking the corner of his lips. God, he tasted amazing. Like cognac, me, and delicious sin.

"Are you on birth control?" I couldn't help but smile internally. We were having this conversation entirely too late. We'd had so much sex that if I wasn't, I had no doubt I'd be pregnant.

"Implant."

"We'll get rid of it," he growled, his palm on my belly as if he was already imagining me pregnant. It was lunacy, but it made me feel hot. This man was dangerous, unscrupulous in getting what he wanted. After all, it was the reason we were married now. Yet somehow, I had been caught and had no desire to escape him.

"Yes, eventually," I agreed.

Liam entered me slowly, my slick core allowing his cock a smooth entrance. He was big, filling me without being all the way in. I shuddered with pleasure, the sensation of him pushing deeper into me, gripping me, and tearing through my walls.

I watched the spot where our bodies connected, him pushing inside me inch by inch, and a throaty moan filled the air. It was fucking erotic watching our joined bodies, his hard length disappearing inside me.

"Fuck, I love hearing your moans," he groaned. "I'm going to fuck you every day for the rest of our lives just to hear your sexy, throaty voice."

Our gazes met, and his pulled me into their beautiful dark depths. I went willingly because I wanted to enjoy every second of being his. He rolled his hips until his cock was all the way inside me.

"I've waited a lifetime for you."

I gasped at his words, his cock stretching me in the most delicious way. He waited for *me*. And as strange as it sounded, I'd waited for him. Maybe I'd searched for him too. Despite our age disparity.

My arms circled around Liam's neck as he drove slowly into me, the position giving him depth and hitting all the right spots with each thrust. His mouth on me was gentle, almost riveting as if he wanted to worship me. Love me. It was the first time that we had taken it slow, and it felt dangerously close to lovemaking.

This Liam triggered something deep inside of me, something I had feared my entire life. That all-consuming feeling that would make you do anything and everything for the person you love, even at the cost of your own life. Yet, I knew there was no stopping it. *I love him!*

Each breath, each kiss, and each second brought me closer and closer to admitting my love for him. The consuming, corrupted, blind kind of love. But it was my love to give to whomever I liked.

And Liam Brennan, my husband, was the one I chose.

"Open up to me, céile." He gently nipped the sensitive skin on my neck, then followed up with a lick. "Let me all the way in."

He was so big that I felt the delicious burn with every thrust. I was soaking wet, my body a depraved temple only for him. His fingers dug into my ass as he pounded inside, claiming every single inch of me.

I whimpered against him, rolling my hips. "L-Liam," I breathed. "I love"—*you*—"this."

The words almost slipped, the feelings swallowing me. I captured his lips as his rhythm increased, the ferocity of his slams growing. Deep and unhurried. Fast and merciless.

I might have robbed this man of a million dollars, but he had robbed me of all my senses and reason. He had robbed me of my heart; it was his.

"Ride me, céile," he growled.

He rammed into me faster and harder, the power of his hips driven by animalistic force, fucking me deep and frantically. He became my air and my lungs, his mouth consuming me. I held on to him like he was my lifeline.

"Aaah... Liam... I'm coming..."

The orgasm slammed into me so hard, I rolled my head back and my lips left his. It was so intense that white dots swam in my vision. I swore I fluttered up into space where nothing existed except for this feeling and Liam.

"Fuck, fuck," Liam grunted and his hands on me tightened. He powered into me, fucking me through my orgasm as my pussy clenched around his shaft. "Who's fucking you?"

"You," I moaned. "You, my husband!"

The orgasm swallowed me whole, my heart fluttered away from me, and I was certain it went to him. This orgasm was unlike any other we'd shared, and I rode the wave, hungry for such an out-of-body experience.

My fingers dug into Liam's shoulders, holding on to him. His shoulders tightened and he came, his cum filling my insides.

I closed my eyes, relishing in all the sensations swirling inside me. This man was in the center of them all. His head rested in the crook of my neck, his breathing matching my own.

My whole body laid slack against him and I inhaled his scent deeply. Two heartbeats drummed as one. It took a while for my mind to settle and for our earlier conversation to come back to the forefront of my mind.

Seconds stretched into minutes and a strange kind of peace washed over me with these latest revelations. All this felt so right.

Slightly shifting away from me, my gaze sought out his.

"Why did your father put that clause in his will?" I asked him curiously. "From everything I've heard from Juliette, she always says you don't want more kids and never wanted to marry."

I didn't expect him to answer honestly. I wasn't even sure what prompted me to ask him. He held my gaze, turmoil replacing earlier lust.

"In our family, blood relations are everything," he started, and I stilled in his arms. "I'm not saying it's right, but Killian and Juliette won't be recognized as my descendants. Not in the Brennan family. Not in my slightly illegal businesses." I scoffed at his terminology, but I didn't interrupt. "Unfortunately, my father has earned us a few enemies that would take the first opportunity to strike once we weaken."

I frowned, not following his meaning. "Aisling, Wynter's mother, is my half-sister. My father seduced the daughter of a powerful Pakhan." When I gave him a confused look, he explained. "The head of the Russian mafia. Father smuggled her out of Russia and kept her as his mistress."

I gasped. "While your mother was alive?"

His hands roamed my back, the movements soothing.

"My mother had been in a coma for several years by that time," he explained. "A traumatic head injury. In our world, marriage is for life, and getting remarried wasn't an option while she was alive."

I nipped his chin gently.

"That would have been good to know before I said my vows," I teased him, trying to lighten the mood.

"My Davina," he purred. "Once I got you, I wasn't going to let you go."

It was definitely wrong that his words didn't make me want to run away screaming. Coming from parents that couldn't commit to each other or me, this commitment made me beam. I knew he'd never abandon his children like my parents abandoned me. And deep down, I knew he'd never abandon me either.

"Back to your father and his marriage," I reminded him before I could get sidetracked.

"My parents' marriage wasn't a happy one. It was arranged. Nobody blamed my father for finding himself a woman, least of all me. I just wished it wasn't that specific woman, because it started a war. Although, Winter Volkov was amazing. Gentle and kind. Kind of hard to believe her father was the ruthless Pakhan."

"Winter?" I gasped in shock.

"Yes, Wynter was named after her grandmother, just spelled differently," he explained. "Anyhow, my mother died a month before Aisling was born. My father married his mistress, but she ended up dying a month later while giving birth to Aisling. God gives and God takes. My father loved Aisling's mother more than anything on this earth. He has never been quite the same since her death."

So much tragedy. My arms tightened around him, hoping to offer comfort.

"I'm sorry," I murmured, my fingers brushing through his thick hair. "For the loss of your mother and your father's loss." I thought back to my grandfather and how much he talked about my grandma. He loved her very much and there wasn't anyone else for him after she passed away.

"Thank you." His nose brushed against mine, the move so tender. He seemed to do that frequently, like his own personal telltale affection. "Anyway, the Pakhan wanted Aisling back, to replace the loss of his daughter. He blamed my father for her death. We wouldn't hear of it, and the feud escalated. I slowly pushed all the Bratva out of New York; however, when Aisling became old enough, she caught the eye of another rival mafia family here in the city. And then more bloodshed followed."

"Jesus," I muttered. "Talk about drama."

He nodded his agreement, and for a moment, both of us were lost in our own thoughts.

"Why can't Killian be your heir?" I asked, even though remembering what the girls had said, I suspected the answer.

"I consider Killian my son and thought he would follow me when the time came, but I was aware of the possibility that people would hold it against him that he isn't related to me by blood. He has proven himself. Multiple times. But families in this organization are old-fashioned. They insist on someone of blood relations to inherit."

"D-didn't your father have brothers?"

He shook his head, his fingers brushing my hair off my shoulder.

"If I don't produce an heir, others within our organization will try to take over. Fight over it. It will put my sister and Wynter in danger. Juliette and Killian too."

"B-but why?" I didn't understand his reasoning. "And if you had a baby, he or she won't be able to help you for decades to come."

"It is human nature to fight for power, and people within my own organization are no different. But they fear me and respect me. It won't be the same with Killian if I appoint him as head of the family. Some might see Juliette and Killian as obstacles and eliminate them. The Russians will try to exploit weaknesses in our organization and then they'll attack, get their hands on Wynter and her mother."

"Jesus Christ," I breathed. I had to admit that this world scared me slightly. After all, I'd only been a criminal for a few weeks. "And you want to bring a baby into this world?"

"With a baby, they'll see the future for our family and organization. And I can count on Killian to help until our children are old enough."

Goddamn, that was a lot to digest. When he blackmailed me into this marriage, it didn't even occur to me that babies would be involved. I thought he had two grown children and starting over was the last thing on his mind.

But Juliette, Wynter, and Ivy always came through for me. If I could protect them with this simple act, I knew without a doubt that I had to. Just as Liam was protecting them.

"Why didn't you marry sooner then?" I whispered. He was one of those men that attracted women's attention everywhere he went. I knew it without a doubt. He wouldn't have had issues securing a wife.

"I never caught a woman stealing from me," he teased, affectionately taking my bottom lip between his teeth. He nipped it, then eased the sting with his tongue. A shiver coasted through me. He tasted like my happiness. "And there has never been a woman that made me remotely interested in taking that leap," he mused.

I narrowed my eyes. "Are you mocking me?"

"Not at all. Your sassy mouth makes it hard to resist you."

Goosebumps broke through my skin and his arms wrapped around me, his body providing me the needed heat. The last few weeks had all gone awry, but somehow in all the clusterfuck, I felt happier now than I ever had.

"I guess we're having a baby," I rasped, emotions choking me. Jesus, if I was emotional before the hormones kicked in, I'd be a mess during pregnancy. I shifted so I could lock gazes with him. "I'll make an appointment to have my implant removed. All I ask is that we don't rush it."

"Just like that?" he asked, disbelief evident on his face.

"Well, you got my grandfather transferred to a fancy facility here in the city just like that," I told him. "This is no different. You do for me, and I do for you."

His eyes studied me, his piercing gaze seeing deep down into my soul.

"It's so much more." He cupped my cheek, holding my gaze. "Having a baby is a lot more than me helping your grandfather. You care for him, and bringing him close allows you to see him more frequently. Like I told you, I had a selfish reason behind it too."

I blinked, tears filling my eyes and threatening to spill over. "It means so much to me," I told him softly. "He's doing so well. The girls and I visit him almost every day. He's happy, and you'd think he gained years back. Selfish or not, you've made me so happy."

He pressed a kiss on the tip of my nose. "Good, that makes me happy," he said, his voice warm. "Your happiness means the world to me."

I grinned stupidly. "Control freak."

"You know it, woman. You're mine, and I'm not letting go."

I pressed my cheek against his. "You're mine too, then."

"I am." Not an ounce of hesitation or delay. This man knew what he wanted, and I was it. I'd never been happier. *He's mine*, I thought giddily. I just had to get this heist done and then we'd be working on having a baby. To protect all the people I love in my life.

"The girls have been there for me a lot over the last four years," I admitted softly. "If having a baby with you keeps them safe, along with your sister, Killian, and you, then we do it." I brushed my nose against his. "I always wanted a big family. And I kind of like the idea of being yours. Maybe having baby duty will tire you out sooner in the bedroom and I won't have to beg for a reprieve."

"You're a unique woman, Davina. And I'm so goddamn lucky you decided to spy on me in the shower." My cheeks heated at that memory that seemed like a lifetime ago.

"So am I," I confessed shyly. This man fucked me six ways to Sunday and I blushed at the memory of watching him jerk off.

His mouth skidded over my forehead, down my cheek, and then hovered over my pulse. The pulse that was my lifeline and beat for him.

My eyelids grew heavy and I felt fatigue settle into my bones. After all, we'd been physically active, and I'd been busy with the girls scheming our next heist.

"Liam?" I murmured sleepily, nuzzling into his chest.

"Hmmm."

"Wynter asked me to spend the next two nights with her. She's lonely and needs someone to record her while she's skating. I'm usually the one doing it. It helps her spot her mistakes."

Silence stretched.

"Is that okay?"

"I don't like not having you in my bed," he grumbled.

"She's almost done with her exams and that project she's helping with." That was true. And if Wynter was right about this next heist, we'd be set for a long time. "Then that'll be it," I added.

"Davina, we have to tell them." I knew he'd demand it. Honestly, I was surprised he let me get away with it for this long. "The longer it goes, the harder it will be to explain." He was right, I knew he was. "Besides, what will you say when you're pregnant? Blame it on the Holy Spirit?"

"I kind of like that plan," I said wryly.

"Davina," he warned.

"You're right," I caved. I had only decided it myself mere hours ago in my sleep. "We'll tell them." *Soon.*

"One week."

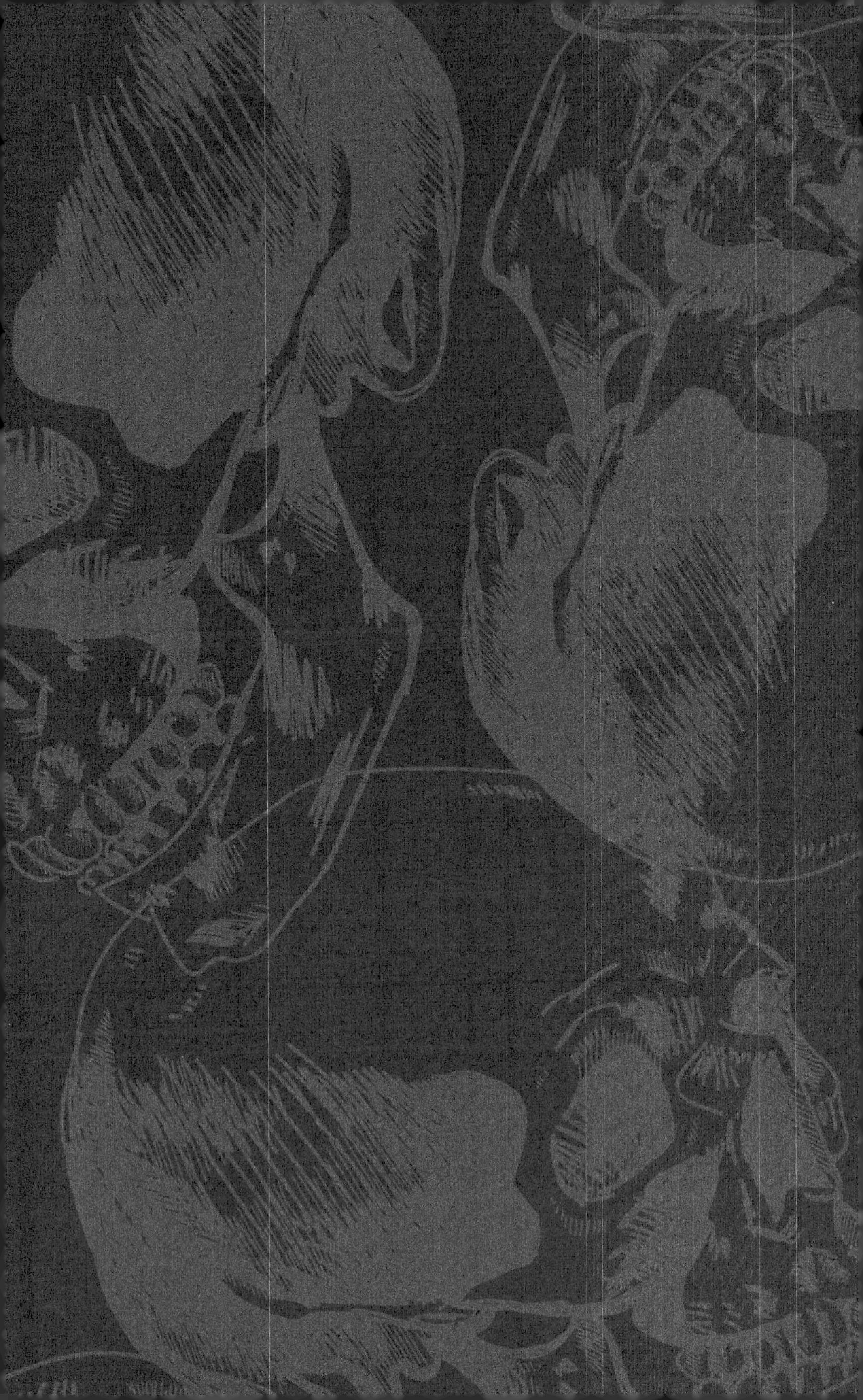

CHAPTER 48
Davina

"Welcome to Philadelphia!" The radio announcer timed it perfectly. The words echoed through the speakers of Wynter's Jeep just as we traveled over The Benjamin Franklin Bridge that crossed the Delaware River.

Good sign.

"Yes!" Juliette shouted from the back seat.

"This city is giving me good vibes," exclaimed Ivy.

"Definitely a good sign," Wynter said, glancing in the rearview mirror and smiling. Her eyes glanced my way and winked. "I think after this job, we can narrow down the property for the school."

"I'm thinking we'll want about ten to twenty acres," I added.

"Why so many?" Juliette frowned.

"Well, it will be like a college. We'll need dorms, study halls, probably a lot of gyms to teach some fighting skills, and grounds around the school for privacy and for kids to roam around," Wynter responded. "Rule number one: we won't tolerate any bullying. There will be kids from all different organizations. But in our school, they won't be rivals. They'll be teachers and students. Nothing more and nothing less."

"You actually read my texts," I teased.

"Of course I did. I'm all in," Wynter replied.

"We're *all* all in," Juliette chimed in. She and Ivy leaned over from the back seat, Ivy directly behind Wynter and Juliette behind me. "And I know there are women married to mobsters who are educated and strong. We could hire them to teach some of the classes so we don't risk exposure."

My head snapped her way. "That is actually a brilliant idea," I commended Juliette. "We'll need a list of all crime families and then we can start an evaluation of their skills."

My heart sped up at all the possibilities. *Look at us growing up!*

Juliette grinned, proud of her idea, and she had every right to be.

"I know of an FBI profiler," I added, the words slipping through before I realized.

"Oh, that's good. Profiling is going to be important to teach our little criminals," Ivy noted.

My eyes traveled over my four friends, and somehow, I found the timing to be appropriate.

"Okay, I have to tell you something," I started quietly, and everyone tensed.

"Jesus, don't tell me you found your birth certificate too," Wynter teased.

I gently slapped her on her forearm. "Well, it's associated with my birth," I admitted.

"We're all ears, D," Juliette announced.

"Have you heard of Senator Ashford and the Ashford family?" I questioned.

Ivy and Juliette shook their heads. "I think I have," Wynter replied. "His daughter, an FBI agent, married a mafia killer or something. It almost destroyed the Senator's career. His sons are known as the Billionaire Kings."

"I've heard of the Billionaire Kings," Ivy chimed in, excitedly. "Hot. Sexy. Throbbing with raw masculinity and arrogance."

I snickered at her description. She really knew the Ashford brothers. At least what the papers reported.

"What about them?" Juliette asked curiously.

CORRUPTED PLEASURE

I took a deep breath and slowly exhaled. "Apparently Senator Ashford's my father. And his kids are my half-siblings."

The girls were rendered speechless, the city noise seemed to be even louder. Admittedly, I just dropped a bomb on them.

"Holy shit," Ivy muttered, breaking the numbing silence. "The Ashford brothers are your brothers? The hot, sexy, super rich and single Billionaire Kings?"

"Yep, but don't forget their sister," I said.

Ivy waved her hand. "Yeah, but she's a girl and not single. But your brothers…"

"You're a horny virgin lush, Ivy," I reprimanded her teasingly. "The point is that she's an FBI agent, or an ex-agent. Whatever the case might be, she'd be an awesome addition to our school." When everyone remained quiet, I continued, "You don't agree?"

"I think it's a great idea," Wynter continued. "I'm just still processing the news."

"I feel like there have been so many skeletons coming out lately," Juliette muttered. I had to agree with her.

"How are you holding up, D?" Ivy asked.

I looked out at the horizon, down the river that ran south. "You know, I'm fine," I told them all. "I got all I need here. I have all of you and Liam—"

The words just slipped out, and gasps sounded around, followed by a deafening silence. My heart stilled and frustration at myself flickered in my chest. Liam and I were going to tell them all together. How could I have been so stupid to let it slip?

I met their gazes, confused looks in all their eyes.

"I'm sorry." My voice was hesitant. "I'm so sorry," I whispered. "I don't know how that happened."

Well, I kind of did. It all started on the night I peeped on him in the shower.

"You're seeing Uncle?" Wynter flicked a hesitant gaze to me then returned it to the road.

The cat was out of the bag. I might as well tell them everything.

"I married him," I answered hesitantly.

"Get the fuck out," Ivy rasped.

"I haven't told him anything," I assured them all quickly. "He caught me stealing that day at the Eastside. I didn't want you all stressing about it. Then, one thing led to another, and I married him."

Well, technically he forced me, but no need to go into those details.

"You've told him nothing?" Juliette stammered.

"I didn't tell him that you found your birth certificate," I quickly replied, hoping she'd hear the honesty in my voice. "Or that we're robbing mobsters." Though he was too smart and found out on his own. "I didn't tell him it was all of us robbing him."

I said *all of us*, but luckily none of them picked up on it. So theoretically, I was honest.

"But you married him?" Juliette asked again. "I mean, I knew you thought he was hot. But do you really like him?"

"Yes, I do. A lot. We kind of had sex and—"

"Eeew," Juliette cut me off. "He might not be my biological father, but we still don't want details." Then she took my hands into hers. "Holy shit, does that make you my stepmother and Wynter's aunt?" Her eyes shone mischievously.

I grinned. "Don't even think about calling me Mom," I warned her.

"Well, technically you can't be my stepmom since he's not actually my dad." She said it too casually, but I knew her latest finding still bothered her.

"Oh my God," Wynter mumbled. "I'm in such shock, I don't know what to say."

"That you'll forgive me for not telling you right away?" I suggested hopefully.

"I'm kind of upset you got married without us," Ivy complained, though her wide smile ruined her complaint.

"But we'll do everything else together," I vowed to them. "Kids. Birthdays. Holidays. I should have told you. It was stupid. I haven't told Grandpa either."

"Oh, man. He's gonna have your arse," Juliette warned, uttering the word *arse* purposely, just as Liam did. "He said he wants to be the grandpa at all our weddings."

"Maybe we can have a small ceremony to appease him?" Wynter suggested, grinning. "Don't get knocked up before we do."

"God, I love you girls." I beamed. "Who needs the Ashfords when I have such a wonderful family here?"

"Damn straight," all three answered in unison.

"But we'll have to meet your brothers," Ivy said. "We need to keep our prospects open."

A round of chuckles sounded in the car, then giggles and cheers.

"Okay, let's get back to the task at hand," I said. "Otherwise, our heist will go down the toilet."

Wynter reached for her phone and started scrolling through it, keeping her eyes on the road.

"Okay, this is the guy we're robbing," she announced, handing Ivy her phone. "They call him Priest."

"Wow, I hope he's not a real priest," Ivy murmured, her eyes full of lust, locked on the screen. "That body shouldn't go to waste. I'd worship it like it was my temple. So fucking hot."

Wynter and I scoffed. She'd find him hot for a day and then change her mind. Just mere minutes ago, she was salivating over the Billionaire Kings. She moved on quickly.

"Well, wait to worship that temple until after we've robbed him," Wynter retorted dryly.

"And some months go by afterward," I added wryly. "So the dust settles."

Ivy grumbled about abstinence. Why? I had no clue, because the girl was still a virgin.

"He looks kind of familiar," she added as she passed the phone to Juliette.

Juliette's gasp had all of us looking at her. "What?"

"That's the guy from Chicago," Juliette whispered. "The blonde one."

I blinked then snatched the phone from her. I recognized him the moment I saw the picture. The man wasn't the type you could forget. Just like Wynter's man and Dante DiLustro. Just like my husband. These were all unforgettable men. Not because they were gorgeous but because they exuded that raw power and ruthlessness.

"Are you sure?" Ivy questioned. "Granted, I only saw their arses in Chicago."

"Yes, I'm sure," she snapped. "I offered to let them both fuck me. At the same time. It's not something you easily forget."

Wynter slammed on the brakes in the middle of the bridge traffic. Ivy and Juliette gripped the headrests of the front seats to prevent themselves from flying through the windshield the same moment a blasting horn echoed from behind us.

"You what?" Wynter shrieked.

"Well, we said distract at any cost," Juliette muttered. "I distracted them. My boobs weren't easily accessible in that dress I wore, so I couldn't just flash them."

"Jesus Christ," I mumbled. So much for a good sign. "You couldn't offer them drinks or something? You're a damn virgin, how did you think you'd pull that one off?"

Juliette rolled her eyes. "It was all talk. I wasn't seriously going to let them fuck me."

"Fuck," Wynter cursed. "If you did that, he's sure to remember you." Another blast of a horn and she stuck her hand out the window and flipped a bird.

She resumed driving, muttering something under her breath.

"Say it clearly," I groaned. "I have to hear what you're saying."

"Yeah, stop muttering like an old lady," Juliette added.

"It's the way she thinks best," Ivy clarified, like we didn't know.

Wynter shook her head. "First thing, when he saw me—"

"Who?" Juliette, Ivy, and I asked at the same time.

"This guy that owns this casino and runs Philadelphia... Priest," she clarified. "Try to keep up." The three of us rolled our eyes.

"Why do I get the feeling that Wynter will be a slave driver when we start this school? She'll be whipping us all into shape whether we like it or not," Ivy muttered dryly.

Wynter glared at Ivy, but she ruined it with her smile. "Anyhow, when he saw me, he didn't recognize me from Chicago."

"When did he see you?" Juliette asked.

Tap. Tap. Tap.

Her fingers tapped against the steering wheel. "That's not the point right now," Wynter finally continued. "It's clear that Juliette was very successful at distracting the men in Chicago," she concluded. "Which means we need to get Priest out of the city; otherwise, he'll be suspicious if he sees you."

"Is his name really Priest?" Ivy questioned.

Wynter shrugged. "No clue."

"Is his name really important now?" I blurted out. "We have the entire plan laid out. This was supposed to be in-and-out. And now we have an unplanned obstacle at the eleventh damn hour!"

Get to the club. Block the exit with the Jeep. Dance while waiting for a call to unblock the exit to the money truck. Follow the money truck to their scheduled refill gas station. Distract the two men while the other goes into the gas station. Ivy's turn to seduce and possibly drug her victims. Then we steal the truck and take the money. Violà. Easy peasy.

"Umm, it's actually only five in the afternoon," Ivy muttered, never quite successful in overcoming the American slang or phrases.

"No need to panic, Davina," Wynter interrupted my little panic attack.

"How about if we call him from a Chicago number and say there is an emergency in that casino?" Juliette suggested. "Wynter can ask her mysterious guy for his number."

"Are you fishing for information on Wynter's man?" Ivy teased.

"Oh, I have Priest's number. And Dante DiLustro's. But let's focus on this Priest problem," Wynter interrupted. "Calling from a Chicago number is actually a good idea."

"Except none of us have a Chicago number," I grumbled.

Juliette and Wynter rolled their eyes, then Wynter blew a piece of curly hair out of her face.

"We'll get a burner phone," she concluded. "I saw mobsters use those to conduct their illegitimate activities," she clarified.

"How do you know that?" I questioned, narrowing my eyes.

"You're right," Juliette exclaimed. "Killian never calls his associates from the same phone that he uses to call Wynter and me."

"Okay, so we need a burner phone," I said.

Twenty minutes later, we had a burner phone, and the four of us stared at it like it was alien technology.

"Why is this so damn complicated?" Juliette's frustrated groan echoed in the car. Parked in the Hilton Philadelphia hotel at Penn's Landing, we were only ten minutes from our final destination. But we kept fucking with the burner phone.

Note to self: add burner phone set up and operation to part of the introduction class at our future fancy school.

You'd think four students from Yale University could figure this shit out. But no, we struggled to assign it a Chicago number. The guy at the store said it was easy. Well, he fucking lied.

"I think I got it," Wynter murmured with a frown, the iPhone in her left hand as she read directions. Her finger pressed a button, then another and another. "Chicago number it is!" she exclaimed victoriously. "We'll be the best criminals yet."

A bubble of laughter formed in my throat. I couldn't contain it and it burst out. Then all four of us cackled, laughing slightly hysterically. We were nervous, and that was putting it mildly. Our nerves kept us on the edge of our seats, ready to put this adventure behind us.

Wynter wiped her eyes. We laughed so hard, tears appeared. "We have to keep our cool," she cackled. "We break after the performance. That's what Mom always says." Her eyes traveled over us. "Keep it together until it's over."

She was used to pressure, performing from an early age.

Ivy and I nodded. "We'll keep our shit together."

"Okay, now download the voice changer and add some effects," Juliette instructed. "And I'll ask Killian to divert the phone number from the Chicago guy to this burner."

Killian was one of the best hackers in the world. And lucky for us, he owed a favor to Wynter and Juliette. So he agreed to do it without any questions, if the two brats—his words not mine—considered the debt paid. I had no clue what they held over his head, but it must have been worth a pretty penny.

As Wynter worked on the frantic recording that sounded like it came from a male with gunshots in the background, Juliette typed vigorously back and forth with Killian, giving him the details he needed to know.

"Okay, Killian has it diverted. Don't answer the burner if it rings," Juliette told Wynter.

Before the latter could even acknowledge that, the phone rang.

The four of us shared a look and held our breaths. It stopped ringing and a round of exhales traveled inside the car.

"Let's go over there, then we make a call and see if Priest leaves." Wynter put the car into drive and left the hotel parking lot.

"Pay cash," I told her as she readied to pay for the parking ticket.

"Good thinking," Ivy commended, twisting her fingers.

Just as we merged into traffic, the burner phone rang again. And again.

"Jesus, this guy is popular, huh?" I muttered.

"They don't believe in texting," Wynter mused, rolling her eyes. "It would have been interesting to read the messages." And just like evil criminals, we cackled.

Ten minutes later, Wynter parked in the back of the fancy casino.

"Is this the exact spot where the truck will park?" Juliette asked her.

"The armored truck comes from the other side," Wynter explained, pointing to the road. "Like I said, it's one way." She took a deep breath and then exhaled. "Okay, are we ready?"

Four heads nodded. We exited the vehicle, the sun setting behind the large, glass building. We estimated we'd be called to move our car in about an hour. Plenty of time to cause havoc in the club and distract the men.

"Okay, I'm calling Priest now."

Ring. Ring. Ring.

"Hello?" a deep man's voice came through. We held our breaths, not daring to blink.

Wynter pressed the button of her iPhone and the recording started.

Priest, need you now. Chicago.

Fake gunshots sounded in the recording and Wynter cut it off, then ended the call.

A round of exhales.

I swallowed. "Do you think it worked?"

"I fucking hope so," Juliette grumbled. "Otherwise, we did all this for nothing."

"Well, it's better to do it for nothing than get killed," Ivy added. It was the first sane thing she had said in a long time.

"To tell you the truth, I was going to say hi to him," Wynter admitted. "We'll be following the truck and robbing him, so it wouldn't have hurt to be friendly. But you ladies failed to mention Juliette made such an *impression* on the two men in Chicago. One who happens to be Priest."

"Sorry," Juliette muttered.

"Don't be," Wynter retorted. "You distracted them. Really well, because the guy never even noticed me. I never noticed any of it."

"Juliette actually blushed," I chimed in, grinning. "First time I'd ever seen her blush."

We all snickered. "I mean, what are the odds that it would be the same guy here and there," Wynter scoffed.

We waited, watching. The assumption was that Priest was in the club. Wynter said he attended his club every Saturday to ensure everything ran smoothly.

As if on cue, the burner phone rang. And again. Then again.

Sure enough, a tall figure came out, and instinctively all four of us slid down into our seats.

"That's him," Wynter whispered, regardless that the windows were closed and there was no chance he'd hear us. Not unless he was spiderman and had high-frequency hearing.

"Jesus, why are they all so damn hot?" I commented, peeking out my window. "It's like their parents paired with gorgeous people to produce super hot babies."

A round of giggles burst from the back seat. "No wonder Juliette offered to service them both," Ivy teased. "I mean, two gorgeous men fucking you. It's the preferred way to die and go to heaven."

"Shut up," Juliette grumbled. "I'd only consider the other guy. This one is too damn scary. And can you imagine moaning his name while he's eating your pussy?" she asked.

"Actually, I could," Ivy cackled. "Oh Priest," she started moaning, like he was really eating her out. "Please, don't stop. Oh, Priest! Oh, oh... Priest."

The Jeep shook from our laughter as we rolled against our seats, careful not to be seen as the guy entered his fancy black car.

"Oh shit," I mumbled.

"What?" Juliette retorted dryly. "You want to moan his name too?"

Ivy giggled like a lunatic in the back seat.

"Shhh," I hushed them. "He's looking our way."

Instantly, the inside stilled. "There's no way he heard us," Wynter whispered. "Right?"

I didn't think so, but maybe the Jeep shaking from our dumbasses caught his attention.

"He can't hear," I murmured. "But maybe he thinks someone is having sex in here."

"Maybe he wants to join in," Juliette scoffed and Wynter snorted, then giggled. She pressed her hands over her mouth, trying to stifle it.

Then the door slammed and a car engine roared to life. "Fuck, that was close," I muttered.

We remained hiding in our Jeep for another five minutes, just to ensure he was gone. Did it make sense? No, but none of what we did made sense. *Better safe than sorry*, my grandfather always said, so we applied that here.

"Are you sure it wouldn't be wiser just to wait here?" Juliette asked.

"It'd look suspicious," Wynter reasoned. "We don't want someone to wonder why we're sitting in the parking lot."

So, after we were certain Priest was long gone, the four of us exited the Jeep, wearing identical black sleeveless mini-dresses. The point was to distract men, and by the glances thrown our way as we made our way to the main entrance, I was certain we'd succeeded.

We got several whistles, but none of us paid them any mind. We were on a mission. We walked around to the front entrance where a line was already forming even though it was barely seven. Eager partygoers.

Wynter paired with Ivy, while I had Juliette with me. We strutted into the club like we belonged there. Two bouncers blocked our entrance when Wynter regaled him with her famous ice stare.

"I was here before with Bas," she announced, her chin raised like the Queen she was. Jesus, she could put on a performance.

"She's still messing around with this Bas?" Juliette whispered in my ear. I shrugged.

The other bouncer nodded. "She's good, I was here when he brought her," he told him. "It's his woman."

Both men's eyes traveled over the four of us and then stepped back respectfully. Jesus, who in the fuck was Bas to be able to enforce such respect?

"Go ahead," they urged, and Wynter glanced over her shoulder, ensuring we were coming.

She tilted her head at both of them and murmured her thanks. We walked past the cloakroom tinged in reddish lights and a bar area. Behind it, the doors opened to a dark dance floor and a large skull sign on the farthest wall.

Kingpins of the syndicate.

Music blasted toward us and we walked into the club. The beat vibrated under our feet, but the dance floor wasn't quite crowded yet. A few bodies writhed and we made our way between them toward another bar.

"His woman?" Juliette asked, narrowing her eyes on Wynter.

Wynter just shrugged. "It's Neanderthal talk," she explained, which told us absolutely nothing.

We ordered a round of sodas and as we waited, my eyes traveled over the club and the people in it. It was clear the club was geared toward the upper echelon of society.

Ivy and Juliette set their drinks down and moved onto the dance floor while Wynter remained next to me.

Juliette and Ivy grinned widely, throwing their heads back laughing as they started writhing to the beat. We watched them move their hips and butts, shaking and rolling their hips like they were professional dancers. Or strippers that didn't quite get to taking their clothes off.

"They need a pole," Wynter muttered, giving me a side glance, and we burst into a fit of giggles.

"So Bas, huh?" I asked her.

Even under the dark of the club, I could see her blush attractively. "Yeah."

I took her hand into mine and squeezed. "I'm happy for you," I told her before letting go of her hand. "It was about time there was something for you other than ice skating."

She chuckled. "You make it sound like ice is my entire life." It was pretty close, but I didn't say that. "I have the three of you, a wonderful family. I have a lot."

I smiled. She was right, but I bet none of it compared to her man. Now that I knew some of the tragic history of her mother, I wished Wynter would find her full happiness. On and off the ice.

Her eyes came to me. "And you and Uncle, huh?"

"I really like him," I rasped, emotions choking me. "A lot."

This time, she took my hand into hers. "No judgments from me, Dav," she said and leaned over, pressing a kiss onto my cheek. "No matter what. We, the four of us, we're friends for life. We might disagree or even bicker, but we're family. Blood or not. Family for life."

I smiled, encouraged by her words. Inhaling deeply, then exhaling, I pushed the words out.

"We talked about a baby," I blurted out. "In the future. No rush or anything. Maybe in a year. There is pressure for him to have an heir, for lack of a better term." I couldn't tell her about the dangers lurking in the shadows, threatening his family. He told me that in confidentiality. "I love him."

It was the first time I'd said those words out loud, yet there was nothing that would make me take them back. Nothing and nobody.

"Yes, I love him," I repeated. "And I love the idea of having an extended family with all of you."

Wynter had perfected her emotionless look for the public over her years of performing. She hid it all, knowing what it could cost her. People could be brutal and relentless. Yet, right now, she gaped at me with a shocked expression on her face.

She moved her lips but nothing came out. She closed her mouth, then opened and closed it again.

"I know it's a lot," I whispered.

"Y-you want babies?"

"Yes. I've always wanted kids. Of course, not at my age, but Liam said he's fine to wait."

"Like little babies?" I barely had time to blink before she pulled me over and hugged me. "Holy fuck." She beamed. "Holy shit. Oh my gosh!"

My eyes flashed to the dance floor, but neither Juliette nor Ivy paid us any mind, then I focused on Wynter.

"Is that a good or bad holy shit?" I asked, though she didn't look mad at all.

"I think that's wonderful," she exclaimed, grinning. "I want kids one day too. All of our kids can grow up together."

I chuckled, suddenly feeling so much lighter. "Yes, they will."

"Uncle's good to you, right?" she asked. It was my turn to blush, and Wynter's eyes shone mischievously. "Not to worry, no details needed," she said. "And you know what the best part is?"

I couldn't wipe the smile off my face even if I wanted to. "What?"

"Juliette will *never* ask you to share any sexual details," she mused, chuckling. "Like ever!"

Both of us laughed, throwing our heads back. We laughed so hard our bodies shook and our cheeks hurt. The relief of disclosing my secret made me feel lighter, and ten times happier. I was looking forward to the future.

The song "Morning After Dark" by Timbaland came on, the beat loud and vibrating. The two of us shared a glance and she tugged me onto the dance floor.

"Our celebratory dance," she shouted, grinning widely.

Our bodies were close, our eyes locked and both of us smiling. Juliette and Ivy joined us, and I knew this moment would forever be part of me. The four of us looked happier than we had in a very long time. We laughed, mimicking each other's dance moves, shaking our hips and pushing our butts out.

Men watched us, their hungry gazes on us, but they didn't dare approach us. None of us returned their looks. Then we started shouting the lyrics. One dance turned into two, then three and four.

Juliette and Ivy managed to sneak in another gin and tonic before Wynter scolded them, but we continued dancing and having fun.

The hour passed by too quickly. "Okay, any moment now," Wynter whispered, the four of our heads rounded together. "The announcement will come."

"I have to use the restroom," Ivy glanced around. "I'll be super quick."

"If you hear the announcement," I told her, "don't come back here. Head straight to the car."

A jerky nod and then she scurried off while Juliette, Wynter, and I danced. My eyes connected with Juliette's and she grinned.

"I don't remember ever having so much fun," she exclaimed. I glanced at Wynter, and she nodded encouragingly. Juliette caught our shared look. "What? You two are hiding something."

Wynter shook her head. "She just told me, but I think it's wonderful news."

Juliette grinned. "What? More news? Jesus, we're full of news. Are you pregnant?"

Our dancing stopped and now the three of us stood in the middle of the dance floor, none of the other people around us mattered.

Before I lost my courage, I blurted, "Liam and I talked about extending our family in the future." Fuck, I loved saying *our* family.

"The traditional way?" she spoke slowly, as if she was having a hard time comprehending it.

I covered my face with both my hands. "Yes. With lots and lots of sex."

The music faded into the background, the only thing I was aware of was Juliette, Wynter, and my own heartbeat. It was as if we were in a bubble, the whole world cut off. I peeked through my fingers, watching Juliette, but she kept blinking again and again. As if she couldn't process the words or the concept.

"He loves you. Nothing is going to change that," I said, worried she'd reached a breaking point.

Wynter held Juliette's hand and shook it gently. "Say something."

"Ewww," Juliette finally murmured. "Like ewww. Can't you adopt?"

"I kind of like the sex part," I muttered. "At least with him."

"No wonder you've had this post-orgasmic look on your face for weeks." I rolled my eyes but couldn't wipe the grin off my face. "Marriage is for life in our world," Juliette warned. "Having a baby will forever bind you to him, you know?"

I took a deep breath, then exhaled. "Yes, I know."

"What about our school?" Wynter questioned.

And Juliette chimed in, "Yes, what about our school?"

"I planned to have our kids go to that school," I told them both. "And our plans are not changing. We're still doing it. But I love him."

"Holy crap, you really are into him." Juliette gasped.

She had no idea.

"Well, I guess that's okay then," Juliette mumbled. Tension seeped out of my shoulders and I hugged her. "Now it's official. All our kids will be going to our school and we're all stuck together for life."

"I thought we were stuck for life beforehand," I joked.

"But now you can't escape." She grinned.

Before another word could be uttered, the music was interrupted and all three of us stiffened.

"Will the owner of the Jeep out back please move the vehicle immediately?" The announcement came through, then he proceeded to recite the tag number. I searched for Ivy, but she must have still been tied up in the bathroom.

"She'll come to the back," I told them. With a jerky nod, we rushed out of there.

CHAPTER 49
Davina

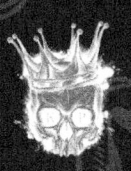

The four of us followed the truck until they made their regularly scheduled stop. Don't ask me why they always had a scheduled gas refill at this specific station, but it worked for us.

The gas station was located in a bad part of town, its fluorescent lights flickered on and off. Half of the sign didn't work at all, and the driver parked the truck exactly there.

"Okay, Ivy," I told her. "Distract them. Do as good of a job as Juliette did in Chicago."

Wynter snickered. All of us did; we couldn't help it.

"Offer to fuck them both," Juliette suggested. "That's sure to distract them."

"Such pressure to perform," Ivy groaned. "How do you do it with skating, Wynter?"

"Okay, less talk, more action," I scolded, though humor colored my voice.

The three of us watched Ivy exit the Jeep and saunter to the truck, swaying her hips. Then she got right in front of it and started unzipping her dress.

"Oh, wonderful," Juliette mused. "She's stripping. Let's hope the police don't drive by and mistake her for a prostitute."

"If they do, we'll just bail her out. I think eventually we're bound to be bailing someone out. Might as well gain some experience in that arena."

Wynter and Juliette snickered, but I was dead serious.

We watched as the guy got out and approached Ivy, his eyes hungry on her. She said something to the guy and he scratched the back of his head. They exchanged a few words, then strode to the back of the truck.

The door shut, blocking Ivy and the two men out of our view.

"Oh my gosh," I rasped. "She's doing it. She convinced him to take her to the back of the truck."

"She probably suggested a ménage," Wynter mused. "She did admit she felt rather horny. Should we give her an extra minute?"

"Hell no," I said. "The third guy is inside the gas station. Unless you want to bone him, let's get rid of those two men."

"Don't stress, D." Juliette chuckled. "Ivy probably has them dead by now."

Juliette and I jumped out of the Jeep. Wynter remained behind the wheel to ensure we had a speedy escape. Juliette was the expert at picking locks, so once at the armored truck, she readied to go straight to work while I was her lookout.

My heart thundered. Noises came from inside the truck, and I prayed they weren't in the middle of fucking. I didn't think Ivy was serious when she suggested she'd have a threesome. She was a damn virgin, for Christ's sake. That would be like going from zero to one hundred in a sports car in less than three seconds.

I kept glancing toward the gas station for the man that'd be back any moment.

It took Juliette thirty seconds to have the back door unlocked. We found Ivy grinning widely next to two unconscious men.

"Please tell me you didn't kill them." I placed my palm on my forehead.

"Don't worry, they're alive" she assured. "And no, I didn't let them fuck me."

"Thank God," Juliette and I said at the same time.

"Help me dump their big bodies out the back." She started pushing one of them.

I nodded. "Ivy, you go to the front and start the truck," I ordered her. "I'll be right over."

She scurried over to the driver's seat while Juliette and I huffed and puffed, pushing the two unconscious bodies and rolling them over like sacks of potatoes.

"What the fuck did she give them?" I inquired. "They're dead weight."

Juliette snickered. "It's a powerful drug. They won't remember a thing when they wake up."

One body out of the truck. We rolled the next one when he groaned. "Fuck, I should stab him with the third needle," she spat out.

"No," I objected. "Just push him. He can't do anything. We don't want to overdose him."

And another body out of the truck. "Okay, ride with Wynter," I told Juliette. "See you at our destination."

I shut the back door and ran over to the front seat of the armored truck just as Ivy successfully connected wires from under the steering wheel. Sparks ignited and the truck started.

She drove off the parking lot and we took off like the devil was on our heels.

Wynter and Juliette were right behind us, following us. I had no idea where Ivy learned to steal vehicles, but I didn't bother asking. I was fucking glad she knew what she was doing. While she drove, I climbed into the back, my dress hiked up and barefoot. Once in the back, I unlocked the vault and my heart just about stopped. There were bags and bags of money.

I started moving all the bags of money closer to the door. I couldn't even fathom how much money was in here.

"Call Wynter and tell her we're all set for at least two years," I told Ivy breathlessly as she sped down the highway, grumbling to herself about fucking Americans driving on the wrong side of the road. "We fucking scored a jackpot!"

We smiled all the way down to the spot we planned to stop and dump the vehicle.

Trenton, New Jersey. Delaware River.

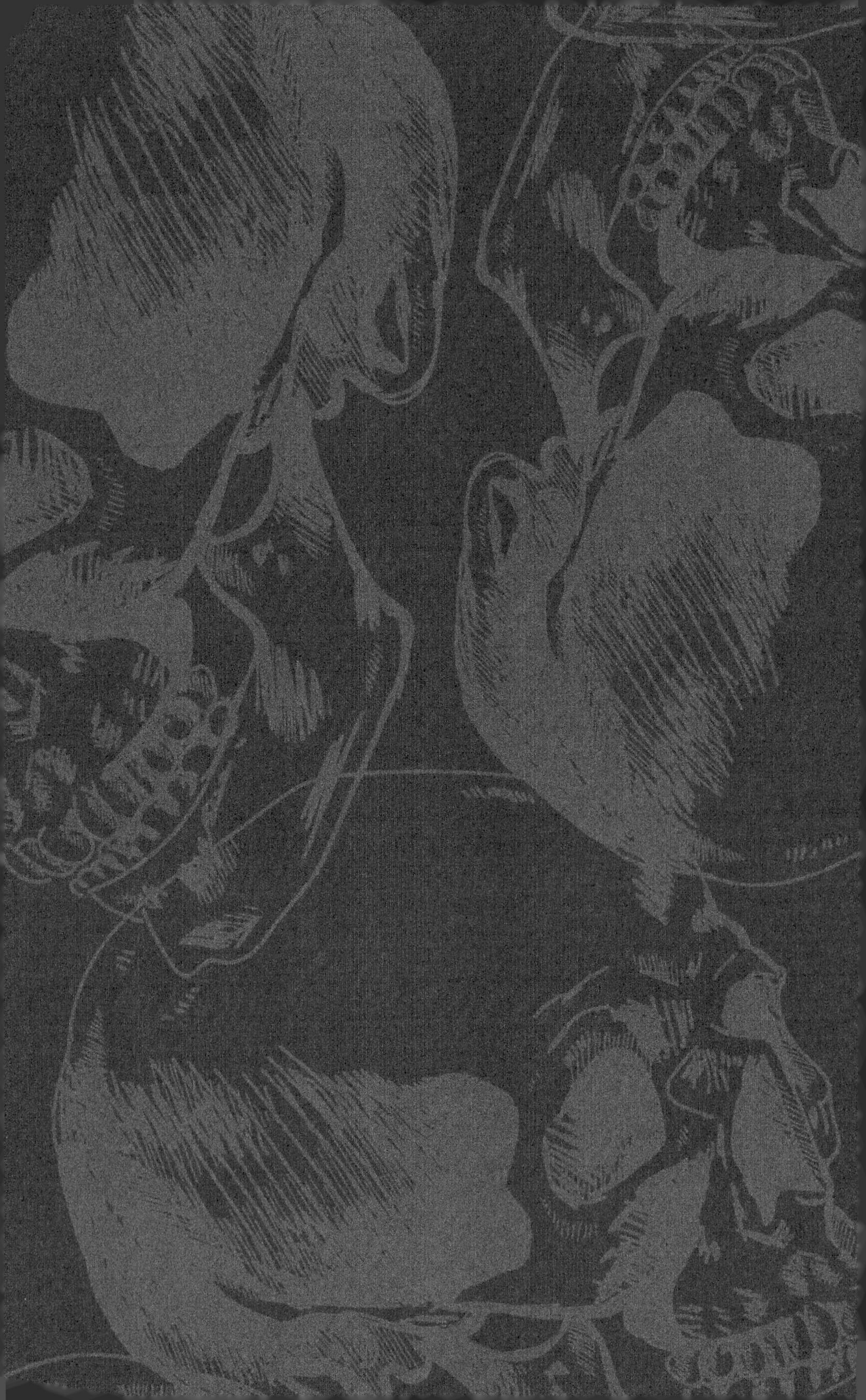

CHAPTER 50
Liam

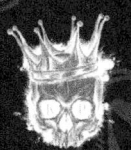

I t was almost midnight when Quinn and I left my office located on the last floor of the skyrise building on the Upper West Side of Manhattan that overlooked the Hudson River. It had been a long day of blueprint review and dealing with the architects.

My phone buzzed. Then buzzed again. And again.

Worried that something happened to the girls, I pulled out my phone and my lips curved up.

> Wynter: You break her heart, and we'll kill you and bury your body in a shallow grave so animals can get to you.

I honestly didn't know my niece had such violent thoughts. Then she followed up with a more proper message.

> Congratulations, Uncle. I'm so happy for you both. Love you.

Juliette's message was even worse.

> Yeah, that's just gross. Just thinking about you and my best friend makes me want to be celibate for the rest of my life.

I typed the message back.

> Good. Then my mission has been accomplished.

An emoji with an eye roll followed, along with another message from Juliette.

> Congrats. Make her cry, and you're dead.

I had to admit, it pleased me that Davina told them about our marriage. It was about time my whole family learned about this.

Then a message came from Davina.

> They're happy. Can't wait to see you tomorrow.

I didn't like not having her in my bed. Nevertheless, I agreed to her spending the night with Wynter in the dorm, but tonight would be the last night. Lost in my thoughts, I walked out of the building and stepped on the sidewalk. Before I even had a chance to inhale fresh air, bullets started flying.

Quinn's body slammed into me and got me out of the way right in the nick of time.

"Fuck," I grumbled, bracing for impact. Once my body slammed into the ground, I reached behind me and pulled out my gun tucked into the back of my pants.

Everything happened fast.

The sounds of gunfire filled the air.

"Take your right," I hissed. "I'll take the left."

I could see my driver from here. He already had a gun in his hand and had started shooting. One man down.

I surveyed the situation. We were outnumbered. By a lot. There were about twenty men surrounding us.

Focusing on the left side, I pulled the trigger and hit one. Quinn lifted his gun and fired.

Pop. Pop. Pop.

The bullets flew all around us. It was like a goddamn war in the heart of Manhattan.

From the corner of my eye, I spotted a shadow moving and I shifted, pointing the gun at the guy.

"Fuck, Cassio," I gritted. "I almost shot your ass."

He chuckled. "Not before I shot yours."

Then I noticed his brother Luca behind him. "Why didn't you invite us to the party, fucker?"

I smirked. "It's a surprise party."

Now all three of us were shooting, and bodies started falling. Blood sprayed over the New York City sidewalk, and honestly, I was surprised no innocent bystanders were around.

"Russians?" Cassio asked.

"Probably." Which meant they knew Wynter was in New York. "Fucking Russians," I muttered under my breath as I aimed at another guy. Their numbers were quickly dwindling thanks to Cassio and Luca's support. Five against twenty gave us better odds.

I spotted one of the Russians slam his body into my driver and I was quick to follow. Then I aimed.

Bang.

The sound of shots rang through the air. The enemies were almost subdued. My driver was in the wrong spot. I kept firing bullets, eliminating targets around him. It was almost over when a bullet hit him right in the skull, and I watched the life leave his eyes even before he hit the ground.

Fuck! I hated losing men. Good men in particular.

Quinn gasped for air behind me, and I turned around to find him on his ass, his back against the building, and it was only then that I realized he was bleeding. A lot.

"On your right," Quinn warned, and I whirled around just in time to duck as a bullet flew above my head.

Cassio lifted his gun and fired, and the last man flopped to the ground. The four of us were breathing hard, the adrenaline still rushing through our veins.

"Thank you," I told him and Luca, extending my hand. We shook hands and rushed over to Quinn. I hunched down to check on him, his skin pasty as he struggled to keep his eyes open.

This was bad. His shirt was soaked with blood, and there was blood coating his hands.

"You better not fucking die on me, you old bastard," I demanded. Quinn had been through a lot with me.

"Says the other old bastard."

"Let me take you to my place," Cassio offered.

"No, I have to get him to my compound." We had a state-of-the-art hospital room, and Quinn needed to be somewhere I could keep an eye on him.

I lifted Quinn's big body and we rushed to the black Mercedes.

Once we were all settled inside Cassio's car, he sped up while I kept pressure on Quinn's wound.

My phone rang and I answered it without checking who it was.

"Yeah."

"Liam." Alexei's cold voice came through and cold dread filled me inside.

"Tell me the girls are fine," I gritted. If something happened to them, I'd burn fucking Russia to the ground if I had to and kill the Pakhan once and for all. I couldn't lose my wife, my niece, or my daughter.

"They robbed a Philadelphia club that belongs to DiLustro."

"They fucking *what*?" I barked.

Quinn chuckled weakly. "Are the girls stealing again?"

Despite the fucked-up situation, I smiled, because if Quinn had the energy to chuckle, I knew he'd pull through.

"They hijacked their armored vehicle," Alexei clarified, his voice monotone, like he was discussing the weather.

"Fuck. Goddamn fuck. I'll call Nico and ask him to wipe out surveillance and any evidence of them," I added.

"All done," Alexei assured. "Nico took care of the casino

surveillance. Sasha took care of the gas station and eliminated the witnesses."

"Gas station? What did they do to the gas station? Blow it the fuck up?" Fuck, did I even want to know? "What the fuck are they doing now? Burning a motherfucking city down?"

Alexei's emotionless voice came through. "They are trying to push a stolen truck into the river."

They had gone too far. Twenty-one-year-old girls should not be planning heists and destroying properties.

"Get them." I had let them get away with too much already.

"There is one of me and four of them."

"Don't tell me you're scared of them," I scoffed. "Four girls freshly out of college. They'll shit their pants when they see you."

Alexei didn't miss a beat. "I won't manhandle them and scare my sister-in-law."

"For fuck's sake," I grumbled. "I have a bleeding man here. I don't care how you do it, just get them here."

"Fine," he acknowledged. "Sasha is in this area. I'll have him scare them."

"Sounds like women troubles?" Luca mused once I hung up.

"You have no fucking idea."

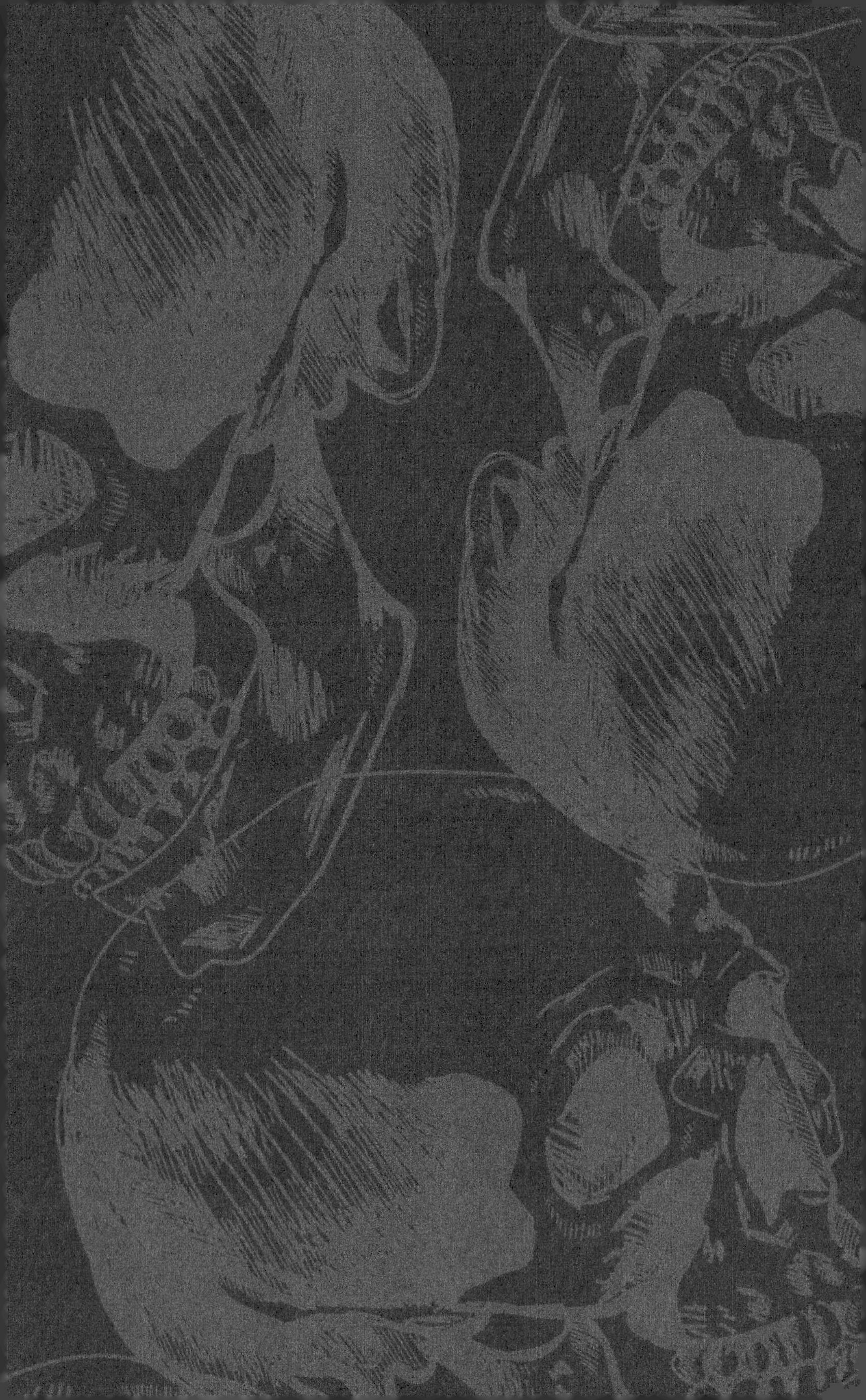

CHAPTER 51
Davina

"H-holy fucking shit," I stammered, watching the truck slowly sink into the Delaware river. It was almost ten at night, but we didn't need any of the flashlights we packed. The full moon glowed over the river, allowing us to see very well.

"You can say that again," muttered Wynter.

"Holy fucking shit," Juliette repeated.

The money was now all piled in the Jeep. We'd be crammed in for the rest of the drive to the dorm, but we had enough to buy ten properties. Probably in the range between twenty and forty million, just by eyeballing it.

"Holy fucking shit," I muttered again. Because what else could I possibly say.

The four of us stood in the cool of the late spring night. The truck was almost fully submerged. And out of nowhere, Wynter chuckled softly. "This is the part where the Bluetooth picked up a phone call in *Good Girls*."

Juliette groaned. "Wyn, you're weird."

She shrugged. "It's a good weird." She smiled softly. "At least that's what I hear."

"Keep telling yourself that," Juliette teased her.

"*Good Girls* is more mature than using Rue's whistle as our warning signal," she retorted without missing a beat.

"Ummm," Ivy broke the silence. "I hate to break up this weird conversation, but I have to tell you something."

We all looked at her, the truck forgotten. "What?" we asked in unison.

"Ummm... when I went to the bathroom, I ran into a guy," she mumbled.

I frowned. "Yeah, so?"

"Priest," she muttered.

"What?" we all squealed. "That guy left!"

"Yeah, I guess he came back," Ivy pointed out the obvious.

"Was he around the dance floor?" Wynter asked her, narrowing her eyes. "This was something you should have said before we hijacked the truck. If he saw Juliette, he'd know it was us. The same person in two different places that were robbed is a pretty strong clue as to who did it!"

"Well, I don't think he ever made it to the dance floor area," she muttered, her eyes darting away from us. It was uncharacteristic of her to avoid eye contact. And just like Juliette, she was never embarrassed.

"Why, Ivy?" Juliette asked her quietly, narrowing her eyes.

"Somehow, we... um... We may have started making out in the hallway."

A choked laugh bubbled in my throat. "Like making out with your mouth?"

Ivy glared at me. "Yes, with my mouth, and maybe my hands," she snapped.

"Oh."

"Yeah, oh," she murmured, then pressed her palms to her heated cheeks. "Jesus, we should stop doing this."

"Ivy, did he—" My voice faltered, and my heart clenched in my chest. "Did he do more than kiss you?" my voice choked out, the lump in my throat caused by fear for what she might have gone through.

She shook her head.

"N-no. I lost my head," she admitted softly, her shoulders slumped. "I-I almost let him fuck me right there in the hallway. I know I talk shit, but I kind of want to save myself for marriage." A gasp sounded next to me. I thought it was Juliette's, but I wasn't sure. "For a priest, he was so damn good with his hands," she said, shame coloring her voice. "If that announcement hadn't happened, I think I would have gone all the way."

Wynter stepped forward and put her hands on both of her shoulders. "So fucking what?" she remarked. "Did you like it?"

Ivy blinked, holding back tears threatening to spill. "I think so. Yes. But—"

"Fuck but," Wynter sneered. "You lost your head. So what? You liked his hands on you and let him touch you. All that matters is that you enjoyed it."

"God, I think Wynter is completely corrupted," Juliette mumbled next to me. "But I agree. If you liked it, what the fuck matters where he touched you?"

"I think I liked the thought of someone watching us," Ivy admitted in a whisper. "I came all over his fingers."

God, if she knew half of the things I'd done with Liam.

Juliette scoffed. "Well, that sounds rather exciting. I bet you Davina did that and much, much more with her husband. Though, please no details. Like ever!"

Wynter giggled, unable to contain her amusement. Truthfully, neither could I. I attempted to glare at Juliette, but my stupid face wouldn't cooperate, and I ended up grinning.

"I bet he spanks you," Juliette drawled, and my head snapped to her.

"How did you know?" I questioned her, shocked.

A second of silence and then we all burst into hysterical laughter. We laughed so hard, I thought I'd pee myself.

My phone buzzed. "That'll be Daddy calling to check on his young wife," Juliette snickered. "Come home, baby, so I can spank your ass and fuck you."

"I thought you didn't want any details." I smirked as I dug through my bag.

My smile fell. It wasn't Liam. It was Garrett.

"Fuck, that loser is still nagging you?" Ivy sounded annoyed on my behalf. She had no idea.

My phone rang again, and this time, I answered it.

"What is it, Garrett?" I snapped into the headset.

"You burned down my house," he shouted, his words slightly slurred.

"I have no fucking idea what you're talking about," I retorted calmly. "But I can hear you're drunk. Stop harassing me, or I'll get a restraining order against you."

He started laughing maniacally. "You are a criminal that burned down my house. You and your stupid girlfriends. You won't be going to the police."

I felt anger rise within me.

"Again, Garrett. I have no idea what you're talking about," I told him, barely keeping my calm. "But I assure you, I won't hesitate to show all these calls and texts you've been sending me over the last few weeks to the police. Trust me, there's plenty of evidence for a restraining order."

I ended the call, not bothering to listen to whatever he had to say.

"That guy really needs a life," Juliette broke the silence. "If he doesn't stop harassing you, we'll burn down his next house."

"The four of you need a life," a deep voice said from behind us, and the four of us whirled around.

CHAPTER 52
Davina

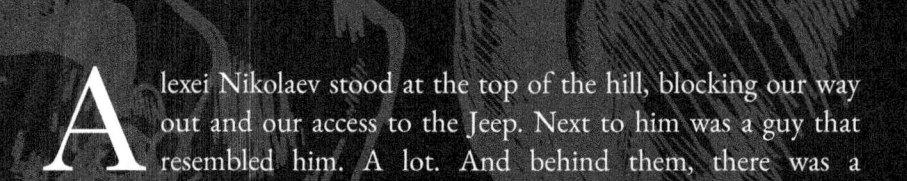

Alexei Nikolaev stood at the top of the hill, blocking our way out and our access to the Jeep. Next to him was a guy that resembled him. A lot. And behind them, there was a woman... with a fucking baby.

"Hello, ladies," the Alexei-looking guy greeted us, looking amused as fuck. "I'm Sasha."

"Holy fucking shit," Ivy muttered. "Did we just fuck up?"

My eyes traveled between Alexei and Sasha. They had to be brothers. That kind of resemblance was freaky. They both looked scary as fuck, for completely different reasons. One reminded me of a psychotic guy and the other of a reckless lunatic.

"Hello," I attempted to use some manners.

Juliette shoved her shoulder into me. "Don't talk to scary Russians," she whisper-yelled.

Truthfully, Sasha didn't have an accent. Not that I could hear over my ears buzzing with the adrenaline pulsing through my veins. Jesus, he looked no less scary than Alexei Nikolaev.

"Umm... listen, we don't want any trouble." Wyn tried to sound firm and sure, but her bravado failed big time. Nonetheless, she earned points for trying. "Just let us get to our car and we'll be on our way."

Sasha looked amused and Alexei's face held no expression at all. I shifted from one foot to the other, anxious and unsure how to interpret their presence.

"When did that *ever* work?" Ivy hissed.

"We need a fucking gun," Juliette huffed. "Now these fuckers will take all our earnings and we'll be back to square one."

"Shush," I hushed them. "These are the Nikolaev men."

Wynter's head whipped around and her eyes bulged out.

"Get the fuck out," she spat out. "Small world, huh?"

"Too small," I murmured.

"Why are you here?" Wynter demanded, her eyes narrowing on them.

"Why couldn't they fucking show up when we were doing nothing?" Ivy complained.

"And why is there a woman with a baby hiding behind them?" Juliette demanded. "You guys better not be some freaks hurting her. I'll get my brother to kick your fucking ass."

The three of us scoffed. Killian was badass and all that, but these guys had at least ten years on him.

"Why couldn't less scary dudes come after us?" Ivy whined. "We get some fucking MMA fighters."

"You ladies know we're right here, right?" Sasha drawled. A soft woman's chuckle sounded behind them. Alexei's eyes shifted, and mesmerized, I watched as his expression softened.

"Why are you here?" I demanded in a strong voice, my insides shaking.

"Keeping you all safe," Sasha deadpanned. "It's obvious you four needed saving. You have trouble written all over you."

Wynter scoffed. "So do you! I bet you get in trouble all the fucking time."

"She knows you already," Alexei said, almost sounding amused. *Almost.*

I shoved my shoulder into Wyn and gave her a pointed look. "They are keeping us *safe*," I accented the last word.

"Well, who sent you?" Juliette demanded. "We don't deal with the Russians."

"Liam Brennan."

"No!" Juliette and Wynter muttered at the same time. "He doesn't like Russians."

Sasha shoved his tattooed hands into his pockets. "He seems to like us enough."

"It could be a set up," Ivy argued.

I gave an exasperated look. "If they're here to keep us safe," I told them all, "we technically get to boss them around."

Sasha chuckled and Alexei's lip tugged up. At least somebody was having fun.

"I don't think so, Mrs. Brennan." Sasha snickered. The four of us shared a glance. It was weird being called Mrs. Brennan. It made me feel so much older.

"We're taking you all home."

I stood up straighter. "No need. We got this."

A woman came around to Alexei's side and a soft gasp escaped me. It was Aurora Ashford. No, Aurora Nikolaev. My sister. With a newborn baby in her arms.

Wynter recognized her too, because her hand slipped into mine and gripped it tightly.

"Hello, girls," she greeted us, but her eyes were locked on mine. She was beautiful, with dark hair and eyes. The coloring was even more stark next to the two Nikolaev men. "I'm Aurora."

Juliette and Ivy glanced at me, their eyebrows raised. "Is that..." Juliette whispered, and I nodded. "Did she hear us talking about her?"

I shrugged, unable to look away from my sister. It seemed surreal. My sister was right in front of me.

"Hi there," Wynter greeted her. "I'm assuming you know who we are then."

Aurora nodded, and something in my throat squeezed so tightly I couldn't get enough oxygen. It made no sense. I didn't know I had brothers and a sister until recently. I shouldn't be so emotional about a perfect stranger.

Yet, something about seeing her hit me right in the chest. She wasn't a stranger. She was family. *My* family.

"I do," Aurora answered softly, her eyes on me. "Hello, Davina. I've been hoping to meet you for a long time."

Fuck, I already liked her.

CHAPTER 53
Liam

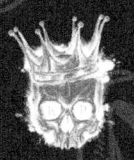

The moment the Nikolaev men pulled up, I was striding toward them. I opened the door to the Mercedes G-Benz, seeing Sasha behind the wheel, and Alexei driving Wynter's Jeep.

The girls slid out, glaring at me.

"What in the fuck were the four of you thinking?" I barked the second their feet touched the ground.

Wynter's eyes flashed in defiance, and I silently cursed. I knew that look. I'd seen that look before. Juliette had perfected it.

I narrowed my eyes on Davina and she shrugged her shoulders. "Don't give me shit, Liam. You had us followed! You kept secrets too."

My lip curved despite the hours of worry I'd endured. First, to ensure Quinn would be okay, and then that the girls would get home safely.

"Somehow I think your secrets trump mine, wife."

"Who's competing?" she muttered under her breath.

The four girls stood in the driveway, unsure what to do or say as I strode to Alexei. Sasha had left his car to come stand next to his brother and a woman, who I recognized as Aurora Nikolaev, Davina's sister. Somehow, I wasn't surprised.

"Thank you," I told both Sasha and Alexei. "I won't forget this."

"I'm sorry," Aurora chimed in softly. "I happened to be in town with Alexei, and I couldn't stay away."

I couldn't fault her for trying. "It will be up to Davina if she wants anything to do with that side of her family," I warned her quietly.

Alexei growled softly, but his wife's hand took his and squeezed.

"Of course," she assured me. Then she tilted her head at her little newborn in her arms. "I brought ammunition, though. Nobody can resist a baby, right?" She smirked.

I shook my head. "Nobody. And congratulations."

Seeing the little baby in her arms, I couldn't help but envision Davina with our baby. Things were moving fast, and there were secrets we had to unfold—including no more heists—but I looked forward to seeing her swell with our child.

"Maybe you can talk some sense into these women," I said, then turned my attention back to the four troublemakers. "Before they get themselves killed."

"Oh, please," Juliette retorted, rolling her eyes. "If you wanted us safe, you'd have told us the truth."

I frowned. "What is that supposed to mean?" I groaned. I was fucking tired. The goddamn sun would be coming up soon, so the chances of sleep were nil.

"We know, Uncle," Wynter snapped, her tone unapologetic. "You even had a chance to come clean. Remember, the morning we went for a jog? So don't fucking preach to us about keeping us safe."

"What the fuck are you talking about?" I gritted, barely holding on to my calm. It was like these girls crammed the toddler, teenage, and college years all into one month.

"I know you're not my dad," Juliette yelled.

The silence that followed was deafening. We all stood still in the driveway, the sound of the city faint and distant. This was not how I imagined our secrets unraveling.

"Well, that was unexpected," Cassio's voice came from behind me, but I ignored him. This had been my fear for the past twenty years. I did it all to protect her. Protect my family.

My eyes turned to Wynter. How much did she know?

"Don't look at me, Uncle," Wynter grumbled. "I'm not saving you."

Wynter's eyes traveled behind me. "Though, I'd like to know why we have all these criminals shadowing us?"

A snicker sounded somewhere in the courtyard, and I couldn't determine whether it was Sasha or Luca.

"I'm taking that personally," Sasha complained, though amusement danced in his eyes.

Wynter narrowed her eyes on him. "Well, tough shit. How many things aren't you telling us, Uncle?"

"Huh?" Juliette jumped her cousin, glaring at me. "All of you are just deciding shit on our behalf without even bothering to consult us."

"We're legal adults." Wynter put her hands on her hips, glaring at me. "Newsflash, Uncle. We have the right to decide things for ourselves."

"You're fucked, Brennan," Luca chimed in, unhelpfully.

"And who in the hell are you?" Juliette snapped.

"Cassio and Luca King," I introduced them. "And Juliette, show some respect."

Her answer was another eyeroll.

Davina walked over and slipped her hand into mine. "I promise, I didn't tell them," she rasped in a whisper, her eyes on me. Maybe I was an idiot, but I believed her.

"I found the birth certificates," Juliette announced. "Both Killian's and mine." Her eyes shimmered, and something in my chest clenched. I wanted to protect her, not upset her. "Does he know?"

I almost wanted to lie and protect Killian, but he really didn't need protection. "Yes," I admitted softly. "He was older when I took you in. He remembers your biological parents." I reluctantly let go of Davina's hand and took two big steps toward my daughter. "It was all new to me. Killian helped, and so did your aunt. I was way out of my element. I missed them, hungered to find their killers, and had a newborn and a son overnight."

"You could have just left us," Juliette murmured.

"First, fuck no. I might not be your biological father, but I am your godfather. Both yours and Killian's. And secondly, I made a promise," I told her. "To my best friend. It was the only way to protect you. By letting the world believe both of you died."

So many damn years of keeping them all off the radar. I was fucking tired. I knew it would be a necessity for today. Tomorrow. Maybe even years. But I'd find those responsible for their deaths and kill them. I'd kill two birds with one stone, because the same threat lurked over Wynter and my sister.

"You should have told us a long time ago," Wynter accused. "You all just expect us to be oblivious to everything. You think you're doing us a favor, when in fact, you're putting us in more danger by not telling us. You should have told us when we were old enough. Both you and Killian."

Of course she was right. Except, what day do you pick to tell your children and niece all the shit that threatened them? My sister knew it and still ended up damaged by our way of life.

"I agree," Juliette muttered. "We shouldn't find shit out this way. Wynter wants to know about her dad. She has nothing, just his name. Do you ever stop to think how that makes us feel?"

"No," I admitted. "I dread to think about it. But I hate even more having to put worry on your shoulders."

"Well, you should at least teach us how to fucking survive," Wynter grumbled. "Because we struggled to set up a goddamn burner phone."

A choked laugh escaped me, trying to envision these women setting up a burner.

"I can teach you shit like that," Sasha volunteered, and I wasn't quite sure how to feel about it.

"That'd be great," all four of the girls answered in unison, beaming like hundred-watt light bulbs.

Wynter walked over and wrapped her arms around me. "I still love you, Uncle."

"I love you too." I tugged on her blonde curls, just like when she was a little girl. "But you have to straighten your ass back up," I continued softly. "Otherwise, there will be hell to pay with my sister."

Juliette joined in and all was good. There was so much shit coming down the pipeline, but for now, I'd enjoy this. Both of them made me proud. They'd need their strength.

Juliette reminded me of her father with her reckless character. But she was strong and loyal, just like he was. I worried about Wynter. Deep down, she was too soft.

Leaving the two cousins to hug it out, I went back to my wife and took her hand. Knowing they were all safe grounded me.

"Why are you stealing money?" I asked. My eyes traveled over the four of them. "And no more lies."

I watched as the four of them gulped in unison. It was almost comical. Then they shared a glance.

It was Davina who answered. "For a school."

I blinked. "A school?"

"Yes, a school," she confirmed. I shifted my gaze to Wynter, then Juliette, then Ivy. There was hope and excitement in their eyes, but I had no idea why. I was missing a key piece of information.

Cassio and Luca leaned against the Jeep, watching the entire exchange with intrigue. I hoped the fuckers were taking notes. Their time was coming.

"What kind of school?" Aurora ended up asking. Thank fuck I wasn't the only one confused.

"For criminals," Wynter answered with a wide smile.

"Well, their kids," Juliette clarified.

"It would be a university for boys and girls from any criminal families," Davina added. "So the kids don't find themselves clueless like we've been. We've learned our shit on the go. But this school will teach them the necessities they need to survive in this world... as well as the things they'd learn at a regular college. You know, math, reading, history, science."

It actually wasn't a bad idea.

"I like the idea," Cassio chimed in.

"Me too," Luca announced. "If you need money, I'd be interested in investing." All four of them instantly shook their heads. "No? Why not?" Luca asked curiously.

"We don't want anyone controlling who can or can't join the school," Davina told him.

"No discrimination," Wynter announced.

Another two heartbeats of silence.

"How in the fuck did you four come up with an idea like that?" Sasha inquired curiously, leaning against the Mercedes.

The girls' eyes darted away from us, refusing to look our way. "Davina?" I growled.

"We kind of burned down a house," she murmured quietly. "My ex-boyfriend's. He was blackmailing us, so we needed the money, so we stole from Liam first, but then a friend came through and erased the surveillance evidence. And that's how the school idea came about."

"Well technically, I burned the house down," Ivy chimed in. "I dropped the match."

"I gathered the alcohol and matches," Juliette admitted.

Burned down a house! They fucking burned down his house? Why in the fuck did nobody tell me this?

"I tried to extinguish it," Wynter said.

"Why?" Alexei asked.

Wynter blinked, confusion on her face. "Why did I try to extinguish it?"

Alexei shook his head. "Why did you try to burn down the house?"

"Davina's ex-boyfriend cheated on her," Juliette reasoned, like it was a perfect reason. "It was either that or we cut his dick off."

Then she gagged, like just the mention of it was going to make her puke.

"We're not killers," Wynter reasoned. "Though, we've gotten pretty good at stealing."

I scoffed. "No, you're not."

"When the prick blackmailed us, we came up with a plan for the blackmail money," Ivy grumbled.

Davina's ex-boyfriend would be dead when I got my hands on him.

CHAPTER 54
Davina

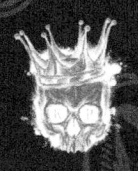

"Can we keep the money?" I asked bravely.

A round of chuckles sounded. I had to admit, this was not how I envisioned meeting my sister. In the middle of a heist. Definitely not a good first impression.

"We're not asking," Wynter added. "We *are* keeping that money."

"Damn straight," Juliette added. "You have no fucking idea what we went through."

"You'll have to clean it," Liam answered. He didn't look mad. Truthfully, when Sasha pulled into Liam's compound with the four of us in the back seat of his Mercedes, Liam stormed out looking more worried than mad.

"Luciano's wife can do it for them," Cassio suggested. My eyes shifted to him. He was a good-looking guy, closer to Liam's age. I had no clue who he was, or who Luciano or his wife were. But there was doubt in my mind about using someone he suggested, because Cassio was lethal. He must have caught my curious look because he added, "Your husband can put you in touch with Grace. Through the dark web. She launders money, and so does her husband."

"Get the fuck out." Juliette gasped. "How do we find the dark web?"

Liam groaned. "Stay away from the dark web, Juliette. I'll get you in contact, and you ladies do it the old-fashioned way. Face-to-face. Grace Vitale lives close by." Then, as if he realized he'd let us all off the hook too easily, he continued, "No more robbing people," he warned.

"No more," the four of us murmured. The rest of the men watched us all, amused. Maybe they ran into stuff like this all the time. Hell if I knew.

Glancing around, I caught Aurora's eyes on me again. Admittedly, I kept glancing her way too. To her and the little baby wrapped in a soft blue blanket.

"You want to hold him?" she asked, smiling softly as she approached me. Her husband kept a watchful eye, ready to pounce on anyone who even looked at his wife and baby wrong. Honestly, I was scared to hold the baby with papa bear nearby.

"You good?" Liam asked.

I nodded, and he strode away to talk to the men while Wynter, Juliette, and Ivy joined Aurora and me.

"He's so small," I murmured as she put him in my arms.

"I have a feeling he'll be the same size as his father," she said dreamily. All our gazes darted to Alexei and caught him watching all of us while talking to Liam and Cassio. Sasha and Luca had gone to the far end of the yard.

"So he'll be huge," Ivy commented.

"And kind of scary," Wynter added.

Aurora chuckled. "I thought so too when we met, but he's the best." She was totally in love. "I hope you don't mind that I snatched this opportunity to see you, Davina."

I scoffed softly. "I just wish it wasn't in the midst of our criminal activities."

She waved her hand like it was nothing.

"Aren't you an FBI agent?" I inquired hesitantly. Wouldn't that be something if my sister arrested me. *FBI motherfuckers!*

"I'm a mother, wife, and sister first," she explained.

"Your brothers..." I faltered, but then continued, "Are your brothers like you?"

She chuckled. "They are a pain in the ass, but just like me, they like you already."

I frowned. "They do? They don't even know me."

"After they learned about you, they began keeping tabs on you. So did I."

"You did?" I asked, surprised.

"Yes, I'd always wanted a sister," she admitted softly. "Our dad is an asshole, but at least he gave me you." Her eyes traveled over my friends. "I hope all of you come and visit us in Portugal. We spend most of our time there, except when Alexei has a job to do."

"Is he really a contract killer?" Juliette blurted out, and I shoved my shoulder into her.

"Don't answer that," I told my sister.

"Yes, don't. Otherwise, Juliette will have nightmares," Wynter quipped, and we all chuckled. The baby stirred in my arms and I immediately shushed the girls.

"Don't wake up the baby," I whispered.

"God, I can see it already," Juliette whispered, careful not to wake him up. "Davina will be shushing us all day and night once she becomes a mother."

I rolled my eyes, ignoring her.

"About the school," Aurora started, and the four of us instantly stiffened. "Can I help? I can donate. Alexei would too. No strings attached."

The girls and I shared a glance. We were adamant about not taking anyone's money.

"Actually, would you consider teaching in our school?" I wondered instead. "Since you worked in the FBI, I bet you have great knowledge and resources."

Aurora's eyes lit up. "Seriously?"

I nodded.

"You're family. I'd do anything for you." Aurora hugged me, careful not to wake up her baby. Then her eyes went to my best friends. "All of you, because you were here for Davina when I couldn't be."

And just like that, Aurora became part of our team.

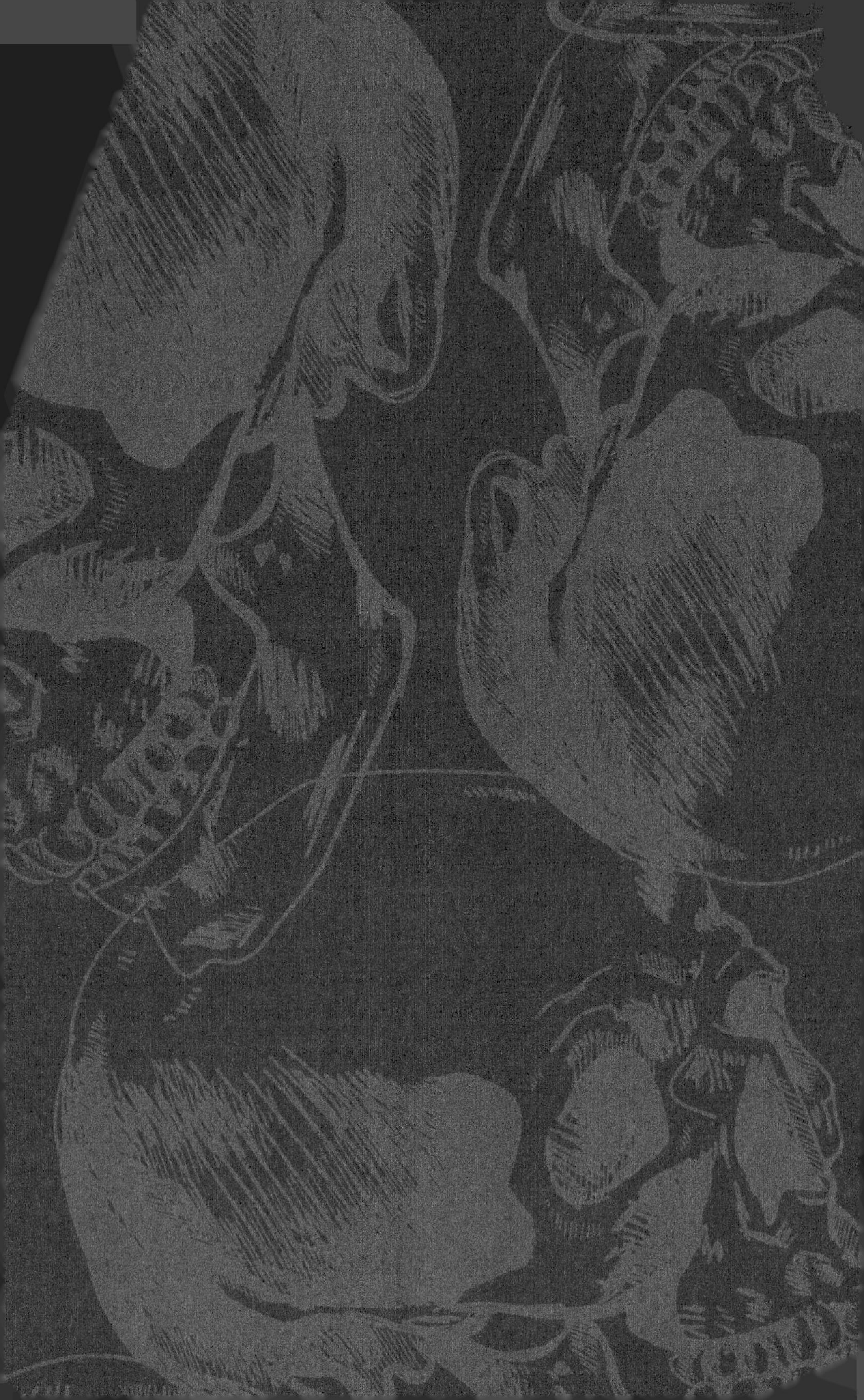

CHAPTER 55
Liam

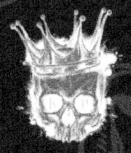

I climbed into bed fully expecting to find Davina asleep. Instead, I found her wide awake and waiting for me.

"Why aren't you asleep?" I asked.

"I can't sleep without you," she whispered softly, and fuck if I didn't love her admission.

"I went over some details with Alexei and checked on Quinn." I pulled her closer to me, loving her body pressed against mine.

"Is Quinn going to be okay?" she asked, worry etched on her face. "I don't even want to think about that being you."

"Don't want to be a widow yet?" I teased her. Today was a close call, and it opened my eyes that a war was coming whether I liked it or not. It might be here already.

"No, I don't," she growled. "Don't even joke about it."

I pressed a kiss on her nose. "How did you like your sister?"

Her eyes lifted, and even before she responded, I knew her answer. "I really, really like her. And the baby."

"I'm happy to hear that."

Truthfully, in our world, bad shit happens every day. It could have been me shot instead of Quinn. I wanted to make sure Davina, my niece, and daughter would have someone looking out for them if something happened to me. And now I knew they would.

"She'll help us with our school," she said, yawning.

"I know you four can make the school happen," I told her. "If you need anything, you tell me."

"I'll have a dedication," she teased, "to my gangster husband." I couldn't help but chuckle. Somehow, I didn't think she was joking though. "And if we have kids, I want them to be part of that school. Both boys and girls."

"You got it," I agreed. "Maybe I should have taught Wynter and Juliette more about this world instead of shielding them."

"You did what you thought was best." Then she met me with a stern look on her face. "But our kids won't be pampered and sheltered to the point of being vulnerable."

I grinned like a teenager, and for the first time in my life, I looked forward to a long life with a woman I loved by my side.

"Are you sure you want children with me?" Her happiness mattered to me, and I wanted her to be sure.

"Yes, I'm sure. We don't need to rush it, right?" She pressed a kiss on my chest. "I want to get a business plan put together and things like that."

I loved how she made plans for our future. For us and our children.

"We have time. I'll teach our kids everything I should have taught Wynter and Juliette," I admitted begrudgingly.

"You didn't know." Davina's voice was soft. "Juliette loves you. Wynter too. They both admire you so much. I don't think secrets do them any favors, though."

It was on the tip of my tongue to ask her what all Juliette and Wynter think and know, but that'd put my wife in an unfair position. She was their friend and my wife. I would get our issues ironed out directly with them.

"So, what are your plans for tomorrow?" I asked her. "Now that there is no more heist planning."

She chuckled. "I'm recording Wynter ice skating in the morning. Then I thought you and I could go visit my grandfather together." Her voice faltered and hesitancy laced her voice. "If you want."

"Yes. We'll visit him and tell him about our marriage."

"Yes," she agreed softly.

"Now that everyone knows," I told her, "nobody and nothing will keep me away from you."

She chuckled softly. "So demanding."

"Always, céile," I growled.

"But you don't want strangers here, right?" she questioned.

"It's your home as much as mine," I told her. There was nothing more I wanted than to see her happy in our home. "You can invite whoever you want, but keep it to people we know. I do have enemies, my love."

Silence followed, and I wondered if it was because I called her love or the admission that I had enemies.

"Do you have a lot of enemies?" she asked.

"I try not to make enemies," I admitted softly. "Unfortunately, in my line of work, they pile up."

She exhaled heavily. "But they'd never come for my grandfather, right?"

"Two men are watching your grandfather at all times."

She scoffed. "Why am I not surprised?" Then her eyebrows furrowed. "I don't like the idea of being stalked, Liam. You won't do it again."

Somehow it didn't surprise me she'd demand that. No wonder she got along with Wynter and Juliette.

"There is shit happening, and there'll be even more coming," I told her. She tensed lightly and I took her chin between my fingers. "I'm going to protect my family, but I need you and the girls to stop being reckless."

"My control-freak husband," she murmured, but her eyes told me she took my words seriously.

I wanted her to understand this was serious. "If something happens to you, I won't be able to live on." She blinked, and I watched her neck bob as she swallowed hard. "You're everything I want and need, Davina. My wife. My family. My home."

She nodded, her throat bobbing and tears shining in her eyes.

"Same," she rasped.

"I trust you, Davina." It might be stupid, but I really did. "The Russians are coming, and they'll come after everything I care for." Our relationship had shifted quickly. It wasn't just sex anymore, there was trust there too. "I have enough money. No strings attached. You take what you need for your school. I just want you and my family safe."

"You're overprotective."

"You got that right." I wouldn't apologize for keeping my family safe, and I knew she appreciated it. She might have liked giving me a hard time about it, but she liked being protected. "I want to keep you safe."

"Don't worry, my hubby," she teased affectionately. "I appreciate your protectiveness. And if someone ever attempts to kidnap me, I'll leave you breadcrumbs."

"Breadcrumbs?"

"A trail for you to follow," she clarified.

"I know what it means, céile. But if you pay attention to the fairy tales, you'll remember that breadcrumbs get eaten."

Davina chuckled in disbelief. "I didn't mean it literally. But if you want to be specific, let me think about it." She got quiet and hummed for a few seconds. "Okay, I'll drop pieces of my clothing."

I frowned at that weird logic. "Clothing?"

"Yes, I'll drop my bra. My panties. Maybe my socks."

I growled. "If you're kidnapped, you better keep your clothes on. I'll always find you. And I'll kill the fucker who dares to take you."

She chuckled softly. "Well, that's intense." She thought I was kidding, but I was dead serious. "How about you? If someone kidnaps you, how will I know where to find you?"

Her question surprised me. "You care enough to come for me?"

"Of course! Now tell me how to find you," she demanded.

"Baby, if someone kidnaps me, it means I'm dead." Because I'd never let anyone take me alive. And my enemies knew it. Either they'd be dead, or I would be.

"You better not be dead." Her soft voice trembled. "I didn't marry you just to become a widow."

"Not even death will keep me away from you," I growled. "Every inch of you is mine. In life and death."

"Okay then. In life and death, I'm yours." I grinned at her agreement. I loved when she gave in. "Let's just talk about lighter subjects, like us practicing the act of making a baby," she rasped softly, and damn if my cock didn't jump at the possibilities.

I stifled a chuckle. My wife had a peculiar way of changing the subject, but I loved her suggestion.

My wife would be waiting for me at home for the rest of my life.

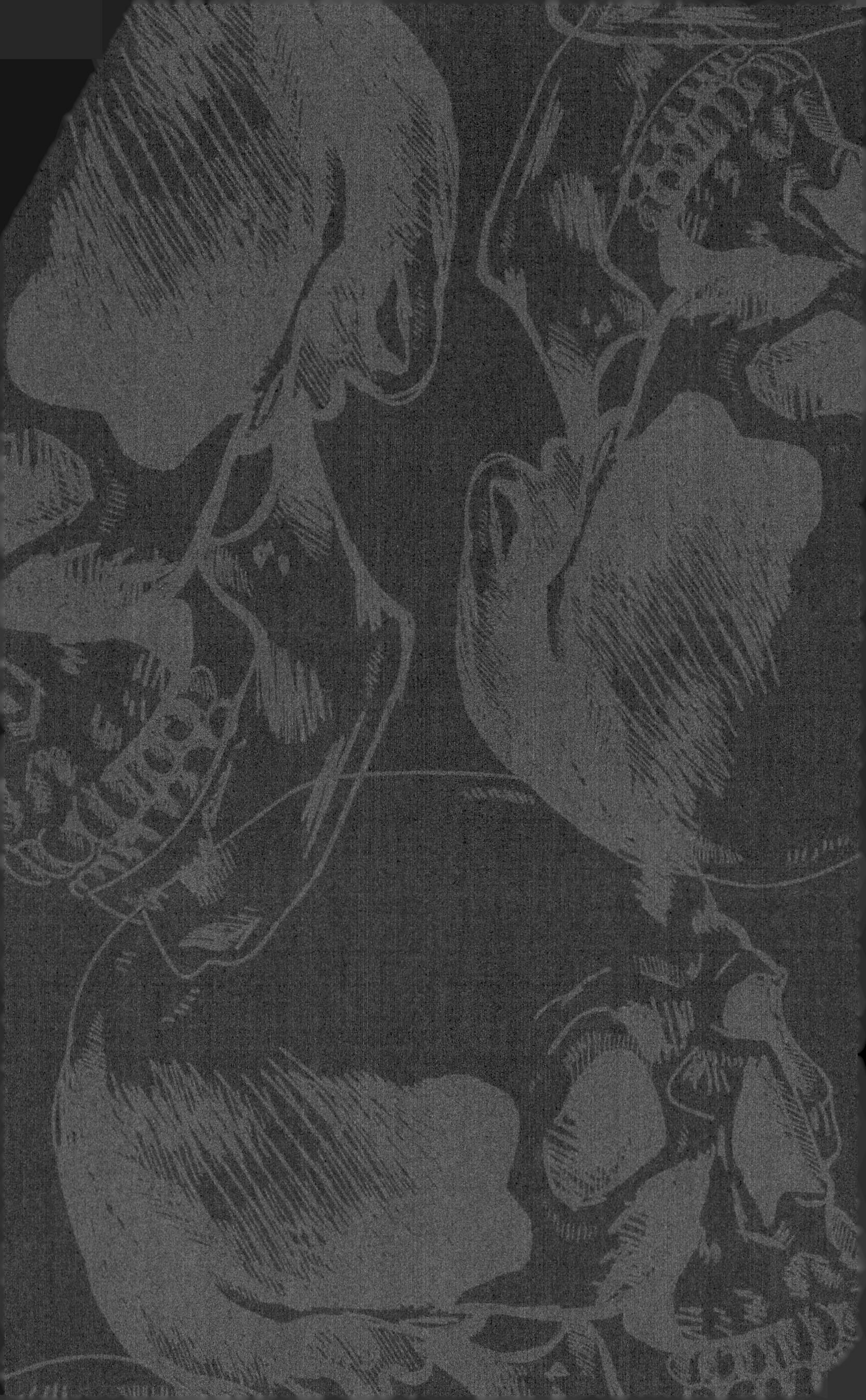

CHAPTER 56
Davina

I yawned, exhaustion heavy in my bones. Needless to say, I got only a few hours of sleep. Wynter got even less.

We'd been at this for hours. It was almost eleven in the morning and I was eager to get to Liam, then head to see my grandfather.

But Wynter had begged for another ten minutes, and I couldn't deny her. Wynter was nothing if not a perfectionist. Something was off though. She was stressed as fuck, and it was showing in her skating. As always, she woke up at four in the morning. Went for her regular jog. Then she did pilates and a workout session. By eight o'clock, she was ready to head to the rink.

We'd piled into the Jeep and then headed for Northwell Health Ice Center. It was where the New York Islanders practiced, and they were more than familiar with Wynter's long figure skating career.

She'd been skating for the past two and a half hours, working on her technical elements—jumps, triple Salchows, spins, more jumps. But more often than not, she'd fall. I had watched her skate for the past four years and had seen videos of her skating since she was a kid. She rarely, if ever, fell. Yet today, it kept happening.

Another fall.

She rolled over, sprawled over the ice. I turned off the camera and got on the ice, careful not to fall. I knew if I got caught without skates, someone would ream my ass, but it'd take too long to change.

I lowered to my knees, right next to her.

"Wynter, how about you take a break?" I suggested. "No sense in bruising your entire body. We had a long night yesterday. You just need a good day of rest."

She stared up, her face tilted to the ceiling. The rink at Yale had her name up there. More than a few banners. But here, the evidence of her amazing career was non-existent. I wondered if she even noticed, because it was clear she had something on her mind that was messing with her usual concentration.

"Yeah." Her eyes remained glued to the ceiling, something sad crossing her expression.

Taking her face between my palms, my fingers cold, I made her look at me. "What's the matter?" I asked her. "Is it the money we stole?"

A heavy sigh slipped through her red lips and a cloud of hot breath dusted through the cold air. It was warm and beautiful outside, but cold as fuck in here. She always dressed in leggings for her practices, but I'm the idiot that never dressed appropriately, even with as many times as I'd done this with her. I wasn't pumping my heart rate like her either, so I was always freezing my ass off whenever we were at the rink. Every. Single. Time.

"Is it about your guy?" I whispered, glancing over my shoulder to ensure nobody was around. Not that anyone was sane enough to be in this freezing rink on a beautiful Sunday morning.

When she didn't answer, I continued questioning her. "School? About what happened yesterday?"

"I'm glad it all worked out yesterday. And we met your sister."

Shifting her head, she focused on the ceiling again, worry still etched on her face.

Last night, we searched the internet for large properties on the east coast. Aurora seemed just as excited as we were as we scouted the possibilities. Locations, acres, buildings. We came to the conclusion that the school would most likely have to be built on a large piece of land rather than buying an existing building.

"Tell me, Wyn," I pleaded with her. "I'm worried about you." Something was clearly bothering her, and I hated to see her like this.

She sighed, her skates picking at the ice as she folded her legs. "I don't want to go back to California," she finally mumbled. "But my mom won't come here…"

She didn't finish the sentence, but I understood. She told me a few years ago that her mother refused to step foot in New York. Now that Liam had given me some of the history, I understood why. Wynter wanted to stay for love, but her whole skating career depended on her mother. In California.

Those two were close, and finding another coach wasn't an option. Wynter skated as much for her mother as herself. Both her parents were ice skaters. Her father died before she was born, and her mother's career ended at the same time.

"I see."

Slapping her hands on the ice, she grunted softly as she got to her feet, balancing on her blades. Her eyes traveled behind me and lit up. I followed her gaze to the man in a three-piece suit with coal-dark hair.

"Your Bas is here," I told her, smiling. At least something made her smile. Her eyes glinted with happiness.

She nodded, her eyes never leaving him. She was head over heels for this man.

"Well, at least he can get you off the ice," I teased her. I shuffled off the rink with her right alongside me. "Your triple Salchows can wait."

We headed toward the short wall surrounding the rink and Wynter winced. I guess the pain was slowly registering now that she was no longer pumped full of adrenaline.

"Ouch," she muttered under her breath, rubbing her left hip and butt cheek. She kept falling onto her left side and I was certain it hurt like a bitch.

"You're taking my Jeep, right?" she asked right as we approached the gate where her skate guards were. And where the object of Wynter's infatuation stood in all his glory.

"Yes." She never even spared me a glance. "He's hot," I commented under my breath.

"He's great," she whispered.

She radiated under this man's gaze. Her face glowed like candlelight and her eyes shone like precious stones.

Once we reached him, I tilted my head in greeting. "Hello."

"Hello," he greeted me in a deep voice, but his eyes never left Wynter. These two would burn down the world together. I had no idea where the thought came from, but it was a conviction I'd stake my life on.

"I'll talk to you later, Wyn." I pressed a kiss on her cheek.

"Sounds good." She glanced my way, smiling. Then, as if she couldn't resist, her eyes shifted back to him.

Leaving the two of them behind, I headed for the parking lot where her Jeep was parked.

It was a gorgeous day. The sun was shining and a light breeze traveled through the air. I'd be seeing Liam. We'd go tell my grandpa we got married. I felt like my feet were barely touching the pavement.

Life was great.

I neared the Jeep and couldn't wipe the grin off my face, thinking about my husband. Lost in my thoughts, I reached for the door handle, but before I could pull it, I felt a presence at my back.

Glancing over my shoulder, I froze. Garrett was behind me. His eyes looked slightly unhinged with several days' worth of beard growth on his face.

"Hello, Davina." His breath brushed my ear, and I hated feeling him so close. "You've been avoiding me."

Well, duh, I wanted to say, but thankfully I kept my mouth shut.

"I'm in a rush, Garrett," I said, trying to keep my voice casual while various scenarios ran through my head.

"You're not ignoring me anymore."

I stilled. *Fuck.*

Keeping calm, I prayed maybe Wynter and her hot-looking man would be coming out any second. But I couldn't count on it. I had to save myself.

Somehow.

"I wasn't ignoring you. I've been busy."

He scoffed, an ugly and disgusted expression on his face.

"We're going to head to my car," he growled. "I'm done with your excuses."

I glanced around, but the parking lot was empty. Only two cars parked here. Wynter's Jeep and a shiny Honda. Garrett's fucking car. If I'd paid attention instead of daydreaming, I would have noticed it earlier.

"Alright."

Just keep him appeased.

He jabbed something into my back. "Go to the back of my car."

"C-can I leave my bag in the Jeep?" I muttered. "That way Wynter will have the keys to her car, and she won't wonder why I left the car behind and not the keys."

He thought for a moment and then agreed. "Don't try anything funny," he warned. "Otherwise, I'll shove this knife into you."

Garrett had gone batshit crazy.

Swallowing the lump in my throat, I opened the driver's door and put my bag on the seat, in plain sight. My bag was wide open, so I grabbed my sports bra from yesterday and let it slip down the front of my body.

I just told Liam last night that I'd leave him clothing as clues, so this should work. Right?

"Okay, done," I told him, impressed that my voice was calm.

He shifted me away from the Jeep. Five steps and we were by his car. But when I reached for the back seat, he jabbed at me again, then clicked his tongue.

"The trunk."

Rude bastard.

He pressed the button on his key fob and the trunk popped open. As I climbed in, I attempted to kick off my shoe, but unfortunately, I wasn't that graceful and only managed to piss Garrett off.

"Get in the fucking trunk," he snapped.

I was in the trunk the next second, bringing my knees up and curling into a ball.

The trunk door slammed shut, and darkness followed.

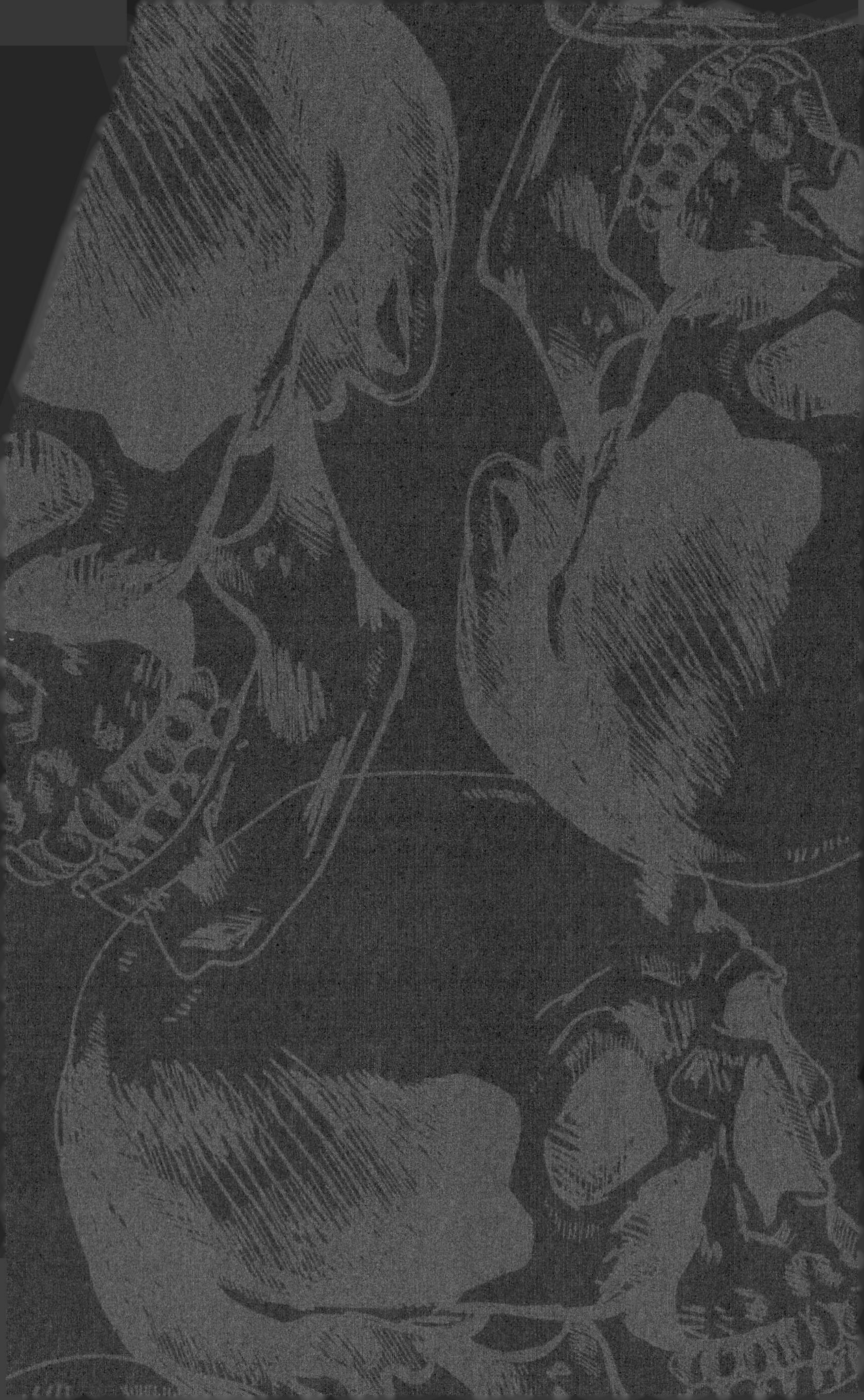

CHAPTER 57
Liam

"Calm down, Wynter."

The truth was I had a hard time keeping my own cool, but it wouldn't help my wife if Wynter lost her shit and couldn't give me all the details.

"Davina was supposed to take my Jeep," she said, her voice still shaking. "But it's still here. And her purse is here. That was an hour ago!"

"Where are you?"

"Northwell Health Ice Center."

"Get to a public place," I ordered her. "Leave everything as is in that parking lot. Do not go back inside the rink. I'll send someone to fetch you."

"But—"

"Wynter, do as I say," I said firmly.

"Okay," she agreed. "I have a friend here with me, so I won't be alone. Don't send anyone to fetch me. I'm fine."

I wouldn't leave her out there, vulnerable. I owed it to my sister to keep my niece safe. I wouldn't fail her too. "Shoot me your address, and I'll have one of my men come and get you."

"No, no," she protested. "I won't leave my friend's side. I promise."

"Wynter," I barked. "I don't have time for this."

"I'm safe," she assured. "My friend won't leave my side."

Who in the fuck was this friend? "What friend?"

"Ummm, you don't know him," she muttered. "From college." She was lying. I'd stake my life on it. But considering Wynter never had an interest in boys, maybe she was worried we'd scare him away.

"You guys go look for Davina," she continued in a breathless tone as if she was scared I'd take something precious away from her. Fine, I'd let her spend time with this boy, but the moment my wife was safe in my arms, I'd find out his name and everything about him. "I-I think…" she trailed off, never finishing the sentence, and an unease climbed up my spine.

"Did you girls do anything stupid? Anything I don't know about?" I growled.

"Umm, no. I don't think so. Nothing other than what you already know." That wasn't convincing at all.

"Wynter," I warned. "Whatever it is, I need to know so I can find her."

She hesitated and it took all I had not to bellow into the phone, demanding she tell me everything. But I knew it wouldn't work. Not with Wynter.

"I-I don't know, but maybe Garrett came for her." Finally! It was good that I kept my temper in check.

"Her ex-boyfriend?" I inquired. I furrowed my eyebrows, unsure why the guy would bother with an ex-girlfriend. That would be an extremely poor way to handle a breakup. "Why would he do that?"

"He's been harassing her ever since we burned down his house," she explained. "Texting her and calling her. Still trying to blackmail her. Even yesterday before…"

Two heartbeats. My blood boiled, but I kept my cool. "Keep going, Wynter."

"Davina's bra is on the ground," Wynter choked out. My fingers tightened the phone so hard, a protesting crackle warned me I was close to breaking it. I forced myself to loosen my grip.

"Go with your friend, Wynter, and don't be alone. When it's safe, I'll send you a note. If something happens, you call me or Killian." Her soft gasp came over the line. "He's back," I clarified.

"Oh, okay. I will."

"Good. Now get out of there, and don't take an Uber," I warned her. "If this friend of yours cannot bring you home, you call me. Got it?"

"Yes."

And the line went dead.

I stood in front of Wynter's Jeep, Davina's bra in my hand.

Fuck, I should have kept Alexei on her. Or somebody else. Anybody. If I had, Davina would be here.

It was definitely my wife's. Our last conversation played in my mind. The timing was suspicious. Or maybe I was paranoid because I forced her to marry me. Yet, deep down, I didn't think Davina was a woman that committed to something and then bailed on it.

I dialed the facility where her grandfather was.

The receptionist's voice came through. "Sunrise. How may I help you?"

"This is Liam Brennan." I got straight to the point. "Has my wife come to visit yet?"

She wouldn't have gone without me, but it didn't hurt to go through the process of elimination.

"No, Mr. Brennan. Not yet."

"Thank you." I ended the call and dialed Nico Morrelli.

"Liam," he greeted. "At this rate, we'll be best friends in no time."

I ignored his comment. There was no time to waste. "I need all the addresses for Garrett Davison."

"Who the fuck is Garrett Davison?" he spat out.

"My wife's ex-boyfriend," I grumbled. "The girls burned down his house."

"Jesus fucking Christ. You weren't joking before, were you?"

"Fuck no!" I spat out. "My niece thinks he kidnapped Davina." I kept turning Davina's bra over and over in my hand. I probably looked like some fucking pervert.

"Give me five minutes and I'll text you."

I clicked the end button and climbed into the Jeep, glancing around for any other signs. I took Davina's purse and dug through it. Phone left behind. Little toiletry case. Her wallet. An old-fashioned calendar.

I opened it to today's agenda.

> Liam. Grandpa. Sex.

If I had an ounce of doubt, I no longer had it. She was coming home to me. Someone took her, and Wynter seemed to be convinced it was her ex-boyfriend. I trusted my niece, and if her sixth sense told her it was Garrett, I believed her.

And he'd been harassing her. My wife!

I'm coming, my céile.

My phone beeped with a message from Nico, sending me two addresses.

> The first address is the burned-down house.

Second address it is, I thought silently. Davina left me a sign. She was counting on me to keep her safe. And I would. At. All. Costs.

My phone started ringing, and Nico was calling me. This couldn't be good.

"Yes," I answered.

"Liam." Nico's voice was cautious, and alarms blasted in the back of my mind. "Gio DiLustro transferred two hundred grand into Garrett Davison's account a week ago."

"Motherfucker," I gritted. "Give me the rundown."

I'll get you back, my céile. Safe and sound.

CHAPTER 58
Davina

I didn't spend a lot of time in the trunk. Twenty minutes, tops. Thank God!

It was pitch-black, and I didn't want to become scared of the dark. I kind of loved what Liam did to me in the dark. I mentally scolded myself.

"Stay focused on saving your own ass, Davina. Not your husband's sexy ass," I muttered to myself as I roamed my hands around the trunk, hunting for anything useful. Maybe I'd get lucky, find a gun, and shoot my crazy ex.

The car came to a sudden stop and my body rolled. Garrett never did know how to drive. Fucking moron.

I heard the car door opening, then footsteps walking around to the trunk.

As soon as it opened, the sun hit my eyes, blinding me. Before I could recover and start fighting, Garrett's hand wrapped around my hair, gripping it to lead me out like a damn dog.

Ugh, I'm gonna kill him.

He yanked me out of the trunk and I landed on my feet. Thank God. I'd need to keep injuries to a minimum so I could bolt out of here.

Glancing around, I noted we were parked in front of a small, log cabin like the ones used for a hunter's temporary shelter. Woods surrounded us, and the only way out seemed to be the way he drove us in. A dingy little one-lane blacktop road.

If I ran that way, he'd find me in minutes, if not seconds.

"You're going to stay here until you admit what you've done and give me the money you owe me," he growled, pushing me forward.

"I have no fucking clue what you're talking about," I told him, playing dumb. I knew he got the money from the insurance company because Wynter's boyfriend confirmed it. But hell if I'd admit to it.

I mean, Garrett could buy another house. What more did this greedy motherfucker want?

Yeah, yeah. The irony of calling him a greedy motherfucker after stealing almost forty million dollars in cash didn't escape me, but we were doing it for a good cause. A decent cause. Well, it was a cause—just unsure what kind.

"Yes, you do. Admit it," he screamed like a madman. "You owe me."

"Geez, Garrett," I mumbled. "What happened to your house? I don't know what you're talking about."

"You had no right," he growled.

"I didn't do anything." I stood firm, though on the inside, I was quivering. So much for being a badass criminal.

"You and your friends burned down my house," he shouted.

I gulped. Gosh, I really didn't know this guy at all. Maybe Juliette and Ivy saved me by starting that fire. Otherwise, I might have still been with this jackass.

"Listen, Garrett," I said, trying to buy time. "My husband is expecting me." His eyes popped out of his head. "He won't be happy when I'm not there. And you know who's gonna pay for that?" I drawled my question, my Texas accent coming out a bit. Without waiting for his answer, I continued. "You, buddy. Because guess what? He fucking hates it when other men talk to me."

"You got married?" he asked, his expression almost shattered.

I scoffed. "I told you, I've been busy. I fell in love and got married. We're having a baby." Okay, tiny lie, but if it knocked some sense into Garrett's thick head, it'd be worth it.

"But we've barely been broken up." It had been almost a month, and there was no appropriate time to move on after a break-up. After death, yes. But not moving on from a cheating scumbag of an ex-boyfriend.

Garrett turned around, as if he had to process my words without looking at me.

This was my opportunity. My open window to bolt.

I sprung away from him, running into the woods but keeping in the general area of the road. It would have been easier to run on the road, but then he could follow me in the car, and I had no intention of getting caught.

"Fucking bitch," I heard him cuss behind me, but I kept going.

My feet crunched over the pine needles and branches, giving my location away. I didn't care, I kept running. I might not be in good shape like Wynter, but I was in better shape than Garrett. I stumbled a few times, but I always dragged myself up and shuffled away. The bottom of my palms burned from catching myself each time I fell.

I heard the start of an engine. As expected, he'd try to catch me by following me in the car. Lazy fuck! I wished he'd follow me on foot so I could hit him upside the head with the biggest log I could find.

It only took another ten minutes before I was heaving, totally out of breath. I bent over, my hands resting on my knees, feeling the oxygen burn my lungs. Or maybe it was the lack of oxygen that burned my lungs.

What-the-fuck-ever.

I just knew I couldn't breathe. I'd ask Liam to start waking me up in the morning so we could train together.

After I got plenty of rest from this past weekend's activities.

It was hard work undertaking a heist.

I could see Garrett's car through the branches, then my confirmation came.

"Get in the fucking car, Davina," he yelled, dark warning in his voice.

Yeah, I'd get right on that. He'd have to catch me first. I attempted to run again, though it wasn't as fast this time. God, I wondered where we were. There were so many trees around, but we couldn't be far from the city. We didn't spend that much time in the car. Trying to watch where I stepped, I rushed through the woods, realizing my mistake too late.

The tree lines disappeared, and I was out on the road. A squeal of tires. Slamming brakes. Garrett!

I whirled around, but as soon as my feet hit the soft dirt ground, my shoes slipping on the pine needles, I realized how stupid I was not to pay attention. The car door opened, but I didn't bother checking behind me. It would slow me down, and I was already too slow.

Before I even got to the first tree, Garrett tackled me so hard, it stole my breath away. My lungs burned and I couldn't take a single breath. If I thought that was bad, what followed was ten thousand times worse.

Bullets sprayed above our head and filled the silence of the woods. Birds chirped angrily. My ears buzzed. I thought I heard gurgling sounds. I squeezed my eyes shut as a wave of terror hit me. Garrett's body still covered me, though I was surprised he'd bothered.

More bullets tore through the air. *Dear God.*

This was something that happened in the movies. Not in fucking New York City or Long Island. Or wherever the fuck we were.

My heart hammered in my chest, threatening to break my ribs. Adrenaline surged through my body, and despite my reason telling me not to look behind me, I did. If Garrett was trying to protect me, I should at least ensure he was alright.

My eyes darted behind me and horror slammed into me. Garrett's blank, empty eyes stared, unseeing. Blood trickled from the corner of his mouth. A terrified cry left my lips and I cringed, but I was too scared to scoot away.

Can a bullet go through him and into me?

I felt like such a selfish bitch. I struggled to shift and make my way out of here. Otherwise, I was a sitting duck. Whoever was shooting, they'd get me. Gunshots already sounded too close.

"Stay down, Davina!" A familiar voice traveled through the air. *Liam!*

Without hesitation, I put my head back down, my face kissing the earth. As long as I could smell the dirt and feel it against my cheek, I was alive. The gunshots continued, and every single shot made my body jerk and my heart jump with fear.

For my husband.

The terror of losing him tasted like a mixture of gunpowder and heart-wrenching sorrow. The kind that would tear me apart.

Tires burned. Doors slammed. Silence dropped like Garrett's dead weight crushing my body. Slowly, I turned my head, glancing to my right, sending a silent prayer to the heavens. I needed more time with him. A lot more time.

A familiar figure ran toward me, and a sob erupted out of me. My throat constricted the flow of air into my lungs and each desperate inhale sent a dizzying relief washing through me.

I struggled to crawl out from under Garrett's dead weight. The next thing I knew, the weight was gone and Liam's hands gripped my shoulders, yanking me to my feet.

The shock of what just happened set in, knocking my feet from under me, but Liam caught me. He crushed me against his solid chest, supporting my weight. Burying my face into his chest, I lost the fight and my sobs tore through me.

"I got you, my céile." Liam's voice was hoarse with relief. "I'll always come for you."

My eyes landed on Garrett's dead body and bile churned in my stomach, a tense ache settling into my muscles and bones.

"He's dead," I croaked as I hid my face against Liam, not wanting to see the face of death.

"He led the Italians to you," he said, rage coating his words. "If he wasn't dead already, I'd kill him with my bare hands," he growled.

"Garrett?" I rasped, confused. How would he know any Italians?

"Yes."

He lifted me up in his arms, and I wrapped my arms tightly around his neck. I held on to him like he was my sanity. My rock. He held me as he climbed into the backseat of a black SUV.

I clung to him tighter, needing him now more than ever.

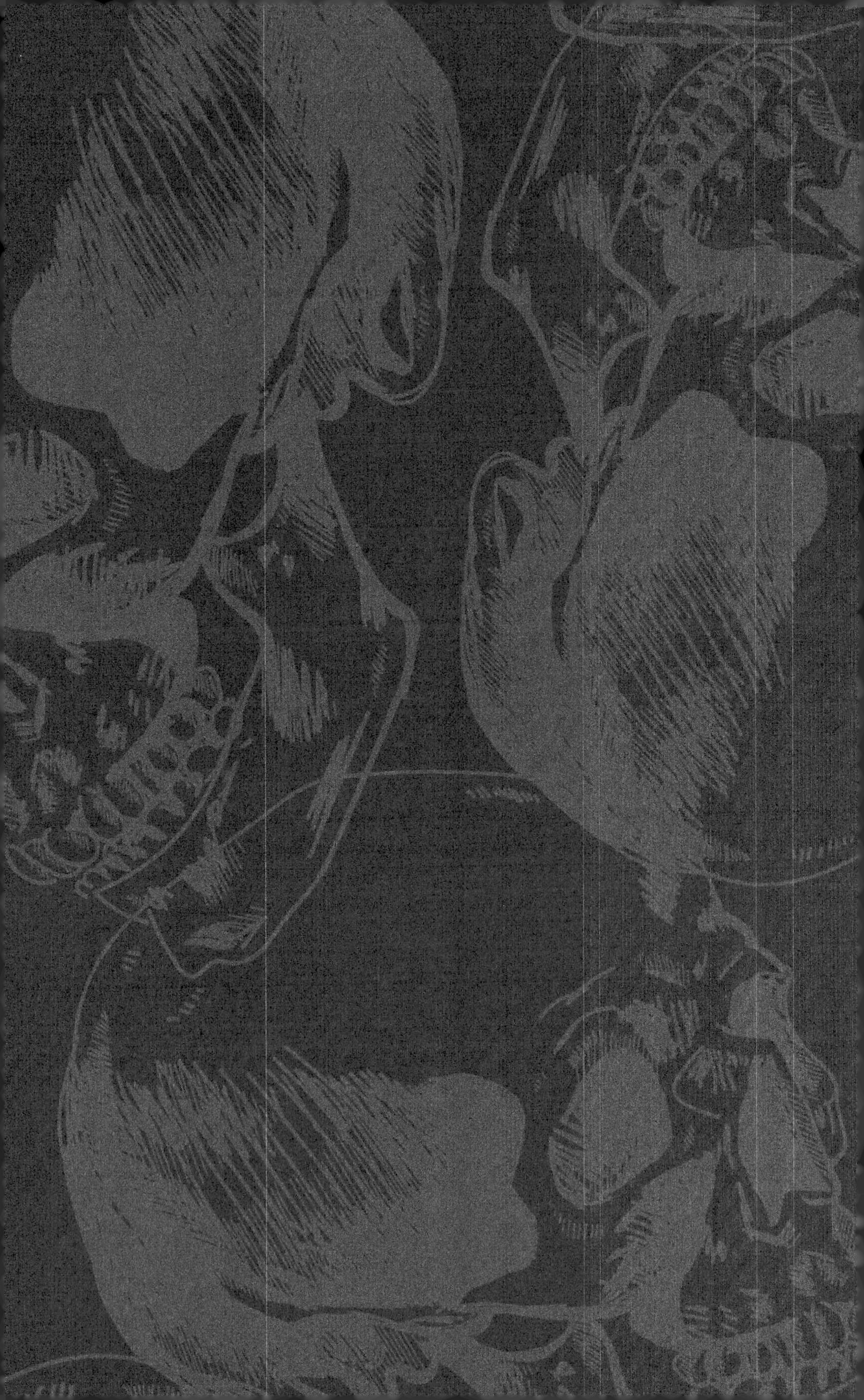

CHAPTER 59
Liam

Motherfucking DiLustros. They tried to kill my wife. Goddamn cowards. Every single fiber of my being burned with rage, wrath vibrating in my chest. I wanted to tuck Davina safely into my tower and then go on a warpath.

"Liam." Davina swallowed, unused to seeing me so enraged.

I didn't trust my own voice. Every ounce of rage ran through my bloodstream, and I was sure it'd spill into my words.

"Liam." She took my hand and shook it gently.

"It's okay, love." I tried to soften my voice but failed. I gently sat her on the couch. Her arms came around her waist as she tucked her legs underneath herself.

Pulling my phone out of my pocket, I dialed Alexei. Aurora had been blowing up my phone for the past thirty minutes.

"You got her?" His monotone voice was a welcome reprieve to the fury boiling inside me.

"Yes, tell your wife that Davina's unharmed."

"Are you okay?" Alexei asked.

"They shot at her," I roared, unable to hold my rage back any longer. "They fucking shot at her. Tried to kill her!"

"They didn't succeed," he stated calmly. "You know what to do to eliminate the threat to your entire family."

"I do," I gritted. "I'll check in later."

The call ended, and I started pacing around the room. Davina's eyes were wide, following my every move. For the first time in my life, I felt like losing something or someone would be the death of me. My breathing ragged, my vision tunneled, and my body trembled with the all-consuming rage. And fear.

I almost lost her.

Jesus. I almost lost her. I'd go to church and thank anyone above and below who spared her. She was my other half.

Finally, I understood why my father became a shell of a man after Winter died. She was his oxygen, his heart.

I dialed Wynter, and thankfully, she answered on the first ring.

"Yes." One word and fear etched through its every syllable.

"I got her."

A sigh of relief that mirrored my own breathed through the headset.

"Can I talk to her?" she asked.

I handed my wife the phone and her icy fingers brushed against mine. Jesus, while I was busy fuming, Davina was cold with fear. She held the phone to her ear, nodding even though Wynter couldn't see her.

"I'm fine," Davina assured her.

Fine, my fucking ass. I sat down next to her, picked her up, and lifted her onto my lap. I pressed my lips to her neck, her pulse strong under my lips. It was the best comfort, because she was alive.

"No, no need to worry," Davina continued. "Nothing happened. I'm fine. Stay where you are."

"Are you sure?" I heard Wynter's voice, soft and concerned. "I don't mind. I can stay with you."

"I'm fine, I promise," Davina repeated. "I just want to be at home, alone with my husband."

Wynter chuckled. "Okay, if you are thinking about *that*, then maybe you really are fine."

Davina smiled and the first flicker of amusement flashed in her eyes. Lifting a hand, I caressed her cheek. *She is my oxygen, my heart.*

Without her, I'd be a shell of a man. Somehow, she made this life worth living.

The elevator door to my penthouse opened and Quinn walked in with his arm strapped up in a sling, finding my wife wrapped in my arms.

"Okay, I have to go," Davina told Wynter. "Love you. I'll talk to you later."

"Love you too."

The call ended. I was about to stand up and go to the office, but I didn't want to leave Davina.

"How are you feeling, Quinn?" Davina eyed him worriedly. Honestly, I wanted him to rest, but he was a stubborn arsehole sometimes.

"Brand new," he replied. "And ready to work."

"You need to rest," I told him. "You lost a lot of blood."

He sat himself down. "I'm good," he insisted. Like I said, a stubborn arse.

Quinn glanced between Davina and me, as if he was waiting for her to leave. She must have picked up the signal.

"I should know what's going on," she protested, her eyes locked on me. She knew who to appeal to. "I'm married to you and—"

"Davina, I don't want you wrapped up in all this," I soothed her.

"I *am* wrapped up in all this," she retorted stubbornly. "From the moment I married you." I leaned closer to press a kiss to her temple. I didn't know if I should be proud of her or scold her for trying to be too brave. "Actually, scratch that," she corrected herself. "I have been wrapped up in this shit from the moment we stole from you. I appreciate you for protecting me, for protecting all of us, but we have to be aware of the threats. Don't leave me blind, Liam."

"I'm trying to protect you. The Italians have even sucked Garrett into their scheme for revenge," I barked out. When she gave me a confused look, I explained, "He received a payment from the Italians."

"But why?" she questioned. "Let me help."

"Remember the old man from the club?" I asked her. She nodded, her delicate brows furrowing. "He's been trying to hurt my family ever since Aisling refused him. My sister paid a big price for it," I clipped.

Just thinking about it had my blood boiling. "He knows how much you mean to me, and I won't let him get to you too."

She gasped, her eyes like stormy clouds, zoning in on my face.

Maybe it was time to go after the Pakhan and Gio DiLustro.

Because I had no intention of losing my young wife.

CHAPTER 60
Davina

Liam had been on the phone with everyone under the sun. He was ready to go into attack mode, but he had to play his cards right. There was so much more at stake here. It could destroy Wynter, and I couldn't help but worry for her.

With the phone calls done, the silence in the penthouse was too loud. Just as my thoughts were. Garrett's actions were incomprehensible. It was such a waste of life, but he had chosen his path when he decided to work with Gio DiLustro and kidnapped me. It all still seemed so odd to me.

"Okay, my love." Liam came back after walking Quinn back to the elevator door. "I know you have many questions."

My eyes lifted to his tall, strong frame, standing in front of me. Thank God he came for me, just as he promised.

"Why would Gio DiLustro go to such lengths for me? He saw me for barely a minute," I inquired.

"Gio DiLustro enjoys inflicting pain on people. He won't rest until he destroys us all. I failed to protect my sister from him, but I'll be damned if I fail again." I held his gaze, and I knew he blamed himself for not protecting his sister. "You mean everything to me, Davina."

"Really?" I asked, hopeful.

I reached my hand for him and he jerked me up, engulfing me in his huge arms.

"You mean the whole world to me, my céile." His eyes shone like blue sapphires. "You're my oxygen, my heart, and my lungs."

His lips pressed against mine, consuming me. Devouring me. Like he truly couldn't breathe without me.

"I want to see you for the rest of my days on this earth," he breathed into my mouth. "Your place is at my side, and my place is at yours. I love you, my céile. Forever."

"Forever," I repeated.

Then Liam grinned, and the entire universe glowed. "The night that you peeped on me in the shower was the best thing that ever happened to me."

A strangled laugh escaped me, remembering the night that started it all.

"I love you," I whispered against his cheek. "I have no idea how or when it happened. Maybe when you spanked me." He smirked in that hot and bothersome way. "I just know that my heart and my body are yours."

He kissed me again, and the entire world tilted.

I knew whatever was happening was far from over, and somehow all our lives were going to be changing soon. But whatever this threat was that loomed over us, I knew we'd survive it. We had to.

Nothing would come between Liam and me, and nothing would hurt our family. Whatever this war was... We'd survive.

For him and me. For our family.

Three Months Later

Epilogue
DAVINA

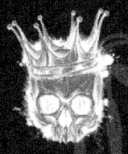

I fell in love with Ireland and my Irish man.

Life had been a whirlwind, but I wouldn't trade it for anything. This family was what I had always craved, what I had always hoped for. I had everything I needed right here.

My husband. My grandfather and father-in-law. My best friends. My sister and her family.

I breathed in deeply, the scent of fresh air invading my lungs. It was July, the perfect time to visit Ireland. And I hoped Wynter would take this time to heal. My eyes flickered to my friend where she sat by the lake. I was worried about her.

Oddly enough, it was Sasha that sat with her and seemed to be able to pull her out of her depression. He even went running with her in the morning while here. Lunatic, but I was glad for him. He seemed to be able to distract her at least a little bit.

"She'll be okay." Liam's voice pulled me back, his arms wrapping around me, and instantly I leaned back, soaking up his strength. His hand snaked down to my belly, gently rubbing it. I was six weeks pregnant, due next March. Right after Wynter's Olympics.

The little bundle of joy timed it perfectly.

Yeah, so much for not rushing it.

Glancing over the large backyard that was surrounded by an old stone fence, I marveled how life had changed. Grandpa and Liam's father had been alternating between playing chess and poker together. I had never seen such sore losers in my entire life, but they got along great.

Juliette and Ivy worked on burning down the house with their cooking. It'd be another night to visit Ivy's ancestral home if we were going to get fed.

Alexei and Aurora sat on the big swing with little Kostya making cooing noises. We'd spent a lot of time together. Somehow it was easier to relate to Aurora, but I had yet to rip the band-aid off with my brothers. One day I'd venture into meeting the Billionaire Kings face-to-face. For now, we only exchanged texts.

Green hills and valleys stretched for miles and miles around us. It was breathtaking.

"This place is beautiful." I beamed, feeling relaxed despite everything else happening.

Liam's breath skimmed across my cheek, his mouth trailing over my skin. "Nothing is as beautiful as you."

I snorted softly. "You won't say that when I get big and round."

"Oh I will." He grinned, brushing the hair back from my face. "Because you're mine, and I'm so fucking in love with you."

"So in love that you like to smack my ass?" I teased him, pushing my butt back into him.

"I smack your ass because it makes you scream for my cock," he purred in my ear. "And I'm all about making my wife happy."

I gasped, feigning shock. "Mr. Brennan, those kinds of words are not fit for our baby's ears."

I felt his smile against my ear. "Should I sweet-talk you until our little lad is born?"

I gave him my most stern look. "You shall have to, husband."

"I promise you the first bite of my meat and first sip from my cup, wife. I pledge your name will always be what I scream aloud in the dead of the night." My lower lip trembled hearing his pledge in a deep voice and soft look in his eyes. "And when I jack off." I playfully shoved at him for being so crude, but it worked. My hormones and emotions peaked. "I promise to honor you above all others, Davina. Our love will remain forevermore. I'm yours, and you're mine."

"I'll love you forever."

"And I'll love you. Until my dying breath."

Without a doubt, I knew this man would keep his promise and love me until the end.

Because I would love him until my own crossed my lips.

THE END

Villainous Kingpin

PROLOGUE - BASILIO

Cruelty ran in my veins.

It was part of me. Just like blood, oxygen, and hustling. It was who we DiLustros were. People shit their pants when they saw me.

Yet, the girl with the golden curls didn't even bat an eyelash. She literally fell off the balcony and straight into my arms, then turned my life upside down. She tilted my world upright, and for the first time in my life, it wasn't all about blood and money.

It was about a woman. My woman.

I had never felt so goddamn happy. So right, and it was thanks to her. Wynter Star. And just like her name, she had become my star. My guiding light in the darkness of my underworld.

The last few weeks had been hands-down the best days of my entire life. And now that she pledged her love and allegiance to me, I knew our future would be happy. Together.

And it was all thanks to her. My angel with golden curls and big eyes that shone like beautiful, precious stones when she looked at me. Only at me.

I've seen and done enough fucked-up shit and ended more than a few miserable lives to know when you found *this*, you had to snatch it and keep it. My one shot at happiness.

She was my once-in-a-lifetime chance at keeping humanity in my soul. Unlike everyone else in my world, she was untainted and gentle, giving love without wanting anything tangible in return. Just me.

She held power over me without trying. I wouldn't fuck around and chance losing her.

To anyone—cousins, family, rival mafia, or anyone else.

I'd put a stop to the thieving schemes she had going with her friends. Fuck it. If those four had some kleptomania issues, I'd set up stores they could rob that were mine. I had plenty of money to go around for the next twenty lifetimes.

I pushed my hand into my pocket, the little velvet box burning through my three-piece. I patted it for the hundredth time since I'd fetched it.

I couldn't wait to slide a promise onto her finger. As long as she wore my ring, that was all that mattered to me.

My lips curved into a smile thinking how I left her. Naked. The softest smile I had ever seen on a woman's face. Her skin flushed from what we had just done. Her eyes shining like the most beautiful emeralds. And her hair. Jesus, her golden curls sprawled all over my black satin sheets. She was like an angel captured in a devil's bed. A willing angel in the devil's bed.

Mine.

I'd never give her up. I didn't give a fuck who I'd have to ruin or kill. She was my perfection. The best part was that she'd let me because she wanted to be mine.

My enemies called me the villainous kingpin. A devil in a three-piece-suit. She just called me hers. She loved me, just the way I was. And God knew I loved her just the way she was. My most beautiful perfection.

I turned the corner to my street and an instant alert shot through me.

My father's car was here.

What the fuck was he doing here?

Dread climbed up my spine and my sixth sense set off warning alarms. He never came to visit. Fucking ever. Every cell of my being went on alert, and I unbuttoned my jacket to ensure I had easy access to my gun.

Then I shoved the front door open. *Blood.*

Bloody handprints decorated the walls of the foyer. Small hands. The taste of fear was new. Something I hadn't felt in so long, I forgot its bitter taste in the back of my throat. Like metal and gunpowder that was sure to take something you loved, more than anything in this world, away from you.

It took hold of my throat and choked the living daylights out of me. My vision blurred and a red haze descended over everything.

Like a fucked-up bloody film.

I pulled out my gun, and with each step I took, my feet crunched on broken glass, shattering the ominous silence. The kind that brought news that changed you forever.

Just not her, I prayed for the first time in my life. *Take it all, but leave me her.*

I heard men's hushed voices, grunts, and I screwed the silencer onto the muzzle, never pausing my steps. Each second counted right now. I rounded the corner to my living room.

Then I saw him.

My father, bleeding like a pig in the middle of my living room. Two bullets in his right leg. A piece of glass jabbed in his neck, and the right side of his face sliced. Angelo, his hacker and right-hand man, tended to him, wrapping up his wounds.

Both of their eyes lifted my way. One wary set, and one furious. The latter one belonged to my father.

"Where is she?" I asked, my voice vibrating with rage as I glanced around. Dread was like a chain around my heart, squeezing harder and harder. "Where the fuck is she?" I bellowed, my voice bouncing off the walls and returning my own echo in answer.

I had to keep my cool, otherwise the rage would blind me and I'd stop thinking rationally. But the adrenaline rushing through my veins refused to heed the warning. It only cared to find my woman.

The living room was in complete disarray. The hardwood floors were stained with blood and broken glass and overturned furniture was scattered across the room.

"Russians," my father spat out, blood spurting out of the corner of his mouth. "They took her."

He had an ugly slash across his face, blood gushing out of it, and two bullet holes in his leg. It wouldn't kill him though.

"Names," I growled, kneeling to lock gazes with my father.

I had to swallow down the burning rage until I had the facts so I could get my girl. I wanted to kill him for allowing them to take her. For not laying his life down to protect her.

Fury rushed through me, blood drummed in my ears. My control was slipping.

"Didn't recognize them." Something about the tone of his voice warned me he was lying. "She tried to run," my father said. "Fucking girl tried to run, and you know how they love the chase."

The red haze in my vision darkened to crimson, picturing how terrified she must have been. The images of how fear would have flooded her big eyes kept playing in my mind. I swear to God, if those fuckers laid a single finger on her, I'd burn down their homes, their cities, and kill their families.

"Where were you two?" I growled. "Did you lead them here? How come they didn't kill you?"

Bratva didn't leave survivors. Just as none of us kingpins left witnesses behind. For a reason.

"We caught them on their way out," my father retorted, spitting blood on my floor. A tooth bounced off the hardwood. "Fuckers," he cussed.

I closed my eyes, took a deep breath, and stood up.

They better not have touched my girl. Not a single goddamn piece of her golden hair. And if someone brought her any harm, I'd bring havoc onto them and this motherfucking world.

I stormed out of the living room, the gun still in my hand as I rushed up the stairs to my bedroom. As I climbed the stairs three at the time, my fingers dug into the mahogany rail, the marble stairs echoing loud under my feet, and I couldn't help but recall her teasing me about it. She called it a fancy mobster home.

It was supposed to be the safest goddamn home in this country. I promised her she'd be safe here.

The bedroom door ajar, I pushed through it, but it was as if nothing happened up here. I could still smell her faint flowery scent. The sheets were tousled just as they were when I left her. Except she wasn't between them.

Her duffle bag sat on the windowsill where she loved to sit.

They'd taken her.

My star. My light. My life.

Don't take her, I prayed. Anyone but her. Bring her back.

And for the first time in my life, I dropped to my knees.

Unless I got her back, I'd be the world's most ruthless villain.

There was no life without her.

TO BE CONTINUED

Have you grabbed your copy of Villainous Kingpin? https://amzn.to/3Mq8oVf

Acknowledgments

Another book finished!

Can you believe it? And it is all thanks to you and your support, my awesome readers!

Thank you to my family and friends for not giving up on me.

Thank you to my editor at **MW Editing** for catching my weird non-English phrases.

Thank you to my cover designer Victoria at **Eve Graphic Design** for giving my books a face.

Thank you to **Susan Hutchinson, Beth Hale, and Brooke Crites** for catching my snafus. Where would I be without you?

Thank you to my wonderful beta readers—**Christine Stephens, Jill Haworth, Mia Orozco, and Denise Reynolds**—for not giving up on me.

And last, but certainly not least, to my daughters and my husband. You are now, and forever will be, my reason for everything.

XOXO

Eva Winners

Printed in Great Britain
by Amazon